When the Saints Go Marching In

AN ADAM SAINT NOVEL

Anthony Bidulka

INSOMNIAC PRESS

Cover design by Mike O'Connor. Cover image by iStockphoto.com.
Author photograph by Hogarth Photography.

Library and Archives Canada Cataloguing in Publication

Bidulka, Anthony, 1962-
When the saints go marching in / Anthony Bidulka.

ISBN 978-1-55483-100-5

I. Title.

PS8553.I319W44 2013   C813'.6   C2013-901467-5

The publisher gratefully acknowledges the support of the Canada Council,
the Ontario Arts Council and the Department of Canadian Heritage
through the Canada Book Fund.

Printed and bound in Canada

Insomniac Press, 520 Princess Ave.
London, Ontario, Canada, N6B 2B8
www.insomniacpress.com

The Canada Council   Le Conseil des Arts
for the Arts   du Canada
since 1957   depuis 1957

ONTARIO ARTS COUNCIL
CONSEIL DES ARTS DE L'ONTARIO

Acknowledgments

With a tip of the hat to Adam Saint, I would like to acknowledge the assistance of my own team of disaster recovery agents without whom this book might also have required the services of Saint's employer, the Canadian Disaster Recovery Agency.

My medical experts who generously shared their knowledge to help me make the lives of certain characters very uncomfortable (my doing, not theirs): Rob Hagiwara, Dr. Dee Dee Maltman, Dr. Tyler Maltman, Dr. Joel Yelland (with the help of Carol), Dr. Lesley-Ann Crone (with the help of Alan), and Kim Garchinski. I greatly appreciate your time and kindness.

My horse whisperer, Bev Jutras, who helped me with horse-related jargon.

My agent, Robert Lecker, for immediately taking Adam Saint under his wing.

My publisher, Insomniac Press. And the organizations which continue to support the publishing industry in Canada.

Mike O'Connor for listening to my ideas and creating a great cover.

My editor, Gillian Rodgerson, for knowing when to

tighten and when to loosen. When to cut and when to add. A [Good] here, a [Ha! Ha!] there, really helps too. Helen Mirren, Diana Rigg, and Linda Hunt are waiting for your call.

My friends and family for being interested and demonstrating support in countless ways.

Booksellers and reviewers, bloggers and other media who've heralded the arrival of Adam Saint, making him feel very welcome.

My readers who were excited to meet Adam Saint before they even knew who he was. (Turns out he's a pretty cool guy). I hope I have not disappointed you. Your support is extraordinary and forms a pillar for my work.

My husband, Herb, for the best life I can think of. (And I'm a pretty creative guy).

For those who can see beauty,
where many see nothing at all.
And Herb.

Chapter One

"What would Canada have that I could possibly want?" General-polkovnik Develchko was not a mirthful man. Yet the derision he heard in his own voice almost made him smile. On the inside.

"You might be surprised...no, I misspoke," the voice on the other end of the overseas line said. "You *will* be surprised."

"Now you've piqued my interest," the General lied. Develchko was beginning to doubt this foreigner he'd been negotiating with for the past twenty minutes. Certainly he could trust the associates who first initiated the contact. Couldn't he? Yet it seemed this person was asking for big things when quite obviously they could not afford to pay for them.

"I have no doubt your services are well worth your price. I simply don't have access to that much money."

Develchko mulled this over, his aquiline features straining. After a moment he said, "Why should I believe you have access to something so important, so highly valuable to the government of your country, when you cannot even raise a paltry sum to pay your own personal debts?"

"This isn't personal."

"Isn't it?" Develchko relished the satisfying ping of hitting a raw nerve.

"I'm afraid we've veered off topic. You know what I want. Our friends assure me you can provide it. I know your price. Now I'm making you a counter offer. One which will not only astound you, but instead of me paying you…you will pay me."

Once again the General felt an urge to display hilarity. This one was ridiculous. Making offers that were ludicrous. Out of this world. Fantastical. So full of empty confidence. Just like a Westerner.

"You won't be sorry, General-polkovnik. When we make this deal, nothing will be the same again."

This last statement gave the Russian pause. He would like that. He would like things to change. He deserved so much better than his current position in life, lofty and respected though it certainly was. Almost everyone thought so. Still….

"Tell me more about this deal."

"I am prepared to give you something of inestimable value. In return you will pay me a mere fraction of its worth and give me what I've asked you for."

"How much?"

"Ten million dollars."

"I find your tall tale very difficult to believe."

"As I would expect." The voice grew assured. "Which is why I am fully prepared to give you proof."

Rebecca Castlegard had never felt quite so beautiful. And desirable. And fascinating. She was finally living a life that most people only dream about. She stared at herself in the round mirror above her beloved antique vanity, picked up the brush, probably equally old, and began running it through her thick, dark hair. She should have had it cut as soon as she knew about tonight's visit, but she'd run out of time. Her list of tasks had been long. Pick up wine. Clean the apartment. Choose an outfit.

It was going to happen tonight. She knew it. Even though she didn't quite approve of what she saw in the mirror, someone else did. As her mother had always told her when the boys at school teased her so mercilessly, someday someone would come along who liked her for who she was instead of what she looked like. In many ways she was a catch, of that she was nearly confident. She might not be a beautiful woman, but she was smart, and she had savings, a nice apartment, and an intriguing career. And now she had someone who *did* seem to like her for herself.

It had started off as a work thing. Nothing unusual about that, but what was unusual was that her suitor was someone way out of her league, both in terms of seniority and looks. Rebecca worked in a highly secure facility. No one got in or out without clearance. She'd been toiling late as she often did. Being alone on a Friday night was not unfamiliar or uncomfortable, but when she realized she wasn't, at first she was startled. What began with a jarring first meeting, over the next weeks turned into something quite wonderful and entirely unexpected.

Rebecca checked her watch. It was time to slip into the

new dress and spritz on perfume. The doorbell would ring in a few minutes.

Everything was working out. As usual, Rebecca complimented herself, she'd planned the evening perfectly. Just as she gave her annoyingly unruly hair one last brush, the chime alerted her to her guest's arrival.

It was *really* going to happen tonight. She wouldn't have purchased the new set of overpriced bed linens if she hadn't been sure.

Practiced smile set, she turned the last lock. The door seemed to explode in her face, wiping the smile clean away.

Rebecca screamed.

The two men who burst into the small foyer formed a wall, pushing her backwards so fast she lost her footing. Two strong arms kept her from collapsing in the stampede, pulling her along until they were in the compact living room. Flickering candles, sandalwood incense, and Michael Bublé on the CD player did little to calm the atmosphere.

"What's happening? Who are you?" Rebecca yowled, pulling as far away from the men as possible.

"Rebecca Castlegard?" the darker-haired man wearing a black leather jacket inquired. His voice was deep and serious.

"Yes, that's me. Who are you?"

"You're an agent with the APU?"

She hesitated. She wasn't used to answering questions about her work. Where she worked and what she did there were not common knowledge. Not even her parents knew exactly what their daughter did for a living. She might be relatively new to the unit, but she knew the rules. She knew enough to stop talking.

"Ma'am," the same fellow kept on, his voice warning of some unspoken implication if she didn't cooperate. "Are you an agent with the APU?"

Rebecca gawked. She was so scared she probably couldn't have said anything even if she were allowed to.

The younger, fair-haired man pulled an iPhone from a pocket, tapped it, then held up the device so Rebecca could see the screen.

Haltingly she stepped forward.

What is that?

Rebecca's eyes squinted as she stared at the little screen. Something about it looked familiar. There was a figure moving into...*oh God...it's me!*

"Where did you get this?" Rebecca demanded to know.

"Ms. Castlegard, you made an unauthorized entry into APU secured chamber thirty-four this past Sunday at eleven forty-seven p.m." The questions were done. They'd skipped over accusations. They were now on proclamations.

Until now Rebecca had been scared. Now she was terrified.

She'd been caught.

"It wasn't unauthorized. I have the appropriate clearance to enter that chamber. If I didn't, there is no way I could have gotten in. All sorts of alarms would have gone off. I was working late that night. Like I always do. That's all. I had every right to go in there."

"Did you have the right to leave with this?" the dark-haired man wanted to know.

The other man had tapped the iPhone a few more times and held it up displaying the results.

Never before in her twenty-seven years of life could Rebecca recall feeling faint. But at that moment, she believed she might pass out. Her great dismay must have been obvious because the dark-haired man grabbed her by the shoulder to steady her. If only his grip weren't so firm, Rebecca wished. She was in dire need of some tenderness. *Please. Someone?*

"I can explain," she managed to get out.

"No explanations required, ma'am. Along with this photographic evidence, a full report has been prepared for submission to—"

"You don't understand!" she brushed off the man's hand and did her best to regain the stance of the confident woman she always imagined herself to be. After all, she was beautiful, desirable, and fascinating. "Someone asked me to do this. I don't have it. You can look if you want. I gave it—"

"Yes, Ms. Castlegard. We know who you gave it to. Who do you think compiled this evidence and prepared the report?"

Breath caught in Rebecca's chest. She thought she might never expel it again.

"But…I don't understand."

"Ms. Castlegard, you have only two choices."

"Choices?" she squeaked, once again feeling deflated and powerless.

"Typically in these situations, there is only one option, so I suggest you consider yourself fortunate and choose wisely."

"Oh…?"

"Option one is your immediate dismissal from APU and a criminal charge relating to your theft of goods. Option two is only available due to your impeccable service record with APU to date."

"And what is that option?" she asked weakly, knowing full well she'd take it.

"Accept our assistance tonight in gathering your things in preparation for immediate transport to your new posting with APU in Georgia. The position is a demotion, but at least you will have a job and not suffer the long-term consequence of a criminal record."

"Georgia? You're sending me to Atlanta? I don't know any—"

"No, ma'am, not Atlanta. Tbilisi."

It wasn't the worst thing he'd ever seen.

Geoffrey Krazinski stepped over the charred limbs as if they were nothing more than grey, gnarled branches littering the ground of a dying forest. When he'd first arrived less than an hour ago, he was alarmed to see smoke. Lazy, opaque tendrils rising from the arms and legs and other body parts strewn haphazardly across the muddy field. How could that be? Certainly he'd gotten here quickly. As quickly as one can get to Siberia from mainland North America. But the crash site was nearing a day old.

When finally he found someone who could speak one of the four languages he understood, he discovered that it wasn't smoke but rather the lingering condensation of something once hot meeting cold.

The fog of death.

Simple science. But there was nothing simple about what was happening here today.

The accident occurred ten kilometres northeast of Magadan. Its small airport handled propeller aircraft only, so Krazinski's jet was forced to land seventy kilometres away at Sokol. From there he boarded a Kamov Ka-60 Kasatka Russian transport helicopter, which whisked him to the site. In Toronto he'd left behind a warm, sunny spring day. Here in subarctic Magadan, the optimistic forecast for this gloomy first Wednesday of June was only eight degrees Celsius.

It had been a while since Geoffrey Krazinski had been in the field. Judging by the sights and smells and sounds, cloying like day-old cigarette smoke, he knew it hadn't been nearly long enough. Morbid as it was, Krazinski wished he had video of the carnage laid out before him. If top brass ever again questioned the rich salaries of the Canadian Disaster Recovery Agency's field agents, all he'd need do was push "play" and watch them blanch. Right before they opened their wallets.

The job of a disaster recovery agent was unforgiving. Brutal. Harsh. Meant only for those men and women with the toughest constitutions and steeliest hearts. He'd done it himself for several years until he could stand it no longer. Pension be damned. He'd made up his mind to tell his superiors to take the job and shove it when blessed fate intervened. Krazinski's direct supervisor suffered an acute myocardial infarction. His promotion was made official the day after the funeral. Now he was the one who oversaw the CDRA's team of specialists. He gladly sat behind a desk and watched as the brass-balled stalwarts dealt with this shit, day-in day-out, for little fanfare but lots of reward.

But not today.

He was looking for red. Onsite officials had told him the body he was interested in was further afield. Marked by a crimson "X."

Krazinski's sleep-deprived eyes rummaged about the repugnant landscape as he walked away from the main area of destruction. It was a dull, sad part of the world, he decided, made even more so by the surprisingly widespread debris field—the pitiful remains of a Sukhoi Superjet. The plane had plummeted from the sky into a graveyard of its own making. A graveyard for seventy-three people. Local air transportation safety commissioners were scrambling to determine a cause, or at least something of substance to tell the public and people like Krazinski. Rumours abounded. The one Krazinski feared the most hinted at pilot error. With a determination of pilot error came the greatest cause for concern: at its source could be anything from mistake to murder.

He spotted the red "X" long before he reached it. Instead of striding forward, Krazinski found himself dragging his feet. It wasn't that he was afraid of witnessing death. God knew he'd seen plenty of it before. Probably more than almost anyone, save for soldiers, doctors, and morticians. No, it was the confirmation of this *particular* death that he wasn't looking forward to. For once he made a positive identification, each step he took, each word he uttered, each decision he made would leave an indelible, immutable tattoo on his career.

It shouldn't have been Geoffrey Krazinski on this

frozen, godforsaken, scrubby plain in Northeast Asia. Typically in situations like this one—delicate situations—there was only one disaster recovery agent he would call upon. A special agent. Trained to deal with any situation thrown his way.

But Adam Saint was unavailable. He was currently on a plane, on his way back to Canada from KwaZulu-Natal. He'd been overseeing the cleanup of a tragic, cult-inspired, mass poisoning that had claimed the lives of five Canadians, including a prominent actress. The Magadan disaster required immediate attention. And so, following protocols he himself had installed, and with the support of IIA higher-ups, Geoffrey Krazinski had called himself into action.

IIA, the International Intelligence Agency, is known— by the few who know of it at all—as Double I-A. IIA is not Interpol. Not CIA. Not CSIS. The relationship between the organizations is intentionally vague, with IIA the distant, little-known aunt who irregularly shows up for Sunday dinner, mysteriously wielding unspecified power over everyone else at the table. From Andorra to Zeebrugge, whatever needed knowing, the agents of IIA make it their business to know. Each IIA member country maintains its own head-quarters, housing lead offices for each IIA branch active within that region. Almost all include a Disaster Recovery Agency.

The loftily appointed offices of Canada's IIA fill two floors in the Bay Wellington Tower of Brookfield Place, a major skyscraper in Toronto's Financial District. Top dog on the organization chart is Maryann Knoble. Knoble is a flint-eyed pit bull of a woman. She favours Arturo Fuente

Opus X A cigars, their smoke seeping happily into her Hermès scarves. Geoffrey Krazinski, head of the CDRA, reported directly to Knoble's second-in-command, Ross Campbell.

The mandate of CDRA is deceptively simple. Whenever and wherever a disaster occurs in the world, be it natural or man-made, and Canada or Canadians are involved or influenced, the CDRA responds.

The first response is the deployment of a disaster recovery agent. The involvement of an agent might take hours, weeks, or months, depending on the nature and severity of the disaster. Typically, a disaster recovery agent is amongst the first wave of officials to arrive on the scene. They quickly liaise with local professionals, gauge the situation, and define Canadian concern level on a predefined rating system; five being nominal, one being acute. Based on the assessment, the agent arranges all resources necessary to attend to Canadian interests. Thereafter, they act as liaison between those resources, local officials, and Canadian personnel, civilian or otherwise.

When a train crashes in Poughkeepsie, terrorists blow up a public building in Belfast, a cyclone ravages Bangladesh, or Angola descends into civil war, if Canadians are there, the CDRA sends in an agent; to some that agent is an advocate, to some a hero, to some an angel of mercy on the worst day of their life.

As Krazinski gazed down at the bloody "X" emblazoned upon the dead man's destroyed torso, the lower half nowhere to be seen, he thought of two things. First was how the vivid red reminded him of the maple leaf on

Canada's flag. Second was what he'd say to Jean when they talked on the phone that night.

"How are you?" Jean would ask.

"I'm okay, sweetheart," he'd answer. He couldn't tell the truth. He couldn't say anything at all.

The blank-eyed face looking up at Krazinski, although irrevocably altered in grim repose, was familiar to him. It was familiar to most Canadians. Krazinski shook his head and muttered an epithet under his breath. What fresh hell would come next? he wondered.

The pronouncement could now be made. Flags across the country would fly at half mast. The Governor General of Canada was dead.

"Mr. Krazinski?"

Krazinski turned, surprised to hear his name spoken.

Behind him, thirty feet away, stood a man he did not know. His first irrational thought was that the man must be cold. His chocolate-brown leather coat, thigh cut, was too thin for the weather. His head was covered by one of those Russian-style hats with ear flaps, and he wore a pair of Aviators despite a heavily muted sun.

"Have you made your identification?" the man asked.

Krazinski detected an accent. Slavic, he thought.

He answered with a slight nod, weary.

Here was the first in a long list of people he'd be dealing with here in Magadan. He knew it was vital, especially on foreign soil, to determine at the outset exactly who was who. He would need to quickly sort the useless cast of chaff from the real decision makers.

"May I ask your name and position?" Krazinski asked.

"Certainly," the man said with a smile, approaching. "My name is Anton. I am your executioner."

Geoffrey Krazinski felt the electricity enter his body as sharply as if it were a knife piercing his skin. The last thing he saw was the man standing over him, removing his dark glasses. At that second, Krazinski knew only one thing for certain: he had just reached the end of his life.

Chapter Two

At sixteen dollars a day, minus the four days she'd already been resident, Hanna calculated she could live at the motel for twenty-eight more days. A month! She'd have a home for a month! Her jubilation was short-lived, however, when she remembered she'd neglected to figure in the cost of food. And all the other stuff they'd need.

Shampoo. Coffee. Gas for the car. Every bit of it cost money. Too much money. She did her best to keep incidentals down to a minimum. But certain things, such as tampons and toothpaste, were simply non-negotiable. Sitting at the room's tiny, round table, the edges chipped from years of neglect, she scribbled more numbers on a scrap of paper.

How she longed for a calculator. Not that she was stupid, far from it, but she'd grown up in a world where no one ever needed to do math using paper and pencil. Doing it longhand wasn't easy. Nothing in her life was. Not anymore.

She reached for her purse. She should count the money again. Maybe, just maybe, she'd missed a bill or two.

As she dragged the purse near, she couldn't help but frown at the sorry-looking thing. Once upon a time the purse had been fun and frivolous. All pink and dotted with fake jewels. It was a purse meant for a girl's night out, when all she needed was a roll of cocktail cash, a tube of gloss, and perfume. She was a low-maintenance kind of gal. All that and a short skirt, and she was set for a good night. That was a dozen years ago. Which meant she was a dozen years older now, and so was the pink purse. Neither looked the same. The purse was soiled, the leather distressed and shapeless. The lining was torn in two places. Worst of all, it was embarrassingly out of style. Glancing into the mirror above a nearby bureau, Hanna studied her reflection. She wondered if the same could be said about her. Distressed. Shapeless. Torn. Out of style. Probably.

She couldn't think about that now. Reaching into the purse for its matching, sickly pink change purse, she dumped the contents onto the table. She unrolled the bills and counted them, writing the total on the paper. Then she carefully counted the coins.

Once. Then again. She added that total to the bill total. Damn. She was right the first time. There was no way around it. She would have to find a job if she wanted to set up house at the No-Way Inn for longer than a couple of weeks.

Hanna was very willing to work to pay her expenses. The problem was with potential employers. They had to agree to pay her in cash under the table. She had found early on that these rules severely limited the quantity and quality of jobs available to her. But there was no way around it. She had no choice. Tomorrow she'd have to begin the humiliating process of walking door to door, cleavage on display, from restaurant to restaurant, fast-food joint to fast-food joint, grocery mart to grocery mart, bar to bar, begging for a chance, until she found someone desperate enough, kind enough, or horny enough to hire her.

Hanna started when she heard a sharp rap on the door.

Oh God.

No one knew she was here. Other than the guy at the front desk. And the gal at the 7-11 where she'd done her grocery shopping the day she'd gotten into town. Otherwise she'd spoken to no one. She was paid up for the week, the room had been made up earlier in the day, and most definitely she had not ordered room service, so there was no reason for any motel employees to be hassling her.

Who could it be?

Hanna was frightened. She'd been warned, but she hadn't listened. And now there was someone at her door.

Casting about desperately, Hanna searched the sad little room for something to use as a weapon.

Nothing.

Why weren't baseball bats as common as Bibles in cheap motel rooms?

Another knock.

Stepping out of her once-fashionable wedge platforms, she picked one up, brandishing it as she would a frying pan meant for someone's head, and timidly approached the door.

"Who's there?" she called out. She didn't recognize her own voice. It sounded all high and whiny. And frightened.

Standing on her tiptoes, she scrunched her right eye and peered through the peephole with her left. No one there. Whoever it was, was out of the peephole's line of sight. The big question was whether or not it was on purpose.

"It's your neighbour," came the reply.

The voice sounded tentative. Was she lying?

"What do you want?"

Silence, then: "I live two doors down. Maybe you've seen me around?"

Hanna tried the peephole again. This time she could make out the top of a head of store-bought blonde.

I'm being paranoid, she thought. No one knows I'm here. This woman's merely trying to be neighbourly in a not-very-neighbourly world.

Stepping back, Hanna unfastened the chain lock and pulled open the door.

Standing at the threshold was a short woman (below peephole height at least) with a bad dye job and worse hair-cut. She wore clothes that, in Hanna's opinion, were much too young and much too tight for her. Hanna immediately recognized the sad irony.

Her own clothes were much too old and much too loose. The only wardrobe she could afford now was from the clothing section of the grocery store. And although she didn't bother standing on a scale, as she had at least once a day every day of her life before this hell began, she knew she'd lost more weight than she could afford to.

"Hi there," the woman greeted with a toothy grin. "Sorry to be bothering you like this."

"That's okay," Hanna told her, her eyes making a quick sweep of the parking lot that fronted the two-level motel.

"Like I said, I live right over there." The woman pointed to her right. She was badly in need of nail polish remover. "I saw you move in. When you didn't move right out the next day, I figured you must be one of us."

"One of us?"

The woman cackled. "We call ourselves the Permies. As in permanent residents. You know how it's a motel and all, but we never move out 'cause its cheaper'n renting an apartment or something like that."

"Oh, well, yeah, I see…."

"So you're one of us then? I'm right, aren't I?"

"Well, I don't kn—"

"It's okay, one way or another. I was just hoping you'd be around for at least a short whiles anyway. My boy never gets much chance to play with other kids his age. So when I seen you got a kid too, I knew I had to come over and introduce myself. Maybe we could plan a…what do they call 'em again? The fancy moms have a name for it…oh hell, what is it…oh yeah, yeah, a play date. How about it? Your boy and mine. They can play right out there in the parking lot where we can keep an eye on them. You could come over for a smoke and drink…you smoke, am I right?"

Hanna was shaking her head. "No, I'm sorry." *What am I apologizing for?*

"Oh that's okay. As long as you're not one of those green-ass, anti-smoker environmental types. Are you?"

Hanna's head was still moving back and forth, staring at the woman as if she'd never seen the species before. "No, I mean I don't have anyone for your son to play with."

The woman chortled and elbowed Hanna playfully in the arm. "I know what you mean, sister. Sometimes I pretend like I got no kid either. Pain in the asses they can be, that's for sure. But you gotta love 'em, am I right?"

"I'm sorry…uh…."

"Oh shit, I forgot to tell you my name. I'm such a dozer sometimes. I'm Stella. The boy is Clinton. Like the U.S. president. What's your boy called?"

"I told you, I don't have a boy. You must be mistaken. But thanks for coming over." Hanna began to move back from the door.

"But I saw him. I saw you with him. When you got here. It was late at night, I know, but I sometimes can't sleep because of all the highway noise. I saw you."

"You're wrong," Hanna declared forcefully, slamming the door shut.

With the door chained, Hanna turned and fell back against it. She wrapped her arms tight around herself, as if bracing against a fresh assault from the unwelcome neighbour. She closed her eyes and took in a long, deep breath, held it for a second, then exhaled very slowly. It was a lesson her long-gone yoga teacher had taught her for relaxation. It worked like magic in the yoga room. It worked like shit in a scuzzy hotel room that smelled like urine.

"Jake!" Hanna called.

A ten-year-old boy ambled out of the kitchen nook, where he'd been eating dry cereal from a box. He wordlessly looked up at his mother. He didn't need to ask her what was up. The tone of her voice said it all.

"It's time to go, Jakey," Hanna told the boy, trying to sound light and airy as if this had been the plan all along. "Pack your things, honey. It's time to leave."

To most, Maryann Knoble was an enigma. She was a woman wrapped in a military general, wrapped in a CEO, wrapped in a philanthropist, wrapped in a barracuda, wrapped in a woman. No one, least of all herself, would describe Maryann Knoble as attractive. She had the body of Margaret Thatcher, the hair of Margaret Atwood, and the face of Margaret Hamilton. She was a brown cardboard refrigerator box in a pricey scarf. Born in Switzerland to a Canadian scientist father and a German biologist mother, Maryann was raised in an international, cerebral, and ultimately emotionally cool household.

In school, Maryann excelled at two things: painting and mathematics. Her parents, having no interest or patience for the arts, encouraged young Maryann to investigate the complex world of economics. In her rare rebellious moments growing up, Maryann would secretly visit a museum or dabble at oil painting on canvasses she hid under her bed. But generally she was not an unhappy child, contented by her growing skill level with equations and computations and quantitative analysis. As she grew older, she developed new-found passions for political science and international relations.

By the time her formal education was complete with a doctorate and several highly respected publications under her belt, Maryann Knoble was a highly sought-after candidate at major corporate headquarters worldwide. They needed someone with the breadth of knowledge about how the world worked, both politically and fiscally, that Maryann so impeccably possessed.

IIA U.K. made the earliest and most profoundly serious financial offer. Maryann accepted. Within a dozen years, she rose through the ranks to second-in-command. Prepared for the ultimate power position and thanks to her predecessor-to-be not so gently being forced into retirement due to early-onset Alzheimer's, she received the call to head IIA Canada.

Although Maryann knew the experience would be less enjoyable than usual, she lit her five o'clock cigar seven minutes late. Her office, at eight a.m., five p.m., and any time after eleven p.m., was the only place in the entire building where smoking was permitted. Well, not so much permitted as tolerated by the very few people invited within smelling distance of her sprawling suite.

When the expected knock came, Maryann barely glanced up at the monitor that showed the area directly outside her locked door. Having no patience with the idea of a personal secretary, she buzzed the door open herself.

Her visitor was Ross Campbell. Her lieutenant. Her deputy. The man they'd turn to on that fateful day when she took her last breath. She had private reservations about whether that day would ever arrive. Nevertheless, a second-in-command was a necessary evil in an organization such as this.

Campbell was a handsome man, lanky in frame and indubitably grey. His thick, wavy hair was prematurely grey, his complexion grey, and his eyes grey. Each day he wore one of a battalion of nearly indistinguishable but undoubtedly expensive grey suit and tie combinations. Maryann wondered if she'd even recognize him on a Saturday afternoon wearing shorts and a Bermuda shirt. She grimaced at the thought. That would never happen. Nor would she want it to.

"Ross, take a seat. Drink? You may need it."

Ross sat and looked at his Baume et Mercier stainless steel watch. 5:08. She was right. He needed a drink. But not now. No time for a clouded head today.

"What is it, Maryann? I thought we weren't meeting again until Monday."

"There's been news you need to hear."

The amount of "news" that flowed through a place like IIA was plentiful, oftentimes unpleasant, and readily anticipated by all who worked there. If Maryann was delivering it in person, Ross knew she must consider it to be of great magnitude.

"What is it?" he asked, trying—not too hard—to keep his nose from wrinkling at the noxious odour of the cigar.

Maryann indulged in a leisurely puff, all the while studying her companion through the shiny lenses of oversized trifocals. "I thought you should be the first to know since the CDRA is within your purview."

He hated this dancing around. Get on with it. He had a lot to do today. "What is it?" he repeated evenly.

"Geoffrey Krazinski is dead."

Campbell's face hardened. "That can't be right. Krazinski just left for Magadan."

"There was an accident at the crash site. He was struck in the head by a piece of debris improperly secured. He was killed instantly."

"God, Maryann, that's…that's terrible."

"Of course it is. But this is Disaster Recovery, not accounting. These things happen. What matters is our response. Krazinski's body needs to be recovered. His family—if he has one—needs to be informed. A new agent needs to be deployed immediately to take his place in Magadan. The new head of CDRA should be named within the week. I assume you can look after all of this. Our meeting on Monday is booked for three. I'll expect a report on your progress then."

"Y-yes…you'll have it."

Knoble laid down her cigar and hunched forward on her desk. "Is Saint back yet?"

"Just."

"Call him in. He'll need to know. Then offer him the position. Lucky bastard is about to have a very good day."

Campbell slowly rose from his seat. Knoble was mistaken. Saint wasn't going to have a good day. He was about to have one of the worst days of his life.

Chapter Three

Getting to Toronto from KwaZulu-Natal via Durban and Zurich might seem daunting to some. Not to me. It was 14,000 kilometres, eighteen hours, four meals, and not such a big deal. Flying has become as much a part of my job as it is for the pilot who controls the aircraft and the airline attendant who looks after me. Just like anything else anyone does often enough, a frequent flier gets good at it.

My rules are simple. Number one: whenever possible—and given some of the out-of-the-way hellholes I've been to, it isn't always—fly business class. Not for the food or drinks or priority boarding but for the extra room. If you can't manage business class, book an aisle seat. I don't care how great you think the scenery is going to be, having at least one side of your body free to move and stretch is invaluable, especially if you're a big guy like me.

Number two: drink plenty of water *before* you get on board; save the alcohol for when you reach 35,000 feet.

Number three: pack a damn good carry-on. What you put in there can save your life or at least your sanity. So think about it carefully. In mine I have Tylenol with codeine and a good muscle relaxant for when sleep is not my friend. I include at least three types of entertainment to outsmart my brain by keeping it occupied. For me this usually means an e-reader loaded with reference materials on wherever it is I'm going next, a foreign language CD to keep up my skills (I know seven; although "know" may be overstating my prowess in two of them), and at least three newspapers. And I own a kick-ass noise-reduction headset.

Allow the airline to take care of you…but in case they can't, be fully prepared to do it yourself.

My life, pretty much anytime I'm not aboard an aircraft, is fast-paced. It's occasionally uncomfortable, sometimes dangerous, always adventurous. So a twenty-hour trip across date lines and time zones, from country to country, is more about downtime and relaxation than stress and worry.

Checking messages as soon as I arrived at Toronto's Pearson International Airport, I was a bit surprised to have one from Ross Campbell. He's my boss's boss. It was Geoff Krazinski's job to talk to him. Campbell, I don't know very well. He's IIA. I'm CDRA.

"Saint." Campbell's voice on the message. "We need to talk as soon as you get in. I'll be in my office."

Navigating through the terminal toward the parking garage, I tried Krazinski's number. He'd know what this was about.

No luck.

It didn't matter much anyway. I'd planned to spend the next few hours writing up my reports on KwaZulu-Natal. Something I could do as easily from CRDA as from my home office.

I had everything I needed stored on the laptop I always carry with me. Names. Locations. Details. Photographs.

Recordings of interviews. All else was in my head. Images of corpses curled up and contorted in the final, disfiguring throes of painful death. The sound of relatives' screams as I confirmed their worst nightmare. Why did they always ask the same question: did they go peacefully? Fuck no, you idiot! Your twenty-year-old sister was given poison with her morning juice and told to lie naked on a bed of gravel in the burning hot sun until her leader and saviour, some insane saddhu, pulled her into the afterlife.

And then there were the smells. Smells associated with disaster. Not just the distinctive scent of death—the stench of rotting corpses, the putridness of what a body expels—but something more. I've never been able to put my finger on what it is exactly. But it's always there. It permeates my clothing and skin and hair like campfire smoke but harder to get rid of, just like everything else I've stored in my head since starting this job almost two decades ago. I tried to ignore the memories. Forget about them. Cover them over with other less disturbing images. It never works.

For the right amount of money, Pearson airport will supply a twenty-four-hour, security-monitored, locked-door garage slot, accessible only by the car owner and a very limited number of airport officials. This is not a password you want to forget. In mine was a Koenigsegg CCX, a Swedish-manufactured roadster that can accelerate from 0 to 100 km/hr (from 0 to 62 mph) in 3.2 seconds. This I know from experience. The claim that it can also top out at 400 km/hr (250 mph) I have yet to verify.

The CCX is a two-door targa top. Its handiest feature is having the facility to store the removable roof under the front trunk, which most targa tops do not offer. This can be a real downer if you're driving along on a beautiful day, decide to take the top off, and realize you've got nowhere to leave it while you zoom off with carefree abandon, wind blowing through your hair.

Another great thing about the CCX are the dihedral, synchro-helix actuation doors. Just saying the words is worth the $600,000 price tag. That and the fact that although the doors rotate forward and upward, just like scissor doors, the clever Swedes have engineered out the problem of the open door obstructing passenger entry or exit. A truly sweet car.

Traffic was blessedly light, and I made it to CDRA in less than half an hour. The place was quiet. After hours for most. I reached my office and hit the buttons that activate the lights and open the window blinds.

It took a minute.

There are a lot of windows.

Some days I think about how ridiculous it is for me to have such an extravagant office. Most of the time I am anywhere but here. Then I realize the office isn't really for me. It's for Krazinski. And Krazinski's boss. And Krazinski's boss's boss. To them the office is part of the "perks" package they buy me off with. It makes them feel better when they call me at two a.m., or during a raging winter storm, or on New Year's Eve, to tell me I have forty-five minutes to get on a plane for Abu Dhabi or Idaho or wherever the hell a major disaster is underway. So who am I to complain? In the rare instances I am in the office, I do my best to appreciate the bird's-eye view of downtown Toronto, the supple leather of the chairs, the fully stocked mini-bar, and the full bath-room with steamer shower.

I tried Geoff's line again. He was either gone for the day—unusual for him, even though it was early evening—or not answering. I was about to try Campbell's number when he appeared at my door.

"I heard you were back." His frame filled a good portion of the opening. His commanding demeanour took up the rest of the space.

I smirked. I hadn't seen a soul on my way up here, and yet he knew I was here.

And they say IIA is not a spy agency.

"I was just about to call you."

Campbell stepped inside and made for the bar. He word-lessly poured two three-fingered scotches, handed me one, and lowered himself into the guest chair across the desk from me.

"Good trip home?" he asked.

Not knowing Campbell well, I couldn't tell if he really gave a shit or was just marking time until he said what he really came here to say.

"Good enough."

"Have you talked to Yelchin yet?"

Milo Yelchin. His was another of the messages residing on my machine. Returning his call was low on my priority list at the moment.

"I just got in. Your message sounded urgent."

"Adam...."

I couldn't remember the last time anyone at IIA or CDRA, other than Krazinski, called me by my first name.

Was this leading up to an exchange of Christmas cards?

"...it's about Geoff."

Geoff Krazinski was the kind of guy you called by his first name. He'd definitely get a Christmas card from me. If I ever sent them.

"He's gone, Adam."

"I've been trying to reach him. Where is he?" When Campbell didn't immediately answer, I added: "Are you telling me he's left CDRA?"

"He's dead."

I know death very well. Just as most people know happiness, disappointment, familial love, I know death. I see it all the time. Yet there is something very different about the death of someone close to you. Although I'm generally not a collector of friends, if I had anything akin to a good friend, it would be Geoff Krazinski. We'd worked together for many years. We saw the world in much the same way. We respected the ways in which we didn't. I knew Jean. I knew their children and saw pictures of grandchildren. They'd even had me over to their home for a meal or two, although I'm bad at dinner parties. I just can't manage talking about the latest show at the Royal Alexandra over crudités and white wine when twelve hours earlier I was pulling a body out of a cavern in Yemen.

For the first seconds following Campbell's simple statement, my mind resisted understanding, then quickly reverted to denial, then sought alternate scenarios where the words either meant something else or were falsehoods with nefarious purpose.

"Adam, I know you two were friendly. I can see this

comes as a shock."

Did he think I always come to work expecting to hear about the death of my boss? I suppose some people did. Expecting? Hoping? For me it was different. If it had been a colleague, one of the other agents, it would have made more sense. Our lives are at risk every day. But Geoff had gotten out of all of that. He'd paid his dues. Now he was behind a desk watching from afar. Just the way he liked it.

"There was a plane crash in Magadan," Campbell kept talking. "The Governor General was aboard. As you can appreciate, this was…still is…a delicate situation. Of course Krazinski wanted you on the job. When he couldn't get you, he went instead. I don't know all the details yet, but there was a problem at the site. Something about a rogue piece of debris hitting him in the head. It was an accident."

"That's bullshit, Campbell. Geoff may have been out of the game for a while, but he was nothing if not careful." Geoff might not have liked what he did when he was out in the field, but he'd been good at it. There was no way I could believe he'd get himself killed by a piece of rubble.

"It's not about whether he was careful or not. *It was an accident.* He did nothing wrong. It just happened. I've got people looking into it. The autopsy is being done right now. As soon as I know something more, I'll tell you."

"Where is he?"

"Magadan. As I said."

"I'm going to get him, Campbell."

"There's no need. Davis is wrapping things up in Seoul. He'll be on a plane to Magadan in a few hours."

I stood up. I had to move. Neurons were firing, adrenaline was flowing. If I stayed sitting, I thought I might explode. "Send Davis home. I'm going to Magadan. Has anyone told Jean?"

Campbell hesitated. He looked as if he were trying to figure out a difficult problem. "Jean needs you here, Saint. And the kids. They're all going to need you."

"The first thing they're going to need is for me to bring Geoff home."

Campbell rose, wiping imaginary lint off a lapel as he straightened to his full height. His eyes harpooned into mine. "You're not a goddamned courier, Saint. You've got bigger responsibilities."

"I'm going to see Jean. Then I'm going back to the airport. You can either support this and have someone in Transportation email me flight details, or I can book it myself. Your call." I scooped up my laptop and headed for the door.

"Wait!" It almost sounded like a yelp. "There's something else you need to know, Saint. Something very important. And personal. I want you to call Yelchin. Then you can decide whether or not you're doing this. If you still want to go, I'll support you."

"I've decided."

I left the building.

Jean Lepage and Geoff Krazinski lived in Rosedale, in a spacious 1930s house they'd restored and loved together. Despite all the extras life had bestowed upon him, Jean was the same down-to-earth guy I imagined Geoff had fallen in love with thirty years ago.

As very young men, both had been married to women, and both were widowed early. Their three daughters, two from Geoff's first marriage, one from Jean's, had gone on to successful lives of their own. When Deidre, the last to leave, was officially out of the house, the first thing Jean did was fire the gardener. He went from full-time stay-at-home dad to full-time yard worker and, reportedly, loved every minute of it. During winter months, he traded in his lawn edger and weed whacker for a seat at the local bridge club, a game he played with all due seriousness. Woe be to the opponent who did not follow the rules.

It was Deidre who answered the door.

"Mr. Saint, I...I...." And with that she began to sob.

I pulled the young woman to me. Her slender shoulders shuddered as she let out her grief in great torrents of moans and wails.

"Adam."

I looked up and saw Jean standing in the direct centre of the imposing foyer. He looked like one of the marble statues they'd imported from Greece and posed around the circumference of the large room—lifelike, yet frozen.

Diedre pulled away. "Dad, I'm sorry. I just...I just opened the door and started blubbering. I'm sorry, Mr. Saint."

"It's okay, honey," Jean assured, his voice tender but firm, his French accent almost undetectable. "Why don't you go back into the living room with the others? I'm going to have a word with Mr. Saint."

Diedre left, and I approached her father. Jean was a handsome man in his late fifties. He'd allowed his hair, worn long, to grey naturally into glossy silver. I kissed him on both cheeks, then we embraced.

"Thank God you're here, Adam. I needed to get out of that room. Come," he pleaded, taking my hand. "Sit with me on the front porch."

The well-lit "porch" was actually a wraparound veran-dah with a rich suite of teak furniture and a commanding view of the manicured front lawn and long, private drive-way that led into the property from the street. Gentle shad-ows of evening inched up to the house, impatient for night.

"Jean, I'm so sorry," I said as soon as we were seated.

"It's so peaceful out here this time of day," he remarked, ignoring my comment.

He seemed grateful for the moment to soak up the scenery, along with deep gulps of air.

"Jean…."

"I know, I know," he responded in a quick burst of words. "You didn't have to, Adam, but thank you for com-ing." After a moment, he added, "It's all so fresh. I don't really know what to say or what to do. The girls have been crying for hours. I don't know how they do it. Their poor husbands are skulking around here like ghosts. I'm sure they're wondering how long this is going to keep them off the golf course." He let out a small chuckle to let me know he was kidding. "That's not true. They're good boys. I just…I just don't know what to do, Adam."

"You don't have to do a thing, Jean. Let the rest of us look after it."

"You'd think the least I could do would be to lead the grieving. I should be in there with them, crying and whimpering and screeching at the sky, 'Why God? Why?' But I don't seem capable." Suddenly his Quebecois accent was more evident.

"You're a strong man, Jean."

"No. You're wrong. I'm not strong. I'm weak. Too weak to show my grief. Too weak to show my fear." His hands were resting on his lap, but his fingers were busy, pulling at and twisting the cuff buttons of his shirt. "I'm afraid if I start crying, I'll never stop. I'm afraid if I mourn my lost husband, I will never feel anything else ever again. No happiness. No joy. No love. Nothing. Once I give in…it's over."

I placed a comforting hand on his shoulder. "I understand." I did.

"You know, when Geoff first started in this business, when he was doing what you're doing now, I half expected this would happen. It was like being married to a cop, or a fireman, or a soldier. Every time he went to work or flew off to some disaster site, I thought there was more than an even chance he wouldn't come back. We talked about this, he and I. He couldn't comfort me because he knew my fears weren't unreasonable. We learned to live with it.

"And then it was over. He became the head of CDRA, and suddenly there were people like you taking the risk instead of him. You know, Adam, that was really when we began our lives together. It wasn't when we first met, or had our commitment ceremony, or finally had all the girls living under the same roof with us. It was right then. Suddenly I could believe he was going to come home every night. Suddenly we could imagine growing old together. Did you know we actually went to church and officially got married?

Just us and the girls and their families. It was small and quiet. But so sweet. So full of hope.

"And now this. It isn't fair. This wasn't supposed to be the way it was going to end for us." He studied his hands and the wedding ring that had taken so long to find its rightful place. A pensive look painted his face. "Or maybe it was. Maybe we were fooling ourselves. Maybe these last years were only a reprieve, a short holiday from what was always meant to be. God," he said with a sharp intake of breath, staving off tears. "It went by so quickly. Life. So very very quickly. Now it's over."

With the CCX back in protective custody at Pearson, my BlackBerry confirmed boarding passes arranged by IIA's Transportation Department for my flights to Magadan.

I started with the 10:10 p.m. Lufthansa flight to Frankfurt, arriving at 11:55 a.m. the next morning. After a quick lunch, I caught the 1:30 p.m. to Moscow, then a Transaero flight leaving Moscow at 8:55 p.m., getting me into Sokol Airport just before 1:00 a.m. A car was waiting to take me the rest of the way into Magadan and to Hotel Centralnaya at 13 Lenin Avenue.

Between my Ukrainian and the driver's Russian and spotty English, we were able to communicate well enough. Never one to pass up an opportunity to practice my language skills beyond the standard "Where's the bathroom?" "How much is it?" and "Are you carrying a gun?" I tried out an old joke on Viktor: One farmer asks another, 'How come your cow gives one hundred litres a day when mine gives so little?' The *other* farmer answers, 'You should be kind and tender with your cow. In the morning, I come to my cow and ask her, "What do you have for me today: milk or beef?"'

Jokes are one of the most difficult things to translate from one language to another, but I must have done okay, because Viktor chuckled the rest of the way into town.

We arranged to meet at the front of the hotel at eight a.m.

The fifth floor room was clean, spare, efficient. And cold. My luggage, having just come from South Africa without a stop at home for replenishment, wasn't much help. I wrapped a thin blanket around my shoulders and powered up my laptop. I didn't need to cross my fingers hoping for WiFi. Another perk of my position with CDRA is a powerful laptop that uses satellite communication technology. I punched up my email account and checked for new messages.

There was a long note from someone at IIA whose job it was to figure out exactly how to get a body from Magadan to Toronto. I reviewed the arrangements. It looked surprisingly straightforward. Or rather, it was straightforward when the body belonged to IIA. Another message had come in from Milo Yelchin. I'd deal with that later. The last message took me by surprise.

Kate.

"We should talk. Call when you're back."

That was it.

Delete.

I had a working breakfast. Over coffee I'd had sent up to my room and a PowerBar from the permanent stash I keep in my carry-on, I researched Magadan and whatever I could find out about the Governor General's downed flight. No earth-shattering revelations.

As promised, Viktor was waiting for me at the front doors of the hotel at eight a.m. The air, coming straight off the Sea of Okhotsk, had a dank chill to it.

I'm sure I looked like a lunatic, sporting linen pants and a short-sleeved cotton shirt. A local, standing across the street staring at me, must have thought so too.

I was both surprised and grateful when Viktor handed me a down jacket and gloves. Both fit. He told me he would add the cost to my hotel bill.

Yesterday Viktor insisted I sit in the back seat. Today I ignored his protests and sat next to him in front.

Although Magadan was new territory to me, I'd studied a satellite map of the city and surrounding area. Within minutes, I knew we were heading in the wrong direction. After a reasonable time, in case Viktor was using a short cut I didn't know about, I brought this to his attention.

"I left instructions that I wanted to be taken directly to the crash site this morning."

"Yes, is that right?" he answered in his peculiar Ukrainian/Russian/English mix. "I take you to see General Develchko."

"I don't know Develchko. I don't wish to see Develchko. I wish to see the crash site." Firm. Authoritative.

Viktor's eyes never left the road. I could see worry lines forming on his high forehead. "I take you to General

Develchko."

He must have thought that if he said it enough times, I'd eventually go along with it. Not a bad strategy really. Short of throwing myself out of the car and hailing a taxi (I'd yet to see one), my options were limited. So I settled in for a meeting with the great Wizard of Magadan, General Develchko.

Minutes later, we pulled up in front of a squat building. Like most in Magadan, it was nondescript, only a story or two, circa 1947 or so. Viktor did a lot of smiling and nodding. He made encouraging mumbles as I dutifully exited the car and followed him to the front door. Although shooting the messenger is not something I object to, it wasn't going to get me anywhere in these circumstances. So I was playing the obedient puppy. For now. (I'm also the type of puppy that will pee all over your brand new carpet if I see a need to.)

At the front of the building, Viktor opened the door. He motioned me inside, then was gone. I guess the rest was up to me.

I found myself in a large entry chamber. Unadorned walls were painted an industrial pistachio green that reminds me of hospitals. The air was not much warmer than outside. It smelled more like a long-abandoned building than a government office.

I heard footsteps and turned. Down a narrow hallway to my left, a tall, spectacularly uniformed man, blond, with piercing blue eyes and a prominent nose, approached in an imperious manner. Several paces behind him were two more men. They wore plain, dull uniforms, with corresponding expressions. One fellow was dark-complexioned, the other pale with fiery red hair and a matching Lenin-inspired moustache and pointed beard. When the tall, blond man was close enough, his right hand shot out with the precision of a military salute.

"I'm General-polkovnik Illya Nikoleyevich Develchko. You are Mr. Adam Saint." His English was very good.

"General," I responded, taking his gloved hand.

"Well," the severe-looking man said, obviously grateful to have dispensed with the niceties, "shall we go to my office and begin? We have much paperwork to look after."

With this, he and his guard dogs turned and began marching back down the hallway.

I held my spot. "General Develchko, I am not here to do paperwork. I've asked to be taken to the crash site this morning."

The trio stopped and slowly rotated in unison. By the look painting Develchko's features, I could tell he was not a man used to being disobeyed, especially in front of underlings.

"Mr. Saint," he began, a tight-lipped smile paining his face, "I'm sure you are aware that travel within Russia and between oblasts has had its restrictions in the past. Particularly for foreign visitors." He emphasized the last word, lest there be any misconception that I was anything but a temporary guest here. One who'd already outstayed his welcome.

He went on: "And you've no doubt heard that such things are much simpler now." The guy was not helping his case. "Well, I regret to inform you this is not always true." And there it was. "I cannot allow you to travel to the crash site without proper documentation. It is for your own safety, you understand. Please come with me."

He began to turn again, but this time I was quicker. "As you'll no doubt have heard, our CDRA agent Geoffrey Krazinski already had full access to the crash site. Since he was killed—at *your* crash site—I, another CDRA agent, will simply travel under his documentation."

Develchko's nostrils flared. I was oddly gratified to see it. Still, the man was not giving up easily. "There are also many documents to sign in order to expedite the transport of your dead agent from Russia to Canada."

"I understood from my superiors at the Canadian Disaster Recovery Agency and the International Intelligence Agency…." This was not a time for acronyms. "…that all paperwork in that regard had already been taken care of. I am not a signing authority. I am simply an escort. While I inspect the crash site this morning—as instructed by my superiors…." A lie. "…Mr. Krazinski's body will be transferred from your hospital to the airport at Sokol in time for my flight this evening."

I had to give it to the guy. The aching smile was still on his face. "So you make no time to visit our many tourist attractions?"

Now it was my turn to smile. This man was playing with me. The only tourist attraction in Magadan was the infamous Kolyma Highway, or "Road of Bones." A dark place with a pitiful past. Constructed in 1932—during the Stalin era of the USSR—by inmates of the so-called "Corrective Labour Camps," the road is actually more of a burial ground than anything else. As prisoners died in the harsh working conditions, their bodies were simply laid beneath and around it, literally becoming part of the road itself.

By the look in Develchko's eyes, I had to wonder if he wished me to visit the road or become part of it.

"Next time," I said.

A strained second passed. The two of us eyed each other superciliously. Who would give in first? I always win at this game.

"Perhaps you will allow me a few minutes of waiting in my office? While I make preparations for our voyage to your crash site."

Now it was *my* crash site. Fine with me.

"Of course," I agreed.

I followed the General down the hallway, his two men trailing behind us. At the end of that hallway, there was another. Then another. And another. Finally we reached a door that looked suspiciously like all the others we'd just passed. If I didn't know better, I'd say we'd walked in a circle. Develchko indicated a stiff-backed chair positioned in the hallway. I wasn't to be trusted to actually sit inside his office but rather outside like a truant youngster waiting to see the Principal.

I sat. As he opened the door and made to go inside, I said in fluent Ukrainian, "Could you direct me to the bathroom? Too much coffee this morning."

The guards, who'd already fallen into military poses next to my chair, settling in for a good, long wait, inhaled sharply.

Develchko scowled. Was he losing patience with me? I hoped so. "Of course," he snipped, then told me where to go.

As soon as the General was behind the closed door of

his office—making phone calls about who knows what—I hopped up, gave the pair of ruffians a see-you-soon wave, and headed back to where I came from.

Viktor, leaning against the car, smoking a cigarette, looked surprised to see me.

"All done," I said brightly. I approached the car in a slow, purposeful way, full of confidence I did not feel. I suspected that any second now Develchko or his sidekicks would come storming out of the building to stop me. But I didn't want Viktor to know that. As far as I knew, he was Develchko's cousin twice removed. "You can take me to the crash site now."

"Very good," he responded, tossing his cigarette butt to the ground and rounding the car to the driver's seat.

"Mister?" a voice came from behind me.

Here it goes. I glanced over my shoulder. But instead of Develchko or another uniform, it was a young man, not much more than a boy. He was wearing a bright red cap, the kind a railway conductor might have, with matching suspenders. He stared at me with anxious eyes.

I would have ignored him if he hadn't looked vaguely familiar. But how could that be?

"Hello?"

"I would talk to you," he said in heavily-accented, halting English.

I glanced at Viktor. He was waiting patiently next to the car.

My eyes swung to the front door of the building. I had no time for this.

"Maybe another time," I said in Russian. "Good bye."

"No, please, sir. Now I must speak."

"I'm sorry," I told him. "I'm in a hurry."

I moved toward the car. Viktor got in.

My inner voice was screaming: *Get out of here! Now!*

"Mister!"

"Some other time," I called over my shoulder.

"No. Please. Now. It must be now!"

The urgency in his voice stopped me.

I turned to look back at the young man, then over his shoulders. Through the clouded glass of the building's front door I could see motion. They were coming.

Shit.

I gave the young man an apologetic head shake. I had to go. I dashed toward the car and jumped inside.

In the side mirror, I saw the young man racing toward the car. And Develchko's men exiting the building.

The young man was at my window.

The tall guard with red Lenin facial hair was running toward us.

Develchko's face appeared at the door, impassively watching the action.

"Step on it!" I ordered Viktor, who was mercifully oblivious to what was happening.

As the car sped off, I suddenly remembered the young man. I knew who he was.

Just as the memory struck me, I thought I heard him yell: "I know what happened to your friend!"

Chapter Four

If Viktor knew I was actually using him to escape Develchko, I feared he'd slam on the brakes and turn me over. But there was something about the young man we'd just left behind in front of Develchko's office that gave me pause.

"Who was that boy?" I asked Viktor, doing my best to keep the unease I felt out of my voice.

I'd recognized him at the last second. I didn't actually know him, but I'd seen him before. He'd been standing outside the hotel that morning, watching me. I'd thought it was because I was a foreigner without a proper coat and he was simply curious. But there was more to it than that. As we sped away from Develchko, I was sure I heard him say something about knowing what happened to my friend. It all happened so fast I didn't have time to think, but by "my friend" he could only be talking about one person.

Krazinski.

"What boy?" Viktor asked, calmly directing the car down the street, unaware that Develchko and his men were probably coming after us with a flotilla of Russian war tanks.

"The one back there. He called out to me." I gave the speedometer a pointed glare. "Could we go a little faster?"

Viktor shrugged. "I don't know the boy."

"Have you seen him before?"

He thought about this. "Maybe. He might be one of the boys from where the plane crashed."

"What? Why would he be there?"

"They hired local men to help clean up, you know? There was much…uh, how you say, unruliness?"

Jeez, he was there. The boy had been at the crash site where Krazinski died.

Perhaps he did know something. Something I needed to know too.

"Go back!" I bellowed.

"What?

"Go back! Go around the block!" I ordered.

"I thought you want to visit crash site?"

It was a risk. I had no idea what Develchko was up to. Would he come after me? Or would he let me go, thinking I was just some crazy Canadian who couldn't follow rules? I was hoping for the latter but guessing the former was more likely. He didn't want me to visit the crash site, which only made me want to see it more. But the young man knew something. Something important about Krazinski? About how he died? Were my original suspicions correct? Was his death not an accident?

"Once around the block, Viktor. As fast as you can. I need to speak to that boy."

I checked the side mirror, then craned around to confirm there was no one behind us. Had Develchko let us go that easily? Maybe I was wrong about him.

Traffic was light. Viktor made fast work of getting the car back to where we'd started.

We crept up to Develchko's office building.

No boy. No Develchko. Nothing. They were all gone.

"There!" I saw the boy's distinctive red cap in the distance, about a block and a half down. He was crossing the street. He'd obviously given up on talking to me.

Viktor accelerated.

In the next moment, still a block away, we were suddenly thrown into stunned dismay, horrified by what was happening in front of us. We watched, helpless to do anything about it, as a vehicle plowed through the intersection, mowing the boy down like a recalcitrant weed.

My mouth fell open, but no sound came out. The red cap, whipped into the air by the impact, caught a breeze. It sailed upward, away from the horrific scene.

Viktor uttered a shocked prayer in Russian.

I was about to join the chorus when something violently smashed into our car from behind.

I felt my head whip back, then rush forward. My seatbelt was on, but the sudden force was so great my forehead cracked against the car frame just above the front windshield. No air bags.

Blood began to gush down my face. I fought overwhelming waves of nausea and dizziness.

It would have been much easier to fall into unconsciousness. Instead I forced myself to stay awake. I glanced over at Viktor. I could see a massive goose egg forming in the centre of his forehead where it must have hit the steering wheel. He was swearing in Russian. It sounded like he was going to be okay.

I wasn't.

I woke up in a hospital room painted the same noxious green as Develchko's office. I was surprised to find myself in bed. And pissed off. I had passed out. What a waste of time. Immediately I wondered what happened to the boy. To Viktor. Where were Develchko and his henchmen? Who brought me here?

I could tell by the colour of the light coming through the slats of a window blind that I'd been out for more than a few minutes.

Throwing back covers, I saw I was wearing nothing but a threadbare hospital gown. Gingerly I swung my feet to the floor and stood up, taking things slow.

One step. Two.

I seemed okay.

I found my clothes in a free-standing wardrobe in one corner of the tiny room. I changed, then opened the door into the rest of the world—whatever it turned out to be. There were people milling about at one far end of a hallway. I headed the opposite direction. I found a door with Cyrillic letters, which I took to indicate a stairway.

Down I went, two flights, coming out near something that looked like a reception desk. I nodded at the girl behind it, purposefully striding past, heading for the front door and hoping she wouldn't notice the bandage at my hairline.

Once outside, I took off at a slow jog. I knew exactly where I was going: away.

After a couple of minutes, still feeling faintly light-headed from my stint as Sleeping Beauty, I stopped near an intersection that looked about as busy as it gets in Magadan. No vehicles resembled a taxi. I felt my pocket for my sat-phone and accessed the Internet. I did my best to search for Magadan cab companies. No luck. Not a big surprise.

I checked the cross street signs and tried to place them on the Magadan map I'd studied the night before. Although I can't boast a photographic memory, I do have detailed long-term recall. This has come in handy learning languages, finding my way around strange countries, and impressing dates by ordering five-course meals off extensive menus without referring back to it.

I estimated I could make it back to my hotel in less than half an hour. Jogging.

Forty-five minutes later, I huffed and puffed my way through the front doors of Hotel Centralnaya.

"Mr. Saint!"

I whirled around, ready for anything.

It was Viktor.

"What are you doing here?" I saw the bump on his forehead, red and angry. "Are you all right?"

"I am good. Come with me." He saw my hesitation. "Please."

I followed him back outside. Not my favourite place. I was looking forward to at least a few minutes in the company of indoor heating.

Viktor led me to a car. Not the shiny black sedan he'd first picked me up in but a seen-better-days, dirt-brown Lada.

"Get in."

His manner was much different from this morning. He glanced about nervously as if worried somebody might be watching us.

"Please," he said again when he saw I wasn't moving.

I got in.

We drove in silence for several minutes until we reached a shabby suburban street. He pulled over but made no move to get out of the car.

"Where are we?" I asked.

"A street in Magadan."

Well, that cleared that up.

"I was waiting for you for when you are released from hospital."

I would rather he'd waited outside the hospital and offered me a ride home, but whatever.

I sighed. "Okay, where does Develchko want you to take me now? Another sightseeing tour? Because I'm not interested. I only have a couple of hours before my flight home. Like it or not, I intend to see the crash site before I go. You either help me or you don't."

"I help you."

That was easy. Too easy? "Why?"

Suddenly Viktor was spitting mad. "Those fuckers smash into us. For no good reason. My head hurts like son of bitch!"

"Tell me what happened. What happened to the young man we saw run over?"

"Dead. Very dead."

Shit. "Who crashed into us?"

"Develchko's donkey's assholes. My fucking head! They could have killed me!"

So he wanted a little revenge on Develchko and friends for giving him a boo-boo. I could work with that. "How do you know it was them?"

"It was same car, waiting in front of that office. Where you meet Develchko. They pretend like it is accident. But no accident. No way. The shit holes. I'll piss on their graves one day."

"Was it Develchko's men who ran down the boy as well?"

This seemed to surprise the driver. After a moment of thought, he said, "I don't know. Maybe. The car did not stay. The one that killed the boy. They ran away."

"A hit and run?"

He nodded, getting the gist of the term.

"Are the police investigating?"

"Of course."

"Are they investigating our accident too?"

"They say it is my fault! They say I was going too slow! Those men will roast in hell. God will not take them for telling such lies. I'll piss on them!"

I hoped he was sufficiently hydrated, because it sounded like there was going to be plenty of pissing in Viktor's future. "Did you see Develchko after the accident?"

"No. Never."

I thought about that. Was Viktor right? Was it Develchko's men in the car that hit us? Why would he do it? Had Develchko overheard what the young man had said to me before we left? Did he want to keep him from telling me what he knew? So he had his goons crash into us to keep us from going after the boy. Possible. Did he kill the boy too? But why? Same reason? It all sounded preposterous.

Some situations are notoriously easy to misread. I'd seen

it before. You suspend belief just for a moment, allowing your brain to slosh around in some multiplex, big-screen fantasy rather than the real world. Truth is easily supplanted by something more extravagant and mysterious. I couldn't afford to be fooled.

What did I truly know? I knew a plane went down. I knew the Governor General of Canada was dead. I knew Krazinski was dead. I knew local authorities reported to IIA that both were accidental. I knew Develchko did not want me to see the site. It was this last bit that made no sense.

I'd only asked to see the crash site to have a frame of reference for when, in the future, I'd think about the end of my friend's life. It would help me to reconcile in my mind that he was dead. It would give me something concrete to tell Jean and their girls about how he'd left this world. Instead all hell had broken lose. Why? Was it coincidence? Or was something more happening here?

"Who exactly is Develchko?" I asked.

Viktor shrugged. "I only drive his car for money."

"Will you get in trouble if you take me to the crash site today?"

"Maybe. But I decide if you want to go to where the plane fell down, I will take you. In my own car. In my own car, I have no trouble, I think."

I hoped he was right. I nodded and smiled at my new friend.

The road leading to the crash site went from paved to gravel to dirt, not so much resembling a road as a path worn down by the numerous vehicles that had likely descended upon the remote area since the plane crashed. Although the temperature gauge in Viktor's car assured me otherwise, it appeared to be colder out here in the near wilderness.

The sky was icy blue, the landscape shrouded in cool greys and arctic white. It might have been because of the aged car's poor suspension, but the jolting ride felt as if we were driving over uneven blocks of craggy ice. Even the paltry foliage seemed to be shivering in misery.

As we got closer to an opening in the straggling pines that lined the road, we spotted the first vehicles we'd seen in a long while. Two large trucks lumbered toward us.

"Who are they?" I asked.

"The place you want is behind that opening. They are from there."

The trucks passed by us without incident.

Closer in, a lone guard stepped out of his sentry vehicle, gun ready. He held up a gloved hand, calling for us to halt.

Viktor rolled down his window. He began a fast discourse with the guard. I could only catch about a third of what they were saying. I heard Viktor tell him I was from IIA. That seemed to get us through the checkpoint.

About a minute after that, Viktor brought the car to a shuddering standstill in the middle of a massive empty field.

"Why are we stopping?"

"This is what you wished to see, no?"

"I want to see the crash site. Where the Canadian Governor General's plane went down. Where my friend was killed. I want to go there."

"You are there."

I stepped out of the car but didn't go far. There was nowhere to go.

Other than a roughly manicured crater in the ground, there was nothing here. No wreckage. No evidence of mass death and destruction. No rogue, homicidal shard of debris threatening to end my life as it had Krazinski's.

I could barely contain my anger. This was why Develchko had worked so hard to keep me from coming here. He wanted as much time as possible to complete the utter obliteration of all evidence that would even hint that a plane crash had ever happened here. What I still couldn't understand was why.

I returned to the waiting Lada, opened the door, looked in. I barked at Viktor: "Stay in the car!"

Slamming the door closed, I pulled out my cellphone and dialed the private number for Ross Campbell. It was early morning in Toronto. He answered on the first ring.

"I'm here," was all I said. "They've wiped it clean. There's no plane. No scattered remains. Not even a broken blade of grass, for chrissakes!"

What I heard next staggered me. "I know," he said.

"What do you mean you know? What the fuck is going on here, Campbell? And if you knew, why didn't you tell me?"

"I just found out myself. It's…it's all a big misunderstanding…not to mention a political landmine. Saint, I want you to get on that plane with Krazinski's body and get back to Toronto before this thing turns into some kind of international incident."

"What thing? What's going on?"

"Somehow word got out that IIA was sending someone to Magadan. They believed you were coming to investigate the accident. Krazinski's accident, not the plane accident. By sending you, it made it seem we were accusing them of assassinating Krazinski. Or at the very least that we blamed them for not maintaining proper safety protocols at the site, leading to Krazinski's death. They assumed you were sent to prove it, one way or another."

"And what if I was? Don't we have that right?"

"No. We don't. Not in this particular environment. And certainly not by you, Saint. I want you to get your ass back here. Now."

"So you're just going to allow them to sweep all of this under the rug?"

"Sweep what? There's nothing to sweep."

"Don't you think what's happened here is even a little suspicious? If they had nothing to hide, why get rid of everything? And what *you* don't know, Campbell, is that there may have been a murder here today. Not to mention an attempt on my life."

The line crackled with tension.

"Saint, I don't know what kind of trouble you're getting yourself—and IIA—into out there, but hear this: I'm ordering you back now. Before the Russian army marches in there and sticks you in a gulag for the rest of your pretty-boy days."

"Haven't you heard, Campbell? The Cold War is over. They don't do that sort of thing anymore."

"The Russians have been known to revert to bad habits at the slightest provocation. Don't test their limits." His voice fell an octave as he warned, "Saint, I'm not kidding. Get out of there, while the getting is good."

"I can't." With those two words, I could sense a tidal wave of anger and frustration roaring my way. I didn't care. "If there is something suspicious about Krazinski's death, I have to find out what it is."

"That's just it, Saint. There's nothing suspicious. Except their suspicion that you're over there trying to make them look bad in an already bad situation." He waited a beat, then, "You know what? Maybe you're right. Maybe Develchko knows there was something wonky at the site that caused Krazinski's death. Maybe they sent him in before it was safe to do so. Maybe a piece of the plane dropped on his head. It's terrible. I know. But do you think that's what Jean wants to hear? It's done, Saint. Nothing you can do will change that. We'll never have to deal with these people again. Let it go."

He kept on before I had time to interrupt. "As far as any murders being committed out there, you're right, I don't know about that. But it sounds as if you're not entirely convinced about it either. Bad things happen. You know that better than almost anyone. Get your head together, for chrissakes."

Was Campbell right? I'd gone from a grueling ten days in South Africa to here with barely a moment's rest. And I'd just suffered a concussion. Was I thinking straight? Just the fact that I had doubts worried me. I don't usually doubt myself.

Campbell read my silence as obstinacy.

"Goddamnit, Saint! Why are you making things so difficult? You have more important things to look after!" he blurted. I could tell the man was losing patience.

"More important things?"

"Jesus, Saint, I shouldn't have to be the one to tell you this."

"Tell me what?"

"Saint, you're dying."

Chapter Five

Despite his name, Milo Yelchin was Japanese, adopted and raised by Russian-Canadian parents. Physically he was an interesting mix of nature and nurture. His facial features were undeniably Asian; his body was as thick and muscled as a Russian weightlifter's. His mind was brilliant. At only thirty-nine, he'd held the position of official IIA physician for a decade, overseeing the health concerns of all IIA personnel, agents, and anyone else IIA wanted checked out. Agents had to see Milo twice a year, whether we wanted to or not. IIA couldn't afford to be carrying anyone whose health might jeopardize an operation. With Krazinski gone, Yelchin had no choice but to report my diagnosis to Ross Campbell. Poor Campbell. Now my shit was on his pile.

"We call it GBM," Milo said. "Glioblastoma multiforme. We saw it on your MRI. It's the most common malignant primary brain tumour. And, unfortunately, the most aggressive."

I was sitting in a chair opposite Milo, staring at his serious face across the impossibly wide expanse of his desktop. The chair was soft yet firm, spacious yet embracing, like a consoling cocoon. As I sat listening to the dire prognosis, part of me wanted to sink further into the chair, to simply disappear forever. But why rush things?

"Treatment can involve the typical things: radiation, chemotherapy. There's antiangiogenic therapy. Surgery. There are some experimental procedures out there."

"Experimental? Has it come to that?" I said lightly.

Milo did not smile.

"Treatment is…difficult." He seemed to be the one having difficulty at the moment.

"Tell me," I said. "Tell me everything."

"As you know—"

"No, Milo, I don't know!" I exclaimed. I heard harshness in my words. And something unfamiliar. Uncertainty? Fear? "Milo, I'm sorry. I just…this is just so far out of my area of expertise. I don't know anything about this."

"That's why I'm here," he said soothingly. "Are you certain you want to hear all this?"

I nodded, not entirely sure I wasn't lying to the doctor. And to myself.

"The human brain has very limited ability to heal itself," he said. "A lot of drugs can't cross the blood-brain barrier to do any good. And even if they could, these particular tumour cells—the ones you have—are resistant to most of our conventional therapies. That makes them more apt to damage the brain than heal it."

"You're not giving me much good news, doc."

"I'm sorry, Adam. You said you wanted the straight truth."

Did I?

"But I feel fine."

"Your symptoms will depend on the location of the tumour, more so than its pathological properties. The tumour can start producing symptoms quickly. But for now it may be asymptomatic. We call it being clinically silent."

"Until it isn't."

He nodded. "Until it isn't."

"Then what?"

"Seizure, nausea and vomiting, headache, hemiparesis—a weakness on one side of the body...."

"Like a stroke?" *Good God.*

"Usually not as severe."

I found myself taking deep breaths. One after another. I heard my mind coaching me: *Keep breathing. Keep breathing. Keep breathing.* I recalled reading somewhere that the ultimate revelation of an individual's true identity and personal fortitude comes upon hearing of their impending death.

Who would I turn out to be?

"The single most prevalent symptom is a progressive memory, personality, or neurological deficit, due to temporal and frontal lobe involvement." Was this man ever going to shut up? "Keep in mind, Adam, this may not happen for quite some time." Jolly good news.

"And at the end?" May as well cut to the chase.

"Death is usually caused by a cerebral edema—that's excess accumulation of water on the brain—or increased intracranial pressure."

Breathe.

How could I be sure I wanted to ask the next question? The final question. With Yelchin's answer, my life would suddenly have a defined end. Give or take. This was all happening at a dizzying speed. I was a ball thrown downhill. I couldn't stop myself.

"How long?"

"Without treatment, three months."

Breathe.

"With some forms of treatment, you can last longer, Adam."

"How much longer?"

"Patients have survived up to two years." The look on my face must have begged for pity because he added, "Some even longer." I was betting the "some" were at the way far end of the bell curve.

I was glad it was late Friday by time I returned to IIA. I wouldn't have to face anyone on the way to my office. Most everyone would be gone for the weekend. Off to a cocktail lounge or pub for after-work drinks with friends. Or a store to pick up food for a family dinner. Or maybe to find that perfect bouquet of flowers for a sweetheart. Without a specified end date, life was full of possibilities. It brimmed with joyful experiences. None of which was the case for me any longer.

Then it hit me. The realization was so ridiculously true, I heard myself chortle. Out loud. In the elevator. I was laughing. By myself.

God, is this the first sign of the end?

But it *was* funny. In a ridiculous, sad kind of way.

There I was, throwing myself an impromptu pity party, bemoaning how I now had an expiry date and therefore couldn't do all these wonderful things "normal" people did. Yet for the life of me I couldn't remember the last time I did *any* of them. So really, other than having less time to not do them in, what was I really losing?

Pitiful.

I threw open my office door and slammed it shut behind me, enjoying the thundering, angry sound it made. I didn't think anyone else was on the floor, but just in case, I didn't want witnesses to what was coming next.

What was coming next?

What do you do when you hear news like this?

I needed some cliché activity to immerse myself in. Surely they must work. Or else you wouldn't see them in every movie and television drama.

I should cry.

How does a man cry? Does it just happen? Or did I have to do something to get things going?

It was dark in the room. I didn't want unnatural light. It would feel too…revealing. I hit the button for the blinds. They slid open, filling the office with the early evening shades of a dying day. How appropriate. I stood near one of the floor-to-ceiling windows and stared out at my city.

My city?

I barely knew it.

I never spent time here.

How was I to find comfort from a place that I didn't know, and didn't know me? I turned away and fell into the chair behind my desk. Maybe I should just plow myself into work. Bury myself in it. Until it was time for someone to bury me.

There was a package in my in-box. I only noticed it because its presence there was an oddity. The secretaries knew better than to put regular mail on my desk. Something was either important enough to deliver directly to me, in person or electronically, or else forget about it. So what was this?

I reached for the hefty envelope. Markings on the outside told me it had arrived by courier, not post. Today. I tore open one end. A sheaf of papers dropped into my hand.

Divorce papers. With yellow stickies indicating where my signature was required.

This was not a very good day.

It took me fifteen minutes to get home. Excellent by Toronto standards. My apartment is in the Four Seasons Private Residences in Yorkville.

Once upon a time, Yorkville was its own village. It was eventually annexed by the City of Toronto. By anyone's account, Yorkville is one of Canada's most exclusive and expensive shopping districts. I can personally attest to the fact, having given my credit cards a workout in any number of local stores. But why would I need any of that stuff now? Or maybe I needed it all?

I parked the car and made my way into the plush Yabu Pushelberg-designed lobby. I used a security card to access the high-speed elevator that whisked me away to my suite on the forty-sixth floor of the West Residence tower. When I opened the apartment door, black, deafening silence assaulted me.

I live in a 2,500 square foot tomb made of glass.

Apparently, I was fast learning, I have quite a talent for morbidity.

I punched at buttons on a panel near the entrance, filling the space with fresh air, light, and music.

As a Puccini opera attacked the stillness, I headed for the bedroom. I peeled off my clothes and spent the next twenty minutes in the oversized shower suite. First I allowed fiery hot, soapy water to cleanse me, then ice cold to numb me. As a denouement, I activated a symphony of steam jets and stood with my head hung low, hoping to empty it. Without success.

I threw on a white Frette bathrobe and retrieved the bottle of pills Milo Yelchin had handed me on my way out of his office. I'd mindlessly stashed them in my jacket pocket. *Something to ease the effects should any of the early symptoms we talked about rear their ugly heads*, he'd said. I was barely listening by that point.

Was feeling sorry for yourself a symptom? Why not? I downed one of the pills dry.

Back in the front room, I gave the sparkling skyline a cursory look before heading for the bar. I poured myself a heavy dose of sixteen-year-old Lagavulin. Drank half of it. Topped it up. I knew if I didn't move away from the bar right then, I might never.

I approached the windows, bringing my nose so close the glass began to fog over from my high-proof breath. I stared hard at the view. Most people would gasp at the beauty of it. It meant nothing to me.

I stepped back and fell into my dove-grey Incanto leather couch. I downed the peaty drink. Empty again. I swore. I refilled. Sat back down. This time bringing the envelope containing the divorce papers with me. I swore some more. One of the benefits of a career where I regularly witness the world in tragic circumstances is that I've amassed a startlingly large collection of cuss words, in several languages.

I was born into a middle-class, rural Saskatchewan family. One sister. Lots of farm animals. I was what they called a hellion back then. Reckless. Rebellious.

Early on, I made it very clear to my father that although I was the only son, I would wholly refuse to take over the land when it came time for him to retire. The polar opposite of what every one of my high school buddies intended to do. Most of them simply accepted their agricultural fate without question, as though it was some kind of divine, unassailable, hereditary right, like becoming king or queen of England. They never thought about what they really wanted. Why bother when it's already been decided for you?

Not me. I didn't know what I wanted. Only what I didn't. Of course, this kind of thinking tends to lead to no good. After a brief career in junior hockey that ended badly, I was left directionless. With no sense of who I was or where I belonged, the only thing I became adept at was getting into trouble. Not surprisingly, this led to skirmishes with local law enforcement.

When my transgressions inevitably became serious enough, my parents took action. They sent me to military school. Some people think military school is too tough. Too strict. That it turns spirited kids into robots with bad haircuts who only respond to being yelled at. But for me, it totally worked. I was turned around. I'd been heading down one path and ended up on another.

I never went back to the farm. After my schooling was done, I enrolled in the Canadian military. Five years later, back in civilian life, I returned to Saskatchewan to train as a cadet at the Royal Canadian Mounted Police Academy in Regina. I never worked a day with the RCMP. IIA had recruited me direct from the academy into the Canadian Disaster Recovery Agency.

On my first day as a CDRA agent-in-training, I met another junior IIA agent, Kate Spalding. At 5'10", with long, dark hair, the face of Sophia Loren, the body of Adriana Lima, and a penchant for high-high heels and fitted but staid business suits, she got my attention. And pretty much everyone else's too. But that didn't bother me much. At 6'3", I was one of the few guys with whom she didn't have to "dumb down" her footwear on a date.

At first, our time together consisted mostly of a quick drink at a bar followed by catching a cab to one of our apartments for sex. Kate had a blithe and blissfully cheery attitude toward sex. There were no hang-ups, no restrictions, no unseen ties that bind. Sex was a gift meant for sharing between two consulting adults, and I'm nothing if not a sharer.

As our training and careers progressed, quickly for both of us, things became increasingly complicated. Kate was slotted into the War Crimes Agency. I was a fully trained disaster recovery agent ready for fieldwork. We each consciously and aggressively pursued demanding occupations that left little time for personal lives.

Still, somewhere along the way, we'd become sexually

exclusive. Even though opportunities to be together were decreasing in regularity, we mutually decided we were satisfied maintaining the status quo.

This worked well.

Until the contraceptive industry failed us.

As soon as we confirmed the news, I found a beach house that was much too big for two people and booked a long weekend in North Carolina. We ran away.

After four days of talking and arguing, crying and promising, always followed by fantastic make-up sex, we returned to Toronto resolute.

Kate would keep the baby. We would get married. We would combine our lives into one larger apartment, which we could now well afford. Kate would try to hang on to her job. I would—secretly—hope she'd fail.

I was a selfish bastard.

And then it got worse. Turns out, I was a horrible husband. And an even worse father.

I had a clear choice. Kate and the baby, or my hard-living, fast-paced, lucrative, exciting, worldly, fascinating, endlessly rewarding, personally gratifying career.

I chose wrong. I just didn't know it until it was too late.

When Rowan was five, Kate asked for a divorce. Then again when he was ten. I was a master at making promises I'd never keep. It wasn't that I had no intentions of keeping them. I simply didn't know how to.

A ringing phone jarred me from my trance. A female computerized voice told me: "The caller is…Kate."

I ignored it. I refilled my glass a third time—fourth?—picked up the divorce documents and began reading.

They'd lived apart for two years. In all that time, Kate Spalding never had occasion to use the key card Adam had given her *just in case*. She hadn't wanted to think about what he'd meant by *just in case*. She was quite certain that what he had in mind had no resemblance to what she was about to do.

She knew he was in town. She'd left countless messages on his machine over the past week. None were returned. She knew why. The divorce papers would have been delivered, as she'd instructed, to his office on Friday. She'd hoped to have talked to him long before he saw them. She had no desire to surprise him or hurt his feelings. She loved Adam Saint. Everything had changed but that. Love was no longer enough. Cheesy but true. With his refusal to call her back, he'd pressed her against a wall. She wanted those papers signed this weekend. She'd run out of time.

Kate pounded on the door again.

No answer.

She inserted the key card into the waiting slot. The door fell open. Pocketing the key, she entered the dimly lit interior.

"Adam?" she called, at first lightly, then with more insistence. "Adam, are you here?"

The pretty girl had become a beautiful woman. If anything, she was in better physical shape than she'd been at any other time. She was also smarter. And exceedingly more cautious. Proceeding into the apartment, she moved like a panther, ready for anything.

"Adam?"

No answer.

She returned to the panel near the front door, which controlled pretty much everything in the apartment. She hated the thing. No one piece of circuitry should have so much power. She hit a few buttons to light up the place.

It was a mess, both the kitchen and living room. Worthy of a week-long bachelor party or frat house kegger. She headed down the long hallway that led to the rear of the apartment.

The door to the master suite was slightly ajar.

Once more she called her husband's name.

Hearing no reply, she pushed open the door and found him.

Adam Saint was on the bed, unclothed, tangled in sheets that had come loose from the mattress. All the windows were shaded. The only illumination came from a glow light in the shower suite on the other side of the room.

On high alert, Kate approached the bed, taking in every inch of the man.

Although the lighting was dim, she could see life beating below Adam's naturally tan skin. Skin she'd often thought was incongruously soft for a man who could be so hard. His colour was good. Was he simply in a deep sleep?

Covering his naked body with a swath of 400-thread-count cotton, she sat next to him on the bed and gently laid a hand on his thickly muscled arm. He was warm. But something wasn't right.

Adam was a highly trained agent. Under no circumstances would he ever allow someone to approach, at any time, day or night, light or dark, fully awake or asleep, without knowing it and being fully prepared to respond. Unless….

"Adam, I know you're awake."

"Just barely," he croaked. Half his face was smushed

against a pillow that looked as if it had been used as a punching bag by Oscar De La Hoya.

"What are you doing in here? Why aren't you answering your door? Or the phone for that matter? You smell like a distillery by the way."

Adam turned full face toward Kate. For a second or two, he simply stared at her.

She allowed it without protest, using the opportunity to take her own inventory of the man. She was reminded how, even with his dark, sandy hair horribly disheveled, a ragged three-day beard, and puffy eyes, he was still one of the most handsome men she had ever laid eyes upon. His lips, thick like a Greek god's, were one of his best features. The edges tipped up ever so slightly as he whispered: "Hello, stranger."

She knew he was taking a short, personal moment, pretending things were as they used to be.

"Hello, stranger," she whispered back.

It had been their thing. Their standard greeting whenever they came back together after being apart for any prolonged period of time. They'd make wild, crazy, passionate love, and their first words to each other afterwards were always the same: *Hello, stranger.*

Kate hid a smile. "You're obviously in need of serious assistance." She stood, pulling his arm along with her. "Come on, get up, you big bag of bones."

Adam, unabashed in his nakedness, followed her lead, the two of them heading toward the shower. Once there, she reached in and turned the spigots, testing the sprays of water for warmth. When she was satisfied, she grasped Adam by the shoulders and directed him inside the enclosure. At the last moment, his arm shot out and made as if to pull her in with him.

"Adam, no!"

"No?" His eyes twinkled.

They stared at one another, on the brink of what would come next.

Kate pulled back.

Adam nodded, the look on his face disappointed but accepting. He was about to turn away when Kate kicked off her heels and began unbuttoning her suit jacket. Within a few seconds, she was in the shower with him, naked, back against the textured granite wall as he pressed hard against her.

Ninety minutes later, freshly showered, shaved, and wearing well-worn jeans and a loose-fitting shirt, Adam emerged from the bedroom. He found his wife sitting on the couch, a glass of wine in her elegant hand. A bottle of Dos Equis was waiting for him on the coffee table. Forty-six stories below, Toronto looked splendidly ebullient as it slipped into late-night revelry. Next to the waiting beer were the divorce papers.

Without a word, he sat next to Kate and picked up the documents and a pen. He turned to the first page requiring his signature.

Kate frowned. "No argument?"

She was worried. Something was wrong with her husband. She knew him too well. Their lovemaking had been extraordinary as it so often was. But tonight there was something different. It wasn't just because they hadn't had sex together in over a year. There was something deep and desperate about it. A certain…melancholy? Was it because he knew their marriage was irrevocably broken? Was it because he knew this would be the last time they'd ever be intimate in this way? At this point in the game of a marriage gone bad, a man *should* know those things. But not Adam Saint. Sure, they'd been formally separated for two years already. But he was the kind of man who would never concede easily.

"You don't want to be with me anymore." His voice was uncharacteristically mellow. "It's okay, Kate. I get it."

"Adam, what the hell is wrong with you? I mean, don't get me wrong. I want you to sign these papers, and I'm glad you are, but I know there's something not right here. You're worrying me."

He pulled the pen from paper and settled his eyes on hers. "I'll sign on one condition."

She smirked. "Okay, this is more like it. Shoot. What is it this time? A little couple's counseling? It went so well last time. Remember? How many times did I show up alone? Was it four times? Five?"

"I want Rowan."

Kate was struck mute. Colour drained from her face. She set down her wine glass. It was either that, she knew, or the contents would end up in Adam's face. "What did you just say?"

"I want Rowan. Not forever. Just for a while. Full time. I want temporary, full-time custody."

Kate rose, glad she'd put her heels back on so she could tower over him in this moment.

She laughed. Not a pretty laugh. "You are ridiculous. Do you know that? You are a stupid, ridiculous man, Adam Saint."

Adam looked up at his soon-to-be ex-wife. "I said it wouldn't be forever. I just want—"

"Custody? You want custody? Adam, if you'd paid your son any attention *ever*, you'd know that he is seventeen years old! Seventeen! There is no custody. Your son is about to become an adult. If you want to convince him to come live with you *temporarily permanently*, you go right ahead." She was mocking him now. "But good luck with that. He barely knows who you are."

The words were hurtful, she knew. She hated herself for saying them as soon as they came out of her mouth. Hurtful but not entirely untrue.

Adam sat back, stunned. His eyes dropped to the papers in his hand. He knew he'd made a monstrous mess of things.

Kate lowered herself to sit on the coffee table directly in front of Adam. This wasn't the way it was supposed to be. None of it. The fucking in the shower. The arguing. This was all wrong. "Adam, I'm going to leave now. I hope you sign the papers. When you do, call me."

She moved to get up but stopped when Adam's hand fell on her lap.

"Don't go." His voice was barely his own.

Kate felt tears building up in her eyes. She was not a crier. "Adam, what is going on? You have to tell me."

Placing the divorce document on Kate's lap, he silently, methodically, signed each page marked with a yellow sticky.

When he was done, he placed them back in the envelope and handed it to her. As he did, he said: "I'm dying."

Chapter Six

I think I expected it to go away like a bad cold. I'd wake up Monday morning and—other than the pounding in my head from drinking every splash of alcohol in my apartment—I'd feel much better. Revived. Refreshed. Rejuvenated. Repaired? But a death sentence is not a fleeting virus easily fought off with the right meds and some sleep. It's an invasion. A battalion of emotions, fears, doubts, and unexpected mind games that play havoc with every fibre of your being. I was no longer Adam Saint. Overnight I had become someone else. Someone I did not want to be.

So now what? What am I supposed to do with that?

I woke up Monday morning at my regular time. By eight a.m., I'd worked out in the building's gym, showered, dressed, swallowed a couple of Yelchin's pills—in case my thudding head wasn't entirely hangover related—and driven to work. Forgoing my own office, I began at the office of Ross Campbell. His secretary told me he was in a series of meetings for most of the day. I was prepared if that should be the case. I left her with a letter in a sealed envelope. The letter was short and concise, and it ended with: "I hereby tender my resignation."

My plan was to spend the next few days wrapping up the

KwaZulu-Natal file, clearing up old paperwork, and transferring my open cases to other agents. Then I'd plan the rest of my life. Which isn't as daunting a task as you'd think when the timeline can be measured in months.

Focusing on something other than what was happening inside my body was a godsend. Much of the success I've enjoyed in my career has come from an ability to turn my mind off to factors extraneous and potentially injurious to my end goal. When I'm in the zone, I don't allow the sight of a dead body to affect me. I never permit confrontation or irrational argument to dissuade me from my purpose. I take neither insult nor praise personally. I know what needs doing. I do it. So it was today.

It was after seven when I opened my office door again. I'd forgotten lunch, coffee, the world outside. It felt good.

The halls were quiet. Office doors were closed. I headed for the elevator. The only thing I could think of was how much I wanted to go home and drink myself into oblivion. Again. At least until tomorrow morning when I could do this all over again. Mindless repetition. I'd not been a fan until now.

The CCX was where I'd left it that morning. Still a few yards away, I fingered the fob to unlock the doors. Normally the locks disengaging would be accompanied by a short tweet. This time, nothing. I tried again.

Nothing.

Immediately I was on alert. In my business, the unusual is always suspicious.

I stopped next to the vehicle and tried a third time. The car did not unlock. I scanned the parking garage. There were several cars nearby. No people, or at least none I could see.

I approached the car and felt the hood. Cool.

I dropped to the ground and inspected the bottom carriage. Nothing out of the ordinary.

Back on my feet, I slowly inserted the key into the door lock. Old school.

The key did not turn.

Crouching down, I carefully inspected the area around the lock.

Shit.

I straightened and backed away from the car.

The markings were barely visible to the naked eye. But I could tell. Someone had tampered with my car.

Once again, I made a visual search of the garage. Was someone watching me?

I found the garage security camera. It appeared to be operational. If someone…Develchko?…had arranged for something to be done to my car, or planned a personal attack on me, surely they would be smart enough to disable the camera.

I took the stairs to the vacant lobby and called the elevator. When it arrived, I slipped a key card into the slot that allowed me access to the IIA floors.

The green light indicating access granted did not illuminate.

I punched the floor button. As expected, without a recognized key card, nothing happened.

I began again. Key card in slot. Push floor button.

Same result.

Out on the street, I hailed a taxi.

The streets were busy. It took about twenty minutes before the cabbie pulled up in front of my building.

"Uh, the card's denied, bud," the driver said as he handed me back my credit card.

I pulled cash from my pocket. Once again, old school. I'd never been a Boy Scout, but I'm always prepared.

By the time I was on the forty-sixth floor, my key card failing to get me into my apartment, the game had ceased to surprise me.

I'm sure they didn't expect me to take this lying down.

As a man of action, I was in the mood to meet their expectations.

Farmland until 1929, Toronto's Bridle Path neighbourhood began taking shape after the construction of the Bayview Bridge over the West Don River. Land mogul Hubert Page subsequently built the first home, then encouraged Toronto's elite to join him in the secluded sanctuary. Some eighty years later, Bridle Path still has only a few roads and is enveloped by parks and the peaceful Don River Valley. Most dwellings are sizable, up to 20,000 square feet, with lots between two and four acres. Disgraced newspaper magnate Conrad Black; the co-founder of Citytv, Moses Znaimer; and even the purple one himself, Prince, have purchased homes there. Not to be outdone, so had IIA chief Maryann Knoble.

Several years ago, and not without some effort, I made it my business to find out everything I could about Knoble, including where she lived. I didn't like the idea of working for someone I couldn't find if I really had to.

Like now.

Generally I had little to do with Knoble. As far as the organization chart showed, I worked for Krazinski, who worked for Campbell, who worked for Knoble. But ultimately, I knew, as did everyone who put a brain cell into thinking about it, that Knoble was the final decision maker. She pressed all the buttons and pulled all the levers. IIA and all of its agencies and divisions were under her strict, irrefutable control. So I knew that, although it was likely Campbell who had physically ordered my life erased, with locks retooled and passwords changed, he'd done so on Knoble's instructions. They would be expecting me to take Campbell to task. But why bother with the middle man? I'm more of a straight-to-the-source kind of guy.

Given what had just happened, I imagined Knoble wouldn't be too keen on inviting me inside if I showed up on her front doorstep. I'd have to take care of that myself.

My intel on Knoble included a great deal of information about her private life and habits. Such as her preference for relying on technology rather than real, live human beings to do her bidding. I'm sure if she could have commissioned an army of robots to replace every IIA and IIA-affiliated agent, she would have done so. And maybe she had. Maybe all our pink slips were pending, simply awaiting her final approval of prototypes developed in some eastern European android factory. But in the meantime, other than a three-times-a-week, non-live-in housecleaner, I had no bodies to worry about aside from her own.

Not much of a cook herself, the IIA chief ate out every night of the week. At the same restaurant. It had a fancy name and prices to match. But it was basically a meat and potatoes type of place, meant for the moneyed set whose culinary tastes ran to the basic but who wouldn't be caught dead at The Keg.

Knoble would finish her meal around nine p.m. Then she'd beckon a driver to deliver her home.

That was weak spot number one.

A bad guy (which tonight was me) familiar with her rigid habits could easily sneak onto the gated property without triggering an alarm. Situated just right, all I had to do was sneak through the gates at the same time as the car ferrying Knoble home.

Weak spot number two was the dog. A doddering old basset hound with poor eyesight and a defective nose for smelling trouble. The first thing Knoble did when she got home was to let the poor dear out for a pee and poo. Alarm would be off. Knoble would be unwary and relaxed. And there I'd be.

"Hello, Maryann. I hate to bother you like this, but I was wondering if I could use your couch for the night. I seem to be locked out of my apartment." An excellent opening line. I'd worked on it while I waited.

I had to give the iron maiden credit. Her face, backlit by the porch light, didn't even flinch. The first gravelly words out of her mouth were: "Sophie, get back here."

Of course poor Sophie couldn't hear her. Besides, she'd waited all day for this moment. She wasn't about to hold it for another second. No matter who was in her backyard.

"You've surprised me, Mr. Saint."

"I'm glad to hear it. I wanted to return the favour." I stepped out of the darkness.

I could see she was wondering how I'd managed to get into her backyard. But she was too proud to ask the question.

"Certainly you didn't think you could deliver a letter of resignation and simply walk away from IIA without repercussions."

"I expected to walk away without a job. It was everything else that was unexpected."

"We only took back what was ours. The office. The car. The apartment. The expense account. All ours, Saint. Not yours. Never yours. You have a demanding, dangerous job. You've done it well. You've been compensated handsomely. I hope you've saved some of your money," she recommended like some kind of shrewd Wall Street broker, "because the bells and whistles, they're all gone. As of now. As far as I'm concerned, you are nothing more than a vagrant trespassing on my private property. Which is how I'll be describing you to the police."

I stiffened. I'd not thought of everything.

Knoble smiled coldly as she fingered the pendant around her neck. A panic button. Knoble was a woman who did dangerous work with dangerous people in a dangerous world. I should have known that someone in her position would never allow herself to be too far away from protection from unsavoury forces.

"I want to know why you're doing this."

Her thin lips twitched. The night was dark, her eyes were darker. "It's simple really. Think of it as an operation.

I'm merely excising a rotting piece of flesh before it infects the rest of its host. And just in case I don't make myself perfectly clear, in that analogy, IIA is the host, and you, Mr. Saint, are the rotting flesh."

"I need more time. There are...extenuating circumstances."

"Your impending death," she stated with a scoff. "I'm well aware."

Note for my file on Maryann Knoble: *She's a heartless bitch.*

"Have you come to ask for your job back? Is that why you're here?" She narrowed her eyes. Without waiting for the answer she expected to get, she said, "I don't approve of your methods, but if so...." She tapped her pendant. "...I suppose I could call off my friends. But we won't talk about this now. Tomorrow morning. In my office."

This surprised me. "Why would you want that? You know I'm going to die. I'm of no use to you anymore."

"Or maybe," she began, sounding cryptic, "in the time you have left, you could be more useful to IIA than you've ever been before."

What was she saying? What use was a dying man...? My mind began to spin with crazy possibilities.

"Good girl, Sophie," Knoble called out to her returning dog hobbling its way up the porch steps, barely giving me a second glance. Knoble cocked her head. "I believe I hear sirens."

"Fuck you," I said.

A Cheshire Cat smile. "Well then, I'll take that as a no. Please inform someone of your forwarding address. We'll

send your things. And one more thing, Mr. Saint." She
dipped her chin in the direction of the sirens. "I suggest a
smartly paced jog might serve you well right about now.
Good night." She turned and disappeared inside, Sophie at
her heels.

It really wasn't so bad. Sure, she had to work evening shifts.
But because it was usually quiet at night, they allowed her
to bring Jake to the restaurant with her. He even helped fill
water glasses and clear tables when he wasn't studying for
the pop quizzes Hanna administered on a frequent basis.
Hanna didn't know which one of them she felt worse for.
Him for having to miss out on a regular kid's life of going
to school, where he'd have friends and teachers who were
actually trained to teach. Or herself for having to study
grade five math and science all over again in her spare
time—what little there was of it—so she could home-
school her son.

Today had been a good day. Right now was a good time.
The restaurant was quiet. Jake was sitting at one of the outdoor, street-side tables reading a book. It was a beautiful
evening. The tips had been good over the dinner rush. If
she squinted hard enough, she could almost imagine they
were living a normal life.

The job had been a stroke of good luck. Just as she was
dropping off a resume—most of it lies and fabrication—
the owner, Elmer, had just heard the news that his best waitress had gone into premature labour. He had no one to
replace her. He told Hanna that if she could start that night,

she was hired. She told him that if she could bring Jake, it was a deal. That first night she'd made forty-seven dollars in tips.

The Mediterraneo Inn was supposed to serve Mediterranean-inspired cuisine. But the only thing that came close as far as Hanna could tell were mussels in a white wine sauce. The rest of the menu was basic, good food at good prices. And Elmer had a big heart, offering her a forty per cent discount on anything she ate there (whether she was working or not). Jake ate for free.

Hanna knew she'd stumbled upon a good thing. She didn't want to screw it up. Good things weren't easy to find. Not when the most important thing was to stay out of sight. Thankfully she and Jake were a needle, and Canada was a mighty big haystack.

At first she'd been tempted to stick to major highways. There was comfort in being on roads she knew well. But there was also danger: danger of being found. So she'd veered off the Trans-Canada, switched up directions, and headed into unknown territory. She passed towns with curious names such as Justice, Wheatland, Beulah, Isabella, and Foxwarren. But a big problem dogged her every stop. Money. Hanna realized she'd need to find a way to make some cash before she and her son perished in the hinterland. The smaller the town the safer she felt but the less likely she was to find a job. She'd have to risk a bigger centre.

Just past the Manitoba/Saskatchewan border, she found Esterhazy. It was far enough off the Trans-Canada to be an unlikely place for anyone to come looking for her. And she liked the place. Despite its lofty claim to being the Potash

Capital of the World, Esterhazy had a decidedly small-town prairie feel to it. It was perfect. Small enough to get around in and to be affordable, yet big enough to get lost in.

Maybe, just maybe, this would be the place she and Jake could stay for a while. She really hoped so. She knew the constant moving around was beginning to get to her son. At first she'd been able to sell the whole thing as a big adventure. After all, what ten-year-old boy didn't want an escapade that included racing from place to place, making secret moves under the cover of night, creating fictional names and back stories. But sometimes a boy just wants stay put, live in a house, and sleep in his own bed. And so did she.

As Hanna wiped down the counter near the cash register, keeping one eye on Jake through the restaurant's front window, she heard the chimes over the door jangle. Three women walked in. Hanna knew exactly who they were. The women were her age, early thirties. They'd probably been friends since high school. They'd married and had babies at about the same time. And here they were on a Wednesday night. The husbands were at home, looking after the kids. They'd gone to some chick flick at the local theatre. Now they were stopping by the Mediterraneo for coffee and dessert and a few, last precious moments of girl time.

Showing the trio to a nice corner table in the nearly empty restaurant, Hanna listened to their laughter and easy chatter. As they gabbed on about nothing and everything, she felt a dull stab of pain in her heart. She hated these girls. For what they had. For what she'd lost. Good friends, nice clothes…happiness. All that was gone. Forever. Every giggle, every smile, every pat on the arm or kind word shared between the women was like the scratch of a nail across a chalkboard. It was as if they were here on purpose, flaunting their abundant riches in front of the poorest girl in town. She wanted to tell them to shut up or leave.

Instantly she regretted the thought. It wasn't their fault they could enjoy their lives in a way Hanna once had but never would again. Instead she smiled and said, "Is this table okay? I'll leave the menus and be right back."

Back at the register, Hanna caught sight of herself in the mirror that hung behind the counter. She choked back a distressed gasp. *Who is that woman?* Once upon a time she was the girl people mistook for Bar Refaeli. Now, after chopping off most of her hair and losing weight, she was Anne Hathaway playing Fantine in *Les Misérables*.

The door chimed again. Two men walked in. Hanna checked on Jake as she walked by the window to greet the newcomers. He seemed to be thoroughly engrossed in his newest find at the library. An Arthur Slade book, something about a "hunchback." She smiled and waved at him, even though she knew he wouldn't see her.

"Hello, Hanna," one of the men said when she offered to show them to a table.

Hanna froze. No one knew her here. How did this man know her name? *Oh God. Jake. I have to get him out of here.*

Seeing her expression, the man gave her a crooked smile and pointed at her name tag. "Sorry about that. Name tags. They make strangers more familiar than they should be, I suppose."

Hanna let out a relieved breath. "Oh, wow, yes. I keep forgetting about this thing." Feeling sheepish, she grabbed a pair of menus, almost dropping them, and led the men to a table.

"Is that your son sitting out there?" the same man asked when they were seated.

"No." Lying came easy to her now. "I'm just looking after him for his father." They'd be looking for a mother and son.

"He seems to really be enjoying his book. I like to see a kid who reads."

What was up with this guy? Why all the questions and comments? Hanna regarded the other man. He'd said nothing so far. Was he staring out the window at Jake?

"Let me leave you with the menus. I'll be right back with some water." She waited a beat, half expecting one of them to say: "We already know what we want: you and the boy."

Walking away, Hanna felt her skin quiver. She thought for sure if she turned around she'd catch the men watching her every move. Something wasn't right about them. Or was she just being paranoid? God, when wasn't she paranoid? But so what? It was paranoia that had kept them alive so far.

As she took orders from both tables, the chattering women and the suspicious men, Hanna kept an especially close watch on Jake. She wondered if she should ask him to sit inside. But she didn't want him any nearer to the two men than he had to be.

Once coffee and dessert were up for the women and she'd served the men a couple of beers and hamburgers, Hanna used the free moment to go outside to visit Jake.

"How's the book?" she asked, scanning the street for

anything or anyone suspicious, as had become her habit.

"It's pretty good. Could I have another root beer?"

"Jake, did you see those two men who came into the restaurant about half an hour ago?"

He shrugged. "I dunno. I guess I saw them."

"Did one of them talk to you? Ask you any questions?" She hated doing this to the boy. She knew she was passing her obsessive mistrust on to him. But maybe that wasn't such a bad thing. Whether she liked it or not, sooner or later her son would have to learn how to look out for himself.

"No. Why would they?"

Hanna shrugged back. "No reason. Just thought I'd ask."

"Just being a mom?" he asked.

Hanna smiled. It was her typical response whenever Jake wondered aloud about why she'd done some of the whacked-out things she'd had to do over the past months. Like abandoning their life. And friends. And family. And everything and everyone they had ever known. *Why did I do it? Well, Jakey, I'm just being a mom.* As if all moms did that kind of stuff.

"Yeah, that's right. Just being a mom."

She gave Jake a quick hug and headed back inside to check on her customers. As she closed the door with its jingle-jangle tune, she shot one last glance at her son.

Something caught her eye.

What the hell is that?

Insect?

Firefly?

Something was buzzing around Jake's head, like a large

mosquito preparing to alight.

But why is it bright red?

Like a light.

Laser!

"Jake!" Hanna's blood-curdling scream shattered the night as she crashed through the door, back outside.

For one horrible second it seemed as if time stood still. She didn't seem to be moving. At least not fast enough.

She could see the assassin's rifle's laser gunsight fall squarely in the middle of Jake's forehead.

She hurled herself forward with all the power she could humanly muster.

She heard Jake screaming. Hanna landed squarely on top of the young boy, sending both of them flying to the ground, then rolling away in separate directions. The customers came rushing out of the restaurant, quickly followed by the cook from the back, who must have heard the commotion.

Oh God, no! Jake! Am I too late?

Hanna scrambled to her son's prone body. She covered him with hers as if to hide him from prying eyes, the air, the moon, everything and anything that could possibly harm him. Only she could look at him. Only she could protect him.

"Jake! Jake!" She checked his forehead for a bullet wound.

Nothing. Just the smooth, soft, white skin of a ten-year-old boy.

Then she saw the blood.

She reached down to touch the back of his head.

"What did you do that for?" his little voice croaked.

"Why did you jump on me like that?"

"Thank God! Thank God!" Hanna lifted her face to the sky, crying out to a God she no longer believed was up there.

"What happened?" "Are you okay?" "Is he okay?" This from the customers who were huddling around the mother and son on the ground.

"You're bleeding, Jakey. Tell me where you're bleeding," Hanna asked, ignoring the concerned bystanders.

"I think I hit my head. That's what happens when people jump on you."

Hanna beamed. Jake's dry, sometimes sarcastic sense of humour appeared intact. "I'm going to call 911," one of the women announced, pulling a phone from her purse.

"No!" Hanna shrieked at her. She knew her reaction was more forceful than what would have been appropriate. But these people didn't understand. The police would ask questions. Questions she could not answer. "He's okay. It's just a scratch. He fell. I overreacted. Just being a crazy mom, I guess. I can take care of it."

"Are you sure?" one of the men asked. "There seems to be quite a bit of blood on the ground there."

"Thank you. Really. It's okay," Hanna answered back, trying for honey rather than vinegar. "You're all so kind. But I know he'll be okay."

"What happened, Hanna?" the cook asked.

Suddenly she remembered the red laser beam she'd spotted on her son's head. Someone had just tried to kill him. There had been a shooter out there, and maybe there still was. She had to get Jake out of there. For the moment, the assembled crowd was forming a protective barrier around them. No one in their right mind would shoot into a crowd. But what would happen once they dispersed?

Gingerly Hanna pulled herself into a standing position. Jake, with a great deal more sprightliness, followed suit.

"I think I need to take Jake home to look after this," she said to the cook. "Are you…do you think you could finish up for me?" She looked at the customers, most of them only halfway through their food and drinks.

"Don't worry about us," one of the women kindly offered. "We can just leave, or help clean up, or whatever you need us to do."

Hanna felt even worse for her earlier uncharitable thoughts about the women.

They were all being so nice.

"It's okay, Hanna," Jan, the cook, said. "I can take care of things for the rest of the night. You go."

If Hanna had learned anything over the past months of their gypsy life, sometimes you just had to ask for a helping hand. If anything good had come out of the nightmare they'd been living in, it was the realization that there were a lot more good people out there than she'd ever expected, people who wanted to help with no expectation of anything in return.

Even so, she wasn't stupid. Innately, right or wrong, she trusted the women over the two male customers. Looking at the women, she said, "My car isn't too far from here. Do you think you could walk me and Jake to it?"

They were only too happy to oblige.

Hanna strategically placed herself and Jake between the women as they walked. It was awkward but safe. If the shooter was still out there waiting for a chance to finish his job, she would make it impossible for him to do it. The poor women. Little did they know they were being used as human shields. If it wasn't for the fact that she was a mother protecting the life of her son, Hanna would have been ashamed of her actions. But tonight it was simply what she had to do.

Along the way, the women asked questions such as "Are you okay to drive?" "Are you sure you shouldn't go to the hospital?" "Is there anything else we can do?" Finally they reached the car. Over the past months, the vehicle had become more than a mode of transportation. It was the only familiar and consistent presence in their lives. It had faithfully ferried them from one hiding place to another, town to town, city to city, hauling their woefully small handful of worldly possessions along for the ride. Just seeing its dull shine in the glow of a nearby streetlight gave both of them comfort. As they climbed inside, they thanked the women, who waved as they drove off. Hanna hoped Jan wouldn't charge them for their dessert and coffee. They'd certainly earned a freebie.

Soon they were on the next street, out of sight of the café and heading toward their motel. Hanna floored it. If there was a killer out there, intent on following them, she wanted to know.

She watched the rear-view mirror almost as closely as the road in front of her.

Seconds passed.

A minute.

No one.

Yet.

At every red light, she bit her lip, waiting to see if another car would zoom up behind or next to them, the driver aiming a rifle at her son.

But none of that happened.

No one seemed to be following them, or even the least bit interested in them.

Onward.

The pressure of her teeth against her lower lip nearly broke the skin as Hanna recalled the horrific moment when she'd spotted the miniscule red dot of light on her son's forehead. Marking him for death. She didn't want to cry. Not in front of Jake. But the thought was unbearable. A deep, deep anguish was bubbling up inside of her, like a boiling pot ready to overflow. She glanced over at him, sitting patiently in the seat next to hers, buckled up for safety. She knew he must be filled with a thousand questions about what had just happened. Yet somehow he sensed it was best not to ask them. Not right now. God how she loved her son. She'd crawl to the ends of the earth for him. And maybe that's exactly what she'd have to do.

After ten minutes of circling city streets, Hanna allowed herself a deep, deep intake of breath, followed by a long sigh. Had she scared them off by her actions at the Mediterraneo? Or had she lost them? Had they given up? For good? Or just for the night?

It didn't matter. For the time being, they were safe. Sadly it was only temporary. They'd found the Mediterraneo. They could never go back. Once again, they would gather up their shallow roots and head for new ground.

Chapter Seven

There is a section of Pearson airport's Maple Leaf Lounge with signs displaying a cellphone with an angry red slash across it. This is where I usually sit. The number of people in airport lounges who are constantly on the phone speaking in voices loud enough to wake the dead could drive any man mad. I haven't figured out if they're oblivious, believe their business is the most important thing in the world, or simply don't care. I don't sit next to any of those people.

So when my cell went off, I immediately jumped up and headed for the noise maker's section.

"Saint," I answered.

"Saint, it's Ross. Where are you? Can you come by my office?"

"I suggest you check your memos, Campbell. My status at CDRA has changed."

"I know all about it."

I knew he did. So what did he want with me?

"Saint, I think if you came in, if we talk about this, you and I can come up with a plan to get Maryann to reinstate you. I know that all she wants is to hear you didn't mean to quit. You were distraught about your…your…."

"My plans to die in a few months?"

"Saint, just get in here. We can fix this."

"There's just one problem, Campbell. I don't want to fix this. I don't care what sort of nefarious, diabolical plans Maryann has in mind for me. Not that I'm not charmed to know she wants to squeeze every last bit of juice out of me until the very day I die. But I think I'm going to go a different way."

"Different? What sort of different are you talking about?"

"Campbell, just give it up. Thanks for your concern. Really. But it's over."

"Saint, IIA and CDRA need you. You can't just walk away like this. Who knows what could happen?"

Odd thing to say. "What could happen?"

Campbell paused. "I'd like you to reconsider. It doesn't have to be forever. You can go off and do whatever you think you should do at some later date."

"Ross," I said, swallowing before I continued. "My later is now."

"I think you're making a mistake."

Fortunately I didn't care what Ross Campbell thought.

"Where are you going, Saint?"

I sighed, wondering whether I should tell the truth or make something up. This was a new day. I was turning a new leaf…the last leaf. Rules were changing. There was no time left for lies.

"I'm going home."

When the steward announced the pilot was taking the Air Canada Embraer 190 in for a landing at John G. Diefenbaker International Airport, I experienced an uncomfortable feeling (which seemed to be happening a great deal recently): doubt.

I dislike doubt. Generally, given any new situation, I am a man who studies the circumstances, assesses all possible courses of action, considers all advice voiced, then makes up his mind about what to do and does it. No further questions asked. Doubt is for sissies.

I am a sissy.

My last visit to my hometown of Saskatoon, Saskatchewan, was five…six…no, almost seven years ago.

I am a bad son.

On that occasion, all those years ago, I attended my mother's funeral.

Eva Saint was not as sweet as her name might suggest. She was a handsome woman but stern, powerfully built—mind and body—and was known around the farming community where she and my father lived for their entire married life as sharp-tongued, opinionated, and someone who did not suffer fools gladly.

By using a little basic math when I was older, I learned that my mother married my father when she was in her first trimester. That unplanned—unwanted—start to my life was also the beginning of the complicated relationship I shared with my mother. The experience of my birth must have taken some getting used to, as it took almost seven years for my parents to come up with my only sibling, Alexandra.

As a boy, I watched my mother try everything under the sun to…well, I'm not sure why she did what she did:

entertain herself? Earn a little extra spending money? Escape a life she didn't want to live? Over the years, she tried her hand at selling Amway, peddling baked goods at farmer's markets, working in a grocery store. Turns out she was lousy salesperson, lousy cook, and a lousy employee. I think my mother just couldn't find a place to fit in.

And then she found hockey. Actually I found hockey, but with my father too preoccupied with the farm, she became the sports version of a stage mother. She came to every practice, every game; she came on the road with the team as a chaperone, and when I was drafted to play league junior hockey in another town, she moved with me, leaving my father and Alexandra to fend for themselves. It was a bad decision. By the time my mother and I were back on the farm, I'd given up hockey for good, my father was more distant toward me—and my mother—than ever before, and my sister was well on her way to becoming a crazy little animal.

I'm sure everyone thought—she most of all—that with a constitution such as hers, Eva Saint would easily live to be a hundred. She was off by almost forty years.

My mother died young. I think she died of disappointment. Disappointment at finding herself in a life she never wanted and could never find a way out of.

Mom and Dad were born in Canada to immigrant parents, making me second-generation Canadian. Grandpa Saint landed on the east coast at the ripe old age of eighteen. As he told it, he rode the rails until he found someplace that felt like home. For him, that was Saskatchewan. As an old man, he regularly boasted about knowing exactly what he was doing when he staked his claim on a piece of land that wasn't even part of a province yet.

Those several sections of prairie dirt were situated near a fledgling community with a population of 310. Today that same community, Saskatoon, is up to the quarter million mark. The family's land—which I had infamously refused to dedicate my life to, as my father and his father before him had—was now probably worth a pretty penny. Not that my dad gave a damn about that.

Oliver Saint is your typical strong-but-silent farmer. A man whose greatest love in life is the land. Happiest when getting his hands dirty carrying out the endless chores a working farm demands. Or so I deduced from observation. The number of conversations I can recall having with my father can be counted on one hand. Especially once I'd decided to make my own footsteps rather than follow in his.

My guilt at not having set foot on the farm in the seven years since my mother's death was amplified by another fact. The only other family member available to provide my father with emotional support in the wake of the loss of his wife—and whatever other support he might require as he grew older—was my sister.

Alexandra is not someone you want looking after you. She could barely look after herself most of the time. Her own son would no doubt concur. First off, the kid began life saddled with the inexplicable name of Anatole. You can't even shorten a name like that to make it sound any cooler. No guy wants to go around being called An, or Tole, or, God forbid, Ana. When I'd asked my sister where she got the name from, she bristled and said she named her son after a famous author. She could not, however, recall said famous author's last name or anything he'd written. And then there's the fact that for most of his life Anatole lived with and was raised by his grandparents, not his mother.

To be fair, this lack of parental skill wasn't entirely Alexandra's fault. Absent father. Distracted mother. And a brother so much older than herself that by the time she was old enough for us to really get to know one another, I was living in another town playing hockey. Then as soon as I was back, I was making plans to get out of Dodge. When my own bad behaviour got me sent to military school at sixteen, Alexandra was only nine. I never came back to live on that farm or in that family.

Alexandra's acting out and mood swings intensified after I left home. Eventually she was diagnosed as bipolar, but by then the damage had been done. Underage drinking led to drugs led to sex led to becoming a single parent of a screaming baby boy. Not unlike our mother, this was probably not the life Alexandra wanted for herself. But unlike our mother, there was an escape.

When I'd called my father's house to say I was coming home for a visit, it was Alexandra who'd answered the phone. She was likely there mooching food or money—two things she excelled at finding. She'd seemed underwhelmed by my news. Promising to inform Dad, she hung up. Just in case, I booked myself a room at the Bessborough Hotel. So there I was. Inside a plane. Spiraling gently downwards into a little-known, remote prairie city. Doubting my sanity. Guilt-ridden. With no assurances anyone would be expecting me. On the upside, all these conflicting emotions were taking my mind off the fact that I had a murderous tumour in my head, which was turning constant low-grade nausea into my new best friend.

I didn't expect anyone to greet me with open arms beyond the doors that opened into the baggage claim area. And they weren't.

I stood alone at the carousel, waiting for my duffle bag. When it arrived, I'd figure out what to do next. Large plate glass windows running across the front of the terminal showcased a beautiful summer day. If worse came to worst, I'd find a nice outdoor deck somewhere and drink too much beer.

"Adam."

I turned to see a man standing nearby. He was just beyond the circle of clambering passengers awaiting their own bags. He was older, handsome, fit for his age, with wavy, silver-grey hair. He wore tailored dark brown pants and a black shirt.

My father.

I forgot about the luggage and approached him warily. I had never seen my father wear anything but a pair of Mark's Work Wearhouse work pants in navy or dark green, with a matching long-sleeved shirt, work boots, and a soiled United Grain Growers baseball cap. Had he actually dressed up to meet me?

"Wow, Dad, I barely recognized you," I said, sticking my hand out for a shake.

No one else would have noticed, but my father hesitated as he warily regarded my hand before finally accepting it. The handshake was quick and brisk. We got through it.

He stepped back, looking over my shoulder at the luggage carousel.

"My bag should be here any minute," I uselessly commented.

He nodded stiffly, turning his attention to a passing family whose bags had the good sense to be amongst the first to arrive.

"I wasn't sure you'd get my message. Alexandra didn't seem too excited to hear I was coming."

He waved it off. "Oh, you know how your sister is. She told me this morning."

I had called two days ago.

Dad waited while I shuffled through the remaining crowd to retrieve my bag. Then we were off.

Why did I do this?

"I wasn't sure how much luggage you'd have with you, so I brought the half-ton," Dad said as he led us to the open-air parking lot.

The half-ton was a nondescript, decades-old rattletrap he probably used for hauling fertilizer and chicken feed. I threw my bag in the back and resisted the urge to jump behind the wheel. Riding passenger is something I rarely do.

"I hope you don't mind my coming out on such short notice," I said once we'd paid the parking fee and were on our way. "I know seeding is over, but I'm sure you're still pretty busy around the farm. Harvest isn't too far off." I may not be a farmer at heart, but I could talk the talk.

As a boy, I'd feel relief when the crop was finally in the ground. I'd erroneously thought it signaled the end of the endless long days of toil. I'd finally have time to slack off and enjoy summer. How wrong I was. Anyone who has ever been around farmers knows one thing is certain: work is never done. There'd be spraying, and summer fallow, fences to fix, rocks to pick, gardens to weed, and machinery to prepare for the upcoming harvest. The list of jobs needing doing was limitless. The nearest day off didn't arrive until first snow. Farm kids are the only ones I know anxious to get back to school in the fall. They need the rest.

"So how're the crops looking this year?" I asked. It was a favourite topic of my father's. A good way to fill in the continuing awkward moments. I checked my watch. My visit thus far could only be measured in minutes. How could that be, when it already felt like days?

A quarter of an hour later, I glanced out the truck's side window. We'd left behind the airport and nearby industrial area, hopped onto the new Circle Drive extension that allowed us to skirt the city's edges until we were offered an exit depositing us on the south side of the city. After that, the farm was only ten kilometres beyond city limits. I leaned my head back against the truck's fabric seat. Closing my eyes, I attempted to will away the subtle thudding signs of an impending headache. A malady I was becoming overly familiar with.

"I don't have the milk cows anymore," Dad unexpectedly broke a nearly five-minute silence. "Turned them in for some horses."

"You have horses?" I did my best to keep the incredulity out of my voice.

"Three."

One summer, not long before I left home for good, my sister and I had joined forces to ask Mom and Dad for ponies. We presented a logical argument that included their usefulness as both pets and a means of getting exercise. My mother's immediate and unwavering response was: "Horses are only good for riding and looking pretty, useless on a farm unless they can be put to work, like Clydesdales." I didn't recall Dad having an opportunity to weigh in on the matter.

"Clydesdales?" I asked.

My father shot me a side glance. The look on his face told me he remembered the same thing I did. "Nah, I got some nice Paints." Then he added a sly aside I wouldn't have thought my father capable of: "Good for nothing but riding and looking pretty."

"That's great." And I meant it.

Falling into another mutual silence, Dad took us the rest of the way home.

I wondered what else might have changed since I was last home. How could I know about any of this stuff? I'd been busy dealing with horrific car crashes in Dian Chi and disease outbreaks in Somalia.

I suppose I could have found the time to pick up a phone now and then. *That's how, Saint.*

But who wants to have a conversation on the phone with someone famous for one-word replies and long, uncomfortable silences?

Was that the way it had to be? Could things have changed if only I'd tried harder, reached out?

I could debate the issue all day. But what was the point? Bottom line was, I was home *now*. I was with my father *now*.

Why I'd made the decision to come home *now*, however,

was still up for debate.

To some, it might seem obvious. I had no job. No home. No car. Pretty dreadful prospects for the future. Given all that, of course you go home. That's what people do when times are tough, when they have nowhere else to turn. They go home. Yes, I'd been cut off from the spectacular sports car, the dazzling apartment, the exciting career. Yes, my wife wanted a divorce and my son didn't know me. And yes, I had a terminal illness. But I also had choices because I had money. Two decades of perks and bonuses and guilt payments had inflated my investment portfolio quite nicely. I didn't need to be sitting in a half-ton truck heading toward a rambling, old farmhouse on the prairies. I could have been at Hotel du Cap-Eden-Roc on Cap d'Antibes, in a room that costs $4,000 a night. Or sailing a sixty-metre superyacht with three super-models priced out at about the same.

I guess I wanted something different. Maybe I was reaching out for something once familiar, hoping it would somehow comfort me. Perhaps somewhere in my tumour-riddled brain, I decided it was high time I faced the doubt, the guilt, the sadness, head on.

What a putz.

Driving into the farmyard, I was surprised by the familiarity of the place and glad for it. As I had known it, the yard was nothing more than a place to keep buildings—the house, some chicken coops, a machine shed, barn, and a few grana-ries. One for people, one for chickens, one for machines, one for cows, and one for grain. Simple. Efficient. Pragmatic.

My mother wasn't one for gardening unless it had something to do with feeding the family. Every year, she planted a huge garden filled with endless rows of potatoes, corn, beans, cabbage, beets, peas, cucumbers, and radishes. Aside from a stray pot of petunias here and there, she never bothered with flowers. They took up too much time and water, she'd say, two resources often in short supply on a prairie farm. And one more thing she didn't really want to take care of.

They were subtle, but there were signs a new sheriff was in town. I remembered the yard being what I thought of as country-coloured: all greys and browns, muted greens and dull yellows. Now the buildings were painted in complementary hues of a more imaginative palette. In a nook here and a cranny there, I spotted flowerbeds stocked with plants whose only job was to look pretty rather than provide nutrition for anyone other than a bee. The grass looked greener. Even the sky seemed bluer.

The biggest change was the house itself. It was L-shaped, two stories tall, with a deep porch strung along the front of the lower level. Even before I was old enough to notice such things, the paint had already begun to peel and the shingles were curled up at the edges. The place was the definition of weather-beaten. But no more. To the best of my recollection, the house had been some tone of grey or beige. Now the building stood proudly clad in a surprisingly harmonious combination of lilac, maize, and clover. Where once stood a rotting post-and-barbed-wire fence encircling the yard, there were now smart, snow-white pickets. My father must have had a visit from Sherwin

Williams and Martha Stewart. Nothing too fancy but a definite improvement.

Dad parked the truck in the shade of a massive poplar tree, moulting its last few fluffy, white seedpods.

I was pulling my bag from the truck's bed when the rumbling commenced. At first I thought it was my headache making an especially grand entrance. But the noise continued to grow until it seemed like several aircraft were making an approach to land on top of our heads. Instead a fire-red Dyna Low Rider glided into the yard, coming to an exacting halt in front of the farmhouse.

Together we watched as one long leg ending in a spike-heeled boot swung over the low-slung seat. With the same smooth motion, the driver removed her helmet.

Curious, I slipped my Ray-Bans down my nose and peeked over them to get a better look.

"Screw off!" the new arrival greeted two exuberant labradoodles who seemed intent on licking the black off her leather pants.

"Doris! Judy! Get over here," Dad called off the dogs.

Doris? Judy? I didn't remember these dogs the last time I was here. I recalled a Lassie and a Trixie. Obviously my mother had been the superior dog-namer in the family.

"Well, well, well," the woman said as she swaggered over. "The prodigal son returns."

I winced. It was meant to be a smile. "Hi, sis," I said.

Chapter Eight

The last time I saw my sister—at our mother's funeral—she had arrived late, wearing an outfit not too different from her current biker chick chic. With circles under her eyes that would have made a clown proud. She was also high.

Until some doctor settled on bipolar, speculation about Alexandra's "condition" ranged from multiple personality disorder to the more colourful GD—grandiose delusion, or delusions of grandeur. None of these diagnoses were accurate from my humble point of view. Her problem? She's just a little bit crazy with a healthy dollop of permanent irritability thrown into the mix.

Still a few yards away, I opened my arms to my baby sister. She smiled and trotted into them.

After a quick hug, she pulled back and said, "You look like closing time at the bar."

"Now I'm really glad to be home."

She flicked an eyebrow to say she only told it as she saw it.

"Nice bike. Yours?" I was guessing it was several years old, but still it would have set her back ten or fifteen grand.

"I get to use it," she said in a vague that's-all-I'm-going-to-say-about-that way, at the same time pulling a pack of Player's from a pocket.

She lit up. "I have to work tonight, so let's get on with

this little reunion of yours."

I assessed my sister more closely. Some might say she bears a resemblance to Angelina Jolie—the Billy Bob Thornton years. Her features were brooding and dark. Except for her eyes, which were ashen. Her mouth was too big for her face. As were those eyes, capable of staring holes into a block of ice. Her frame was naturally slender, but somewhere in her varied life experiences, she'd developed powerful shoulders and biceps. Her thick hair was wet chestnut, and when she bothered with it—which was far less often than she should—it had the ability to transform her from wild child into gorgeous woman.

Alexandra had her baby at sixteen. Our mother talked her out of an abortion. Even though my sister warned us she wasn't expecting an overwhelming infusion of maternal instinct or super-gooey love stuff once the child arrived. And she was right. It just didn't happen for her. She never wanted or sought help from Anatole's father. So it was up to her to raise the kid. In her mind, because she wasn't the only one to make the decision to have the baby in the first place, the responsibility also extended to my mother and father. But she did try to provide for her son. At seventeen, she began a career doing the only thing she really seemed good at—and tended not to get fired from—serving up drinks at Saskatoon's less reputable drinking establishments.

"Well, thanks for coming over."

Alexandra shrugged. She took a puff off her cigarette, pssted away a randy tomcat that was rubbing itself up against her legs, and said to our father, "Did you say something about supper? Are we going to eat, or what? I gotta go soon."

Inside, the house I grew up in was just as I remembered it. Utilitarian. Drab wallpaper. Time-scarred furniture. Cracked linoleum floors. Dim overhead lighting. Every window hidden behind dusty drapery.

My room—the same one I slept in until I was fifteen years old—was on the second floor. From there, I had a bird's eye view of the backyard and the garden, a thicket of unruly caragana and a rickety tool shed.

Everything was still there. Even the garden.

After a speedy unpack, I changed into a pair of age-faded jeans, a soft cotton shirt, and slip-on loafers and headed downstairs to dinner.

The kitchen, a corner room with long expanses of windows facing the backyard, was empty. I took a moment to take it in. Same old appliances. Same cupboards stained dark brown. I checked inside the refrigerator. Aside from the usual fare, there was a plate of leftover ham and a bowl of potato salad. I spotted a Labatt, pulled it out, and left the kitchen behind.

Puttering about the house, room to room, sipping my beer, I found that I was alone. About to head back upstairs to knock on some bedroom doors, I heard voices outside. I stepped through the back door off the kitchen onto the deck. No one there. I made my way around to the front of the house.

In the shade of a paper birch, my father and sister were sitting at a wooden picnic table. At the centre of the table was a blue, lidded pot sitting on a trivet. I remembered the table but not a single occasion when any of us sat at it. To me, it had been nothing more than a big, heavy hindrance that had to be moved each time I cut the grass.

"It's about time," Alexandra crowed when she saw me.

I ignored her as I crawled into the spot next to her. "Who's the fourth bowl for?"

"Me."

I turned to see a tall, gangly, almost-worrisomely thin young man joining our alfresco experience. It took me a moment to realize it was Alexandra's son, Anatole.

"Anatole," I said, standing up. "I'm your uncle. Adam."

Without meeting my eyes—not that I could have seen his, hidden beneath a heavy swath of dark bangs—he limply shook my hand and slipped unceremoniously into the spot next to my father, mumbling, "I know who you are."

Quickly doing the math, I realized this wasn't some shy, surly youngster we were dealing with here. Anatole was nineteen. He was a man. Sort of. His thick hair was jet black against translucently pale skin. He wore nondescript jeans that didn't fit him very well and a black t-shirt emblazoned with the name of a band that, although I'd never heard of it, I was quite certain was either heavy metal or goth rock.

"I'm glad you're joining us for dinner." Had they forced the poor guy to come over just because it was my first night?

"Where else am I supposed to eat? I live here." He did not look up when he spoke. Instead his attention was focused solely on a hand-held electronic device.

"Oh, I didn't know that." At the time of my mother's funeral, Anatole would have been thirteen. In her life of booms and busts, Alexandra was in one of her upswings, and although I never visited the place, I was told that mother and son were living together in an apartment in the city.

"Why should you?" he said. I searched the words for some hint of accusation or blame but found none. It was a statement of fact, nothing else.

"We moved in with Dad after Mom died," Alex said. "You were gone, so someone had to." I didn't have to search too hard to find the intended meaning behind her words.

"Oh," was my only response, playing it safe. We were dancing on a landmine.

"What else were we supposed to do? Someone had to be here with Dad." I noticed Dad busying himself readjusting the placement of his utensils.

"You made a big sacrifice," I said. I suspected the move was more Alex's decision than Dad's request. "I'm sure Dad really appreciated you doing that."

Dad nodded. "I did."

I regarded my sister. "But...you don't live here anymore?"

"I have my own life, you know." Defensive. "I couldn't stay here forever. So when Anatole graduated high school, the deal was I could move out."

There was something oddly screwball and backwards about that deal, but again, I felt it wise to refrain from comment.

"He graduated early; at seventeen," Alexandra continued. "He decided to stay here. It was only supposed to be until he got his business going."

I turned to my nephew. "You have your own business? Good for you. What is it?"

Alex wasn't done. "He's been doing pretty well for quite

a while now, haven't you, Anatole? He could afford to move out any time. But I think he just likes living here with his grandpa."

"Where do you live?" I asked my sister.

Her grey eyes razed me like a bush fire. "I live in the city. Why do you ask?"

Touchy. "Just wondering. Trying to catch up on things since I've been gone."

"There's lots of time for that later," Dad said as he began ladling hot, thick stew into our bowls. "Anatole, you want root beer?"

I smiled at the memory of my father's homemade root beer, so cold it was mere degrees from freezing. It was the only thing I could remember my father ever making that was close to belonging to a food group. Mom did all the cooking and baking. She wasn't great at it and didn't appear to enjoy it, but it was definitely on her duty roster.

I held out an empty glass. "Anatole, I'd like some too please."

I marveled at how my nephew was able to fill our glasses while simultaneously typing a text message. All without spilling a drop.

"Dad," I said, "I don't remember you and Mom ever eating outside before. Didn't she used to say eating outside was for animals?"

Alexandra chuckled at the memory. "Yeah, she did. She never wanted to go on picnics. She said she didn't want to go to all the trouble of preparing a meal when the ants would eat most of it."

"I like it outside," Dad said quietly. He handed around

a chunk of bread.

I tried the stew. It was a hearty mixture of juicy beef and thick knots of half-softened farm vegetables. Simple but delicious.

"Dad, did you make this?"

"And the bread," Alexandra added, chewing some in a rather unladylike fashion.

Dad nodded, waving his hand in a dismissive gesture.

The changes in my father were understated but undeniably there. I couldn't help but notice that much of the change was in the opposite direction of who he'd been when my mother was around. As if he suddenly wanted to do all the things she never wanted to, or would deride as being wasteful of time or money, silly or useless. Had he been so repressed during all the years of their marriage? Or had her death brought out something new in him? Something he hadn't known was there before? The mother and father I knew were black and white, practical, serious people living in a serious world. This man before me now was still serious and silent but beginning to show signs of living in a world of colour and light.

How long had this been going on? By the looks of the place, this metamorphosis hadn't occurred over the past days or weeks. This had been happening for years. Years I had casually missed. As part of my career—the one I used to have—it was my job to find answers, investigate disturbances to the norm. This situation with my father was one such disturbance. I found myself keen to find out more.

"Anatole has a very good business on the computer," Dad said.

"Oh," I said, unsuccessfully trying to find at least one of Anatole's eyes. I knew they were there somewhere. "What exactly do you do, Anatole?"

Still thumbing away at his iPhone, he responded with: "I'm a genius on the computer."

Now I knew everything.

Dad nodded his agreement.

"He helps people with their computer problems," Alexandra elaborated. "They call him up at all hours of the day and night. You should hear how desperate people get when they can't get their computers to do what they want them to. If it were me, some of these people, I'd just tell them to go fuck themselves."

"No swearing, Alexandra," Dad calmly stated.

"That's a superb business plan, Mom."

I shot Anatole a look. So the boy had a bit of a backbone when it came to his mother. Good for him. He'd likely needed it.

Alexandra laughed it off. "Yeah, you're right. That's why I'm not doing your job, and you're not serving up pints."

I turned to my sister. "I'll have to swing by to see you in action while I'm here," I said.

An odd expression crossed her face. Then, "Why *are* you here, anyway?"

"I've come to see Dad. And you. And Anatole. It's been too long." I hadn't really thought about how to answer that question yet. Going with the truth would be fine, I suppose. If I knew what it was.

Alexandra snorted. "Seven years. Yeah, I'd say that's a bit long. Sometimes too long is just too long, bro. You know what I mean? If someone is missing seven years, don't they declare them dead? Because that's what we thought, you know." She was suddenly agitated, attacking the bottom of her bowl with a spoon, as if to leave behind even a morsel was unthinkable.

"I wasn't missing, Alexandra. I was busy. I called. I talked to Dad every so often. And Kate, I know she talked to you, and to Dad too."

She stared at me. I could never figure out my sister's eyes. Sometimes in them I saw nothing but the slow burn that could easily turn into anger, disappointment, resentment, or a hundred other unhappy sentiments. Other times I saw the eyes of a little sister who used to look up to her big brother with undisguised adoration.

"Where is Kate? Why isn't she here with you? And Rowan. We haven't seen him since he was little. He and Anatole wouldn't even know each other anymore. It's crazy for two cousins to be strangers."

She was right. "I'm hoping he'll come out this summer for a visit."

Alexandra's mouth dropped open.

"What is it?" I asked.

"You're staying for the summer? The whole summer?"

Had I just said that? Is that what I wanted?

Alexandra stood up from her chair. "If that's the case, then what am I doing here? I gotta get to work. I was only here because I thought this was some kind of one-time deal, you being here for supper. But if you're staying forever, then I gotta get out of here." Then for an instant the little sister eyes were back. "Come by sometime if you want."

Alexandra stomped off toward the Harley, her stiletto heels pegging holes in the lawn.

"Thanks," Anatole muttered at his grandfather before getting up and carrying his empty bowl and his mother's into the house.

I regarded my father. He was occupied swiping up stew gravy with a chunk of bread.

Doris and Judy, finished with seeing Anatole and Alexandra off, came by for a nuzzle. They were sweet dogs. One charcoal, the other apricot, but otherwise identical.

"Nice dogs," I commented idly.

Dad looked up at me and said, "You stay as long as you want. This is your home too."

A confused and sad man, I was. But I was home.

Later that night, I threw myself down on my childhood bed and gazed with unseeing eyes at the spiderwebs decorating the peaked ceiling. In an odd way, I felt like the boy I once was, lying in this same spot, staring into space, considering my future. I'd been resisting taking the medication I'd gotten from Yelchin. Something about swallowing that little pill made my bleak future more real to me than did the headache and nausea that caused me to want to take the pill in the first place. Right now I felt good. Maybe it was the root beer.

"When are you planning on telling them?" the voice came from the doorway.

I sat up fast. Why hadn't I sensed someone was there?

Even though he was thin as a bicycle spoke, at 6'4" and

with the cool, shadowy features of his mother, Anatole looked rather imposing from my position.

"What are you talking about?" I asked him, noticing that for the first time I could see his eyes. Dark. Intelligent. Startlingly intense.

He said, "I know your secret."

Chapter Nine

I'd forgotten the striking magnificence of an early Saskatchewan summer morning. I awoke at five thirty a.m. to a sun already hard at work for more than half an hour. I threw on jeans, a denim shirt, boots, and a light jacket and headed outside for the barn.

Doris and Judy were happy to see me. I found the saddles just where Dad said they'd be, selected my tack, and hauled it to the small corral.

American Paint horses combine the characteristics of western stock horses with pinto spotting pattern. The three waiting for me in the corral were a riot of blotches and colour, one black and white, one white and bay, the third mostly a light creamy colour I'd never seen in a horse before. According to Dad, they answered to LaVerne, Maxene, and Patty.

As soon as she saw me, Maxene sauntered over and nuzzled my neck. I like a brash and ballsy female. We were bonded for life.

As a youth, I'd spent very little time in the undulating, heavily treed land that surrounded our farmyard. Without a horse to ride, I had little call to. Most of the acres were used as pasture land for the small herd of dairy cattle we kept for milk and cream and the occasional steak. Somehow the cows knew exactly when to come lowing home, first thing in the morning and early evening, just in time for milking. They say cows have small brains. Yet I've known plenty of humans who can't get to where they're supposed to be on time.

High atop Maxene, I felt like an eleven-year-old boy on an adventure, setting out to discover a foreign land. The dawn air was bracing. Each breath met my lungs with an intense burst of pleasure, like water on parched land. The sun was strong this time of year, yearning to warm up the newly budded trees and carpets of crocus and wild grasses. Maxene seemed to know where she was going. So I allowed her to lead the way, using the time to take in my surroundings. I was raised on this land but didn't know it at all.

Some time later, the yard long left behind us, with nothing but trees and grassland and Mother Nature in front, behind, and on either side of me, I noticed something unusual. My shoulders had dropped. My breathing had slowed. My mind felt freer than it had in a very long time. I could feel the muscles of the horse ripple beneath me, her smooth, plodding gait massaging my lower back. The air smelled fresh and clean. The noise of the world was gone. I could think.

Last night, when my nephew told me he knew my secret, my gut immediately tightened. I had one thought: Which secret does he know? Did he know that Kate and I were getting a divorce? That my son Rowan and I were veritable strangers? That I had a tumour in my head preparing to kill me? That I had no idea what I was doing here or what I'd do next?

I had to laugh when he popped me with a whole other secret.

"I know you've been canned from CDRA," he told me.

Apparently Anatole wasn't exaggerating when he said he was a genius on the computer. As soon as he'd heard his Uncle Adam was coming for a visit, he began researching me. Until then, he had no particular interest in who I was or what I did. But if I was about to enter his world, he wanted to know why and how it was going to affect him.

The kid definitely had Saint blood in him

What surprised me was the depth of his research. He'd made it his business to find out everything he could about IIA and CDRA and my role therein. In the process, he did some sneaking—hacking?—into areas he should not have been looking into. He discovered I was no longer on CDRA payroll.

I was impressed.

I was also a little nervous that someone from IIA IT Department was on their way to Saskatchewan to find the bandit who'd infiltrated their system; I was even more nervous that they weren't.

Before I had a chance to say anything, Anatole assured me my secret was safe with him and left.

And that, apparently, was that.

As I rode, I reflected on the evening with my family. My family. Even thinking those words in my head felt odd. My father. Alexandra. Anatole. They were my family. The Saints. And yet somehow we felt like strangers. The conversation, especially once Alexandra and Anatole were gone and I was left alone with my father, had been stilted. On the positive side, even that was a marked improvement on any of our past conversations. Still, nothing of any import had been discussed. Instead of using the time to learn about each other's lives in the intervening years since we'd last seen one another, my father—after some coaxing from me—commented as briefly as possible about the neighbours, how spring seeding had gone, where Doris and Judy had come from, and the weather forecast for the balance of the summer (apparently a warmer than usual season was expected by the prognosticators at *The Old Farmer's Almanac*).

But it takes two to tango. I'd volunteered nothing more than a trifling anecdote or two when he asked about Kate and Rowan or my work. I asked no deeper questions about him, about the change I sensed in him. The whole evening had gone this way. My father, Alexandra, Anatole, me—we talked, but none of us really *said* anything. And why should we? We were strangers suddenly thrown together again as a family unit. There was no reason Alexandra should welcome me home like the hero brother she once thought—hoped?—I was. Anatole needn't have spoken more than a word or two if he didn't feel like it. My father shouldn't have to reveal to me why he'd changed after my mother died. And there was no reason for me to share with these people the fact that my life was falling apart right in front of my eyes. And that once that was done with, I would die.

So why was I here?

"Why am I here?" I bellowed, letting the cry rise up and disappear into the impossibly blue sky.

Maxene stopped but did not startle. She was no doubt wondering what sort of command she'd been given and what was expected of her.

Patting her neck, I slipped off the horse and tied the lead to a nearby low-hanging branch.

Except for the twitter of flitting songbirds, busily searching for goodies to fill the yawning mouths of newly hatched offspring, the dell was quiet. I needed to walk. I needed strenuous exercise. Something to take my mind off my mind.

From the moment Ross Campbell gave me the news that I was a man on death row, a grand battle had begun inside of me. It was not only a physical battle of strong, healthy tissue rising up against a malicious, invading army of cancer cells but a mental battle too. I was desperate to make sense of what was happening to me and happening fast. I needed to find a way to deal with this, create a process to move forward in a logical and efficient manner, as was my way. In most battles I've fought in life, I've been the victor. But now the unthinkable would occur. Defeat.

What now?

What now!

Had I made a giant mistake in coming back to Saskatchewan? Back to my parent's home? What did I expect to find here? Was my sister right? Was a long time sometimes too long? Was it too late for me?

I hadn't even decided how or when—if ever—to tell my father about my illness.

Why should I?

Why should he suddenly have the burden of his son's sickness laid upon him? Not only the mental burden of knowing about it, but was he also expected to take on the physical burden of caring for me? Taking me to the doctor? Administering my drugs?

Cleaning my ass when I no longer could? Carrying me when I couldn't walk? Why put him through that? Why put anyone through it?

I should go.

I should leave today.

I could fly to Tahiti. Have a few incredible weeks, then check myself into a clinic somewhere. I'd give them all of my money and tell them to look after me until I'm gone.

I began to run.

Faster and faster.

I shrugged off my jacket and tossed it aside.

I hit my stride. My focus was laser clear. The terrain was uneven with obstacles at every turn—willow branches ready to whip my face, rocks prepared to trip me—but I dealt with each hurdle with ease, almost anticipating them before I saw them. Chilled, dewy air cooled my skin, my muscles pumped, my heart kept pace. Then, womp!

Down I went, rolling into a shallow ravine.

Even before I came to a stop, I knew I was not alone.

We'd literally run into each other.

Shaking my head and managing to get up on all fours, I realized two more things. First, the bottom of the ravine was home to a damp, piddling creek. Second, the woman accompanying me on my sudden trip down here was wearing only a half-slip and a bra with one strap hanging loose. She was barefoot and breathing heavily. Her chest moved up and down in an uneasy rhythm as she pulled herself to her knees and stared at me. Her eyes were so blue they were almost translucent and rimmed in red as if she'd been crying. Her hair was a vivid mess of red curls. As I looked closer, I could see abrasions on her arms and across her taut belly, there was dirt under her fingernails and smudged on her cheeks. Above all, the woman, quite obviously, was petrified.

For a moment, we were frozen in place, assessing one another.

"Don't," she pleaded in a ripped-to-shreds voice.

"What is it?" I answered back, trying my best to control my own breathing after the unexpected fall. "Is something wrong? Do you need help?"

Her brilliant eyes moved from fear to desperate hope then to weariness. "Are you…are you one of them?"

"One of who? Miss, I can help you."

As if I'd suddenly become a buoy to someone who was about to drown, the woman fell into my arms and began to sob and talk at the same time. "There are two of us…in the house…I got away, but she's still there…there are three men…oh God, you've got to help her…please! Help her!"

I was immediately on full alarm. I pulled the woman up with me so we were both on our feet. I urged her to move out of the soggy ravine bed to drier ground. "Tell me your name."

"Eva," she stuttered.

"There are three men holding another woman captive, is that right?"

"They're with her right now. In the bedroom. I woke up, and I heard them with her. That's how I had the time to get away. I loosened the ropes and—"

"Where is she?" I could hear her story later. Priority was

to save the second woman. "Where is this house?" *Where could it be? We were in the middle of nowhere.*

She pointed a shaking finger in the direction she must have come from. "I don't know," she cried. "It's an old house. Abandoned, I think. Do you know it? Do you know it? You have to help her!"

My mind raced. My father's house was the only one I knew of for miles. This was rural Saskatchewan, beyond the suburbs of Saskatoon. There were no abandoned...wait, there *was* an abandoned house. The house my grandparents—my father's parents—lived in when they first homesteaded this land. I'd only been there once or twice as a boy, but I was quite certain I could find it.

"Eva, do you know where you are?"

The young woman shook her head, eyes glued to mine. I had no time to take her back to the farm. "I want you to stay right here. Can you do that? You'll be safe here." I regretted tossing aside my jacket earlier. The sun was trying its best, but the air was still chilly and the woman was barely clothed.

I tore off my shirt and wrapped it around her heaving shoulders. "This will keep you warm until I come back. Don't wander off, Eva. I'm going to help your friend and then I'm coming back to help you. Do you understand?"

She nodded.

I urged her toward a tree and asked her to sit under it with my shirt covering her like a blanket.

I stood to leave. "I will be back." I hoped I would fulfill the promise. I wanted to. But I knew I couldn't guarantee it. I had no idea what type of situation I was about to get into. "But if it gets too cold or I don't come back soon enough…." I pointed in the general direction of Dad's house. "There's a farm about a kilometre straight that way. My father lives there. I want you to go there. He will help you."

She nodded. The woman seemed to have no words left in her body. She was going into shock. I'd have to come back for her no matter what.

I retraced my steps to where I'd left Maxene. The horse eyed me as I approached. She could sense something was up. I leapt onto her back and set her in the direction of the house where my grandparents had lived and died.

Maxene did her best to gallop, and I did my best to locate the old farmhouse.

Within fifteen minutes we were there. From a distance, the building looked innocuous. The architectural version of the nondescript, seemed-like-such-a-nice-guy neighbour who turns out to be a serial killer.

My best guest was that the men—at best, drunken young idiots who'd taken a date too far, at worst, a group of career offenders who prey on women—had brought Eva and a second woman here because it was so remote. Whether they knew about the place beforehand or got lucky as they drove around the countryside looking for somewhere to assault their captives didn't really matter. But as I brought Maxene to a standstill behind a nearby copse of trees, it did raise an important question. Where was the vehicle? How did three men bring two women out to this abandoned farmhouse with no car or truck in sight?

Was I too late? Had they noticed Eva had escaped and

took off before she brought help? Or was I at the wrong place? Maybe my grandparent's house wasn't where the woman was being held at all. If that was the case, I had no time to waste.

With as much stealth as the topography allowed, I closed in on the house and eventually the front door.

Fortunately old houses on the prairie were built to keep weather and pests out, so there weren't many windows to worry about, and the ones there were had been boarded up. I knew this was a simple four-room house. Kitchen and living area. Bathroom. One bedroom, which was where the men would have the second woman. There was no second entrance, so I was going to have to blast my way in through the front door.

With one ear against the rough wood surface of the door, I listened for telltale noises inside.

Silence.

I stood back, took careful aim, then drove my foot forward.

The door gave way easily, and I was inside within one second.

Empty. The door to the bedroom was slightly off its hinges but closed. I rushed against it screaming with aggression and show of brute force.

Empty.

Silent.

Nothing.

No one was here.

The state of the place confirmed that no one had been for a very long time.

Goddamit!

I was at the wrong house.

Where? Where? Where?

Eva would have to direct me.

With lightning speed, I was back atop Maxene and rushing toward the ravine where I'd left the young woman.

Maxene had not yet come to a complete stop when I slid off her back and ran over to the tree where I'd left Eva.

My shirt was the only thing left. Hanging limply on a branch.

I stumbled to the tree, catching myself against it. Like a violent intruder, a sudden sickness welled up in me, the ferocity of it nearly overwhelming. I held on, doubled over, and threw up on the ground.

Arriving home, I saw Dad and Anatole having breakfast on the deck.

As I pulled up, atop the horse, I called out to them, "Have you seen a woman? Her name is Eva. She was supposed to come here for help."

Dad stood up, alarmed. "Eva? Adam, what's wrong?"

I told him what had happened. "There was a woman out on the trail. She and another woman were abducted by three men. She escaped. I thought they were holding the other woman at Grandpa's house. But I went there, and the place was empty."

"Of course it was empty. No has lived there since—"

I cut him off. "I know. There has to be another abandoned house within a kilometre or two of here. Can you think of any?"

"No, son, there isn't."

"Dad, you have to think harder. There must be some-place. It doesn't have to be a house. Any other kind of building?"

He shook his head. "Adam, I know this area pretty well. There are no other places like that. Closer to Saskatoon maybe."

"You need to come with me." There was no time for politeness. "I'd like you to show me anyplace you can think of."

"I will. Of course. But not on Maxene."

I looked down. The scene must have read preposterous. I was on my steed, sweating, shirt undone, blasting out my bizarre story like something out of one of my disaster re-covery cases. I nodded at my father. "The half-ton?"

Anatole, nose twitching like a nervous rabbit, watched unmoving from his seat as my father joined me in my search.

It was one o'clock by time my father and I returned to the farm. Unsuccessful. No abandoned house. No Eva. No kid-nappers abusing a second woman. We eventually filed a re-port with the Saskatoon Police Service about what I'd witnessed. They promised to look into it. But the whole time they looked at me as if assessing whether or not I was either intoxicated or otherwise under the influence. It didn't help that my father remained silent as a stone throughout the ordeal. Then again, what did I expect him to say? He hadn't seen or heard anything. All he was doing was driving his son around the countryside looking for an abandoned house and a blue-eyed, red-haired woman running around in her bra and panties.

It appeared Anatole hadn't moved since we'd left hours earlier. Except now, instead of breakfast, he was chewing on a ham sandwich.

"So what are you up to today?" I asked my father as I settled into a chair next to my nephew.

"I'll be out for the rest of the day."

"Oh?" I wasn't going to let him get off that easy. "Where?"

"Going into the city for parts."

A little bell chimed in my head. "*This is a moment, Adam,*" it told me. If I was here to spend time with my father—to make up for the past seven years, to get to know him better—here was an opportunity. I'd been too focused on finding the woman that morning to even think about engaging my father in any kind of meaningful discussion.

"I've got nothing to do," I said. "Why don't I come with you?"

For just the slightest moment, I caught an unusual look in my father's eyes.

Recovering quickly, he began what was one of the longest speeches I'd ever heard him give. "No need for you to do that. You're on holiday. You should sit back and relax. It's a nice day out there. You could go for a walk. Your mother left some books on the shelf in the living room. Or take one of the other horses out. They could use it. You wouldn't be interested in a farm implements store anyway."

I pushed one more time. "I'm happy to come along, Dad."

He took time for a deep breath. "I'm just going in, getting the part, and coming right back," he told me.

I was dumbfounded. Not only was my father suggesting I spend a hot summer day reading—he may as well have told me to go pick daisies and pet a unicorn—but he was actively suggesting things for me to do that didn't include him. I wanted to spend time with him, but he obviously wasn't interested in spending time with me. Or maybe he didn't want me to meet his buddies down at the farm implements store? When I hadn't been home for years, had he trash-talked me in front of them in order to save face? And now he didn't know how to backtrack, how to explain that the long-lost, ungrateful, deadbeat-of-a-son was back.

"You know," I stuttered after a moment. "Now that I think about it, I did bring a good book I'd like to get to. Maybe I'll just…do that."

"Good then."

Didn't take much convincing.

He made haste toward the door, anxious to get away from me. Stepping outside, he stopped and turned to say, "There's plenty of food in the fridge. Anatole can fix you some lunch."

I looked at Anatole. He was chomping on his sandwich, seemingly engrossed by something on his screen. But I could have sworn I saw his pointed chin move right then left.

"We'll be fine," I told Dad. "You go and have a ball getting your parts."

He looked at me quizzically, as if he wasn't sure what I meant. I wasn't sure what I meant. He turned and left.

"Brutal," Anatole mumbled under his breath.

"What?" I asked gruffly.

"I'd say you just got dumped by your own dad."

I stared at my teenage nephew. I debated whether knocking his block off would be considered an inappropriate response. Instead I said, "This is a farm. There're always chores needing doing. Mucking out the horse barn. Cleaning out a granary. What do you think? Feel like getting dirty?"

For the first time, Anatole looked up from his computer. His black eyes were as wide as a new born calf's. "You talking to me?"

"Yeah. Why not? You've been working on that thing long enough. Wouldn't you rather spend some time outside on a day like this? You don't want to be holed up inside your room all day again, do you?"

"Uh, yeah. And I don't *hole up*. I'm working up there. I've got clients, y'know."

"Come on, play hooky with me."

Clicking the iPad shut, he rose from the table, looking down his nose at me. "Hooky? What are you? Fourteen?" As he walked away, I heard him grumble, "Besides, I don't have anything to wear for getting dirty."

He was probably right about that. All I'd ever seen the kid wear were black jeans, a black t-shirt with a band logo on it, and lace-up work boots that were definitely not meant for working. I, on the other hand, did not have the same problem. Even if all I had with me was a $1,700 Canali suit,

I'd happily get it dirty, just to delve into something physically strenuous. I wanted nothing more than to be dead tired.

By that evening, I'd gotten my wish.

And so my new life as a farmhand began. Every day looked much the same as the one before and after it. In the morning, I'd take one of the horses out for a sunrise ride (Maxene continued to be my favourite). At breakfast, I'd cajole Anatole about considering joining me in my labours. He'd tell me to fuck off (but in much cleverer terms). I'd ask Dad what needed doing around the farm. At first, he'd always say he was taking care of things and I should just relax, so I'd head out and find something. I'd fertilize and weed the flowerbeds, clean out the chicken coop, mow the lawn, feed the horses, paint an old shed, mend fences. Eventually Dad saw there was no use fighting my desire to be useful. One day, he began by giving me something to do. The next day, it was two somethings. Then the floodgates opened. Most days, Dad and I worked at separate tasks. But now and again he'd need my help. On those days, we worked side by side. Not much was said, but I could tell he was glad for the help if not the company.

Around noon, he'd go inside and fix lunch for the three of us. Sandwiches with potato salad or coleslaw. Sometimes he'd fry up some garden potatoes if he thought the day called for something hot in our bellies. Every day we'd empty at least one jug of his ice-cold homemade root beer. Then it was back to work. By six or six-thirty, we'd head back inside and get cleaned up for dinner.

The manual labour was good for me. The headaches

and bouts of nausea were few and far between. Although I thought about what was happening in my body all the time, I would go for days without even considering taking one of Yelchin's pills. I knew I wasn't being cured. But I hoped I was doing something right.

There are days when an innocently cloudless sky hints at inclement weather. Something about its colour, the smell of the air, tells you that today it will rain. It was chilly for a July morning. I'd had to go back to the house for a heavier jacket after saddling up Maxene for our usual ride. I didn't want to have our time cut short just because I was getting cold or wet. By the time I returned to the barn, I was surprised to see I had a guest. Anatole, wearing a bright orange rain jacket over his usual black attire, was preparing LaVerne for riding.

"Grandpa says the horses need more exercising. So I thought I'd, y'know, come along with you."

I shrugged as if it made no difference to me. Inwardly I was smiling. I'd been trying to get the kid out of the house ever since I got here. A little bit of exercise and time outside would do him the world of good.

"If you can find an extra lead rope, we may as well bring Patty along too. She'll get lonely if we leave her here all by herself."

"Horses don't get lonely," Anatole countered.

"You're wrong about that. They're just like people that way. They like to be around others just like them. They like the company."

We worked at readying the horses for a bit, then: "Is that why you're here?"

The question took me off guard. The little shit.

"I'm here to visit with your grandfather. And you and your mom."

"Where is Aunt Kate? And Rowan? Why aren't they here too? With you?"

"Rowan's done with school now. You know how it is. He's not that much younger than you. He's off doing other things that teenage boys like to do."

He stared at me. That was all he was going to get. Kate was none of his frigging business. I stared back that answer.

"Let's go if we're going." I jumped on Maxene and directed her out of the corral. Anatole and LaVerne followed, Patty in tow.

"How was last night?" I asked when we were clear of the yard and the horses were slowly navigating a slight rise.

"Last night?"

"Friday night. When I asked what you were up to, you said you were hanging with friends. Where did you go?"

"I didn't *go* anywhere."

"They came to the house? I didn't hear anyone drive up." Shockingly enough, I'd found a copy of an old Nelson DeMille paperback and gotten quite into it—along with a bottle of scotch—before I fell asleep on the couch. "Don't Judy and Doris bark when a car drives into the yard?"

"What are you talking about? There was no driving. We were online."

"You spent Friday night with friends *online*?"

His laugh sounded like a jeer. "What? Did you expect

we'd all go down to the Soda Shoppe for a pop and cheese-burger before heading out to the sock hop?"

How old did this kid think I was? "No. But it might be a good idea for you to leave your room every once in a while. Come to think of it, Anatole, I don't think I've seen you leave the yard even once since I've been here. And that's been almost two weeks."

"So?"

"So I think you're a young man. You should be out there spending time with *real* people. Meeting girls. Getting laid. Getting high. Whatever it is nineteen-year-olds do these days for fun. I mean, have you ever actually met any of these 'friends' you spent Friday night with?"

"That'd be pretty hard to do. They live in places like Beijing and Perth and somewhere I can't pronounce in India."

"Don't you think that's a little screwed up?"

"Because I'm spending time with people from around the world, learning about how they live, their culture, their social issues? You think that's screwed up? Maybe I haven't been anywhere or traveled all over the place like you, but I have a better education about the world than most people my age. Besides, I need to be at my computer for my clients. My clients need me. They think I'm great. They say so. So you know what? I don't care if you or anyone else thinks I'm weird."

"I never said I thought you were weird."

"Screwed up then."

I nodded. "Yeah, that's more like it. I'd say you're a little screwed up." Before he had a chance to start in on me, I added, "But, man, you got nothing on me."

Anatole reigned in his horse.

Maxene and I stopped too.

He glared at me. I glared at him.

I laughed. Anatole joined in.

My attention was caught by a sudden movement over my nephew's shoulder. I focused my eyes on small grove of wild sandcherry.

"Anatole, did you see something?"

He turned to study the area over a hundred feet away. He shook his head. "You mean like a hot redhead in her underwear?"

"Smartass," I muttered. "It's starting to drizzle. We should head back."

I turned my face to hide the worry. Was Anatole right? Had I imagined the whole scene with the redheaded damsel in distress? Was it imagination? Or hallucination? I'd take a pill when I got home.

Chapter Ten

"Saint?"

Milo Yelchin. My doctor.

"I'm here."

"Saint, I'm glad I reached you. I hope I'm not disturbing anything. Campbell told me you were planning a visit home to see family."

"Yes." The more the man talked the less I wanted to hear him. Something about his voice was causing me to feel tense, uneasy, angry. This was the man who'd told me I was going to die. And now he was here in my home…my old home… my new home…whatever the hell this place was to me…or at least his voice was. And I didn't like it. I knew it didn't make sense, but I blamed him for my diagnosis. Besides, he'd forgotten about the time change between Ontario and Saskatchewan, and it was way too early in the morning for a consultation with your physician. "What's up?" I asked, clipped, hurried, as if I had much better things to do. And I did. Like get a cup of coffee.

"I wanted to check up on you, Adam."

Why was everyone calling me Adam now that I was dying?

"I'm fine."

"When you were in my office, we discussed possible

treatment options. I'm wondering if you've made any deci-sions in that regard?"

"You mean aside from taking your damn pills? Which aren't doing much for me by the way. Aside from that, no I haven't."

"I want to reiterate my earlier offer. Whatever you de-cide, wherever you are, I'd like to be the doctor who treats you. Ross Campbell agrees."

"Campbell only wants that so you can keep an eye on me," I responded, sounding harsh. "He wants me back so I can do his and Maryann Knoble's evil bidding until they've worked the last breath out of me."

Shocked silence quivered over the phone lines. I'd given the poor doctor a little more to chew on than he could manage.

"Tell Campbell I'm not coming back."

"I think he already knows that, Adam."

Oh, so the good doctor did know a thing or two about behind-the-scenes shenanigans at IIA.

"He just wants what's best for you. After all the years you've given IIA, he feels you deserve at least that much. I do too. Let me help you, Adam."

"I wasn't with IIA. I was CDRA." Now I was splitting hairs just for the petty satisfaction of it.

"Okay, whatever you say. But you should know that we are here to help you through this. I'll fly out to Saskatchewan tomorrow if you need me to. I'd like to anyway. Just to check on things. I've looked at flights, and I cou—"

"There's no need for that, Yelchin. I'm fine."

"I can prescribe—"

"I have plenty of pills left."

"There's more we—"

"I do have a question for you."

"Oh? What is it?"

"With this…thing I have, is it likely I could be having hallucinations? Seeing things that aren't there?" I neglected to add: "Like scantily clad young women in distress."

Yelchin was silent. Then he asked: "Exactly what kind of hallucinations are you taking about?"

"Nothing yet. Just curious."

"Adam, I think it's best I come out there. Or you come here. Whatever you're more comfortable with. We can talk about this."

"Is that a yes?"

Another short silence. "Anything is possible. It depends on where the tumour is. And if it's growing."

I sighed. So that was it. Pretend people in make-believe situations could come and go from my world, and there was nothing I could do about it. What a pain in the ass.

"Yelchin, I appreciate the call. As I've said, I don't know what I plan to do yet. When I do, you'll be the first to know. I'll call you." I hung up before adding, "Don't call me."

Rain or shine, there is always something to do on a Saskatchewan farm. Even Anatole had begun to occasionally leave his computer in order to pitch in. I'd pestered him into buying some grubby duds at Walmart. It's astounding what freedom comes from owning clothes that beg to get dirty.

It was coming to the end of another dirty day. I was ankle deep in mulch in a backyard flowerbed when Dad stuck his head out a window to call me inside.

I made my way to the deck, opened the door a crack, and yelled inside: "Dad! If I come inside now, there's no going back out again. Your lilies will have to wait until tomorrow for their mulch! You sure you want that?"

"I don't know about him, but I simply can't wait to get a glimpse of Mr. Tough-As-Nails in a bed of lilies."

And suddenly Kate was at the door.

"What are you doing here?" It was the best I could manage. Seeing as my whole body wanted nothing more than to wrap her in my arms and squeeze her until tomorrow.

"What do you think?"

She gave me a meaningful look. It was one of those looks. The kind dying people give as a reason for not telling anyone they're terminal. The kind filled with pity and sadness. The kind that made you less of who you were and more of a human vessel for disease. The kind of look you could imagine that same person wearing at your funeral.

I grabbed Kate's arm and pulled her outside.

"You didn't say anything to him, did you?"

"To who? Oliver?"

"Yes. Or anyone else around here."

"No, of course I didn't. But not because I was being careful. I thought they'd already know. Adam, haven't you told your family yet?"

I shook my head.

I saw tears well up in her eyes.

I'd seen Kate cry more in the past month than for the entirety of our marriage. I guess death does that.

She drew in her cheeks and tightened her lips. She was shoring herself up. Sucking tears back into those selfish ducts. "I wanted to know how you were."

I smiled. "You could have called."

"And I brought Rowan."

My heart nearly stopped. My son.

"He's here?" I was smiling.

She nodded.

Then another thought. "Kate…does he know?"

She nodded. "He knows you're sick."

I looked down. I understood. "It was the only way you could get him to agree to come out here to see me. Isn't it?"

She said nothing.

Oh man. My cheeks heated, my stomach lurched with that horrible, hollow feeling you get when, in the heat of the moment, someone you love slaps you for doing something really stupid. What I'd done was more than stupid. I'd lost my son. And now, in a last minute act of desperation, I wanted him back. God how I wanted him back.

"Where is he?"

"Ollie took him and the dogs to see the horses."

I didn't move.

"Listen, you should clean up. Then go find your son. You need to talk to him."

I nodded, feeling numb.

"Do you know what you're going to say to him?"

I felt a flash of anger. "You just got here. Give me a chance to breathe."

Kate sparked just as easily. "I thought that's what you've been doing out here in the boonies for the last few weeks. Thinking about how to deal with this. Sorry if I screwed up your schedule. Maybe we can come back later."

I swallowed. Took a deep breath. "I'm sorry. I'm just…. I'm just not the guy I used to be. I'm not always prepared."

"Adam…."

"But I will be. I'm going to take a shower. Tell him… tell him I'll see him in a bit."

"Adam, after that, there's something I need to talk to you about. It's important and can't wait."

Suddenly I couldn't think of one thing that wasn't important and could wait.

Miraculously, by the time I returned downstairs, cleaned up from my backyard toils, it was clear by Dad's demeanour that Rowan hadn't said anything to him to make him suspect my illness.

My son, at seventeen, clearly favoured his mother. He was beautiful to look at. Impeccably groomed. He kept his dark, wavy hair combed back from his high forehead, no strand out of place. Perfect teeth. Perfect posture. His Brooks Brothers persona was, as always, fully intact.

I knew better than to go for a hug. We shook hands across the kitchen table, where he was sitting with Kate and Dad. Anatole had disappeared, probably retreating to his beloved cyberworld.

"I suppose we could go for a walk," Rowan suggested without skipping a beat. His voice sounded mature, diction precise. "Grandpa, do we have enough time before dinner?"

"Sure," he said.

I could tell Dad was trying to figure out exactly what was going on. He must have wondered why I showed up here without my wife and son. I had passed off my lack of knowledge about Rowan to his being a grown up now. He was a budding adult, off spreading his wings, trying on his coat of independence, wanting as little assistance or interruption from his parents as possible. Certainly after his experience with me, Dad could understand that. But did he believe it?

Doris and Judy at our sides, Rowan and I headed off for the pasture. We followed a path that had become my favourite over the past weeks. With its winding route along a creek bed, through thick groupings of majestic pines and whispering aspens and fields of wildflowers, it offered the ultimate in both privacy and beauty.

"I understand you have some sort of illness," he began right off the bat.

I was used to being the one in charge of conversations. Apparently my son had come with an agenda. I decided it best to let him play it out.

"That's right," I said. "I wanted to be the one to tell you, but I guess your mother beat me to it."

"It's probably something you shouldn't have left up to chance."

I felt my neck colour at the comment. Was it meant to be admonishing? Blasé? Hurtful? Kate had been right. I did not know my son at all.

"I suppose you're right."

"How serious is it?"

"It's quite serious."

"Will you die?"

"We're all going to die some day, son."

"Oh, come on. Don't give me that. I'm seventeen. Not some kid."

I'm not ready for this. I'm not ready for this. Suddenly I was furious with Kate again. How dare she spring this on me? This was too important to screw up. And that's exactly what I was doing. Screwing up royally. Everything coming out of my mouth was wrong. I could hear the bullshit in my voice. Rowan could too.

"The answer to your question is yes."

"And Grandpa doesn't know yet, does he?"

"No."

"Who knows?"

"Your mother. You. The doctor."

He seemed to think about that, then, "What happens now?"

I stopped walking. I pulled Rowan to a stop, turning him to look at me.

"I don't know. I really don't. But I don't want you to worry about it."

"What about college? If you die, will there be enough money for me to go to college?"

I felt the blood rushing out of my cheeks. This was no accident. I had done this. I had turned my son into this cold, harsh, selfish, unfeeling boy pretending to be a man. And a dick.

"You'll be fine, Rowan. So will your mother," I told him, my voice low.

He turned and started back in the direction we'd come. "That's good to know. We should go back now. Grandpa will be wanting to start dinner soon."

I followed, Doris and Judy at my side.

Chapter Eleven

It was night's version of day. The horse's flanks shone like fine pelts of silk, and trees seemed to be lit from within. Kate was on Patty. I had Maxene, LaVerne in tow. We rode in silence for many minutes. Freshly cut ditch hay and clover flavoured the air, mixed with faint wafts of the bug repellant Dad insisted we bathe in before heading outside after dinner. It was the first time I'd taken the horses out after dark. There was a subtle but distinct change in the forested pasture. Gone were the songbirds and curious squirrels. Gone were the verdant green and vivid russets. I'd thought riding at dawn was quiet, but this was silence much deeper and true.

Our family dinner had felt awkward and forced. Even though Rowan and Anatole were only two years apart in age, in countless other ways their differences separated them like a chasm. Forgoing his customary black costume, Anatole had appeared wearing blue jeans and a dress shirt. But clothes don't always make the man. His manner was still brooding goth-boy. He'd spent most of the meal studying his iPad. Neither Kate nor Rowan paid him much attention. Instead Rowan dominated the conversation by having a one-sided exchange with his grandfather about his trip to Europe the previous summer and plan to return there in upcoming summers between his terms studying fine art at college in Toronto.

As soon as his final forkful of saskatoon berry crisp had been devoured, Anatole vanished upstairs to seek better company with a screen full of digital beings. I'd suggested Rowan help Dad clean up while Kate and I headed outside.

"This is really beautiful," my ex-wife broke the silence after several minutes. "I had no idea."

"Actually neither had I. I'm seeing this place in a whole new light."

"The yard looks different. The house..." she began with an easy laugh—she'd never been a fan of my mother's interior decorating skills, "...looks pretty much the same. But even Ollie, is he dressing different? It's like he's changing the outside but neglecting the inside. You know I hate to say it, Adam, but your mom's passing seems to have done him a world of good."

I nodded agreement. "I see it too. I'm actually beginning to enjoy being here with him. Before it was like spending time with a rock. Now he's more of a...friendly rock."

She laughed. "It's true. I think I actually heard him humming in the kitchen. And the man makes a mean pot roast."

"Should we talk about the weather next?"

Kate expelled a puff of forced air through her nostrils. It was a habit I recognized. A sure sign she was vexed with me. "Can't we just enjoy a little idle chat?" she snapped.

"You said you had something important to tell me that couldn't wait. I know you're only here for the weekend, so...?"

"First, I want to know how your talk with Rowan went. He seemed okay when you two got back from your walk."

"He's fine. I'm the one with scorch marks."

"Uh-oh."

"He's just being a typical teenage asshole."

She shot me a look. "I wonder where he learned that from."

I shook my head, knowing she was probably right. "I'm worried about him. I don't think he's dealing with this very well. All he's thinking about is whether I'm leaving enough money behind so he can afford to go to his precious art college."

Kate looked stricken. "Oh, Adam, I'm sorry. He's a kid. Try to remember that. Even when he shows you his horns and spiked tail, he's still a teenager. He's still your son."

I chuckled. "Don't I recall you once calling him 'spawn of the devil'? Very nicely including both him and me in your utter disdain."

The tight smile on her face told me she remembered the moment very well. I knew she'd break speed records changing the subject. "Adam, tell me how you're feeling. Physically, I mean."

"I told you. I'm fine. Some headaches. Nausea. Maybe a little problem with my vision, but otherwise everything is okay."

"I heard you're not taking treatment."

"How the hell do you know that?" Maxene could sense my consternation and whinnied her concern.

"You're not the only IIA agent in the family. I have my ways. Besides, it doesn't matter how I know. What I want to know is if it's true."

"Yelchin gave me some pills…." I stopped there. I'd

known Kate a long time. There was no use in skirting the truth. "It is true."

"Can you tell me why? I know you fancy yourself Mr. Tough Guy who needs no help with anything, but Adam, this is cancer. It's going to kick your ass."

For the next minute, the only sounds were the footfalls of hooves on the ground muffled by the thick mat of last autumn's leaves, moss, and clumps of plump, summer grass. I appreciated Kate's allowing me time to formulate an answer. She knew me well enough to know that if I replied quickly, there was a high probability it would be a lie, or only some portion of the truth.

I began, "Kate, long term, I have no chance of survival. None. There is no happy ending to this story...."

She tried to interject. I held up a hand to silence her.

"All I can control are the chapters that lead up to the end. They can either be about happiness, mending fences, seeking bliss; they can be about working in the field, getting to know my father, late-night horse rides with my beautiful ex-wife... or they can be about hospitals and clinics and treatment facilities, needles and pills and radiation machines." My sigh was heavy. It wasn't cancer kicking my ass. It was truth. My truth. Spoken for the first time. "I've made my choice."

And then came the words that would change everything.

"Adam, what if I could offer you a different ending?"

Maxene, LaVerne, and Patty were tied to a tree near what had become my favourite spot in the pasture to sit and think. The bank was soft with tender swaths of grass, the slope gentle enough to sit on without fear of toppling into the creek, which at this spot ran fast over a bed of river rocks, filling the air with a soothing burbling. Kate and I were cross-legged, facing one another, taking turns swigging from a cold bottle of Cuervo Gold I'd brought along. I wanted to reach out and take her hands in mine. Yet despite our closeness, I was very aware that those hands were no longer mine to hold.

"Before I tell you anything more, you have to promise me one thing, Adam Saint."

"I never make promises I don't know if I can keep."

"Liar."

She said it in mirth, but the single word stung just the same. Once again, truth was taking the stuffing out of me.

"What is it?" was all I said, followed up with a healthy dose of liquid numbing agent.

"I need you to promise, Adam. If you don't, I could lose my job. And that is not happening, do you understand?"

"I do." I swatted at a mosquito, hoping it wasn't the first of an approaching nighttime army.

"Ever since you told me about your tumour, I've been doing some nosing around IIA."

"IIA? What do they have to do with any of this?"

"Shut up and listen."

"Yes, ma'am."

"For a short time, about eight years ago, I was seconded from the War Crimes Agency to work for another IIA department."

"How did I not know about this?" We were together

then. As far as I knew Kate, had worked with War Crimes for most of her career with IIA.

"That was part of the deal. And part of the reason I didn't last there. Complete secrecy. I couldn't tell anyone what we were doing. Not even my own reflection in the mirror. Our marriage was faltering. I wanted to save it. I realized I couldn't do both. So I went back to War Crimes."

"Which department?"

"The only agents who know about it are those who've worked or currently work there. The only secret I was ordered to keep after I was done was the department's existence."

"Until now?"

"Oh God," she said, playing with her now naked ring finger. It was a nervous habit she'd had ever since I met her. Putting a ring on it, or taking one off, hadn't made a difference. She yanked the tequila bottle out of my hands and downed a couple of ounces. "I can't believe I'm going to do this. Adam, this could be very dangerous. For both of us."

"Dangerous how? Dangerous as in you may lose your job? Or dangerous as in ice picks in our eyeballs?"

A small smile crept on her lips. "You do have a way with words."

"And the answer is...?"

"I don't know exactly. It doesn't matter anyway. I've thought about this, and I'm going to do it. You have to listen carefully. Out here in this godforsaken swamp is probably the only safe place in the world for us to talk about this."

"Have you scanned the crabapple trees and gophers for listening devices? And this is a pasture, not a swamp."

Laying aside the liquor bottle, she reached out and grasped my hands. "I need you to take this seriously."

"Believe me, I am."

"Good, because what I'm about to tell you may save your life."

She had my attention.

"The department I worked for was called the Asset Protection Unit, APU."

The world has too many acronyms. "You're right. I've never heard of it."

"Every IIA member country has one. The main goal of APU is to protect its so-called *assets*."

"Protect from whom?"

"The rest of the world."

"I don't get it. What kind of assets are we talking about?"

"Think of it this way. Suppose you win a million dollars in a lottery. What's the first thing that happens after you get all the money? Second cousin Marvin and crazy Aunt Suzy are suddenly on your doorstep asking for a piece of the prize. Everybody wants some of what you have. Doesn't matter what they want it for—to buy a new car, live in Tahiti, get a facelift, whatever—they want it, you have it, they believe they deserve some of it. They'll do whatever it takes to get some."

"So you're saying APU protects Canada's money?"

"No. It protects *anything* Canada has that IIA deems valuable. That others might want if they knew we had it. Things we aren't willing to share. Or even use ourselves. We protect them—and by protect I mean hide—for the good of the country, and really the overall good of the world. I would tell you more or give you examples, but I can't."

"Because you're sworn to secrecy."

"That and because I didn't work for APU for very long. APU agents are specially trained to look after one specific asset. One agent may spend their entire career protecting a single asset. Identification of Canadian assets is on a need-to-know basis only."

"Why are you telling me all of this?"

"Do you know what the single most common downfall of any intelligence agency is?"

"The involvement of humans."

"Yes." She stopped there, as if debating whether to take the next step.

"Kate," I urged, "what is it?"

"During my time with APU, one of my colleagues was a man named Nigel Congswell. He had a thing for me." She pasted three fingers over my about-to-open mouth. "He thought he could get somewhere by impressing me. First it was his muscles. Then it was his encyclopedic knowledge of fine wines and French cheese. When none of that worked, he confided in me."

The road was still foggy, but I was beginning to see where this was going. "He told you about his asset."

Kate nodded solemnly. Even in the dark, her eyes were flashing a curious mixture of excitement and fear.

"Tell me." She was no longer my wife. Or ex-wife. Or co-worker trying to help me. She was a reluctant source with something I needed to know.

"His asset...was a cure for cancer."

A hundred questions circled my mind after Kate's revelation. Was she lying? Had Congswell lied to her to get into her pants? Why would the Canadian government—which at the end of the day controlled IIA and all its departments and agencies and sections, clandestine or otherwise—want to hide the cure for cancer from the rest of the world? And last but certainly not least: What could this mean for me?

"Kate, how can you be sure this is true?"

"I couldn't. I didn't. I tossed it off as just another of Nigel's attempts to get closer to me by telling me a big secret. I left APU soon after and never saw Nigel or heard about his asset again. If IIA is good at anything, it's controlling rumour and maintaining secrets. I've never heard another peep about a cure for cancer—or any other APU asset for that matter—ever again. To tell you the truth, I forgot about it. Until you told me your news."

"Kate, what did you do?"

"I told you. I did some snooping. I have significantly more resources at my disposal today than I did back then."

"You contacted Congswell?"

She shook her head. "I tried. He's long gone. But I used a few other contacts I've cemented along the way. I can't tell you more than that. But, Adam, it's true. There is some kind of cure for cancer out there that APU is protecting."

"But why would they do that? Why would a country—especially Canada with its reputation for merciful actions and foreign aid—ignore an opportunity to destroy a scourge like cancer?"

"I've asked myself the same question. It's still unclear what exactly this 'cure' is or what form it takes. But from the little I've been able to learn, my understanding is that it's difficult to procure and even then highly unstable. There are hints that APU is not in full control of this…substance or whatever it is. From what I've been told, the whole thing is causing IIA a lot of headaches."

I was shaking my head, not wanting to believe as much as I did.

The birth of hope can be a dangerous thing.

"This has nothing to do with drug companies lining IIA coffers? A cure for cancer would slam some of the world's richest corporations into sudden bankruptcy. Not to mention all the spinoff industries getting fat off of people dying."

"Adam, to be honest, I don't know the answer to that. I'm not hooked in high enough to know. But at this point, I don't care. All I care about is—" She caught herself, swallowing any further words. She turned away and flicked away an imaginary bug.

"What do you care about? Why are you doing this, Kate? I'm not stupid, you know. I loved our making love the last time I saw you. I think about it all the time. But you still let me sign those divorce papers. And you still…you're still seeing someone else."

Her face swung back, sharp eyes hooking into mine like a barb into a fish. "How do you know that?"

I smiled as kindly as I could bear. "Look at you. I knew you wouldn't be alone for long, Kate."

"None of this means I don't love you, Adam. Because I do. And I love our son. I know he loves you too. If you just disappear, if you die, it will damage him forever. If there is any way I can stop that from happening, if there is any way I can guarantee my son his father for the foreseeable future, I will do it. I'm willing to take the risk. And so should you, damn it."

"Exactly what kind of risk are you talking about?"

Kate stared at me hard. "I think you should go after the cure. I think you should find it, take it, and live."

"How am I supposed to do that?"

"I think I know a way."

"How?"

"Nigel Congswell."

We spent the next hour lying side by side on the grassy bank, making good progress toward the bottom of the bottle of Cuervo. Intermittently we'd discuss potential plans for going after Congswell. Then, silently, we'd stare up at the night sky's brilliant display of dippers, big and small, and the Northern Cross and think.

Was it possible? Could I find this mysterious cure for cancer and heal myself?

I raised myself onto my elbows intending to ask Kate another question she likely had no better answer to than I. Instead I leaned in and kissed her.

She kissed back.

I rolled over on top of her so that I was straddling her, looking down at her beautiful, starlit face. Slowly I unbuttoned her blouse and pulled the fabric aside. I lowered my face between her breasts and breathed in the heady scent of her. I felt her left hand at the back of my head pulling me even closer, the other at the zipper of my jeans.

Everything else disappeared from my fevered brain except one thing: "I love you, Kate."

I felt her jerk beneath me.

She was pulling away.

I sat up and looked at her.

"Get off, Adam," she said.

"Kate, I...." I felt like a fool.

"Get off, please."

I lifted a leg to free her. As I dropped back to the ground, she moved away, then stood up. I stayed put, flat on my back, studying her face against the dizzying backdrop of a million stars. As well as I thought I knew her, I couldn't read what I saw there.

"Kate, I know you love someone else now. But that doesn't mean I can't still love you too."

She didn't wait for more. She dashed over to Patty and mounted her in one swift move. A kick of her heels set the animal in motion, horse and rider quickly swallowed up by the dark of night.

Chapter Twelve

"Text me when you're done," Anatole instructed in a dry tone.

Despite his apparent dislike for doing anything kids his age should be doing—like going to a bar at midnight even when you've already had too much to drink—he'd offered to drive me into the city under those exact circumstances. At the moment, it seemed like the best thing to do. I couldn't be in the same house with Kate sleeping in the room next to mine. I needed a change of scenery and more tequila.

"You're not coming in? Come on, I'll buy you a drink."

"I don't drink."

"I'll buy you a soda pop then."

"Get out."

I did.

"Text me!" I heard him yell as I slammed the door.

There is nothing subtle or dishonest about Dirk's Tavern. What you see is exactly what you get.

Located under a freeway overpass just inches from the southern outskirts of the city, Dirk's easily lives up to its reputation. Part biker bar, part skanky dive, it's where anyone can go when in the mood for dark, dank, and dangerous. The regular clientele are one beer away from skid row, living social assistance cheque to social assistance cheque, heavy smokers, eaters of potato chips, and likely on a first-name basis with at least one member of the Saskatoon Police Service. Fortunately or unfortunately, depending on your point of view, the regulars do not make up much of the crowd on any given night. They're usually either out of money, in jail, or passed out in the back alley. Mostly the crowd consists of an eclectic mix of self-respecting bikers, university students looking for adventure and cheap beer, and singles who are either too old or too undesirable for the swankier clubs downtown.

I've been in my share of places just like this one. Every now and then, when a job is over and there's nothing monumental that has to get done the next day, well, there's nothing quite like spending an evening in a scuzzy bar. Saskatoon, Singapore, Saigon, they're the same the world over.

Midnight to two a.m. is the shank of the evening for most bars. Anyone who's making a night of it has settled in and is nowhere near to thinking of leaving. As I waded through the large crowd milling around the parking lot, chain-smoking and hiding illicit bottles of beer under their shirts in case I was a cop, I was pretty sure I'd find a seat inside.

Even though smoking bylaws prohibit the vice indoors, Dirk's still managed to maintain the smoky ambiance and distinct odour of day-old ashtray. The crowd indoors was still thick. The place was dim, and a steady diet of rock anthems and pseudo-ballads kept the joint hopping. I muddled past the random scattering of tables and hightops through a morass of cheap perfume and sweat to reach the bar. The bartender was a head atop a mound of muscle. I was about to call for his attention when I felt a claw of nails down my back.

I turned and caught my breath.

I knew I'd drunk a lot of tequila already that night, but I can usually hold plenty of liquor before falling into total mental disrepair. Yet still, I could have sworn the woman standing in front of me was the same woman I'd seen in the pasture, battered and dirty, barely dressed, having just escaped her abuser. Or was it? That woman had fiery red hair and stunningly blue eyes. This woman was a brunette, her eyes brown. But everything else about her looked exactly the same.

"Eva?"

At first, she frowned, but she quickly turned coquettish. "Who told you my name? Was it Cindy? Did she come over here and say something? I'm going to kill her!"

My mind felt numb. "Your name *is* Eva?"

"Yes, you silly!" she giggled.

The woman looked like the woman in the pasture, but she certainly didn't act like her.

"Have we met before?"

I asked.

"Maybe," she responded, batting long eyelashes. Her voice was like a cheeping bird. "Where do you think we met?" I shrugged.

"Oh. You mean like in a different life or something?" She seemed to find the possibility fascinating.

"No. I'm sorry. I must be wrong."

"There's nothing wrong about you, honey," purred the young woman.

In seconds, her mouth was on mine.

I recoiled, attempting to step away.

Suddenly her hand was at the nape of my neck, clamping on like a steel vice. She pulled me closer still, smashing our lips together.

Eva's eyes were open. Taunting. Teasing. Daring. Dangerous.

In a blinding flash, the woman was yanked away from me. Her lovely face and inquisitive tongue rudely replaced by the ugly puss of someone who I immediately concluded had to be none other than her jealous boyfriend.

"What the fuck do you think you're doing, asshole?" the guy wanted to know. I guessed he'd had KFC for dinner.

I could feel something sharp at my neck. Chicken Little was holding a knife to my throat. Looking over his shoulders, I saw he wasn't alone. It was going to be four against one. Not very fair odds.

For them.

"I just came in here to get a drink," I politely answered the question.

"From my girlfriend's mouth?" his voice rumbled.

"I didn't know she was your girlfriend."

"Well, you do now."

The knife ground into my skin. I felt a trickle of blood run down my neck. That is what I call hostile behaviour.

In a smooth choreography of moves, I buried my knee in Chicken Little's groin, brought my left hand up to block and push back his knife hand, and with my right, pushed up on his chin and propelled him back, then around, just as he was losing knee strength from the gonad crushing. As he dropped to the floor, I gave his head a bit of assistance, so that it didn't miss hitting the edge of the bar on the way down.

I turned to face his friends.

"Anybody else?"

I didn't really think they'd take me up on it.

But they did.

All at once, the men descended on me like a swarm of hornets. They were yelling and screaming and spitting with outrage over what I'd done to their buddy.

Shit.

I was doing pretty well for the first few minutes, fending off the volley of fists and feet and blaspheming. But I knew victory would not be mine in the end. These were big guys. One of them actually had some fighting skills. Another had absolutely no qualms about fighting dirty, including pulling hair and scratching eyes. He was the worst.

I was going down.

Abruptly the tide began to turn. Suddenly there were only two guys on me.

Where was the third?

Out of the corner of my eye, I spied a whirling dervish landing a punishing round of karate chops mixed with foot jabs on the missing man. He was turning into a helpless, whimpering lump of pulp. More surprising still, a series of high-pitched yips told me it was my sister going all *Crouching Tiger, Hidden Dragon* on the guy.

With only two to handle, I was in a much better position to win back the upper hand. I landed a lucky backhanded punch upside the nose of one guy—eliciting an impressive spray of blood—at the same time as a powerful kick to the flabby abs of the other.

And then it was over as swiftly as it had begun.

By this point, the front man, Chicken Little, was struggling to his feet.

My co-combatant was in his face like gravy on chips. "I don't have many rules around here, but one of them for damn sure is NO FUCKING WEAPONS!"

"He was kissing—"

"I don't care if he was fucking her in the ass with a pool cue. No weapons! I want you and your friends out of here right now. Or you'll never be allowed back."

"But he s—"

"Do I have to call the bouncers?"

I had to smirk at that one. Alexandra quite obviously needed no assistance from a bouncer. Even Biceps on a Stick behind the bar had stayed clear of the action while she took care of business.

"Forget it," he grumbled. "This is so not worth it."

"Hey!" I called out to get the guy's attention. "Tell Eva I—"

"Eva? Who the fuck is Eva?"

"Your girlfriend."

"I don't know who you're talking about, dude, but my girl's name is Crystal."

I stared at the bloody hoodlum. He stared back. My eyes moved to my sister. She was eyeing me like I was an alien, her lip curled up in a what-the-fuck? sneer.

Chicken Little helped his mates off the floor and guided them to the door. I scoured the bar for signs of Eva. She was long gone.

The rest of the place and its patrons returned to normal in the blink of an eye. Knife fights and blood sports were nothing to get too excited about around here.

"Thanks," I said, returning to the bar.

"Fuck you and the mule you rode in on."

I smiled. My sister. Always the scrapper. Apparently in more ways than one.

"Where did you learn to kick ass like that?"

"Comes with the territory," Alexandra answered, flipping the barman a look.

"What territory?"

"The territory of being me."

I studied my sister's face. I didn't know if I wanted to know what she meant by that.

"Well, anyway, thank you."

"He had a right to be pissed off, you know."

"She kissed me. Not the other way around."

"Listen, if you want to make out with some girl half your age instead of your own wife, I'm not one to judge. But as the owner of this place, I reserve the right not to want that shit in here."

"You own Dirk's?" I was incredulous. My sister had never so much as owned a pet gerbil. If she had, the popular bet would be that it would be dead within a month.

"I know what you're thinking. And you're right. Dad helped me. But I'm paying him back. Probably faster than he expected. Faster than I expected. The shithole business is booming."

We shared a grin. And in that moment I saw the resem-

blance between us. When we smiled…a rarity for us both…
we looked alike.

"Kate and I aren't married anymore."

Alexandra opened her mouth, then closed it, then
opened it again. "Dad said she showed up and was staying
the weekend." It wasn't like her to care about whether anyone's marriage survived or not. Not even her own brother's.
Alexandra and Kate hadn't spent a lot of time together, but
I sensed they liked each other.

"You talked to Dad on the phone?"

"Yeah, so?"

"But you won't come over? I've only seen you…what is
it? Twice since I got here?"

"So?"

"So, if I didn't know better, I'd say you weren't interested in spending time with me."

Placing hands on hips, she responded with: "Well, let
me put your inquiring mind to rest. I'm not."

The bartender handed me a dampened cloth. I swabbed
dribbles of blood off my neck, cheek, and knuckles. Only
some of it was mine. "Thanks," I said. "Do you have anything for a wounded heart?"

"Oh, ha ha ha," Alexandra jeered, circling around to the
back of the bar. She shooed away the barman, pulled down
a bottle, and poured out two shots of Canadian Club.
"Here," she said, handing me one. "For the pain."

Raising glasses in a tight, wordless toast, we downed the
alcohol.

"So tell me about all this," I said, hands raised to en-
compass the bar.

"I think it's none of your business. Obviously you have a lot of other things to be interested in. You know what I think, Adam? I think you should go back to your highfalutin life in Toronto and take care of your marriage and whatever else it is that you do. If you couldn't find even one chance to come back in seven years, it must be real important stuff, whatever it is. So go do it. Dad told me the garbage about you seeing some woman in the pasture who miraculously needed your help. And now this? Both of them Evas? Mom's name? What's wrong with you? Are you fucked up or what?"

"You saw her. She told me her name was Eva. They both did."

Alexandra regarded me like an alley cat who might be rabid. "I didn't, Adam. I didn't see her. All I saw was my brother getting the shit kicked out of him in my bar."

She didn't see her.

I took that in, with nothing to say.

"If you're so desperate to get back to your life as a super-hero, go already."

"Now why would I do that? When things are getting so interesting around here?"

"That's ten bucks for the shot," she said, leveling her gaze at me.

I pulled a fifty from my jeans pocket and tossed it on the counter. "In that case, I'll have another. I'm all for supporting local business."

Alexandra poured two more shots. "Including my two shots and a tip, I hope you have more where that came from." She raised her glass.

174 — Anthony Bidulka

"Wait," I stopped her. "I want to propose a toast."

"Go to hell."

"Nice, but I had something a little different in mind."

She stared at me but did not drink.

"I want to propose a toast to my sister. I want to say I'm sorry for not seeing her for the last seven years. I'm sorry for not being here more...at all...since Mom died. And I want to say how proud I am of you for doing everything you've done. For taking care of Dad. Raising a son. Starting a business. And making it all work. You're quite the broad, Alexandra Saint."

For a moment, I wasn't sure if she was going to spit or cry. In the end, she responded with a curt nod and said, "Go to hell."

"Okay. Let's stick with that."

We both grinned once more and took our shots.

As promised—and having no other way to get home—I texted Anatole to pick me up. The half-ton arrived at the front of the bar less than ten minutes later.

"So where have you been?" I asked when I took my seat next to him. I'd had several glasses of water and three cups of coffee by this point, but I decided to let him drive anyway.

"There's a twenty-four-hour comic store not far from here," he told me with a baleful glare. "Do you want to hear more?"

"Nope. That's good."

"Home, right?"

I rolled down my window. "Wait."

"Wait? For what?"

As is my habit, I'd been taking stock of my surroundings. It was late. There were still plenty of vehicles parked on the streets but not many people. Except one. A man, about a block away. He was leaning over a car as if talking to someone inside. I wouldn't have given it much attention—probably some guy trying to arrange a last minute hookup with a girl he met in the bar—but he was wearing a trench coat and some sort of cap. In summer. In Saskatchewan.

"What are you looking at?" Anatole asked.

Suddenly the man yanked open the door of the car and pulled out the driver. Forcibly.

The driver, a woman, began to flail about wildly and, with some expertise, landed a hit to the guy's solar plexus. Within a split second, a second man was on the scene. I jumped out of the car and began running in the direction of the attack. Halfway there, I stopped short, not believing my eyes.

"Eva?" I called out. The brunette version.

The trio froze in mid tussle and stared at me, still half a block away. This gave the woman just enough time to shove away the assailant nearest her and jump back into her car. Before the two men could react, she'd hit the gas. As the vehicle blasted by me, I got a decent look at the driver. It was definitely the same woman I'd met in the bar. Eva. Her brown eyes wild.

I looked up just in time to see the two men jump into an SUV and give chase.

What the hell is going on here?

I raced back to the half-ton, opened the driver's side door, and told my nephew to shove over.

"Are you certain you're below point-zero-eight?"

"Oh for crying out loud!" I barked as I circled the car and jumped into the front passenger seat. "Just do whatever you have to do to catch up with that SUV."

Pulling a pretty decent U-turn, Anatole took off.

"What are we doing, Uncle Adam?"

"Looks like they're headed up Lorne Avenue. Just stay behind them."

"Exactly who are 'they'?"

How to answer that one? I stared ahead as I said, "The guys in the trench coats."

"Ooooooookay." He waited a beat, then, "Why exactly are we following two guys in trench coats?"

The SUV made a sharp right turn onto Maple, an otherwise quiet suburban street, most definitely not a major thoroughfare. Although we were too far back to see Eva's car, I knew she was trying to lose them by circling around short streets and perhaps hoping to slip up a back alley without their seeing her. Interesting that she wasn't simply making for the nearest police station or public area with lots of other people around. At that time of night, her best bet would have been 8th Street. Instead she'd chosen to elude her pursuers rather than scare them away.

"Make the right! Make the right!"

"I see it!" Anatole shouted back, his eyes bugged out beneath his curtain of dark hair. "Why are we doing this?"

Since I was involving him in a high-speed car chase, I supposed I owed my nephew a bit of justification. "Those men are chasing Eva. We either have to get them off her tail or be there when they catch her."

"Eva?"

"Yeah, didn't you see her?"

He gawked at me.

"Keep your eyes on the road! Right, they're making another right!"

"Yeah! Got it! Are you saying we're chasing the same woman you found in the pasture that day?"

Fucking hell! How was I going to explain this? It was the same woman—in appearance…sort of—but not, and she just happened to have the same name….Nope, no way to do this with any clarity…or sense of dignity.

"Right again!" I called out.

We were going in a circle. Eva wasn't having any luck shaking the trench coats. The streets were too empty. There weren't enough deviations from the simple grid pattern of streets in this part of town. She'd have to get out of here.

"We're almost back to where we started, Uncle Adam. How much longer do you think this is going to take?"

"You have somewhere else you need to be?"

"Ha. Funny. Just saying: This is weird."

Understatement. This was more than weird. And revelatory. My nephew was actually doing a pretty good job— for a computer nerd—at keeping up with the SUV, matching them for speed and hairpin turn by hairpin turn. Especially since he didn't have much to work with. Dad's half-ton had to be thirty years old and burnt oil like a decommissioned refinery.

The SUV appeared to be slowing down. We were on

Ruth Street heading west.

"Something's happening." The trench coat's vehicle had slowed to a snail's pace as if not sure where to go. Had she done it? Had Eva successfully lost them?

"What do we do?" Anatole wanted to know.

"They're turning into Prairieland." Prairieland was a large events centre park, basically a series of huge buildings surrounded by vast parking lots. The place would be a ghost town this late at night. "Follow them in."

Anatole made a left through the main gates into the park.

"Where are they?" he wondered aloud as we both scoured the large empty lot.

The SUV occupants must have extinguished their lights, either in the hope of sneaking up on Eva…or us. I ordered Anatole to do the same.

"How will I know where I'm going without lights?" he complained.

Tall lampposts dotted the area with circles of light. The SUV would be hiding outside the circles. If you can't beat 'em, join 'em. "Just do it, Anatole."

Anatole turned off the half-ton's lights, slowing our pace accordingly. Within a few seconds, our eyes adjusted to the new lighting conditions.

"There," I whispered.

"I don't see anything."

I pointed to a spot ahead of us and to the left. They'd picked a good spot, away from illumination in the shadow of a building. The SUV was sitting still. Idling. Waiting. Watching. And then, as we got closer, I saw the second vehicle. Eva's car. Also parked, lights off. It sat twenty yards away from the SUV, at a right angle.

A worrisome thought entered my brain. Were the trench coats and Eva working together?

Had they lured us into a trap?

"Stop," I told my nephew.

The Chevy came to a halt at a right angle to Eva's car. Our vehicles now roughly forming three sides of a square.

"What now?" Anatole asked.

"Get ready to gun it."

Under his breath, I heard, "Fuck me."

"No swearing." My father's voice.

Thirty seconds passed with no movement from anyone.

Forty.

Fifty.

Then three things happened at once. A shot was fired, at us, from the SUV. I lunged across the seat and pulled my nephew's head out of the line of fire. Tires squealed as Eva's car made a run for it.

I had no weapon. Nothing to defend us with. Running suddenly sounded like a pretty good idea.

With both our heads below the dashboard, I shoved the truck into drive and used my hand to push down on the accelerator. Being in an empty parking lot, my hope was that we had a little distance to go before we hit something. I counted to five—a long time when driving blind—then I manhandled Anatole into the passenger end of the front seat, told him to stay down, and popped up behind the wheel.

Shit. All I saw ahead of me was black.

I found the switch for the lights just in time to discover

the half-ton barreling toward an uninviting-looking ditch at a far edge of the parking lot. I slammed on the brakes. Adam flew into the cubbyhole beneath the dash. Probably not a bad spot for him.

"You okay?" I called out to him.

"Why wouldn't I be?"

Raw sense of humour intact. Good sign.

I spied a look through the rear window to see what was coming. A speeding SUV? More gunfire?

They were gone. Eva. The trench coats in the SUV. Gone.

"Fuck!"

"Don't swear." Anatole. "Can I sit up now?"

My eyes made one more trip across the abandoned field. "Yeah. But put on your seatbelt."

Anatole unfolded his lanky body and repositioned it on the seat next to me. "There aren't any."

I didn't want to go into why not. I pointed the truck in the direction of the park exit and peeled out of there.

"We're not going home yet, are we?" Anatole concluded as he grasped on to the door handle to keep from getting jostled about by the admirable speed I was coaxing out of the Chevy.

"They can't have gotten too far."

"Who? The guys in the SUV or the woman?"

"Either. Keep your eyes peeled."

I was racing down Ruth Street in the hope the SUV drivers would stick to what they knew.

"Do you really think we should be chasing guys with guns?" His voice was remarkably calm, his thinking irritatingly logical.

What was I doing? This wasn't a CDRA assignment. I wasn't on the mean streets of Beirut hunting a suspect who'd blown up a car full of Canadian journalists. I was in Saskatoon with my sister's child. My priority wasn't to figure out whether these mystery women all named Eva were anything more than tumour-induced hallucinations. It wasn't to chase down some gun-wielding villains. My first duty was to keep my nephew safe. Anatole was right. I needed to stand down.

"Do you hear that?"

I lowered the window. Sirens.

I'd stand down later.

I made a left onto Broadway and headed south toward the wailing. We caught a green at 8th Street and kept going.

"There." Anatole pointed at a speeding police cruiser cutting us off at Main Street. "They're heading west."

I followed the police car, past Eastlake, then right onto Victoria.

"Uh, oh. I bet I know what happened," Anatole said as we approached what was obviously the site of a very recent car crash.

"Try to get as close as you can," I said, straining to get a good look at the vehicle.

"Whoever it was probably didn't know the Traffic Bridge is closed."

"Closed?"

"For a long time now. Years, I think. Stupid, right? Having a bridge in the middle of the city out of commission."

We were nearing the accident. Several police cars had arrived, but the constables hadn't yet had time to cordon off the area. An ambulance was pulling up.

"If you're speeding down Victoria too fast and don't know the bridge is out, by the time you're up and over the hill right before the bridge, you don't have a lot of time to stop before you'll smash into the wall of cement blockades."

My eyes surveyed the wreckage, steam spewing from an accordioned front end. I swore under my breath. It was Eva's car.

"Find a place to park."

The police were getting organized in a hurry. As our truck moved by the scene, a uniformed officer waved us on. Anatole found a spot half a block away on 11th. I got out.

"Wait here," I said.

"Uncle Adam, they're not just going let you walk up to the car and look inside."

I winked at him and closed the door.

I jogged back to the accident site. A fire truck had joined the brigade as had a few late-night revelers who'd probably been making their way back home from the bars and restaurants on Broadway and downtown.

Anatole was right. The officials weren't about to let me anywhere near the wrecked car. But I had to find out if Eva was okay. Had she survived the crash? I circled the area until I found a decent vantage point that gave me some height to observe the scene. The evening had grown surprisingly cool for a summer night, and I put my hands in my jean pockets.

There was something wrong. Paramedics were loitering about instead of tending to the accident victim. Police officers were actually scratching their heads. I looked closer at the car. The driver's side door gaped open. The car was empty.

Once again, Eva had pulled a disappearing act.

Who the hell is this woman?

Other than her chameleon appearance and appetite for making me think I was losing my grip on reality, I knew nothing about her. But I did learn something about her tonight. She wasn't from Saskatoon. Only out-of-towners, like me, wouldn't know that bridge was out.

She couldn't have gone far. Especially now that she'd likely sustained injuries. I had nothing to lose by taking a quick look around. *Where would I go if I were her?*

I didn't have far to look.

Next to me a sign prohibited not only vehicular traffic across the Victoria Bridge but foot traffic as well.

That's where she'd go. The bridge. It was perfect. On the other side of the river was downtown Saskatoon with a million places to hide.

I jumped over the barricades and headed down the condemned bridge. It was like walking into a tunnel of tar. Suddenly the stars and moon I'd been admiring a few hours earlier with my ex-wife were nowhere to be seen, sucked up by the city's ambient light.

At least I knew that as long as I stuck to a straight line, I was pretty much on the right track. I tried for a slow trot, all the while keeping my ears on keen alert.

I thought I heard a sound ahead of me. It could have been anything. I hoped it wasn't.

"Eva?"

My eyes adjusted. In the foggy shadows ahead of me, I could make out a shape moving away.

"Stop!"

The figure was listing to one side. She was hurt.

"I can help you, Eva. If you'd just stop."

I was easily gaining on her. With every metre I progressed, she'd only cover half the distance.

And then she did the unexpected.

Still too far away to be certain it truly was Eva, I watched the dark figure crawl up the side railing of the bridge.

Oh no you don't! "Eva! Stop!"

I quickened my pace, careful not to trip on the uneven, deteriorating surface.

"Stop it! Eva! Stop!" I shouted.

As I got closer, the woman straightened to her full height on the precarious ledge.

Closer.

"Eva!"

Closer.

"Stop!"

I was within arm's length. She turned to face me.

Suddenly the moon was back, come out from its hiding place behind a bank of night cloud. The silvery light played across Eva's beautiful face. She smiled when she knew I was near enough to recognize her.

I stopped. Held out my hand to help her down.

She crooked one arm as if to salute me, then waggled her fingers…and jumped.

There was a time when Alexandra Saint wanted nothing more out of life than alcohol, sex, hard drugs, loud music, and to do every possible thing to piss off anyone close to her.

Those were the good old days.

Alexandra didn't understand *normal* society's aversion to even a trifling amount of drug use. Why shouldn't people have the right to go off the deep end every now and again? Most people have shitty lives. They have crappy jobs, working too hard for too little money. They suffer through bad relationships. They live in shitholes. Why not grasp any chance available to get away from it all? Who cared if it wasn't reality? What was so bad about drug-induced fantasies? Or drinking enough alcohol to make you forget all the bad shit? As long as you weren't hurting anybody. Alexandra had never been a proponent of drinking and driving. But drinking and walking? Drinking and cycling? Drinking and having sex with whoever looked good that night? Why the hell not?

All her life, Alexandra had been different. Everyone knew it as soon as they met her. There was "something off about that girl," she'd hear them say. Even her parents and brother thought so.

Not that she could blame them. She *was* different. She knew it before she reached her teens. She didn't know why. It wasn't something she'd done to herself. She just thought different thoughts. She saw the world a different way. Most people were so fucking stupid, it drove her bonkers. For a long while she thought that if only she could show them exactly how aggravated they made her—by acting out, showing them up, or simply getting in their face—they'd eventually change and she wouldn't have to be so aggravated anymore. She could settle down and be normal.

Of course, that never happened. Things never changed. People stayed stupid.

Alexandra was only nine years old when her brother was shipped off to military school for being a badass. He never came back. In the short time she could remember living together as brother and sister, to her, Adam was this bigger-than-life, heroic figure. She worshipped him. But ultimately he disappointed her. He simply left and forgot all about her.

With abandonment by her brother, the strictness of a mother who favoured her absent son, the reserved silence of her father, and the complete, utter boredom of life on a farm, childhood for a girl like Alexandra Saint was endlessly frustrating. She'd had no choice but to go out and wreak havoc.

At fifteen, at a high school party, Alexandra discovered nirvana. She learned the perfect way to deal with the intense, unrelenting noise of stupidity that surrounded her on a daily basis. She got turned on to the triple threat: drugs, alcohol, and sex. All in one night. She never looked back.

Of the three, sex was the most complex. She happily indulged in alcohol and drugs without sex. She could do alcohol and sex without drugs. She could do drugs and sex without alcohol. But no way could she do sex without alcohol or drugs or both.

Without mind-numbing substances, sex was hopeless. Sober, she could never hope to find a guy who wasn't annoying long enough for her to want them to take their clothes off and do the deed. Not that Alexandra didn't like sex. It was dealing with idiots that was the problem.

Alexandra's parents took her to more than a few doctors. They were obsessed with figuring out what was going on (or not) in her head. Everyone wanted to put some kind of label on her. They wanted an explanation. Why does she do the things she does? How can we make her stop? They hoped for a pill that would cure her.

Alexandra knew better. There was nothing wrong with her. Some days were simply harsher than others. Some days every colour was dark, some days light. Some days getting out of bed was a mental grind, other days it was reasonably manageable. There were times she understood what it was to feel satisfied, even content. Happy was a stretch. Hopeful only a dream. She didn't believe in silver linings or the innate goodness of people. Instead she expected the worst from others and was never surprised when they proved her right. Sometimes her body physically ached for no good reason. Sometimes she felt like Superwoman. She *was* different. And if people didn't like it, she didn't like them. Simple as that.

Although unaware of the similarities, Alexandra became pregnant in much the same way her mother had when she conceived Adam. In an unfulfilling shuffle with a boy she didn't know very well. Unlike her mother, who married the father of her child, when Alexandra discovered she was pregnant, she never considered telling the father. Why should she? She was a girl. He was a boy. At sixteen, neither was parent material.

But Eva Saint was a forceful woman. She convinced young Alexandra that the right thing to do was to have the baby rather than the abortion her daughter wanted. Her mother told Alexandra she'd done good by having Anatole. Alexandra could agree with the *having*. It was the *keeping* part she had a problem with.

Suddenly there were new doctors. They preached about prenatal shit and postnatal shit, and on and on and on. Alexandra thought her head might explode.

Her mother had steered her wrong. The day she gave birth, Alexandra confirmed her suspicion she was not cut out to be a parent.

Like regular human beings, it turned out that for the most part, kids are stupid and annoying too. Baby Anatole annoyed Alexandra. A lot.

For the good of everyone, the child most of all, Anatole often stayed with his grandparents. Which was a pain in the ass during the fairly regular intervals when Alexandra herself, too broke to afford her own place, would also have to bunk at her parents' house. The four of them together under one roof was tough living.

A doctor she almost trusted eventually diagnosed Alexandra as bipolar. She took the pills. Usually they helped enough to take the roughest edges off. Alexandra suspected there was more to it than that. The medication didn't entirely get rid of the angst, the slightly unbalanced, disassociated feelings she'd struggled with since she could remember. But they were enough to keep her going. Enough to keep the knife away from her wrist. Enough to resist the temptation to abandon her life, her kid, her job, and just hop on the back of the next Harley belonging to whatever low-life came around offering her a ride. She'd blast off into the sunset and see what happened next.

In an attempt to look after her kid, Alexandra began what would turn into a long career of go-nowhere jobs. The only thing she really excelled at was serving beer at the raunchiest liquor dens and holes in the wall in Saskatoon. The darker the bar, the more rundown the venue, the rowdier the clientele, the more she liked it. There was something about the odour of underlying danger or the possibility of a bar brawl that intoxicated her, helped her feel alive. And at least in a low-rent bar, the clientele already know they're stupid and annoying to begin with. That helped.

What didn't help was the piss-poor wage. No one ever got rich being a waitress. More and more, Alexandra relied on her parents for financial aid. More and more, she'd find herself unable to pay rent to some scumbag landlord and have to move back to the farm for a spell. As it was, Oliver and Eva Saint paid for pretty much everything Anatole needed. As grateful as Alexandra was for all her parents did for her child—a charity she could not refuse—she equally hated every time she was forced to hold out a hand for herself. Of everything on the long list of things in life that aggravated her, this was the worst.

Over the years, as they both got older and matured, a surprising thing began to occur between mother and son. Alexandra found herself increasingly interested in the little creature who was her child.

At first, it was the recognition that, despite the pimply teenager who'd fathered the child and whose name she'd pretty much forgotten, Anatole had physically taken after his mother. Even as a bouncing baby boy, he had the same dark, brooding features. And when someone pointed out that Anatole responded to his mother in a way reserved only for her, with atypical giggles and gurgles, the bonding between mother and son began in earnest. All of a sudden, time together was something Alexandra yearned for instead of dreaded.

It was one of her earliest employers who convinced Alexandra that she needed to learn how to defend herself against the never-ending parade of creeps who harassed her at work. The boss couldn't have cared less how Alexandra dressed. He simply believed that if you presented yourself in a provocative manner, you were an idiot if you didn't prepare yourself to deal with the attention—wanted and unwanted. Some people needed school to learn how to type or operate a drill for their jobs. Alexandra needed to learn how to fight and use a weapon.

Although she didn't come out and admit it to anyone, the time she spent in classes to develop her "expertise" in self-defence and offence was some of the best of her life. Not only did she naturally excel at anything that had to do with kicking butt or shooting a gun or directing a switchblade to just the right spot, but her prowess also made her feel special. Powerful. Worthy.

Alexandra Saint fucked a lot of guys. "Fucked" was a crude term, but it accurately described what it was that she did with most men. On occasion there'd be a guy she'd have a relationship-type thing with. But those dalliances were measured at best in weeks. Even on medication, she still found most suitors to be nothing more than little-boy brats in big-boy clothes.

Then along came Dave Steader, known to all as Scruff. He was a biker who made a decent living from running a small gang of petty criminals doing petty crimes across the province. He was big and hairy and looked a little like a cartoon monster. He wasn't all sweet as pie and soft-hearted inside either, except when it came to Alexandra. She was the first person, first anything, that he ever truly loved. He showed it in every way he could think of. Some of them worked, some not so much.

Despite Scruff's life of crime, he did have a strong moral code separating right from wrong, acceptable crime from unacceptable crime. For instance, anything that hurt someone physically—for more than a day or two—was not cool.

Eventually Alexandra moved into Scruff's apartment. The place was small and ugly and smelled a bit off. But it was during this period that Scruff—who refused to take a cent in rent or food money—encouraged Alexandra to start saving her money and eventually make an offer on the bar where they'd first met. The owner was getting old and had no savings to retire on. It was win-win for both parties, especially when Alexandra's father agreed to front a majority of the purchase price with a no-interest loan.

Alexandra and Scruff were together for a few years. Sometimes off but usually on. They even talked marriage, or at least getting a bigger place together. One big enough so that Anatole could move in. They even thought about having a baby together. A real home and a real family. It had once seemed like such an impossible dream to Alexandra.

It was.

With Scruff away on one of his regular trips to Vancouver to visit his mother and sister, Alexandra received a late-night telephone call. Scruff had flown off his motorcycle, doing 145 on the Coquihalla. He was killed instantly. Suddenly Alexandra Saint was abandoned. Again.

She grieved. She started fucking a lot of guys again, but it was never the same. Her heart just wasn't in it.

Although she knew she shouldn't, Alexandra blamed her brother for abandoning her on the farm with their parents. At first, he came home to check on her every so often, and that made it a bit better. But then he moved away for good. Got a job with some big top-secret organization (she didn't really know what he did and sometimes even wondered if he was really just a shoe salesman or something). He got married. Had a kid. Then he *really* got involved in his "career," and that was it. He basically forgot to come home.

Until their mother died. Only then did Adam show his face.

She didn't know why, but seeing her brother at their mother's funeral, with his perfect looks, perfect family, and perfect career, made Alexandra spitting mad. Everything had always been easy for him. Sure he'd been a bit of a troublemaker as a youngster, but in all other ways he was a golden boy living a golden life. It made her nauseous thinking about it. Then he was gone again. Claiming some great emergency that would cause the world to explode or something if he didn't rush off to look after it.

Once again, he didn't come back.

Her guts curdled when the old biddies at the funeral lunch began clucking about how they *expected* that she, as the only daughter, would be looking after her father now that he was all alone in the world. Who the fuck were they to assume anything? To guilt her into doing the *supposedly* right thing? And where the fuck was Adam? Traipsing around the world on jets and yachts. That's where. Why wasn't he *expected* to do something? Why did it have to be her?

Yup. Alexandra Saint was a pissed-off woman.

Chapter Thirteen

Where had the money gone? Where? Where?

Hanna leaned hard against the bathroom sink. She felt a now too familiar ache in the pit of her stomach. She felt this way every time she thought she was about to lose control. Something that was beginning to occur with frightening regularity. Before, every time she was about to hit rock bottom, she'd come up with a new idea, a big plan. Or something that truly smacked of divine intervention would occur and it would be okay. But no more. Hanna was done. Empty. There was nothing. Nowhere left to go. The money from her last job was almost gone. She could think of nothing to save herself and her son from destitution.

She'd been overly confident. She thought she alone knew how best to protect her family of two. She thought she was doing the right thing. The only thing to be done. But she was wrong. So very wrong.

They'd reached the end of the road. Someone had tried to put a bullet through her little boy's forehead. It didn't get worse than that. Only a quirk of fate had put her in the right place at the right time to save Jake's life. But how much longer could she count on that? She'd gambled with her son's life. For what? To end up here? In this filthy bathroom, feeling like she wanted to puke her guts out? All she really wanted to do was crawl into one of the cubicles, lock the door, curl up on the floor between the toilet and the wall, and go to sleep. Forever.

But she had a child to look after. She didn't have the luxury of thinking about what she wanted. This was all about Jake. She had to pull it together. Fast.

She raised her heavy head off the sink and faced her reflection. Looking at herself in the mirror used to be pleasant. All she had to do was add a touch of cosmetics, fluff her hair, then turn into the light, making the picture even more beautiful.

What happened to Bar Refaeli? Did she have sunken eyes, skin that was drawn and pale from too little sleep and too much worry? Was her hair growing lifeless and more and more grey by the hour?

Hanna washed her face with cold water. From her purse she pulled out the last two remaining bits of makeup she owned. A lipstick and an eyebrow pencil. Both were worn down to the nub. Each time she used them she was surprised to find they'd yet more to give. She used the eyebrow pencil to darken her brows and line her eyes. She coloured her lips with the lipstick. She'd bought it for going out at night. It was much too bright for today…or any day of her current life. As a last minute thought she dabbed a bit of the colour on her cheeks and smudged it into her sallow skin. Better.

When she was done, she straightened her clothes and marched out of the washroom with a practiced smile on her face.

Jake was waiting at a Formica table meant for six. He was scooping up the last of his soup. He looks so tiny sitting there, Hanna thought as she joined him.

"You all finished, sweetie? Did you like it?"

"It was okay, I guess. Aren't you going to finish yours?"

"No, gosh, I'm so full. I told you, you should finish mine too. We don't want anything to go to waste."

Jake pulled Hanna's bowl over and spooned up the remainder. He puzzled over how she could always be so full when she ate so little. She was always giving him half her own meal to eat.

A few minutes later, a woman in an industrial apron, her hair in a hairnet, came over to collect their empty dishes. "All done here?" she asked, her voice kind.

"Yes. Thank you so much," Hanna said, trying for another smile.

"Thank you," Jake repeated after his mother, knowing she'd want him to.

"Aren't you a polite young man? Are you two staying with us tonight?"

"No, no, no," Hanna quickly replied. "We have to keep moving along."

The woman looked at Hanna, concern in her eyes. "Oh, well then, you two make sure to have a safe night out there."

"We need the bill," Jake said. "Don't we, Mom?"

The women exchanged glances. The older woman immediately understood that Hanna did not want her son to know that this was the kind of place you went when you couldn't afford to pay a bill.

"Your mom already paid." She smiled at Jake. "Listen,

I might be able to find you an extra piece of puffed wheat cake. Would you like that, hon?"

"That's okay," Jake said. "I had almost two entire bowls of soup."

"That's good, sweetie. That's real good."

There is false hope. There is faint hope. I wasn't sure which I had. But it was hope all the same.

Despite the tequila with Kate, the whiskey with Alexandra, being shot at by two guys in trench coats, and watching mystery woman Eva take a leap off the Victoria Bridge, I awoke the next morning feeling spry and energetic and, yes, full of hope, false, faint, or otherwise.

Suddenly there was the possibility that I could be the old Adam Saint. Not that I intended to push aside all that I was slowly coming to learn about myself. In that regard, I had work to do. In more ways than one. But I could be in control of my destiny. I could do something about what was happening to me.

I rapped on the door of the bedroom where Rowan slept. It was a little past five-thirty a.m. This was several hours before his usual summer wake-up time. I didn't care. Maybe if he was half asleep he'd keep his mouth shut. I could do some of the talking for once. Because that's what I needed to do—talk to my son.

Opening the door, I swept in. I yanked the top covers off the bed, and by pulling open the blinds, I invited in a powerful blast of early-morning sun.

Rowan grumbled something uncomplimentary. Beneath

the bedsheet, he scrunched into a tight fetal position, burying his head under the pillow.

I fell, rather heavily, on the bed next to him. I pawed his shoulder and shook him into wakefulness.

"Come on, Rowan. This is your last day here. I want us to go horseback riding. You're going to love it."

Rowan jerked the pillow off his face. His eyes looked bleary, wild, as they landed on mine. "What are you doing?"

"I want us to go riding together."

"I don't ride! You'd know that if you knew anything about me."

I didn't know that. "Well, I'll give you a lesson."

"At six in the morning?"

"Why not?" I asked, jovial.

Rowan sat up in bed. The sheet slipped down to his waist. "Because I've seen this movie, and I don't want to be in it. Dying father forces recalcitrant son to spend time with him so he can assuage his guilty conscience before he kicks the bucket. Don't you get it? I'm not interested!"

We stared at one another. No sound was needed. The air sparked with electricity.

"That okay with you?" he challenged.

It wasn't. But for now, maybe I'd have to give in. And hope, hope, hope—false, faint, or otherwise—I'd have more time to work this out later.

Rowan slammed himself against the mattress, turned his back to me, and reburied his head beneath the pillow.

Quietly I lowered the blinds. I covered him with the blanket I'd tossed on the ground and closed the bedroom door on my way out.

For one horrible moment I stood outside that door and wondered if this was a battle I'd lost for good. Maybe I just didn't know enough to lower my weapon.

Looking up, I saw Anatole at the head of the stairs. His dark eyes were boring into me.

He'd heard.

I straightened up, cleared my throat, and approached him. As I got closer, I could see the streak of tears that had scarred his pale cheeks. His big hands, slack at his sides, were trembling.

"You're going to die?" he croaked.

"Anatole, I didn't want you to hear this way."

Suddenly he was in my arms. His shoulders were shuddering as more tears flowed. We stood there for a long time. He, sniffling and snorting and saying unintelligible things. Me, not quite sure what to do to comfort him.

As a disaster recovery agent, I am often in circumstances where people needed consoling. They'd need a safe bridge, from hearing the worst news, seeing the worst thing, being part of the worst experience, to get to eventual, grudging, calm acceptance. I could do that for them. I could be that bridge. I'd learned how to remove myself from the emotions of the situation. I'd learned to be compassionate without passion.

Even when it came to my own family, my parents, wife and son, they were all such strong, stoic people, it was never an issue. There were many tears at my mother's funeral; none from us.

More shocking was that it was Anatole dampening the shoulder of my shirt. The geek goth who only cared about electronic beings he could never hope to touch.

The boy pulled away and stepped back. "I thought I'd ride with you this morning." I saw he was wearing jeans, boots, and a long-sleeved shirt under a hoodie. "I was waiting for you in the kitchen. Then I heard noises up here…."

"It's okay. Come on, let's go downstairs."

In the kitchen, I sat Anatole down at the nook where he'd obviously been working on his laptop while he waited for me. I poured two glasses of orange juice and gave him one.

"Anatole, I don't want you to tell your grandfather about what you heard this morning."

"Why not?"

"I might get better."

"Really?" He sounded relieved and almost cracked a smile. "The way Rowan talked, I thought for sure you were totally fatal. So what do you have? We can look it up on mayoclinic.com." He was already tapping away at his keyboard.

"No, we don't need to. I know what I have. It's a kind of cancer. A tumour in my head."

"Oh shit."

"You got that right."

"So it's operable?"

"No."

"It's cancerous but not operable. How are you going to get better then?"

"Well, that's why your Aunt Kate is here. She came to tell me about a guy who might be able to help me. The only problem is I've got to find him first."

"I want to help. I can help, Uncle Adam."

I sat next to him, nursing my glass of juice. "You say you're a genius on that thing?"

"At least."

"Nigel Congswell. I need to find a man named Nigel Congswell."

While Anatole began playing his laptop like a virtuoso, I booted up my own computer and pulled up the online version of the local newspaper.

I was not entirely surprised when the fine members of the Saskatoon Police Service appeared doubtful of my claim that a mysterious damsel in distress was in dire need of assistance. Again. No one else had witnessed her abrupt departure from the bridge. Still, with my status as crackpot still not official, the police couldn't afford to ignore me entirely. Besides, they did have a smashed-up rental car with nobody inside. I was the only one giving them a possible scenario to explain the missing driver. Out came the water rescue teams and divers.

I scanned the news headlines, expecting to see the results of their search and learn the fate of Eva.

Bubkes.

No body. No sign of anyone either entering or exiting the South Saskatchewan River.

There was a small article about the accident and a request for anyone with information about the missing driver to contact the police. The cops likely ran the rental car information and came to a dead end.

I'd taken a dose of Yelchin's meds when I'd gotten home last night, the little capsules I now referred to as Eva-pills. I had no idea if I was hallucinating the woman or not. The bullets from the trench coats had been real enough. Anatole could attest to that. But why they were shooting at us, I had no idea. Had tumour-induced hallucinations mixed with reality? Had we simply gotten in the middle of a lovers' quarrel or family squabble or illicit drug deal gone very bad? Saskatoon did have one of the highest crime rates in Canada. Or was this something more?

When a gentle hand landed on my shoulder, I was surprised to realize two hours had passed.

My orange juice was long gone. Anatole and I never went for our ride. And I was suddenly craving coffee.

"What are you two doing?" Kate asked. "And where did you get to last night?"

As usual with Kate, even after an awkward interaction like last night's in the pasture, she easily bounced back to normalcy without a backward glance. I ignored the second question. "Unfortunately we're not doing too much," I told her. "I asked Anatole if he could help me locate Congswell. But we keep running into brick walls. Like you told me, he left—or was possibly ousted—from IIA about eighteen months ago. After that, it's like he disappeared."

"I'm still trying, Uncle Adam," Anatole said, his eyes never veering off the screen, his fingers madly clicking away at the keyboard.

"I know. You're doing amazing things with that machine. But it seems Congswell is pretty well-hidden." I stood up to make coffee. Kate pressed me back down, saying she'd do it.

"Are you sure you heard nothing more about why Congswell left IIA? Or where he could have gone? Is there anyone else we can talk to?"

Kate shook her head. "IIA is like a dead bird. Not a peep about any of this. Everything about APU is top secret. They like to keep it that way. I didn't think it would be this difficult to track Congswell down. I can't use any more of my resources at work than I already have. If I do, somebody is bound to get suspicious."

"And I no longer have resources."

Kate looked up from where she was spooning grounds into the coffee maker.

"You've got Anatole."

"He's only as good as the info we give him. He needs something more."

I watched Kate wordlessly put the coffee grounds to work. She found cups and reached into the fridge for milk. She knew I didn't use sugar or cream, as any good spouse would. But there was something about the set of her face that made me suspicious. There was something she wasn't saying. I knew it, as any good spouse would.

"What is it, Kate? Do you know something that might help?"

Anatole glanced up from the computer.

"I…I don't know for sure…but—"

"Kate?"

"There was a picture, of a very pretty girl. I asked him about her."

"Him? You mean Nigel? Where did you see this picture?"

Kate stumbled over her words. Her eyes implored me to…do something. I was stymied and stayed silent.

"I saw the photograph in his apartment," she admitted quietly.

Eight years ago, Nigel Congswell had made a play for Kate. He'd flirted with her. She'd responded.

"You were in his apartment?"

She nodded. No words. No denials. No explanations.

I heard a low, "aw jeez, that's rough, man" kind of whistle from Anatole.

I wanted to ask: Did you sleep with him? Instead I said, "What was special about this picture?"

"There were a few of them," she responded, sounding grateful I'd not pursued the obvious avenue of questioning. I was keeping this professional. "Displayed prominently. She was stunningly beautiful. I remember asking him if she was his girlfriend."

Because you were jealous? I wondered. "What did he say?"

"He laughed. He told me the girl was his sister. And that she was a well-known model working in London."

That woke up Anatole. "Do you know her name?"

"She went by Clara Cong."

Kate barely had the words out of her mouth before Anatole was entering them into his search engines. In a frighteningly short period of time, we had all the information we'd need. Clara Cong had been a successful model throughout Europe but especially in the U.K. where she was regularly featured on the cover of fashion magazines such as *The Face, Vogue*, and *Harpers & Queen*. Photos showed her to be tall and appropriately emaciated, with lots of tawny hair and eyes that inexplicably reminded me of an elk. Her reign, though spectacular, was short-lived. After a brief career as a television hostess on a U.K.-based reality series that lasted only six episodes, she disappeared into obscurity. At least as far as the British fashion world was concerned. Anatole found a couple of articles subsequent to her heyday—obviously published on slow news days—noting that Clara Cong had gone on to marry and to bear two children. A little further digging turned up a current address in London.

Pulling the laptop away from Anatole, I connected to the website for Air Canada and booked a ticket.

Chapter Fourteen

As the plane touched down in Toronto, I had a moment of elation. Not until that moment did I know that part of me had not expected to see the city again.

I had gone home to die.

Now I had a chance to save myself.

And when I was done with that, I would rebuild my life. Rebuild my family. I wouldn't have a wife who wanted to divorce me. I wouldn't have a son who couldn't care less if I lived or died. I wouldn't have a father I didn't understand.

Nigel Congswell represented hope. I would find him no matter what it took. In the meantime, I needed to do whatever else it took to keep myself alive and strong. So as soon as the pilot said it was permitted to do so, I dialed the office number for Milo Yelchin. I reached an answering machine.

"Milo, it's Saint. I'm on a layover and only have a few hours in Toronto. You offered to help me, whenever, wherever. I'd like to take you up on that. Other than a few headaches, a bit of nausea, and…some other stuff, I'm feeling great. I know it won't last forever. I'm going…on a trip. But if there's anything more you can prescribe, anything preventative you can suggest, I'm your guy. I'll do whatever you say. As soon as I get off this plane, I'm heading to your office. I hope I can catch you there."

Milo Yelchin didn't work in the IIA building. Although the majority of his practice revolved around providing services to IIA personnel, he insisted—for privacy and confidentiality reasons—that his office and medical clinic be offsite. The building to which the cab pulled up was a two-story house in Forest Hill, much less ostentatious than IIA's swanky downtown digs. The main floor housed reception, examining rooms, and a small pharmacy. Upstairs were Milo's office and patient consultation rooms.

I'd met Beth, the receptionist, a few times before. We enjoyed a pleasant, flirtatious relationship. I was married. She was sixty-three. So our verbal engagements were entirely innocent.

"I see you have no appointment, Mr. Saint. That is very naughty," Beth informed me.

"Do you think you could bend the rules for me, just this once? I'd be forever grateful."

"Explain grateful."

"Well, I could be naughtier."

She winked at me. "In that case, let me call up to Sandy and have her check to see if the doctor has a few minutes for you."

She pushed a button and spoke to someone on the second floor.

Placing the phone against her chest, she said, "She's just going to find him. He's not answering his pager. She'll have to track him down."

I nodded.

A prolonged, wailing moan followed by a blood-curdling scream ripped down the staircase. Beth and I looked at each other. Was there some kind of excruciating *procedure* going on up there? I could tell from the horrified look on the receptionist's face that something was not right.

I raced up the stairs two at a time. Unsure what was coming next, I headed in the direction of the screams. I found Sandy draped against the frame of Milo's office door. Her face was a mess of tears and mascara. She looked as if she was about to crumple to the ground.

Rushing to the woman's side, I enveloped her in my arms. I looked inside Milo's office and saw the source of her distress.

Milo Yelchin was hanging from a crossbeam of the exposed pipe that decorated his ceiling.

By this point, Beth and several others had arrived. I passed Sandy into Beth's motherly embrace. Gingerly I stepped into the office, stopped, and stared up at the man. His slack body was gently swaying, as if buffeted by an invisible breeze. There was no reason to mess up the scene and piss off the cops by trying to get Milo down. I'd seen this before. The doctor was dead.

My eyes made a quick sweep of the room. Even though this was an obvious suicide, it never hurt to look for corroborating evidence. Nothing seemed amiss. Milo had apparently come to work as usual that morning. No one had been alerted by his behaviour or outward signs of anguish. He'd methodically used a rope and his belt to fashion a noose, which he hung from the pipes. Pipes which, ironically enough, were probably part of the initial selling feature of the place.

Noticing the computer screen on Milo's desk, my gaze froze. Milo had done one more thing before ending his life. He'd typed a note.

I never should have done it, Ross.

Tell him I'm sorry.

Sarita, forgive me for my many other mistakes.

I love you.

Milo.

Sarita Yelchin was Milo's wife, but it was the first two lines that attracted my attention. What did he mean? Had he addressed the first line of his suicide note to Ross Campbell? What had he done? To Ross? For Ross? Tell *him* I'm sorry. Who was he apologizing to? For what?

"I'm calling 911," Beth said, handing a still-sobbing Sandy to the next person in line.

"We should call Sarita," someone else suggested.

I turned to the woman and said, "Not until the police arrive and cut him down."

My brain began to work the scene. The police would be here in minutes. As a witness, I'd be detained. Once they heard the message I'd left on Milo's phone telling him I was coming over for help, I'd be further detained. I'd miss my flight to London. I'd miss the first leg of my possible road to recovery.

I couldn't miss that plane. Was I being selfish? Without Milo to help me, my health could begin to falter at any time. To get another doctor's opinion and access to treatment could take days, weeks even. I couldn't afford the time. Besides, there were plenty of other witnesses, better witnesses. People who knew and worked with Milo. The phone message meant nothing. This wasn't a murder investigation. I was simply a patient in the wrong place at the wrong time.

I left. Walked a block away. Hailed a cab and headed back to the airport.

Clara Cong lived in Bromley, in Kent. Idyllic, peaceful, and not that easy to reach by London's efficient transit systems. I rented a car.

Stepping out of the Audi A3 I'd picked up at Europcar near the airport, I wished I'd thought of buying an umbrella. The temperature wasn't bad—low twenties—but the drizzle was unrelenting, the kind that soaks you to the skin if you're in it too long.

I dashed up the steps to the apartment building. I found the ringer for the flat belonging to C Bellows (according to Anatole, Bellows was Clara Cong's married name). I pushed the corresponding button and waited.

"Come up," a female voice rang out through a speaker. "Number three."

A buzzing indicated the front door had been unlocked. Very trusting.

I scurried up the steps and knocked on the door marked with a three.

"Oh, hello," the woman who answered said, looking a little surprised. "I was expecting the FedEx man."

"Sorry, I would have identified myself, but—"

She laughed heartily. "But I didn't give you a chance, did I?" Although her native tongue was likely American or Canadian, she'd adopted a slight British accent that sounded nice along with her singsong voice. "I work at home, you see. Mail-order business. So I get plenty of company from FedEx, Klick, and Swift." She laughed again. This was the woman for whom LOL was made. "Just invite them up, never thinking twice it might be some stranger like you."

"Again, I'm sorry to barge in unexpectedly."

"You haven't barged in yet, have you? You're still standing in my hallway."

"I'm looking for Clara Cong."

Now she really let loose, *LOL*. When she was done, she said, "I'm rather certain you wouldn't even believe it was me!"

I only stared.

"Not every ex-model ends up on a soap or marrying a rock star, you know. Some of us end up here, in Bromley, with two kids, a deadbeat husband, and looking forward to a visit from the handsome delivery fellow."

I held out my hand. "Ms. Cong, I'm Adam Saint. I'm pleased to meet you."

Other than in height, the woman before me did not at all resemble the Clara Cong in the fashion photos Anatole had found. This woman had curves. She was bordering on being slightly overweight. By the looks of her clothes, which did her no favours, she didn't seem to care. Her hair was neatly pulled back into a ponytail. I could see strands of grey mixed in with the brown of her bangs. She was wearing glasses and a pleasant perfume but little if any cosmetics. She looked terrific.

"You know, this is absolutely daft and superficial of me," she said, backing up, a nonverbal invitation for me to come in, "but it's been a while since a fan tracked me down. A real long while. Used to happen all the time. Then one of those rags printed a picture of the real me, and it pretty much stopped after that." She led me into a small living area, just off an even smaller kitchen, talking the whole time. "You're not a reporter, are you?"

"No, I'm not, I—"

"Tea? I just made up a pot. You may as well share it with me. You see, my little guys are at their gran's. She takes them every day so I can get some work done. I'm home on my own during the day until three when I go to pick them up." She tittered as she motioned me into a chair. She trotted into the kitchen to get the tea. "Gawd! I hope you're not some sort of crazed stalker, are you? Here I am telling you I'm here on my own. You must think I'm a total idiot. How did you find me, by the way? I hope you're not too disappointed. Some reporter *should* do a story on retired models—not a bad idea, right? I have to tell you, that time in my life was super. But now—even with a duff husband—this time is the best. I'm so bloody happy. And I can eat!"

Returning with the tea tray and a small plate of ginger snaps, Clara lowered herself onto the couch next to my chair.

"Help yourself," she said, indicating the cookies and taking one herself. "Tell me, who did you say you were again? By your accent I can tell you're from the U.S. Am I right?"

"Canada."

"Oh, I love Canadians. We share a queen!"

I chuckled. "We do."

"Sorry, I'm going on and not letting you talk. Who are you again? Adam, did you say?"

"Adam Saint. I'm a friend of your brother Nigel's."

I saw the light that was Clara Cong-Bellows dim a little. Her first hint that maybe I wasn't there to see her? I immediately felt bad.

"I'll get more biscuits." She grabbed up the plate, still mostly full, and escaped into the kitchen.

"I used to see pictures of you in his apartment." I stole Kate's story. "He was very proud of you." I raised my voice a little so she could hear me in the kitchen. "You must be very close."

She stepped back into the room. No cookies in sight. "We were." Her smile was gone. Her face, caught in a frown, suddenly looked more like the one I remembered from the Internet photos.

"Nigel and I, we lost touch, a number of years ago. I heard he might have moved to London. I'm in town for a few days and thought I'd try to track him down."

"So you just happened to find out where I live?"

Clara was beginning to sound wary. If I was going to get any help out of her, I'd have to do it fast.

"He told me all about you. Sometimes I think I knew more about you—at least back then—than I did about him. Like I said, I'm sorry to barge in like this, without warning and all. But I hoped you might tell me where I could find Nigel. I'd love to catch up."

"I'm sorry to have to tell you this…without warning and all…." I didn't know if she was mocking me or being sincere. I did know she was uncomfortable. "My brother is dead. Car accident. Over a year ago."

Right about the time Nigel Congswell left IIA.

"Ms. Cong, I'm so sorry."

"Stop calling me that. I'm Mrs. Bellows. He may be an arsehole, but that man gave me my kids. And their name is my name."

I stood too. I was no longer a welcome visitor.

"Where did the accident happen?"

"What?"

"Where was Nigel when he had his accident? Was he still in Canada, or was he here? Or somewhere else?"

"He was here," she told me. "Got run over by a lorry." She picked up our tea cups, beginning to clear away the evidence of my ever having been there. "I have to pick up the boys pretty soon. So if you'll excuse me."

"Of course. Thank you for your time. And again, please accept my condolences."

At three o'clock on the nose, Clara Bellows left her apartment building to pick up her children from their grandmother's house. It may have been the only bit of truth the woman had told me.

It didn't take a genius to know she'd lied to me about her brother's death. Not only was she a bad liar—awkward pauses, wide eyes—but there were other signs. She'd changed her story within a span of thirty seconds. First he'd been in an accident, then he'd been run over. More damning was that, if your beloved brother had recently died, wouldn't you have at least one picture of him somewhere in your home?

Having been in the flat, I had the benefit of the knowledge that Clara had no alarm system. The lock on the front door was shamefully easy to pick for someone like me. The only problem would be getting back into the building. This was easily solved. I never left. I simply found a nice quiet corner in the dingy darkness of the stairwell. I squatted there until footsteps confirmed that indeed Clara had left the building.

Back in the apartment, I began a hurried search. I had no idea whether Clara's mother-in-law lived half a block away or several. Whether she picked up the kids and came right home, or stayed for a visit or took the kids to a park. I gave myself ten minutes, then I'd be out of there.

I only needed seven.

There may have been no pictures of Nigel Congswell in Clara's apartment, but there were several postcards hidden in a bedroom drawer. The fronts displayed brilliant skylines, including an observation wheel not unlike the London Eye and a famous Merlion. On the back were short cryptic notes, each signed with the letter "N." The most recent postcard, dated only weeks earlier, featured a graceful, colonial-style facade surrounded by lush, tropical gardens, a place exuding timeless elegance. The hotel, immortalized in the novels of W. Somerset Maugham and Rudyard Kipling, was a place I knew well. On the back, "N" had simply written: *My new job!*

I'd confirmed my next destination.

Chapter Fifteen

Having never lived in a sauna, I can't be sure, but July in Singapore must be a pretty close approximation. The temperature wasn't that unreasonable, a toasty thirty-three degrees. It was the eighty-eight per cent humidity that took things over the edge. In just the few moments it took me to step out of the air conditioned airport into the air conditioned hotel car, I was sopping wet.

Someone once told me that doing business in modern day Singapore was only made possible by a man named Willis Haviland Carrier. Why him? In 1902, Carrier invented the first large-scale, electrical air conditioning unit.

It was late when I arrived, but I knew we were pulling into the driveway of the famed Singapore Raffles Hotel—the *original* Raffles—when I heard the sudden change from pavement to crushed pebbles beneath the wheels of the hotel's Bentley. The car door was opened by a turbaned doorman resplendent in a dazzling white uniform. I stepped out and was greeted by name, as if it hadn't been almost five years since I'd last stayed here. I glanced up at the dramatically lit three-story façade and thought: *Where oh where are you, Nigel Congswell?*

My luggage was whisked off, and I was led inside.

It was an indulgence to be staying at Raffles. But I'd learned that policies had changed since my last stay. If I was going to get to Congswell, I'd have to be a hotel resident. Only paying guests were now allowed into the hotel proper.

Raffles Singapore is not only an historic hotel, but an international landmark as well. It's where film stars mingle with heads of state and top politicians. Much too juicy for curious tourists to pass up. As such, the lobby and other parts of the hotel were constantly being overrun by gawkers and stalkers, not to mention potential terrorists. And, for what you shell out for a room, this was simply unacceptable. So now the lobby and beyond are for guests only, while passers-by have to satisfy themselves with a visit to the attached shopping arcade—malls *are* everywhere—where the famed Long Bar, home of the Singapore sling, was relocated.

Once inside, I marveled at the soaring, sparkling, bright white atrium, dramatically offset by dark polished woods. On one side of the lobby is the Tiffin Room with its famous Indian buffet. Opposite, the Writers Bar, a tribute to literary giants who've stayed here over the years, such as Noël Coward. (In reality, it's not so much a bar as a collection of three or four tables, a piano, a guy serving drinks, and a gold-plated plaque proclaiming its noteworthiness.) At the far end of the grand space, a sweeping staircase led up to luxurious suites that, in daylight, look out on sun-dappled courtyards.

Instead of a regular front desk check-in, I was escorted directly to my suite, where all business would be taken care of in private. Once there, I was impressed to see on the foyer's front table a welcome card from hotel management, a bottle of my favourite Scotch, and a bowl of fresh strawberries. I've heard the service at Raffles Singapore likened to a gentle breeze. You can feel it, but you can't see it.

The suite was old-world colonial grandeur. Large. Sparse. Teak floors. There were easy chairs, handmade carpets, and lazy fans rotating from fourteen-foot ceilings. There is nothing quite so comforting as a well-appointed hotel room.

I was tired to the bone. But instead of allowing myself to be swallowed up by the glorious, big bed, I took a quick shower, then booted up my laptop.

Singapore is fourteen hours ahead of Saskatoon. It was midnight in Singapore. Ten a.m. yesterday in Saskatoon. I connected to Skype. Finally I was the one benefiting from Anatole's obsession with his computer when he answered almost immediately. His face was slightly skewed because of the angle of his webcam, but otherwise the connection was near perfect.

"Are you there?" he asked. Was that excitement I could hear in his typically monotone, bored-with-the-world voice?

"I just arrived. Anatole, I think even you would be wearing shorts here."

"Hot, huh? I looked up the forecast for tomorrow…. I'm emailing you the website now…it's going to get worse."

"I like the heat. The humidity, however, is a bitch."

"How's the hotel? Did you know Raffles is where the last surviving wild tiger in all of Singapore was shot? Did you know the hotel used to be on the water? You can't see it from your window though, can you? That's because they've done all this land reclamation. The shore is like five hundred metres away now. Isn't that cool?"

"Thanks for the research. And thanks for making the room reservation. It's perfect."

"Great. Like I told you, I can help you with this, Uncle Adam. It doesn't matter if I'm on the other side of the world. With my computer skills, I might as well be in the room next door." He added dryly, "Except I'd probably be staying at the Motel 6 down the street. Do you have any idea what you're paying a night?"

I let that pass. "How about the rest of it, Anatole? Were you able to find out anything more on Nigel Congswell? What am I looking for?"

"Well, you were right. He is employed by Raffles."

"How do I find him?"

"He's head of security. I have to give the guy credit. He really knows how to put together pretty convincing fake identity documents and a fake resume."

I nodded. As IIA agents, these were skills we mastered early in our careers.

"He spends most of his time on-site. As far as I can tell, he should be on the property right now…no, wait, with the time change, I guess it will be tomorrow morning for you. He's going under the name John Berry. I couldn't find out much else. No home address or anything like that. But I'm still working on it."

"That's great, Anatole. Thank you."

"You feeling okay?"

"You don't have to ask me that every time we talk, okay?"

"Okay." He waited a beat, then, "What are you going

to do when you find him?"

I took a breath. That same question had kept me awake for the past two nights. I was sure it would keep me up again tonight.

How far was I willing to go to get the information I needed out of this guy?

How far was I willing to go to save my own life?

I had no answer for my nephew. "Good night, Anatole."

I have a love/hate relationship with sleep. I believe sleep is healthy for a body. The more the better. I also believe sleep is a colossal waste of time. Imagine the things one could accomplish with an extra few hours every day. If I had my druthers, I'd prefer two to three hours of sleep a day. I know, however, that my particular body and brain need a minimum of five to operate at reasonably high capacity. At six, I am a beast. With eight hours of sleep under my belt, I can do almost anything. It's a trade-off.

When I'm working, I do my best to get five to six hours a night. I have the added benefit that when I sleep, I sleep. There is no dozing, no tossing and turning, no rehashing the day's events or the day to come. I attribute this to my ability to keep my emotions separate from my work life. I do it to be efficient. I do it so I can perform for the people who need me to.

I do it to survive.

Losing sleep over the past few days, wondering about how I would deal with Nigel Congswell, aka Raffles Hotel Head of Security, was a new and discomfiting experience for me. Combined with jet lag and the general stress of being a dead man walking, I could tell that my body was beginning to degrade. I needed rest.

Once I'd logged off from my call with Anatole, I searched the pharmacy of standard travel drugs I keep in my Dopp kit. I slipped a mild muscle relaxant under my tongue.

The bed, a king with a thick, white comforter, looked intoxicatingly inviting.

I adjusted the ceiling fan to keep me pleasantly cool throughout the night. I circled the rooms, testing the various push-button switches until I hit upon the right combination that extinguished all the lights. The bathrobe came off.

Just as I was about to throw back the cover of the bed and dive in, a subtle movement beneath the sheet caught my eye.

Crap.

Was this an actual, honest-to-God hallucination? Paranoid delusion? Or reality? I was getting fed up with having to decide which.

Either way, this was not the opportune time or place for it.

As I stood there, studying the bed, I had a brief moment of regret. Why hadn't I persisted in finding another medical expert to replace Milo? How long would it have really taken? Maybe I needed more than Eva-pills.

Or maybe I was making a mountain out of a molehill. Maybe there was nothing in my bed. It was dark. I was fatigued. Stressed.

I reached over and turned on the bedside lamp.

Once my eyes adjusted to the light, they roamed the white expanse of the bed.

Nothing.

Nothing.

There!

A definite movement beneath the bedspread.

As a CDRA agent, I would regularly travel with, or locally source, a weapon—usually a handgun. Now the only thing left in my arsenal were two fists. Somehow I didn't think that whatever it was under the covers was very punch-worthy.

I recalled seeing an umbrella stand next to the front door. In a pinch, as far as weapons go, a parasol does quite nicely.

After retrieving the umbrella, I stood over the bed again. This time I waited almost a full minute before seeing the movement again. It was something small, near the centre of the mattress.

Holding the umbrella over my head with my right hand, I slowly reached for the lip of the comforter.

I threw it back.

"Goddamit!"

Snake.

There are not many things I'm afraid of. And I am not afraid of snakes. But I do truly hate the bastards.

Here was my dilemma. I was in a foreign country. I am used to being in foreign countries. I am used to having to adjust my understanding of how the world works based on local customs, geography, weather, politics, rituals, religion, cultural norms, morality codes; the list goes on and on.

Normally I would undertake extensive research before placing myself in any unfamiliar situation. If I am called in to assist in the negotiation for the release of a Canadian held captive in Syria, I know that even though most of the country is desert, it can periodically snow in Damascus. If I'm infiltrating a North Korean village, seeking a missing diplomat with Canadian ties believed to have attempted a holiday visit with his mother, I know that Christmas is a non-event in North Korea. On the other hand, Constitution Day on December 27th is a big deal. If I planned to be in a humid forest somewhere in Asia, I'd be familiar with the type of dangerous insects and reptiles I could expect to run into. Not so much while staying at Raffles Singapore.

What I was looking at now was about five feet long. Its body was dark with light blue stripes running along each side. The head, tail, and venter scales were crimson. The snout was blunt, and the requisite beady little eyes were on each side of its head. I expected its fangs were sharp, but that was just a guess.

How might the snake describe me? About 6'3" long. No stripes. No tail. Pointy snout. Eyes at front of head. Thick and juicy. Then again, it wasn't looking at me at all. Its head was concealed beneath the coil of its own body, its tail in full view, undulating in the air. Unlike when an ostrich hides its head when it senses danger, I did not think this was a good sign.

Ignorant about Singapore's snake population, I had no way of knowing whether my guest was as benign as a Saskatchewan garter snake, or virulent as a viper. If it was the former, all I had to do was pick it up and toss it outside.

If it was the latter, that plan could result in my death.

I had one thing going for me. I had legs. Tired as I was, I was quite certain I could beat this thing in a foot race. I did not, however, care to irritate it, or convince it to make any sudden moves. As far as I knew, this snake possessed powerful abdominal muscles, enabling it to spring up and throw itself around my neck. So with sluggish steps, I moved toward the shelf where I'd emptied my pockets. I reached out and found my iPhone.

"Smile," I suggested as I snapped the snake's photograph.

Hurriedly I tapped out a message and sent it, along with the pic, to Anatole.

I seldom feel awkward when an unexpected situation finds me naked. It has happened before. But something about standing exposed, in the middle of a hotel room, in a faceoff with a snake, felt wrong. So my next move was to unhurriedly find my robe and slip it on. I was knotting the belt when my phone made the subtle donging noise telling me a call was coming in.

"What the hell is that?" was Anatole's greeting.

"That was kind of the point of sending you the picture."

"Where are you? Where is it?"

"On my bed."

"Right now? In your room?"

"Uh-huh."

"Awwww maaaaaan, you have the coolest life."

"Anatole...."

"I know, I know, I'm working on it. I...okay, hold on. I

think this is it. Ohhhh…."

"Anatole, what is it?"

"Hold on, I'm reading…it…oh…."

"Anatole!"

"Okay, you'll have to help me here. The picture you sent me isn't that great."

"My apologies. The lighting technicians were on coffee."

"What colour is the head?"

"Red. Bright red."

"Could it be pink?"

"I'm not an interior decorator."

"The body is kind of bluey-greeny?"

"I'd say more dark blue."

"The bottom of the snake is grey?"

"It doesn't respond when I ask it to roll over. But from what I can make out, the bottom looks reddish. And it has stripes."

"Oh." His voice was small. "I was afraid you'd say that."

"The tip of the tail is red too. Just like the head."

The line was quiet, then: "How big did you say it was?"

I was not liking the tone of his voice. "I'd say about five feet."

"Uncle Adam, get the hell out of there."

Chapter Sixteen

When a resident of the Raffles Singapore Hotel calls the front desk claiming to be sharing his room with a potentially lethal snake, all manner of staff come running. None of which, to my disappointment, were John Berry (Nigel Congswell).

My butler, Saranya, was the first to arrive. Although an unlikely herpetologist, he took one look at the snake and ushered me into the front room. Then in an urgent but hushed tone, he got on his phone and alerted the troops. Within minutes, I was comfortably ensconced in a new, improved, snake-free room, with both written and verbal apologies and requests to give me the earth, moon, and stars from all levels of hotel management.

I'm sure Raffles trains its staff to never utter the word *venomous*, even if a cobra is biting their ass. So there was little forthcoming from them as to what kind of snake was in my room, only that it was an unheard of event in the hotel's history. I was now an unwitting figure in the oft-recounted and sometimes fantastical folklore of the venerable Raffles Singapore Hotel.

Once the hubbub was over and I was alone in my new accommodations, I called Anatole. I wanted to tell him I was safe and find out more about my former roommate.

According to my nephew, based on the photograph I'd sent him and my description, he'd been hoping my snake was the generally harmless Pink-headed Reed Snake. The species is often confused for the Blue Malaysian Coral Snake, which has similar habitat and appearance. There is one small difference. The Blue Malaysian Coral Snake's venom is primarily neurotoxic, which means death, and a sneaky one at that. The initial bite often results in no symptoms. But after several minutes, victims begin to feel numb near the wound. Then they experience trouble breathing. Eventually they die of respiratory failure. See? What did I say? Snakes are bastards.

When Anatole heard that my snake was five feet long, almost three times the size of a full grown Reed Snake, and had a red tail to match its head, he realized—in terms of the snake lottery—I'd come up a big loser.

And now I lay me down to sleep.

Early the next morning, I stepped onto the common verandah that fronts the Palm Court Suites. The verandah itself is a study in old-world simplicity and serenity. It looks out over a cozy inner courtyard lined with livistona palms, graceful casuarina trees (planted in honour of W. Somerset Maugham, whose first book of short stories set in the East, was called *The Casuarina Tree*), and distinctive travelers palms, ever so fitting for a hotel.

Not yet seven a.m., the temperature had already reached the mid-twenties. The air hung heavy with moisture and the fragrant scent of nearby frangipanis. I'd asked for breakfast to be served outside on the small glass-topped table directly across from my suite's front door. While I waited for it to arrive, I fell into the accompanying cane chair and rubbed my eyes. The last time I recalled checking the time on my travel alarm, it was three a.m. Thankfully, once I was down, I was out for the count. The heaviness of my sleep weighed on me now. My brain felt unusually sluggish as it attempted to move into high gear. I was looking forward to the arrival of coffee.

There was no getting around the fact that, despite how swiftly and efficiently the Raffles staff took care of the snake situation the previous night, as if hoping to convince me—and themselves—it had never happened, there *was* a snake in my room. The question remained: Was this simply an unfortunate accident? There was certainly plenty of lush flora on hotel grounds, all in close proximity to guest rooms. A perfect spot for a snake to set up house. So one day he decides to wander into a suite. Just to see what there was to see. Were snakes curious? Perhaps. Still, I couldn't dismiss the possibility that this was no accident. Had the snake been intentionally placed in my bed? Meant to scare me off? Meant to kill me?

Squeaky wheels over creaking, aged, wooden floors alerted me that I was no longer alone. Until now, I'd had the lengthy verandah all to myself. The clamour of my breakfast trolley's arrival would likely put an end to that. As Saranya laid out my coffee, juice, granola, and half grapefruit, he claimed no further knowledge about last night's incident. He repeated management's offer to improve my stay in whatever way I might dream up.

"Actually, Saranya, there is something I'd like," I responded.

"Absolutely, Mr. Saint. What can we do for you?"

"I'd like to meet with your head of security. John Berry I believe his name is."

Saranya looked understandably uncertain. "Is there something wrong with your room, sir? Has something else occurred that we should know about? Was something taken from your room? Perhaps we forgot it when we moved everything last night. I can check this for you immediately."

"No, no, nothing like that. The hotel has done nothing wrong. Everything is just fine. You see, I'm considering bringing my family here next year, and, well, I suppose after last night you'll understand if I have a few security concerns. I'm sure a short discussion with Mr. Berry would give me all the reassurance I need."

"I see. I will look after this. If you please enjoy your breakfast, I promise to return before you are done. At that time, I will let you know how we can help you."

"Thank you, Saranya. That's fine."

When the butler departed, I lifted the shining silver carafe to pour my first highly anticipated cup of coffee. Apparently my head was not so cloudy after all. For in that split second, I knew two things. One, the snake in my bed was no accident. Two, there was a projectile rushing at high speed directly toward my head.

My right hand whipped up like a lever under the control of a highly tuned piston. Just as the round object—about the size of a baseball—was about to clobber me in the temple, my hand opened and palmed it.

I had no regard for the way the bowl of my hand screamed in pain. Instead I jumped up from my table, up-setting my juice and coffee cup and sending them crashing to the ground. I raised my hand that still held the ball in such a way that if I spied the source, I would whip it back at three times the speed.

I was steaming mad. If that ball had made contact, I could have been, at a minimum, rendered unconscious. At a maximum, dead.

The snake was no accident. The ball was no accident.

Someone was out to get me.

Pushing aside palm leaves, I scanned the courtyard and adjoining wings of the hotel. I was on the second floor. I assumed the ball was launched from the same height or higher in order to achieve the accurate trajectory. I guessed the source to be some kind of ball launcher, the kind used to train tennis and baseball players. It had to be sitting somewhere within view. I had to be careful though. Without knowing exactly where my enemy was, I was still a target.

My only hope was that the launcher wasn't quickly ad-justable, at least not quick enough to hit a moving target. I began moving along the veranda, ducking up and down, de-pending on the availability of leafy protection. All the while I searched the other buildings.

And there he was. Second floor. Main building. Directly across the courtyard.

He saw me seeing him.

Excellent. There's nothing like an early-morning foot race.

I scurried down the staircase to ground level. Racing

across the courtyard, I desperately searched for a corresponding set of stairs to take me back up again.

There wasn't one. Damn. I'd have to enter the hotel to find a way to get upstairs.

Time was being wasted. By the time I got up there, of course the ball launcher would be long gone. But I had to try.

It was almost a full minute more before I found my way back into the hotel, up a set of stairs, and to the location of the now-disappeared ball launcher and its operator.

"Goddamn!" I cried out to the cosmos. It helped. An elderly Chinese couple, tottering off to breakfast, were not so impressed.

"Excuse me," I called out to them.

They tottered a little faster.

I tried again in Mandarin. That got their attention. "Did you see a man running away from here?"

They shook their heads and continued on their way.

I thanked them.

About to yell out one more profanity, I spotted a small object on the deck railing. A ball. The same kind as the one I still held in my hand. It was at the exact same spot from where the unidentified man—Nigel Congswell?—had staged his attack on me. Attached to the ball was a hastily scribbled note.

Meet me – Boat Quay – outside Fullerton Hotel – near the naked boys – 8 a.m.

I had less than twenty minutes. I knew the location he was talking about. I'd have to run to get there in time. Congswell was being clever. It was a familiar tactic: keep

232 — Anthony Bidulka

your opponent running. It keeps them off guard. Tires them out. And allows little time for thinking.

I looked up and saw Saranya across the courtyard, his face confused as he surveyed the mess I'd left behind at my once peaceful breakfast setting. He'd come back to let me know if he'd been able to arrange a meeting with the head of hotel security. I think I'd just beat him to it.

I ran.

Down the stairs and out the front of the hotel.

Exchanging waves with the ever-present turbaned door-man, I dashed across the circular driveway. I hit the inaccurately named Beach Road and turned right. I jogged across busy Bras Basah Road against the light, then made a left at the Swissôtel onto Stamford Road. By the time I made a right onto Connaught Drive, I was perspiring heavily. My shirt was soaked through. The enforced exercise after an unsettled night actually felt good. But running full out in stifling heat, without hydration, was not a good thing.

As I neared the water, I remembered that instead of using the main Connaught/Fullerton traffic bridge, which would take me too far west, if I made a dodgy turn here and there, I was better off crossing the Singapore River via the old Cavanagh pedestrian bridge.

Once across, I was on Boat Quay, only a short distance from the meeting place. I glanced at my watch. A drip of sweat plopped onto its face. It was 7:57 a.m.

The naked boys in the note were a well-known bronze statue. It replicated the carefree scene of five naked boys, happily jumping off the quay into the river below, as if to cool themselves off on a sweltering day. The only thing separating passersby from the boys was a series of stanchions connected by two rows of chain that ran the length of the quay.

At this time of the morning, the normally bustling quay was quiet. The only activity were joggers, jet-lagged travelers out for a walk, and people arriving for work at nearby banks, embassies, and trading companies.

Huffing and puffing, I searched the statue for another note. I expected this wasn't the last of Congswell's game. I saw none and frowned. Now what?

I placed a hand on the head of the only bronze boy on the pedestrian side of the stanchions, where he cheered on his mates. Taking a moment to regulate my breathing, I sensed movement to my left, then *whoosh!*

My body went hurtling through air over the stanchion chains.

In a slow-motion moment of dreaded certainty, I looked up and saw the joyful faces of five little bronze boys who would never end up in the Singapore River. Unlike me.

The next sound I heard was a thud.

Instead of in the water, I'd landed on the flat bottom of a bumboat. A burlap bag was pulled over my head. With amazing speed, my hands were bound behind me. I felt myself being pulled deeper into the boat. They likely wanted to get me out of sight and mind of anyone who happened to be watching from the quay. Before I had a chance to even think about what was happening, the boat powered up and off we went. The way I figured it, I'd either just been kidnapped or was being taken away to be killed.

Having a great time in Singapore; wish you were here.

234 — Anthony Bidulka

Bumboats are typically flat-bottomed, wooden, and barge-like; not really built for speed. Old rubber tires fixed to the sides are used as shock absorbers in case of collision with the quay, jetty, or other boats. Which doesn't exactly inspire confidence in the boat or the pilot.

The banks of the Singapore River were once lined with warehouses filled with goods meant for distribution throughout Singapore and Malaysia. Back then bumboats were an important part of the commercial process. They were usually loaded with Chinese workers, shuttling cargo back and forth from ships anchored in the harbour. As time passed, the riverfront warehouses faded into obscurity and with them the bumboat. Eventually a series of commercial centres, Clarke Quay, Boat Quay, and Robertson Quay, were developed. The Quays offered nightclubs, restaurants, and fun attractions along the riverfront. These businesses brought tourism to the area, which had the happy side benefit of giving the bumboat a new role on the river, which apparently included the transport of bound and gagged Canadian visitors.

Soon after I was aboard, I could feel the boat making a U-turn. This was good news. It meant that instead of heading out to sea, and all those hungry sharks, we were motoring back into the city.

As the Singapore River gently twists and turns its way inland beneath numerous bridges, Boat Quay with its chic cafes, high-end restaurants, yuppie pubs, and designer galleries eventually gives way to the wilder and baser Clarke Quay. Clarke Quay is five blocks of industrial-era buildings transformed into eateries and nightclubs, and moored

Chinese junks, or *tongkangs*, refurbished into floating pubs and seafood joints. After Clarke came Robertson Quay. Judging by the length of the boat ride, I was betting we were getting off in Clarke.

Singapore's crime rate is one of the lowest in the world. Even this early in the morning, a guy being dragged through the streets with a bag over his head was very likely to be noticed. So I understood when, once the boat had moored, the bag was replaced with a pair of dark sunglasses and a coat with a hood resembling the Grim Reaper's cloak.

Two beefy dudes escorted me onto land. We crossed the waterside promenade and marched down a side street. Before long, I was directed into a building and ordered up a narrow set of stairs to a second floor. I was shoved into a small, stiflingly hot room, windows boarded over, and pushed into a straight-back chair. Once again, my hands were tied behind my back. The men left, closing the door behind them. I was still wearing sunglasses, and the ambient light was so low I could barely make out a thing.

Within a minute, the door opened again. A single set of steps entered.

"Let's get one thing straight from the start," a male voice said to me. "If you lie to me, or I even suspect you're lying, I will have my friends take you back to the boat and drown you off Sentosa Island. You've heard about how there's no crime in Singapore? That's not because there aren't any criminals. It's because they're too good to get caught."

There were two things this guy didn't know. One, I don't scare easily. Two, I highly doubted he was telling the truth.

Capital punishment is legal in Singapore. The city-state has ranked highest amongst per-capita execution rates in the world, at times coming in at about 1.5 executions per 100,000 of population. That's a lot. Executions, carried out by hanging at Changi Prison at dawn on Fridays, are well publicized.

"Now tell me who you are." His English was perfect.

"I guess that's where I have you at a disadvantage."

He scoffed. "*You* have *me* at a disadvantage? You're the one tied up in a dark room, Mr. Saint."

So he knew my name. My certainty as to the identity of my captor grew. "Maybe you know my name, but I know *everything* about you." Overstatement of truth can be a powerful conciliation tactic. "You really shouldn't be sneaking peeks at hotel guest information records…Nigel."

A sudden intake of breath.

Got him.

"I have no idea what you're talking about. My name is—" He stopped himself just in time. For a former IIA agent, his interrogation skills were sorely lacking. I'd already gotten more information out of him than he'd ever get out of me.

"No need to finish your sentence. You were about to say your name is John Berry. The alias you've created for yourself here in Singapore. You work as the head of security for Raffles Hotel, where I am a guest. But you already know that, seeing as you put a deadly snake in my room, then tried to knock my block off with a speeding ball while I was enjoying breakfast this morning." I added for good measure: "You should know that my hotel satisfaction survey will reflect my great disappointment with your hospitality skills."

"Who the hell are you?" he hollered, at the same time whipping the sunglasses off my face. His nose was two inches from mine. Hot specs of spittle landed on my cheek.

"You're going to be embarrassed when I tell you."

Nigel pulled back, exasperated.

Good. If he could make me run halfway across Singapore, I could make him sweat a little too.

"Your name is Nigel Congswell," I continued, ever so calmly. "You're a former IIA agent, Asset Protection Unit."

Nigel's eyes widened. Mine were beginning to adjust to the light. I could finally get a better look at the man. I'd had Anatole pull up a picture of Nigel Congswell from Google Images. It was likely several years old, but there was no doubt the man before me was one and the same. Just under six feet, his sandy hair was greying at the temples. He sported a set of G.I. Joe biceps and a Ken doll jaw. Many women—my wife apparently being one of them—would find him attractive. Myself, I thought he was a little bland.

Pulling up another chair, Nigel straddled it. His eyes narrowed as he studied me.

"Don't blame your sister. She didn't tell me where you were. I just…kind of figured it out." No use ruining their next family Thanksgiving.

"I was wrong," he uttered after a prolonged silence. "I thought you were someone else. I thought you were after something else."

"What's that?"

"Shut up."

If only my fists weren't tied together.

After another moment of thought, he said: "I'm going

to let you go. But I want you to pass a message to Maryann fucking Knoble. I don't have what she wants. And I'm never coming back. Got that?"

It appeared that Nigel now took me for some kind of messenger. Sent by IIA chief, Maryann Knoble. But that wasn't the reason he'd tried to scare me off. He thought I was "someone else" after "something else." I was probably going to want to know more about that.

"I don't work for Maryann Knoble."

"Fuck!" he raged, jumping to his feet, taking the chair with him and throwing it across the room. "Make up your fucking mind. Who are you? Why are you here? Are you IIA or not?"

The guy was developing a real heater. I needed to calm him down. "I was. Just like you. I was with Disaster Recovery."

"So what the hell are you doing here? Why are you harassing my family? Why are you on my back?"

"Nigel, I think you know why. I know about your asset."

"What are you talking about? Didn't you hear what I just said? I'm not with APU anymore. I have no more assets to protect."

The trained agent was back. If I didn't know how trained he was, I might have almost believed him. "Nigel, I know. I know about the asset. I know why you left APU. I know why you're hiding out in this sweat lodge using a fake name."

With slow, deliberate movements, Congswell retrieved his chair and placed it back in front of me, this time two inches closer. He sat and looked me in the eye while a wide grin spread across his face. "Oh yeah? Well, why don't you tell me all about it?"

I stared back. "Cancer."

I saw the twitch. His brain was so busy I could almost hear it whir. I figured if I used his own story with Kate against him, it would have the added benefit of encouraging him to believe my lie that much more easily. "I have a personal relationship with someone in APU. Pillow talk can be very revealing."

In a sudden outburst, Congswell jumped up and bellowed out something in a language I thought might be Tamil. The two men who'd brought me here were immediately in the room, guns up, pointed at my face. Nigel too was now brandishing a weapon.

"What? What? What?" I yelled as the two men hauled me out of my chair.

"Turns out I believe you after all." The tone was menacing.

"We can help each other, Congswell."

"Oh yeah? You want to help me? Sure you do," he said with scorn.

He uttered more unintelligible words to his men. They dragged me toward the door.

"What is this?"

"You made a mistake, Saint. You shouldn't have told me you don't work for IIA anymore. Because that tells me one thing. If you don't work for IIA, then you're an enemy after my asset. I don't know about you, but I kill my enemies." More shouting in Tamil. "Have a nice boat ride."

Not good.

Next thing I knew, the burlap bag was back, yanked down over my head.

Everything went dark. I couldn't see a thing. One man was pulling me forward, another pushed from behind.

I heard more bellowing. This time it sounded different. The men sounded…surprised.

Without warning, I was thrust violently to one side. With arms tied behind my back and virtually blinded, my balance was off. I skidded to the ground. I heard a gunshot.

Then another.

Followed by a quick volley of gunfire.

Yelling. Swearing. Shrieks of pain.

The door slammed shut.

Silence.

Uh-oh.

Chapter Seventeen

My hood was whipped off. Once again, Nigel's face was in mine. This time he looked alarmed. I could see pinpricks of red on his left cheek. Behind him, one of his men was crouched against the closed door, gun at the ready for whatever was on the other side. On the floor next to him was the unmoving body of the second man.

"Who the hell is out there? Who did you bring with you?" Nigel demanded to know. He had his gun against my nose.

"You brought me here. I didn't bring anyone. Think about it, Nigel. Whoever is on the other side of that door is gunning for both of us. You've got to let me go. I can get us out of here." If only I had a dollar for every time I've said that without having a clue as to how I was actually going to pull it off.

Nigel might be a Ken doll, but he was also ex-IIA. He wasn't stupid. He knew there was no time to waste. For right now I was the least threatening of two threats and quite possibly a useful ally. He pulled me up, then circled behind me to undo the ropes binding my hands.

I did a quick reconnaissance. There were no windows. But like most old warehouse buildings the world over, almost every room has roof access. I looked up and saw it. A small hatch. For the moment, the gunfire on the other side of the door had ceased. It was a standoff. Each side trying to figure out who had whom outgunned.

"Hoist me up. I'll see if I can open it," I said.

Nigel grinned. "And then off you go, scampering away across rooftops, while we're left down here to fight off a team of bloodthirsty assassins. Nice try."

"If you want to give me your gun, I'll happily change places with you. You go first. I've checked, Nigel, there's no ladder in here. This is the only plan. Decide now."

I knew he'd never hand over his firepower.

He said something to the gunman at the door. I had a poor grasp of Tamil, but I was pretty sure he told the guy that if it looked at all as though I was going to leave them behind, his orders were to forget the other guys and shoot to kill me.

Couldn't argue with that.

Nigel lowered himself into a weightlifter's stance, bent at the knee. I scrambled up, balancing myself with one foot on his thigh, the other on a shoulder, my hands on his head. I gave him the go-ahead to straighten up.

Just then, someone on the other side began peppering the door with bullets, splintering the wood. Igor, or whatever his name was, pulled back to avoid being impaled by slivers.

Once Nigel was standing upright, I gingerly began to straighten up. I only had one chance at this. Now that they were making their move, it wouldn't take long before the bad guys (exactly who were the baddest of the bad guys was still up for grabs) blasted their way into the room. Nigel yelled at his man to return fire to hold them off.

Nigel was an admirably steady base. I straightened to my full height. With a hope, a prayer, and a bare fist, I punched at the hatch. It blew open. Glorious fresh air washed over my face. I blessed the multitude of detested pull-up reps I suffer through at the gym for allowing me to hoist myself up and out of the room onto the flat roof of the building.

Did I consider running?

Truly, no. For two reasons. First, this guy had something I wanted. Second, I'm not a fan of anyone getting gunned down in a dark room on a sunny day in Singapore.

Quickly judging the leverage I'd need to pull up a 200 pound man without falling back into the room myself, I shimmied part of my torso through the opening. I reached down with an open hand and smile. I was surprised to see that it was his sidekick, not Nigel, who was waiting atop the chair for me to yank him up to safety. I grudgingly had to give Congswell credit for looking after his man's safety before his own.

As I hauled up the brute, my muscles screaming at the effort, opposing gunfire increased in intensity. Somehow I think they were getting the sense that we were about to escape. I reached down for Nigel.

Just as he was clearing the hatch, the door gave way.

As soon as he was up, he whipped around and fired several shots into the room.

That should make them think twice about following us. For all they knew, we'd be waiting for them, at a perfect vantage point to pick them off like gophers popping their heads out of a hole.

Nigel took the lead. He raced across the roof of the building, and the next two buildings as well. I had no idea what his plan was until he turned and yelled, "Pick one and jump!"

Then he disappeared over the side of the roof.

His companion in arms immediately followed suit.

I dashed to the edge of the building and gazed down. As I'd guessed, we were on Clarke Quay. A long row of canopies belonging to a string of street-side establishments were stretched out below us. Both men had landed safely in the cushion of a canopy. They slid smoothly onto the waiting pavement below.

I glanced back.

The first gopher head appeared.

I jumped.

"You really have no idea who those guys were?" Nigel asked.

We'd come to an uneasy détente. If not in the same boat, we were at least in similar rough waters, reluctantly suspecting we might need each other's help.

We were literally sitting on top of the world, also known as the SkyPark atop the Marina Bay Sands complex. From a Canadian's perspective, the massive structure with its three fifty-five-story hotels connected at the top by a one hectare sky terrace looks a lot like an inukshuk. The SkyPark boasts the world's largest public cantilevered platform. It hangs over the north tower by sixty-seven metres, providing a stunning 360-degree view of the Singapore skyline. Nigel had called in a hurried favour from a friend who works at the restaurant up there, The Sky on 57. It was still early. Other than prep staff, the place was closed, allowing us both privacy and protection.

"No. But I'm guessing you do."

Silence. He hadn't quite figured me out yet.

"Listen, we don't have time to play games. So I'm going to lay my cards on the table," I said. "I know you worked for APU. I know your asset possessed a cure for cancer. I know you left APU. And now IIA seems to be having issues related to the asset. Like, perhaps, your running off with it, and now they want it back?" I decided to risk a guess. I was also manipulating Congswell into talking, without actually laying any of my own cards on the table. I wasn't quite ready to do that. Not until I knew more about what was going on.

"No," he insisted. "I didn't take anything. And I can tell you one thing for sure. That wasn't IIA on the other side of that door. Out and out gun warfare in foreign territory is not their style. You should know that if you really were an agent."

He was right.

Or maybe we were both wrong.

"Then who was it?"

"Since you know what the asset is," Nigel said, "you've got to have figured out that if knowledge of its existence got out, people would do almost anything to possess it. That's who was out there. Some of those people."

"So the information leaked? People…organizations…

other governments…they know Canada is hiding a cure for cancer?"

He shook his head. "No. I don't think it's that widespread. There may be rumours, conspiracy theories—there always are about this sort of thing. But widespread actual knowledge? No."

"But someone *does* know?"

"Yes."

"Who?"

"I don't know. We have our suspicions. But nothing definite."

We. He said we. Did he mean IIA? Or someone else?

"Is that why you're hiding in Singapore? Are you hiding from these people?"

He took a deep, uneasy breath. He wanted to talk. I just knew it. I was betting he hadn't had a single soul to tell his story to. I needed to be that soul.

"Nigel, if I know anything, I know no one can hide forever. Especially if the people you're running from are as powerful and determined as the ones we ran across this morning. They obviously know you have the asset. They want it. And they're willing to do anything to get it. Not hard to figure out. The question is, what are you going to do about it? I can help you."

"Not hard to figure out?" Nigel repeated, snorting in derision. "Except you've got it all wrong. I already told you. I don't have the asset. I don't have the cure."

Damn.

"Then why would these people, whoever they are, and Maryann Knoble, and the IIA—you said it yourself—be after you?" I hesitated, then added, "The cure is missing, isn't it?"

"Yes."

"If you don't have it…do you know where it is?"

He stared at me, then whispered, "Not anymore."

Oh God. The idiot lost the cure for cancer.

"What happened?"

It was about then that he grew his spine back. "Why would I tell you? I have no idea why you're here. Or who you are. If it wasn't for the fact that you helped get us out of a sticky situation back there, we wouldn't be talking right now. You might not be talking ever again." He readjusted himself in his seat. "It's time you told me what you want. If you don't, I'm going to send you back down that high-speed elevator and let whatever happens to you happen. I know Singapore. I have friends here. I can find safety. I doubt you can."

"I'm a pretty resourceful guy," I informed him. "But you're right. We need to trust each other a little more if we're going to help each other."

"I don't need your help."

"You need to get those thugs off your back. They're not going to give up just because we ran away. They'll be back. By now they know where you work, where you live, everything. Nigel, your life in Singapore is over. You can't hide here any longer. You need to get out. And it just so happens, this is the kind of thing I specialize in." Not exactly true but not an outright lie.

He thought it over. "What do you want?"

Oooo boy. Truth time. I debated. With a deep breath, I

spelled it out. "I want what everyone else wants. I want the cure for cancer."

He glared at me but didn't move away. "Asshole."

"Maybe."

"I'm not surprised. Well, buddy, get in line. But don't blame me when you get to the front and there's none left."

That was a sentence loaded with double meaning if ever I'd heard one. "What do you mean?"

"Nothing," he said too quickly. "I mean I don't have it. I told you."

Something wasn't right. He was hiding something.

"Even if I did have it, why would I give it to you? Do you expect me to believe that you, Adam Saint, should be the anointed one, the one to get famous, to make trillions off the discovery, rather than anyone else? Come on, Saint. Think about it. If IIA were keeping the cure from the world, don't you think there must be a damned good reason?"

All good points. "What is it?"

He turned away, staring out at the abyss of sky and cloud over my shoulders.

"Fuck you," he muttered.

"I have cancer."

His eyes were back. He considered the words I'd said. But not for long. "Yeah, well, boo hoo. I don't know you. I don't care if you live or die. There are millions of people out there just like you. Worse off than you. More deserving than you. So you, Saint, are a world-class shit for even trying to get this for yourself."

Another good point.

What am I doing here?

What had I done? Had I allowed the cloud of cancer, cloud of death, to clog my brain and my ability to think clearly? At the first sign that I could do something to control my destiny—as I'd always done until now—I took hold like a dog on a bone and steamed forward. Without due consideration of consequences. Why hadn't I stopped for a moment? Instead I'd hopped on the first plane for London, then Singapore.

The only thing I'd allowed myself to focus on was life. My life. Survival. A chance to save myself. I gave no thought to who else I might hurt, what else I might jeopardize.

I never considered that saving myself might be the wrong thing to do.

I smiled as I recalled a piece of sage advice I'd once overheard: when dying, know enough to lie down.

Nigel Congswell is right. It's time for me to go home and die. Preserve what integrity I have left.

I stood up from the table. I held out my hand.

Nigel looked up, surprised. "You're leaving?"

"Strangely enough, I agree with you." I sighed. "I guess I thought I'd get here, somehow get my hands on a vial—or whatever it is you carry a cure for cancer in—then go back home and live happily ever after." Now it was my turn to look away. "This is…this is all kind of new to me, this dying thing. I guess I didn't think it through." I cocked an eyebrow and held up a forefinger for emphasis. "The first time I've done that, I want you to know." I lowered the finger. "But now I have. I was wrong to come here. To come after the cure. Despite everything that's happened, I trust IIA. I believe in what they do. They have a reason to keep the cure for cancer from the world. I trust that reason, whatever it is."

Congswell did not look impressed. "So now you're going to up and leave a colleague in the lurch?"

I chuckled. This guy was good. "Former colleague. And, if you'll recall, you were in the lurch long before I got here."

"That's where you're wrong, Saint. You may not have intentionally led them to me, but before today, I'd gotten away clean. No one has come after me the entire time I've been in Singapore. I wasn't the one in danger…."

There it was again. "Nigel, who are you protecting?"

"No one. My point is that *you* brought these men to my doorstep. Not me. You. They were onto you. And you led them right to me."

Although I showed no signs of it, I wondered if he was right.

"Someone's behind all this," he insisted. "Someone you know. Who told you about me? Who told you about the asset?"

Kate.

Kate?

No fucking way.

Nigel Congswell might be right about how the gunmen found him. But this was not Kate's doing. She wanted me alive. Not dead.

Or was I just fooling myself? Kate wasn't my wife any longer. I'd signed the papers telling me so. What more proof did I need to know that she and I were no longer on the same team? We didn't have each other's backs. I wasn't the most important person in her life.

There was so much I didn't know about her anymore. What did she think about? What was important to her? What motivated her? Who did she care about?

There was someone else.

Who?

Why?

That night in Toronto, when she first learned I was going to die, we made love. I saw it in her eyes. She did still care.

This wasn't about Kate. Congswell was fishing. But was he right about this? Was there someone else behind this?

I lowered myself back into my seat. "It was me," I lied. "Just me. It's amazing what a tumour in your head will do for determination. I'd heard rumours about your asset. So when I was diagnosed with cancer, I decided to dig into it, see if there was something to it. Lo and behold, there was. I couldn't get anything more out of APU or IIA, so I decided to track you down. Which, by the way, wasn't difficult."

"Great," he replied sourly.

"Nigel, we have to get out of Singapore. We have to get away from those gun-toting idiots. They think we have something we don't. They think the cure is vulnerable because it's no longer under IIA protection. They think it'll be easy pickings. There's only one way I see to get us out of this mess. We have to find the cure. Then return it to IIA, where they don't have a chance at getting their hands on it. Are you with me on that?"

I could see a battle playing out on Nigel's face. He was conflicted. He was also badly outnumbered. If he truly had a selfless attitude toward the asset—and cared about staying alive—he'd know I was right.

Finally he nodded.

"Okay then. But I can't help you unless I have the whole story. Why did you leave IIA? How is it that you lost track of the asset? And, Nigel, don't bullshit me on this; who are you protecting?"

"I'm not protecting anything anymore. Not even, quite obviously, myself."

"So where is it? Where is the cure? If you lost it, where's the last place you saw it?"

Nigel looked me straight in the eyes and said, "The asset is not a substance, not a thing, not an it. The asset...is a she."

Chapter Eighteen

Illya Nikoleyevich Develchko was a teenager during the last years of what is commonly referred to as the Brezhnev Era. It was a period that began with high economic growth and soaring prosperity but ended with a much weaker Soviet Union facing social, political, and economic stagnation.

Still, Soviet society reached modernity under Brezhnev's rule. A social and sexual revolution was taking place. Society became more urban, and people—particularly women—became better educated. In contrast to previous periods dominated by fear, upheaval and war, the Brezhnev Era courted economic development, cultural reform, and personal prosperity. Though *some* areas of life for *some* people improved, disease was on the rise because of a decaying healthcare system, living space remained small by First World standards, and homelessness grew rampant.

Illya Nikoleyevich's parents were the Russian version of wannabe yuppies, interested in anything Western. They ate up the rock music, they wore the jeans, they poured every ruble they earned into owning a refrigerator, a colour TV, and whatever else the flourishing Soviet black market had on offer. Oftentimes, their desire to participate in the so-called new prosperity came at the price of meals on the table and warm clothing for themselves and their children. As with most citizens, they had no power or any real hope of seeing change. They simply blindly tried to make the best of a bad situation.

Rates of alcoholism, mental illness, divorce, and suicide rose inexorably. In turn, Illya Nikoleyevich's parents—first his mother, then his father—fell victim to all of it, in that order. Illya and his sisters were left to fend for themselves. Eventually the girls were sent to live with one set of distant relatives and Illya to another.

Illya got the short end of the stick. His new family did not really want another mouth to feed. They took him in solely to avoid the wrath of the rest of their relatives. His new father was a big brute of a man, a blue-collar worker who acted as if his weakling nephew was a personal affront to his own manhood. Attempts to interest Illya in sports, bodybuilding, or working in a factory were met with little resistance—as Illya wanted nothing more than to please the man—and equally little success. Illya simply wasn't good at those type of things. When the boy was old enough, it was decided that the only hope for him was the army, which had the dual benefit of getting Illya out of the house and into someone else's hands.

Even as a teenager, Illya was proud to be a part of the Soviet Union's military, the sole remaining superpower rival to the United States. The Cold War between the two nations had led to significant military buildup, and by the early eighties, the Soviet armed forces had more troops, tanks, artillery guns, and nuclear weapons than any other nation on earth.

The fall of the Soviet Union in 1991 was devastating to Illya. He vociferously reminded anyone who would listen that it was not because of military defeat, but rather economic and political chaos. The same factors that destroyed his own parents. Funding for the military plummeted. Attempts to revitalize it failed miserably, and a series of treaties between newly independent states divided up its assets. The last vestiges of the old Soviet command structure were finally dissolved in June 1993.

Illya Nikoleyevich just barely hung on, and only through a series of lucky breaks and slipping—or hiding—between the cracks when it was judicious to do so, did he continue his life as a military man. His fortunes and personal stock rose and, more often, fell with that of the military.

During his years as a career soldier, Illya had certainly gained some physical prowess, but undoubtedly his greatest strength lay in his mental abilities. He was bright, a quick learner, and crafty when he needed to be. Above all, Develchko harboured a deep need to prove himself to others; he wanted not only to meet but also to wildly exceed expectations. If he couldn't find approval from a parent or foster parent, then a military superior would do just as well. Greatest of all was his wish to someday return to the little village where he was born and raised by his two foolish parents and show himself off to be the greatest hero they had ever seen.

The rank of General-polkovnik did not exist in Imperial Russia. It was first established in the Red Army in 1940 and still exists today in the contemporary Russian army. General-polkovnik occupies the position between two-star Lieutenant General and four-star Army General. Develchko bristled whenever he'd overheard it said that because of this, General-polkovnik was neither an exceptional or rare rank. Idiots! How many men could claim such a rank? Compared to how many men were nothing more than fishermen, or butchers, or electricians? No, he was proud of his status as General-polkovnik and showed it in everything he did. From the way he walked and talked to the way he treated his many inferiors.

In his career, Develchko had readily and with great eagerness accepted undesirable postings. He'd probably been in every shithole in Russia. But in shitholes lay opportunity. Most men of his stature, or even greater *supposed* stature, were too stupid to realize it. Wondrous prospects existed by taking positions no one else wanted. Along with such stations came a great many things including gratitude. The gratitude of those simply too happy to find someone to do the jobs they needed done, the jobs that neither they, nor anyone they knew, wanted to do. And freedom. And flexibility. And ultimately power.

Illya Nikoleyevich Develchko was powerful. He'd sacrificed greatly and done many indelicate things to attain that power. In certain circles, amongst men and women around the world who also wielded great power, he was known for this willingness to do anything—anything—to keep it. And get more.

Develchko was in a position where he controlled many men, much money, and demanded great respect. Now was his time. Time to make his move. He needed to deliver something big. Only then would the higher-ups truly welcome him into their fold, with wide open arms and a kiss on each cheek. No more would they see him as a lowly or-phan boy who came from the dirty countryside to beg and crawl his way up the ladder of success. He would show them who he really was. A hero. His lifetime wish would be achieved. He could die a happy man.

Only after years of waiting did blessed opportunity pres-ent itself. Opportunity from the West. It was a bitter pill to swallow that the cause of his parents' deaths, his miserable childhood, the defeat of his beloved Soviet army, was also to be his own personal salvation. But Develchko found conso-lation in reminding himself that the opportunity wasn't being given to him by the West. He was taking it from them.

Develchko had never expected to meet Adam Saint. That was not in the plan. But now that he had, he knew he did not care for the man. This mattered little. He did not care for most men. What *was* important was that he did not trust Adam Saint. He could not—would not—permit his great future to lie solely in the hands of this brash and arrogant Westerner.

The cure for cancer was a reality. Adam Saint was after it. Fair enough. The man had access to the world in ways Develchko was practical enough to admit he did not. His new plan was to keep a watchful eye on every move made by the Canadian. And when the time was right, his own men would cut Saint down at the knees. And as Saint fell to the ground, Develchko would personally take from him the prize that belonged solely to him.

Saskatoon and Singapore had turned into bloody messes. The men assigned to follow Saint had moved pre-maturely. They'd been told the cure was neither a drug nor a formula, as most would expect, but rather a person. This person, in some mysterious way, controlled the cure. Unfortunately when his men witnessed Saint—whom they'd been tailing throughout his travels—first meet with a woman in Saskatoon, then a man in Singapore, they assumed the person had the cure. In each case, they had attacked with the intention of kidnapping the person with the cure and bringing them back to Russia.

Regrettably both instances resulted in miserable failure. And now that they'd shown their hand—not once, but twice—their quarry would be extra careful. Develchko was livid. His men were severely reprimanded. One of them would likely not survive his injuries.

It was obvious to Develchko that he could not rely on boys to do a General-polkovnik's work. From here on in, he would have to become personally involved.

The advice had been sound. Either they go to ground to avoid being killed—which could last weeks, months, or years—or they had to get out of Singapore immediately.

Nigel Congswell knew Saint did not have months, and certainly not years, to wait out a murder plot. He had a vested interest in moving now. So did he.

Congswell made a call from the Marina Bay Sands to his people at Raffles. People he trusted with his life. He had one team go to his home to gather a few necessities and important personal documents. Another team cleared out Saint's hotel room. They delivered everything to Changi airport. By the end of the day, Nigel and Adam were on a series of flights that would take them back to North America.

When Saint was booking the tickets, he'd asked Nigel to identify their final destination. Normally this would have been a reasonable request, but Nigel still did not trust Saint. Not by a long shot. Some might say that Adam Saint was quite obviously smart and skilled. But smart and skilled were simply the opposite sides of the coin from cunning and devious. Instead of revealing their final destination, he'd said: "Get us to Las Vegas. I'll tell you where we go from there when we get there." Saint had accepted that... with an unreadable look on his face.

"I'll have a bourbon," Nigel requested, when the steward asked for their pre-dinner cocktail order.

The steward turned his attention to Saint.

"I'll have the same."

The attendant nodded confirmation and was gone.

"Okay," Saint began once the drinks arrived, "now that we're off the ground and sitting side by side for a very long plane ride, I think it's time you started giving me details."

This wasn't surprising. Nigel knew he'd only be able to hold off Saint for so long. And really, he was beginning to wonder, why not come clean with his story? Their plan had obviously failed. Big time. And now they were both in big trouble. He couldn't turn to IIA. He'd burned too many bridges there. In fact, despite what he'd told Saint, when the shooting started in the warehouse, a small part of him did wonder if Knoble hadn't taken out a hit on him, just for the sake of revenge. He wouldn't put it past the woman.

They needed help. Saint's being another ex-IIA certainly counted for something. Maybe he *could* trust him. The only thing holding Nigel back was the fact that the guy had cancer. No matter what Saint claimed about rethinking his motives, when faced with his own death versus life, it wasn't hard to figure out which one he'd choose.

"Maybe after the fifth bourbon we can talk."

"Or maybe now," Saint countered. "You told me the asset was a woman. Who is she? Some kind of super scientist? A researcher who stumbled upon the cure?"

Nigel nodded. "Something like that."

"What happened? IIA found out about her...she's Canadian, right?"

Another nod.

"Then for some reason they decide they don't want her sharing what she knows with the rest of the world...or even her own countrymen for that matter. I haven't heard of any politicians or billionaire Canadians suddenly recovering from lymphoma or leukemia."

"Correct."

"Well, I won't hazard a guess as to why for now. This woman...can you give me a name, please? It's awkward referring to her as 'the woman' all the time."

Nigel took a long slow sip of his drink. He savoured it as he stared at the man next to him. *Oh, he's good. Just slipping in an innocent request for a name.* He smiled and laid down his glass. "Do you think I'm drunk already? Or stupid?"

"Both?"

The men laughed. It was the first time they'd shared anything beyond a glare.

Nigel turned away. He gazed out the window at the unrelenting sheet of blackness. He imagined it hugging the plane, helping to keep them aloft, whisking them away from danger. He felt safe. For now.

"Hanna Billings," he said quietly.

Saint nodded to himself. "You were working for Asset Protection when they called you in to watch her?"

"Yes," Nigel admitted, aware that he'd just crossed a line with Adam Saint. There was no going back now. "It was a difficult situation at first. She was, understandably, resistant. But it was for her own good. Intellectually I think she knew that. Emotionally it was a problem. We were basically asking her to hand over control of her life."

"*Asking* her? Is that how IIA works in a situation like this?"

"It *was* more than asking. But we pretended it wasn't. She pretended it wasn't. But it was. We all knew it. We all knew it had to be done. If anyone discovered…her involvement with the cure, well, life as she knew it would have been over anyway."

"So you began looking after her. This was eight or nine years ago?"

"You did your homework."

"Always do. So how does it work? Did you take her into hiding? New identity, all that?"

"Nothing that extreme at first. You see, other than IIA, no one knew about her. All we did was watch over her. We 'redirected' her lifestyle and living arrangements. Just in case. I became her glorified, long-distance bodyguard. Everything she did, said, everyone she met, everyplace she went, I knew about it, I vetted. We had our ups and downs. But generally everything went smoothly for a number of years."

Nigel signaled for another drink from a passing steward.

"Someone found out about her? Is that what happened next?"

Nigel hesitated. Saint had it wrong. That had happened. But not then. Not for a long time. Something else, also significant, happened first. Something that should never have happened. Something that was his fault.

"We fell in love."

There. He'd said it. Other than Hanna, he'd never admitted that fact to anyone. Not to Maryann Knoble. Not to his sister Clara. Not to any of his friends.

"Thank you," he said when the drink arrived. He knew he should switch to something lighter. A beer maybe. But the whiskey was medicine. A bitter pill his body needed.

Saint was respectfully silent as the meals were served, allowing Nigel time to eat and reflect on his admission. Only when the coffee had arrived did he bring it up again. "Care to tell me what happened when you and Hanna Billings fell in love?"

"She's a beautiful woman. That was obvious from the start, of course. But as I got to know her, I realized she was so much more. I was supposed to be watching her, yet stay as much out of her daily life as possible. I know it sounds corny, but I found myself finding more and more reasons to show up at her door, to be involved in what she was doing. She didn't resist. The day I realized she felt the same way was the happiest day of my life.

"We didn't want IIA or anyone else finding out. So at first it was this big, illicit, taboo thing. Which made it all the more exciting. Sneaking around was fun, you know?"

Saint nodded. He did know.

"Things got serious pretty fast. About two years ago, we decided we needed to stop hiding. We wanted to get married. But that's when things started going wrong."

"Wrong how?"

"I started noticing little things at first. A car parked outside the house too long. Untraceable phone calls. APU started hearing rumours. There were vague reports about someone out there knowing about the asset—about the cure—and planning to steal it. Weeks would go by and nothing would happen. Then Hanna would feel she was being watched in the grocery store, or followed home from work. There was something going on. But I couldn't quite put my finger on it."

"Then something did happen?" Saint guessed.

Nigel nodded. "Something big. There was an attack on her house. Fortunately we were on high alert. It was a ballsy move. Looked like they were trying to abduct the boy...."

"Boy? What boy?"

Nigel hesitated, swallowing hard. "Hanna has a son," he acknowledged. "Jake."

"So they were kidnapping the boy to get to the mother?"

Nigel nodded.

"There was a firefight. I was able to get Hanna and Jake out of there and into a car. We escaped while it was all still going on. If something like this happened, the plan was to get the asset to an IIA safe house. But Hanna refused."

"Refused? Why would she do that?"

"She's smart. She knew what it meant. If we took her and Jake into hiding like that, she knew they'd never come out.

She wanted to run. Far away. Start a new life. Be normal. She wanted Jake to have a regular life."

Saint studied his seat mate. "You helped her."

Nigel's face gave the answer.

"It didn't work, did it?"

"It did at first. I lied to IIA. To Maryann. I told her Hanna and Jake had somehow slipped away from me after we escaped the house. It worked because I was the one leading the IIA team looking for them. All I had to do was put Hanna and Jake wherever my team wasn't."

"What about the people who tried to kidnap the boy? They were still out there. How did you expect you could hide from an enemy like that without IIA help?"

"I know. It was stupid. *I* was stupid. I knew better. But I loved her. I thought I could be the big, strong man who could do everything for her. I wanted to be the one to protect her from everyone and everything.

"I thought I had a foolproof plan. I got some money together. I set Hanna and Jake up in…well, somewhere safe. Everything was okay. For about a month. Then they found us. We ran and hid again. They found us again. And again. It seemed like they were always just two steps behind us. So I decided to leave IIA. I needed to dedicate myself to keeping Hanna and Jake safe. I figured if we could get far enough away, we could make it work. We'd finally be free, be safe, be a family."

"But I found you working hotel security in Singapore. Hanna and Jake are lost. I take it something went wrong with your plan?"

Nigel grimaced. "You might say that. Before I left IIA,

I prepared fake identification documents for all of us. I wanted to ensure we had the freedom to move around, even leave the country if we needed to. But these guys were too good. They were on us like bloodhounds. We could never be sure when they'd show up next. This went on for months. We were desperate. And exhausted. Most of all, I began to realize we were out of options. It was only a matter of time before these people found us, before someone got hurt. Or worse. I wanted to go back to IIA. Just come clean, apologize. We needed their help. Hanna was resistant, but she just didn't have any fight left in her. So I went to Maryann to make the deal."

"Maryann Knoble is a steely broad," Saint said, "but I can't believe she'd turn you away."

"She didn't. She agreed to take us in again. Put us under Asset Protection."

"So what happened?"

"When I got back to our latest hiding hole, they were gone."

"Someone got them?"

"No. Hanna left a note. She told me she loved me. But she loved Jake more. She thought if she could just get away from IIA…from me, maybe they'd have a chance at a normal life."

"She couldn't seriously believe that you or the IIA were responsible for what happened to them? She was an asset. IIA or not, she had to know that was never going to change."

"I think she'd come to believe they were able to track her because they could track me. Especially when I was IIA.

Even after I wasn't. She still thinks she and Jake are two insignificant specs in the cosmos. She thinks if they try hard enough, they'll be able to disappear."

"She's wrong."

"I know."

"Where are they now, Nigel?"

"I don't know. That note was the last I heard from them. You know, Saint, strangely enough, maybe Hanna *was* right. She's been very successful in falling off the radar screen. She's gone so deep into hiding, no one can find her. And believe me, I've tried."

"If you don't know where they are, why are we going to Las Vegas?"

"I never said we were staying there. I just…I need some time to figure out what to do next. When I know it, so will you." He stopped there, then added, "You know the good thing about what happened to us back there in Singapore? It gives me some hope that Hanna and Jake are still safe. If they'd already been captured, there'd be no reason for those goons to come after us."

"Unless," Saint responded, "there's more than one set of goons."

The pinging sound startled me awake. It was a familiar sound, but in my haze, I couldn't quite place it. I fought to open my eyes. Unusual for me.

"Ladies and gentlemen, we'll be landing in Las Vegas in a few minutes. The local time is three p.m. The temperature is forty-one degrees Celsius, which is one hundred and six

Fahrenheit. Please remain seated with your seatbelts fastened until...." *Blah blah blah.*

I blindly felt around for the seat control panel. I pushed buttons until my seat began maneuvering me into an upright sitting position. I shook my clouded head. I tried to remember when I'd fallen asleep and if I'd consumed a bottle of rum beforehand. I'm sure if I could have touched it, my brain would have felt mushy. Which maybe it was. I opened my eyes, wincing at the bright light bathing the plane's interior. My mouth was dry, my throat a little sore. Was I sick? Coming down with the flu? A cold? Another symptom?

I lolled my head to the left.

What the hell? Immediately I was on high alert.

The seat next to me—Nigel Congswell's seat—was empty!

Chapter Nineteen

Congswell was gone.

In one quick motion, I unbuckled my seatbelt and bolted upright. Before I knew it, a flight attendant was in my face, a grim expression on hers.

"Sir, please return to your seat and fasten your seatbelt. We're about to land." Her voice was calm, but assertive.

"My…friend…the man I was traveling with…his seat is empty."

"I'm sorry, sir, we can't discuss this right now. We are about to land. Please sit down and buckle your seatbelt. Now."

I gave the woman a tight smile and did as I was told. The last thing I needed was a sky marshal fitting me with a pair of handcuffs.

He couldn't have gone far. This was a commercial aircraft flying at 35,000 feet. I doubted there'd been an escape-by-sky-diving opportunity made available to him without my knowing. With my head throbbing, I was coming to suspect Congswell had slipped a little something special into my last drink. It was a clever ploy. Pretend to spill your guts, make me believe we're bonding over stories of ill-fated love, then drug me to give you time to…what? Get an aisle seat?

The configuration of the aircraft was such that business class—where we were—and the front section of economy deplaned through the same set of doors. Congswell must have asked for a seat closer to the exit to get a head start. Despite the disapproving glare of the nearby flight attendant, I craned my head to see if I could catch sight of him.

No luck.

So Congswell decided to ditch me. I wondered how much, if any, of what he'd told me about Hanna Billings was true. But why lie to me? Why abandon me, when all I wanted to do was help the guy? Quite obviously he didn't trust me. Frankly I didn't blame him. If he wanted to go it alone from here, it was no skin off my nose. I wasn't lying when I said I'd help him protect the asset, help him keep the cure for cancer from being revealed to the rest of the world (no matter why IIA thought this was necessary). It was my small gesture of contrition, for being such an ass as to consider taking the cure only for my own use.

But now that Congswell was gone, it seemed my duty was done. I'd catch the first flight out of Sin City back to Saskatoon. I'd go home and get on with…what was left of my life.

I took my time leaving the plane. After so many days of non-stop action, running from here to there, eluding venomous snakes and blazing gunfire, it felt rather nice.

It wasn't until I was riding the escalator down into McCarran's baggage claim area that I knew my adventure wasn't quite over yet.

Nigel Congswell was at the far end of the large hall, striding purposefully toward the exit. His carry-on roller was not the only thing behind him. He seemed blissfully unaware that he had a tail. I might not have noticed it myself except for the fact that the tail was a tall man with fiery red hair and Lenin's beard.

Develchko's man.

What the holy hell was the flunky of some Russian general doing in Las Vegas?

Develchko was somehow behind all of this. He must be after the asset. Did he think because I'd been after Congswell that *he* was the asset? How could he have heard about the cure in the first place?

I knew how dangerous Develchko and his men could be. They'd put me in the hospital. I couldn't be 100 per cent certain, but it also seemed likely it was they who'd mowed down the young man in Magadan in cold blood. And maybe…could they possibly have had something to do with Geoffrey Krazinski's death? Was it not an accident after all? Had the young man known Develchko was responsible and been killed before he could point the finger?

As I elbowed my way through the crowd of people clogging the sluggishly descending escalator, many wild thoughts zipped through my brain. None of them made sense. Yet. I needed time to think. This, however, was not that time.

"I'm sorry, sir," I excused myself past the last of the escalator-riding passengers. "Airport security."

I hit the ground running. The last I saw of Congswell and Lenin they were just fifty feet apart, heading for the exit.

A wall of oppressive heat hit me as I burst outside. Just

in time to see Nigel pull an oldie but a goodie. There was, as usual in Vegas, a mind-numbingly long taxi queue. Nigel had forgone the line and marched directly to the front. He showed the taxi captain some kind of official-looking badge, perhaps his old IIA identification for all I knew.

They had a quick chat. Then Nigel, to the hoots and hollers of disgruntled travelers in line, was allowed to jump into the next available cab.

Not far away, Carrot Top jumped into a car that he'd obviously had waiting for him. Off they went in pursuit of Nigel's taxi.

Sons of bitches!

Me? No waiting car. No fake badge. No cab. Unless I wanted to be number fifty-three in line.

I took a chance. Jogging up to the taxi captain, who was reaching to open the back door of the next cab in line, I yelled in my most authoritative tone: "Airport security business! Hold that cab for me!"

The uproar was deafening. Suddenly the crowd in the queue was united in frightful, righteous indignation, raising their voices in joint protest. My life was probably in danger. There were folks in that line who hadn't had a cigarette, or a good meal, or a satisfying sleep in many hours. They were pissed, and they weren't going to take it any longer.

Good agents know when to back away from a dangerous situation they can't possibly survive. I did so then.

Back in the terminal, I found a relatively quiet spot near a bank of unpopular slots. I pulled out my cellphone.

"Anatole," I said when the call was answered. It was an hour earlier in Saskatoon.

"Uncle Adam, are you in Vegas yet?" I'd sent him a text on one of my earlier layovers. My message had been short and concise: "Going to Las Vegas with Nigel Congswell. Why?" If anyone could find a connection between Congswell and Vegas, any reason why he'd be bringing me here, it was Anatole.

"Just landed."

"Have you figured out why you're there yet?"

"I was hoping you'd be able to help me out with that."

"Congswell won't tell you anything, huh?"

"Well, there's good news and bad news."

"I'll take the bad news first. I'm guessing it's gonna be waaaaay more interesting."

"Nigel dumped me."

"Woooooow. I bet you must feel like that's the story of your life lately, huh?"

I didn't even want to begin to think about what he meant by that. Jerk. *Oh, what the hell, Saint, say it out loud.* "You're a real jerk sometimes, Anatole. You know that?"

"Yup. So what's the good news?"

"He did give me a little more information. That being said, we should keep in mind that shortly after confiding in me, he drugged and abandoned me on the airplane."

"On the plane? You mean he jumped? Awesome."

"No, he switched seats. And you watch too many movies."

"Got ya. What'd he tell you?"

"He told me the asset's name. It's a woman by the name of Hanna Billings. She has a son named Jake. Both currently MIA."

"So what you're saying is that this woman has the cure for cancer?"

"Yes. But that's all I know. I don't know where she used to live. Or who she works for. Or who the child's father is. Nigel began protecting her for IIA about five years ago. They fell in love a few years after that. Somebody found out about her. Nigel left IIA to go into hiding with her. It didn't last long. He says he lost track of her and her son. Judging by what just happened, I don't know if any of this is true."

"So she's gone. And now he's gone too."

It didn't sound very good. "That's about right."

"So how are you going to find the cure now?"

I hesitated. I didn't want to tell Anatole over the phone that I no longer considered that an option for me. "I've got a new lead," I told him. "When I get a few minutes with my laptop, I'm going to email you some information about a man named Illya Nikoleyevich Develchko. He's a general in the Russian army. I had a run in with him right before I came back to Saskatoon. I don't know how, but he's tied up in all of this somehow."

"Have I told you how cool your life is?"

I grinned but said nothing in response. Instead I asked, "What about you? Were you able to dig up anything after I texted you?"

"Not much. There's one thing, but I don't know if it means anything."

"I'm sitting at the Las Vegas airport watching Ma and Pa Kettle gamble away their life's savings, it's one hundred and six outside, and I've got nowhere to go. I'll take anything you've got."

"Who are Ma and Pa Kettle…wait, I'm Googling them now…what the…."

"Anatole! Never mind them. What did you dig up about Congswell and Las Vegas? Any connections?"

"It was pretty sparse. But there was one thing. For the past several months, he's been making calls to Las Vegas. About once every two weeks or so. The number that shows up the most is for someone named Sheila Shellbrook. No address attached to it. Probably a cell."

Great. All I had to do was sort through Las Vegas for a woman named Sheila. But I had to do something. "She must be a friend of Nigel's," I suggested. "Or maybe Hanna's. That's just the kind of person he'd go see. Did you find out anything else about her? Anything that might tell me where to find her? Anything at all?" I was desperate.

"Hey, this isn't easy stuff I'm doing here." He sounded a bit miffed. As he should. He was pulling magic bunnies out of his computer. I needed to remember he was not an IIA agent who'd done this kind of thing a million times before. He was my nineteen-year-old nephew sitting in his room on my father's farm in Saskatchewan.

"Anatole, I'm sorry. You're doing an amazing job. I couldn't do this without you."

"Really?"

"Really."

"There *was* something," he gamely continued. "About two or three of Congswell's calls to Las Vegas were made to one other number. The Flamingo Hotel. Shows Management Department."

Ding dong. "Sheila Shellbrook works at the Flamingo."

"If you give me another half hour or so, I should be able to confirm that."

I checked my watch. It was just after four p.m. She could be at work now. If Nigel was in a rush to see her, that's where he'd go. Followed by red-haired Lenin. "I don't have half an hour. You get to work on Hanna. I'll check out Sheila at the Flamingo."

"Okay. Oh, and Grandpa says hi."

For a second, I was tongue-tied. Then I said, "Well, tell him...hi back."

Even the traffic seems to move slower in the blistering heat of a July afternoon in Las Vegas. As the taxi made its way down congested Las Vegas Boulevard, mirage-like panels of shimmering heat emanated from the frying-pan pavement. On the sidewalks, tourists in string bikini tops and short shorts mixed with bangers in three-quarter-length denim shorts, oversized sports jerseys, and baseball caps. There were moms and pops on their first trip outside Oklahoma, and the omnipresent hawkers selling everything from frozen daiquiris to helicopter rides over Hoover Dam and kinky sex shows.

Opened in 1946 by mobster Bugsy Siegel, the Flamingo Hotel is the oldest resort on the Strip still in operation today. Siegel named the resort after his girlfriend, Virginia Hill, whose long, skinny legs earned her the nickname Flamingo. Siegel considered flamingos a good omen, but things didn't work out too well for him. I was hoping I'd have better luck.

As soon as the cab deposited me at the hotel entrance, I muddled my way through the melee of people who seemed to have nothing better to do than stand in my way, carrying cocktails the size of missiles. After a short bit of confusion—a must in any Las Vegas hotel—I found an area that looked more like the business side of things.

"Excuse me," I said to a woman behind a reception desk. She didn't look at all like my idea of a typical denizen of Las Vegas. Her dark skin was without a hint of cosmetics, not a sequin or feather boa in sight. "I'm looking for my friend Sheila Shellbrook. She works in the Shows department."

"Sheila is the Kai props manager."

My face must have registered a blank.

"Kai is Flamingo's new Cirque du Soleil show. It's our first. Our theatre is too small for a regular Cirque production, but Kai is specifically designed for smaller auditoriums."

"Yes, of course. I remember Sheila telling me all about it."

"You should see it." It sounded more like an order than suggestion.

"I will."

"Good."

"Is Sheila around?"

"The theatre is dark tonight. That means no show. But she's always back there, checking and double-checking the props. You know how Cirque shows are. All those pulleys and chains and highwire things. Scares the bejeebers out of me." The woman slid a sheet of paper across the counter.

Her long fingernails were bedazzled. Finally some Las Vegas razzmatazz. "Here's the map on how to get backstage. Are ya'll having a reunion or something back there today?"

Another blank look from me.

"There was another guy who came by earlier. He was looking for Sheila too."

I was pretty sure I knew who that was.

Getting backstage access was easier than I'd imagined. I had been prepared to lie, cheat, steal, flirt. Then again, I suppose there are a great many people, from actors to technicians, delivery people to costume designers, who regularly need to get back there, even when it's not a show day.

Leaving my luggage with the receptionist, I followed the map. The deeper into the theatre I got and away from the hullabaloo of the hotel, the quieter it became. Only in town a short time, my ears were already inured to the ubiquitous chiming of slot machines, the never-ending murmur of a thousand conversations, and the occasional victory scream of someone winning fifty bucks at a craps table.

Opening the final door, I was met with darkness.

I allowed my eyes a moment to adjust. The air smelled of grease paint and face powder and the faint mustiness of a closet crammed with old clothes.

If Nigel and Sheila were up ahead—and maybe Develchko's man too—stealth was required. Moving forward, I used my hands to keep from banging into anything.

There was light coming through an opening at the opposite end of the room. That was my destination. Getting there, I passed by rolling wardrobes hung with plastic-covered costumes, each with a tag bearing someone's name. There were shelves devoted entirely to shoes, another for hats, still another for what looked like varied swatches of cloth. There were more shelves for smaller props—fake phones, fake toasters, fake everything. From the audience pit, these items would look authentic. Up close, quite the opposite.

Having reached the opening, I was keenly aware that I was without the comfort of a weapon. I stood still for several seconds listening for voices. Other than the odd groan or wheeze common to empty theatres, there was only silence.

I stepped through and realized I was in the wings of the main stage. It was still dark here, but the stage itself was fully lit, as if in wait for a performance.

"Welcome, Mr. Saint."

I knew the voice.

I stepped forward into the light. From the shadows of stage right, a lone figure emerged.

Develchko.

"What brings you to Las Vegas, General? Can't resist a good buffet?"

"Our time together in Magadan was…cut short. I thought it time to get reacquainted."

"I'm flattered. Is that why you're here? Buying us tickets for the show? I hear it's pretty good."

"Not quite," he said, lips tight. I was getting the sense he wasn't exactly enjoying my sense of humour.

Enough beating around the bush. "In that case, General, why don't you tell me why you've come all this way? What are you after?"

"The same thing you are."

I stared, not giving an inch.

He stared back. Then, "The cure, Mr. Saint. I want the cure."

"Which you're planning to sell to the highest bidder."

"Of course not," he scoffed. "Russians are not nearly as self-serving as you Canadians."

Was this hoodlum actually making himself out to be better than me?

He leered at me. "You were going to use the cure on yourself. Were you not?"

The man was dangerously well-informed.

Without waiting for my answer, he continued. "You see, I, instead, plan to share this great cure. For the benefit of my beloved country. Forevermore, Russia will be known the world over as the motherland of the cure for cancer. Sick people, dying people, all will be made healthy again. And I, General-polkovnik Illya Nikoleyevich Develchko, will be remembered as their saviour."

"So this *is* all about you after all?"

"Don't be insolent!" he bristled.

"My apologies."

The man pulled in a deep breath, his chest rising impressively beneath his uniform. His blue eyes burned bright under the stage lights. "I know this isn't how you wished for things to turn out. I sympathize with your disappointment. But in life, Mr. Saint, there must always be a winner and a loser. Today, unfortunately, you must be the loser."

"Today isn't over."

"It soon will be." I heard the strain of leather as his hands, resting at his thighs, balled into fists then straightened then balled into fists again. "Once you give me the cure."

"I don't have it. You know everything else. You should know that."

He sighed. "I thought as much. I believe you know where it is though. Isn't that right, Mr. Saint? Tell me where it is."

"Why would I do that?"

A nerve vibrated along the stern line of his jaw as he looked up. With that silent order, a spotlight powered on, its powerful beam directed heavenward.

I followed the path of light, craning my neck to see what the Russian obviously wanted me to see.

Many metres above the stage, suspended in a weave of rope and cables, hung two bodies. They were face down, perpendicular to the stage floor. One was Nigel Congswell. The other a dark-haired woman. Sheila Shellbrook. Their mouths were covered with silver electrical tape. Their arms and legs were bound. Their eyes, however, remained wide open. Staring down at us. Nigel's were unreadable. Sheila's were clear. The young woman was utterly terrified. Justifiably so. She feared she was about to lose her life.

Despite the great distance, our eyes locked. Wordlessly Sheila Shellbrook was begging me to save her.

A thick, dark knot formed in my chest.

I did not know if I could.

My head snapped back. Glaring Develchko in the eye, I stepped closer to him. I asked, "What's going on here? Why do you have them up there?"

"Don't mistake me for a fool, Mr. Saint. Neither of them has the asset. Do they?"

"No."

"My terms are simple. Tell me where it is, and I will free your friends."

"I don't know where it is."

"I don't believe you."

"If I knew where it was, why would I be here?"

His voice was an oil slick. "To stop me, of course. Without me, your precious asset is safe. You must face it, Mr. Saint, there is no getting rid of me. I have the power. I have the money. I have the men. And now I want the cure. You will get it for me."

"How do you even know there is a cure? How can you be so certain?"

"I am ten million times certain the cure exists," he boasted, narrowing his eyes in a face that might have been handsome were it not the home for such a malevolent mind.

"Ten mil…." There it was. This was how Develchko became involved. He was nothing more than a customer. A client willing to pay an astronomical price for a one-of-a-kind good. He was buying the cure for cancer. At quite a deal, I'd say. But more interesting to me: Who was the seller?

"Why are you really here, General? Shouldn't you be waiting at home for FedEx? Isn't that how you were to receive the goods? You know, if you're not home when they deliver, they return to sender."

Develchko's face twisted in antipathy.

"Who is the sender?" I demanded to know. "Who are you supposed to be buying the cure from? And why, General-polkovnik, are you double-crossing them?"

"You should keep your lies of double-cross to yourself," he spit out. "Just like a Westerner to muddle the truth."

"Judging by your defensiveness, I'm guessing I hit it on the nose. If you were paying someone else to deliver you the goods, why would you bother coming all this way yourself? Cutting out the middle man, is that it? That way you get to keep both the cure and the ten million all for yourself. Tsk tsk tsk. You're a very greedy general."

His face darkened. "I am simply keeping a close watch over the operation. This is much too important to leave in the hands of men like you. This you'll understand, I'm sure."

The man was squirming. No one likes getting caught with their hands in the cure-for-cancer cookie jar. "You still haven't answered my question, Develchko. How can you be so certain there actually is a cure? You should know, in cases like this, the return policy is quite unforgiving. Buyer beware and all that." I was enjoying screwing with the man.

"You think I'm stupid?" The words were hot, but Delvechko was remaining impressively cool.

Welllllllll….

And then he said what I least expected. "I have proof."

"Proof? What kind of proof?" I was at a loss here.

Whenever possible, I like to adhere to the rule followed by every good lawyer and interrogator: never ask a question to which you don't know the answer. I didn't even know *what* the cure was. Proof of the same was difficult to imagine.

Develchko had decided there was no harm in coming clean with me…or, if not clean, at least a little less dirty. For some reason, he did not consider me a threat. And that worried me.

"We were sent a specimen," he announced.

I kept my mouth shut.

"The specimen was delivered to a secret Russian medical facility of my own choosing. Tests designed by the Canadian doctors were repeated by my people. We discovered the Canadians were telling the truth. The specimen, a piece of kidney, I believe, proved to be impervious to certain strains of cancer."

I listened and learned. Although it no longer particularly mattered to me one way or another, I now knew Hanna Billings didn't possess *the* cure for cancer. She possessed *a* cure for *certain* cancers. Scientifically this probably made more sense. Still extraordinary, but this explained the rock-bottom selling price of ten million dollars.

The second thing I learned was even more stunning. The cure for cancer wasn't a formula, or a man-made drug synthesized in a researcher's test tube. It was living tissue. The asset, the highly sought-after cure for cancer, was Hanna Billings herself.

There had to be something about the woman's body, her organs and blood, who knows what else, something naturally occurring, but immensely rare, that acted as a cure for cancer.

Not wanting to communicate my ignorance on the matter, I countered with: "So you already have the cure. If you have the specimen, why are you here? Why do you want more?"

"The cure only works when obtained directly from the living host. And even then, unless kept in cryogenic storage, it is only viable for a short period of time after harvesting. The miniscule specimen we received was entirely used up in our experiments. We require more. To conduct further tests, to find a way to replicate it, then commercialize it for use in the general population. Perhaps adapt it for use against all cancers and even other diseases. So you see, Mr. Saint, we know without doubt that the cure is a reality. All we need now is to take possession of the donor."

Donor? Develchko and the Russians weren't interested in a donor. Hanna Billings would be their guinea pig. They would slowly rip her apart, piece by piece, using her up in their experiments and trials until there was nothing left of her. Literally. Suddenly the reason IIA chose to keep Hanna from the world became crystal clear. Even under the most stringent vigilance, a unique being such as Hanna, revealed to the world, would most certainly be forced to give up her life in every way imaginable. She would die so others could live. In a pre-emptive move, IIA, a heartless corporation, had made a decision steered by unusual compassion. IIA had not only been protecting Hanna Billings's life, they were saving it.

Who was I to put a fly in such mighty ointment?

"I hate to disappoint you, Develchko." I shrugged, my

voice resolute. "But I'm afraid you're going to have to go home empty-handed. I don't have the cure. I don't know where it is. I never have."

"Which one?" he asked, face impassive.

I didn't understand. "Which one what?"

Leisurely he repositioned his head, once again gazing up at the two bodies suspended above us. "Which one of your two friends' lives do you wish to lose first? Consider it the price you pay for refusing me."

"Develchko, no." I kept my voice steady. "I'm not refusing you. I simply don't know where the cure is. If you let them down, maybe the three of us can figure it out together."

The man stared at me, his fiery eyes falling onto mine like a vulture on prey.

He did not believe me.

Develchko looked away, at someone standing in wait in the wings.

"No!" I shouted. "Don't. I can't do this without them. I can't find the cure without their help."

His gaze back on me, Develchko calmly raised his right arm so his hand was near his ear.

"Develchko… General…" I pleaded. "Don't do this. I need their help. Both of them."

Develchko dropped his arm with the horrid finality of an executioner's axe.

I staggered backwards, looking up, as a body plummeted to the stage.

Chapter Twenty

As the bands holding Sheila Shellbrook aloft above the Flamingo Hotel show stage uncoiled, dropping her body with breathtaking speed, all I could do was watch, helpless. With her mouth gagged, limbs bound, she made not a sound, no last-minute protective movement or flail, as I'm sure her body and mind were screaming to do. She was the props manager for the theatre. She knew exactly how high she was. She knew exactly what would happen to a body dropped from that height. She'd probably staked her career and reputation on ensuring that what was about to happen to her would never happen to anyone.

Other than the sickly sound of unfurling restraints, the auditorium was deathly quiet as Sheila plunged to the ground.

Then, with less than eighteen inches clearance, the body came to a sudden, jerking halt.

Develchko had rigged the ropes to stop just short of smashing his prisoner to smithereens. This was, after all, the set of a Cirque du Soleil show. As anyone who has seen one can attest, almost anything is possible.

I rushed to Sheila's side, kneeling next to her. She'd stopped in a face-up position, still trussed up like some kind of a restrained mental patient. Her eyes, vividly green, were wild. They danced from my face to Nigel's, still suspended far above us, then to Develchko, who had stepped into her restricted range of vision.

"Are you okay?" I asked.

She didn't even nod. She was in shock. The death drop hadn't killed her, but it had nearly scared her to death.

I looked up at Develchko. "You bastard." I said it, although I was quite certain he already knew it.

Develchko was smart. He knew outright murder in a public location was not as easy to get away with in the United States as it might be in Magadan. I had no doubt that had we been in his playground, Sheila Shellbrook would be dead.

"I wanted you to know," he said in an astoundingly even tone, "that although I am serious about my threats, I am not a monster."

It was all I could do not to jump up and tear into the man like a rabid dog.

"You're wrong about that," I murmured, anger simmering beneath the surface. "Let me take her gag off and get her out of this thing."

"No!" he blasted, a rare chink in his stable facade. Immediately regaining control, he said, "You do not make the rules here. Step away from the woman."

I could feel my breathing getting heavy, my blood running hot through my veins. My fury was escalating. In a minute, I would lunge at the man and gouge his eyes out.

"Vasily," Develchko called out, obviously in tune with my intentions.

The red-bearded Lenin lookalike came in from the wings, followed by another man I'd not seen before. They were on me in seconds, pulling me to my feet.

"You know what I want," Develchko said matter-of-factly. "Now go and get it. In the meantime, I will have your two friends looked after by my two friends."

There was no use telling him, yet again, that I had no idea where the asset, Hanna Billings, was. He'd made it very obvious he did not believe me.

"How do I reach you?" I asked.

His wolf's eyes penetrated me. "I am a ghost, Mr. Saint. You cannot reach me. I will reach you."

Great. The bastard had just announced his intention to keep on me like sour cream on perogies. "I don't want you following me," I said. "What I'm about to do is very delicate. I don't care how good you think you or your men are. The three of you will stick out like matryoshka dolls in a Barbie store. Listen," I indicated his prisoners, "you hold all the cards. You've given me no choice. Just let me do what I have to do. On my own."

I could see Develchko ruminating on this. Finally he responded. "That is fine. I will stay out of the way." He recited a number. "You will contact me in three days."

"Three days? I can't do this in—"

"Then I suggest you make haste. Please remember, Mr. Saint, if I do not hear from you in three days, these two people will be dead. And then, so will you."

My head swiveled up to find Nigel. His eyes were boring into me. What message would he give me if he could? Would he tell me where Hanna was so his life and that of

Sheila Shellbrook could be saved? Or would he tell me to jump off a cliff, protecting his lover's life at the expense of his own, Sheila's, and likely mine? Obviously he'd refused to tell Develchko anything when he'd had the chance. So I was pretty sure I knew which way he'd go.

I made to leave, then stopped. I turned to confront Develchko once more. "Who are you working with? Who told you about the asset?"

He looked at me as if disappointed in the question and said, "Trust no one, Mr. Saint."

For a while, I allowed myself to be ferried along the Strip's sidewalk, buoyed by the crowds of people heading for who knew where, which suited me fine. Because I had absolutely no idea where to go or what to do. And only three days in which to do it.

Eventually, wanting to get away from the unrelenting heat and throngs of jubilant tourists, I crossed the street. I headed for the hip CityCentre complex with its stylish glass high-rises jutting into the sky at every angle but straight up.

Amongst the bunch was the ultra-elegant Mandarin Oriental hotel, one of a chain that is amongst my favourites in the world. For a getaway within a getaway, the Las Vegas version would do perfectly. Although it was mere steps off the Strip, the Mandarin, a non-gaming, non-glitz hotel and residential tower, offered a cool, inviting, quiet respite from the madness just outside its doors.

Nodding to the attendant behind the ground floor welcome desk, I took the elevator to the twenty-third floor.

For me, at that particular moment, the Sky Lobby bar was a much-needed haven. Stepping into the cool, sleek lounge, I released a floodtide of air, pent up since I'd first arrived in Las Vegas hours earlier. I soaked up the floor-to-ceiling stunning views. Low, slung-back, red leather chairs set off against rich, dark floors and cushioned couches invited me in. Most especially, I appreciated the beautiful young woman behind the fully stocked bar—for both the girl and the booze.

The place was half full. Mostly thirty-somethings spiffed up in their sexy best, having a few cocktails before dinner. I lucked out with a seat by the window. From there, I could watch the millions of lights along the seven kilometre Strip come to life as we approached an eight p.m. sunset. I ordered a Scotch and settled in. I am not proud of the fact that part of me wanted nothing more than to sit in that lovely chair, in that lovely room, with my lovely drink, watch the lovely scenery, and end the night with a lovely young woman in a lovely hotel room.

And why shouldn't I? So much had happened so fast. I hadn't even really had the time to admit to myself that, once again, I was a doomed man. A man with a death sentence. Weren't guys like me allowed a little self-indulgence? Wasn't it okay if I decided not to save the damsels—and Nigel—in distress in favour of one last crazy weekend in Vegas? Have some fun before the really serious symptoms of this tumour show up and take over my life? By the time I woke up, Develchko's three-day time limit would have expired, and I could just walk away.

Of course, there was no way I could do any of that. I

had made plenty of bad decisions in my past. I'd ended up on the floor of a seedy joint or two, in the beds of more than a couple of wrong women. I've been ashamed of myself. I've been embarrassed. I've been disappointed. And humbled. But never regretful. Why? Because all those things, every decision, good or bad, they're a part of living a big, full life. Falling down isn't the issue. It's what you do when you get up that's important.

Now, to be fair, cancer is in a category all by itself. Still, I couldn't see it changing who I was. Unless…for the better?

I needed to get my head together and think. I needed a plan.

I opened my laptop and went to work.

A few minutes later, I checked my watch. If I left immediately, I could make the flight. I threw twenty bucks on the table and ran.

When did phone booths disappear? The minutes on her last prepaid cell card had expired. She didn't have the cash to buy another. Hanna circled the downtown block once more. Wasting gas. That wasn't good either. She was making poor decisions. And each time she made one, it seemed to lead her to another and then another. Was this what spiraling out of control looked like?

It was a dreary night. Rain sluiced down the car's window panes, compliments of a dull, dirty sky.

I used to love rain.

Not anymore.

Hanna used to love rain when she could cuddle up on

a couch with her son, a good book, a warm blanket, a glass of wine for her, milk for Jake, and a plate of chocolate chip cookies for both of them. How could it get any better than that? For hours and hours they would sit together like that. Hanna reading a children's adventure story to Jake, the pitter-patter of raindrops on the window providing a comforting background score to their perfect evening.

Hanna pulled into the hotel parking lot. Surely a hotel would still have public telephones. Once she was parked, as close to the door as possible so they wouldn't get wet, she searched her purse for quarters or a loonie.

"I've got one, Mom."

Hanna turned. There was Jake. Sitting in the back seat, faithfully in his seatbelt, his little hand reaching toward her, holding out a golden coin.

"You do?" she replied, trying her best to keep her voice from cracking.

What have I done to my son?

She'd tried her best to keep their increasingly dire circumstances from him. But Jake was a smart boy. She couldn't fool him forever. He knew times were tough. He knew they'd gone from three meals a day to two. He knew that most nights they were sleeping in the car because they couldn't find an affordable motel room. He knew it wasn't normal to have "sink showers" in public restrooms. He knew his mother had grown morosely sad and that when she smiled at him, there wasn't even a hint of joy left in her face.

"I left my piggy bank at home, like you told me," he said. "But I brought the money. Do you need some?"

"Oh no, honey, you save that. Mama just needs to make

a call. I'm looking for change for the phone."

"You trying to call Auntie Sheila again?"

A few weeks after she'd taken Jake and left Nigel, she realized she'd made a horrible mistake. She still wanted to be with Nigel. She desperately loved him. She began sending him emails from miscellaneous Internet cafes. She never used the same address more than twice. She wanted Nigel to know they were okay. And that despite what she'd done, she still loved him and hoped they could be together again one day. Nigel would write back. Only sometimes would she get the messages. She was paranoid. She feared there might be ways for the people who were after them to somehow trace her through email accounts, or through Nigel's. So on a regular basis she would abandon an email account and never use it again.

Nigel told her that he would do whatever he could to find a way for them to be together. A way to guarantee her and Jake a safe life. He understood this was the only way she'd ever consider being with him again. Hanna's first priority was to protect her child. He got that.

Nigel chose Singapore. He said it was far away, easy to get lost in, with plenty of English-speaking people. It would be the perfect place for them to begin their lives anew. But until he could make this new life happen, they came up with a plan to stay in touch. Hanna would call Sheila, her oldest friend, every two weeks. So would Nigel. Sheila would be their intermediary. When Nigel felt he'd established a life in Singapore, and that it was safe to do so, he would come back for them.

In the meantime, Hanna and Jake stayed in hiding. She

thought they were relatively secure, blanketed by anonymity. But then things changed. Hanna began to suspect someone had found them again. So she picked up their pieces and hit the road.

Money became scarce. She had fewer and fewer opportunities to contact Sheila. Now she was certain. Someone *was* on their tail. She had to stay vigilant twenty-four hours a day. She trusted the telephone and email even less.

But today was the day, Hanna admitted to herself. The day they hit rock bottom.

Powerful people with guns were after them. Hanna had no money left. She couldn't take the chance of being out in the open, never mind stay in one place long enough to get a job. They were in desperate need of help.

Hanna studied the parking lot. Dark. Wet. Vacant, except for guest cars long ago abandoned in favour of warm meals, warm beds, warm lives. It was late. Jake was groggy. He should be asleep. Still, she couldn't risk leaving him behind.

"Yeah, honey, I want to try calling Auntie Sheila one more time. Why don't you put up the hood of your coat so you can stay dry. I'll race you into the hotel."

Jake grinned and did as he was told.

Once inside, Hanna spotted a bank of pay phones in an alcove just off the lobby. She settled Jake into an armchair, where she could keep him in sight. She dialed the familiar number. Yet again, the phone in the Las Vegas apartment rang until an answering machine picked up.

"Sheila, it's me," Hanna said into the receiver, as usual not identifying herself.

"I've been trying you all day. I…I hope you're okay." She sighed, worried, then hung up.

She glanced over at Jake. He was waiting patiently in the chair. No video game. No book. No comic. Nothing. He had nothing. She had nothing to give him. And worse, his life was in grave danger. She began to cry. *Again! God I'm so tired! I can't do this anymore. I can't. I can't. I can't.*

Reaching into her soiled, pink purse, she pulled out a badly wrinkled scrap of paper. She hadn't touched it in months. But she always knew it was there. She straightened it out on the counter below the phone. Through tear-blurred eyes she quietly recited the numbers. She inserted another coin and dialed.

A voice answered after the third ring.

"It's me. Hanna. And Jake. We need help."

Chapter Twenty-One

I'd left a window open overnight. I woke up, chilled by early-morning air and serenaded by the cheerful trilling of a Western Meadowlark. I opened my eyes and feasted on the fluttering, sun-gilded leaves of a hearty birch silhouetted against the uninterrupted blue of a prairie sky. As my bare feet hit the ground, I marveled at how rested I felt. It had been the best night's sleep since…well, since I'd left home for London.

On the deck overlooking the backyard, I found Dad handing out plates of scrambled eggs and sausage. Anatole had his nose buried in his laptop. Surprisingly Alexandra was there too. Her hand was lying easily on her son's shoulder. I settled in next to her.

"You're back?" Dad asked, as if his only interest in the answer was to determine whether or not he should fix another plate of food.

"Sit, Dad. I can get it myself in a minute. I want to have my coffee first anyway. Sorry I got in so late last night. I hope I didn't wake you."

He shook his head, taking his place at the table.

"You took a taxi?"

"Yes."

"You didn't have to do that. I could have picked you up."

Our eyes met for a brief moment. I nodded. He nodded back.

"It's my birthday next weekend." He said it so quietly I wondered if I misheard the words.

Anatole's dark eyes made an appearance above the top of his computer. I was heartened to see that although he still wore one of his black, metal rocker t-shirts, he also had on a pair of three-quarter-length shorts and flip-flops. And, if I wasn't mistaken, his hair might have been trimmed so it no longer obscured his eyes.

"Really?" I said.

"Sixty-five."

I added that to the shamefully long list of important things I didn't know. Along with not knowing what to say. Happy birthday seemed a little lame. A lot lame.

Dad's eyes stayed on his plate of food. "I think I might start on some painting inside the house this week."

I thought about what Kate had said when she'd visited and nodded my approval.

"Your sister thinks we should have cake. Maybe have some neighbours over."

I swallowed. I looked at my sister. She looked at me.

"Dad," Alexandra said breezily, "maybe you shouldn't count on Adam being here for that. He's in some kind of trouble. Who knows where he'll be a week from now."

"Trouble?" Dad responded, sounding suitably concerned.

I shot both Alexandra and her son dark looks. I wondered how much Anatole had shared with his mother.

I tried for a big smile. "It's nothing, Dad. I need to take care of some CDRA business before then. But I'll try my best to be here."

"That would be good. The older you get the more important every birthday becomes," he said. "You'll see what I mean some day."

Anatole and I exchanged uneasy glances.

I felt my hand inch toward my father's. I didn't recall ever touching his hand before. I wanted to say: "I really do want to be here."

"He won't be here," Alexandra laid her bet.

"We'll see," Dad said, not in an unkind way.

My sister received the comment with a frown.

Dad wasn't about to let me off the hook quite so easily though. "Where are you going? When are you leaving?"

"I think that's why he's here," Anatole said, uncharacteristically not mumbling. "We're going to help him figure that out."

Oh? Really? We're just going to spill everything out on the table, are we?

Not in a million years was this how I would do things when I was with CDRA. Or could. In my work, confidentiality was key. But like almost everything else in my life, things had changed.

Go with it, Saint. You might like it.

"What are we trying to figure out exactly?" Alexandra asked Anatole. He'd obviously recruited her. Even stranger, she'd accepted. I was beginning to understand that their bond was stronger and tighter than I'd thought.

"Uncle Adam is looking for a woman named Hanna

Billings." All the while as he talked, Anatole tapped away at his keypad. He was bringing up websites and Word and Excel documents. He'd begun an extensive digital file on "my case."

"Who is she? Why are we looking for her?"

I needed to answer this. There were some things I was not yet ready to share.

"Hanna Billings was someone my company was protecting. She and her ten-year-old son went missing. We think their lives are in danger because of something she knows. I need to find them."

"In three days!" Anatole crowed, a little more excited by the prospect than I was.

"Three days? Says who?" Alexandra was asking the right questions.

"Never mind that," I said. "The important thing is that I find her. Anatole's been helping me look for clues that might tell me where she is."

My nephew's computer made the dwoop-dwoop sound that indicated he was receiving a Skype call.

"Oh good," he said. "It's Aunt Kate."

I froze.

My mind went back to a conversation I'd had with Nigel Congswell. He'd pointed a finger of suspicion at whoever it was who'd put me onto him in the first place. Kate. I couldn't believe it. I shouldn't. But a part of me had since constructed a wall of distrust. I had decided to keep my distance from Kate and pretty much everyone else except for the people sitting around this breakfast table. The Saints. Sudden contact from Kate had me troubled. How much had Anatole told her? Why was she calling?

Anatole made the connection and greeted his aunt. He then turned the screen so I could see my ex-wife's face, striking even when pixelated.

"Adam, I'm glad you're back," she responded upon seeing me. "Anatole told me there was some trouble. Are you all right? Do you have the—"

"I don't have the asset." I cut her off in case she had been about to say "the cure." That would lead to a number of difficult questions from my father and sister that I wasn't prepared to deal with. "It looks like that might not work out quite the way we hoped."

Kate's face changed. Her brow furrowed, her eyes grew moist, her jaw tightened.

She still cares.

I could feel the intensity of Anatole's stare. He too would know what my comments inferred.

After two seconds of silence, Kate snapped: "Adam, I need to talk with you in private."

"What's going on?" my sister wanted to know. "We know he's looking for this Hanna chick."

"Who's that?" Kate asked.

I looked at Anatole, wordlessly asking his permission to steal away with his precious laptop. He wasn't happy about it but bobbed his head ever so slightly.

Laptop—and Kate's face—in hand, I entered the kitchen, careful to close the door between it and the deck. I settled in the nook.

"Kate, the asset is not a thing, it's a person. A woman by the name of Hanna Billings. IIA wants to keep her, and the cure, from the rest of the world. They have a damn good reason. And if the world can't have the cure, neither should I."

For a moment, the face on the computer screen looked as if it were frozen. Then, "No, Adam. That's not acceptable!" Her voice grew louder and more forceful. "Someone is lying to you, Adam. The cure is available! You have to get it and bring it back!"

"Yes, Kate, I am. But not for me. I'm going to find Hanna Billings, save the lives of Nigel Congswell and a woman named Sheila Shellbrook, and put an end to a Russian madman." Even as I said it, I wondered how I was planning to do it all. "When I do, Kate, Hanna and the cure are going back to IIA."

Kate seemed to be settling. "This Hanna has the cure?"

"Yes." She didn't need to know more than that.

"And you *are* going to find her? You know where she is?"

"I am. And not yet."

"Okay."

I knew Kate still believed that I would change my mind and take the cure once it was in our possession. Like any good agent, she was thinking ten steps ahead but focusing hardest on step one.

"How can I help?"

"I don't know if you can. Hanna went off the grid a few months ago. The only people who may have had a sniff of where she'd be, where she'd go, are currently being held captive by the same Russian I ran into in Magadan, a General Develchko. He's given me three days to bring him the asset. The problem is, I have no idea where she is."

"That doesn't sound encouraging. APU is pretty tight about stuff like this. But I'll see if there is anything more I can dig up on her. I'll call you." This was the reason I'd allowed a crack in my wall of distrust. This and the fact I'd once loved this woman. Probably still did.

"If you can't reach me, try Anatole. I'll stay in regular contact with him, no matter where I am."

"Adam...."

"Yeah?" I held my breath.

"Good luck."

I nodded and snapped the laptop shut.

Sitting across from one another at the kitchen nook, each pounding away at the keys of our computers, Anatole and I were the digital information version of dueling pianos, without the music or entertainment value. Anatole did whatever it is that hackers do. I did whatever it is ex-government agents do. Both of us used whatever online resources, databases, search engines, information portals we could get our key-tapping fingers on, to search for Hanna Billings.

I'd just poured us fresh coffee when Anatole deliberately pushed aside his screen. "Uh, Uncle Adam?"

"Yup."

"I think we have a problem."

I lowered my screen as soon as I saw the look on my nephew's face. "What is it?"

"I think Nigel Congswell may have lied to you."

I shrugged. This was nothing new. "What about this time?"

"The asset. The cure for cancer. He told you his girlfriend, Hanna Billings, was the asset, right? That she discovered the cure?"

"Something like that."

"Well, I think the real story is something way different."

"Why? What's the problem?"

"Well, I don't know how Hanna Billings could have discovered the cure for cancer."

"Why not?"

"She's a hairdresser."

I sat up, jarring the table with my knee. "How do you know that?"

"I found her."

I stared at Anatole. He was grinning from ear to ear. A new look for him.

"You fantastic sonofabitch!" I proclaimed, moving closer to my nephew. "Tell me!"

"Well, you said we should try tracking her down by finding out where she came from. Where she grew up, where she went to school, anything. If we had some idea where she used to be, it might give us clues about where she'd be today. Makes sense."

I nodded, waiting for more.

"But that was like looking for Waldo. We know nothing about her. Except that Nigel Congswell was her protector guy for several years. I got to thinking that if Congswell was like her bodyguard or boyfriend or whatever, he would have been spending a lot of time with her, right? So maybe it would be easier looking for him instead of her. If they were together so much, wherever he was is where she was. So I started looking into his life."

"Brilliant."

"Yeah," Anatole agreed. "Especially since we already know a lot more about him than about her. I snooped around and got a look at Nigel's Visa bills during the same time period he was acting as her bodyguard…."

"Anatole, you…."

"Don't worry." He held up his hands in a pre-emptive defensive posture. "I've done it before. I know how to be safe."

I sucked in my cheeks and said nothing more. In a situation like this, if I could do on a computer what Anatole could, I probably would.

He kept on. "Up to a certain point, Congswell was spending all his time and money in Toronto. Then suddenly he was making credit card purchases at hotels and restaurants and businesses somewhere else."

My eyes widened. He truly did find her. "Where?"

"Dauphin, Manitoba."

We had her.

"There's no phone listing for a Hanna Billings, but that didn't surprise me. She wants to keep a low profile, or doesn't have a land line. But there were several other Billingses listed. One of them is probably a relative."

He kept on. "I checked, and both a Hanna Billings and a Sheila Shellbrook attended a local high school at the same time. It was good for us that neither of them got married or changed their last names. I guess she never married Jake's dad then, huh?"

I gave that a silent shrug, not wanting to interrupt the intelligence briefing.

"Pre-school records from a while back show that a Hanna Billings pre-registered her son Jake. The registration form gave me her address, post-secondary education history, and work information."

"Finally," I murmured, already formulating a plan in my head. "Something I can work with."

"But, Uncle Adam, what I want to know is how does a hairdresser discover the cure for cancer?"

I spent the next few minutes filling Anatole in on what I'd learned from Develchko in Vegas.

I finished up with: "Anatole, you've done incredible work on this. I couldn't have done it better myself."

He pushed the hair off his face and attempted his second crooked smile of the day. Who was this kid? I reached over and planted one on his temple. He recoiled and made a sound like a sick cat.

Hanna Billings, I'm coming for you.

Chapter Twenty-Two

Hanna Billings was not a researcher, a brilliant scientist, or an oncologist who discovered the cure for cancer. I already knew this. What I had not known was that she'd been a hairdresser in Dauphin, Manitoba.

It was my first bread crumb. My fervent hope was that she'd left more of them in Dauphin.

I had less than three days to find out.

I had two leads to pursue. Hanna's hometown. And Maryann Knoble.

Nigel had mentioned Knoble a number of times. She'd been his primary contact at IIA. More than anyone else, she was sure to have information about Hanna Billings. I was betting that Maryann Knoble knew many things.

I jumped back on my computer and checked flights. There was only one airline, Perimeter, that served Dauphin's small airport. I could fly to Winnipeg and catch the second and last Perimeter flight of the day to Dauphin at 5:55 p.m. But only if I left immediately.

As I powered down the laptop and prepared to leave, I spoke quickly to Anatole.

"I arrive in Dauphin at six-forty this evening. I'll need a hotel. By the time I land, I want you to tell me which of those Billingses in the phone book are related to Hanna. And if there's anyone else in town I can talk to who knows Hanna or Jake or Sheila Shellbrook. If I'm going to spend the night in Dauphin, I want it to be worth it. I'll be back in Winnipeg tomorrow morning at eight-forty. I want you to get me on the next possible flight to Toronto after that. Rent me a car. Something nice. And see if you can get Kate to find out what Maryann Knoble's schedule is tomorrow. As much detail as possible. Clock is ticking. Got all that?"

"Got it!" he shouted, as I exited on the run.

I made a hasty U-turn, ran back into the room, and did what I could to mess up Anatole's new hairdo before leaving for good.

Dauphin, surrounded by fertile farmland, is one of those naturally beautiful Canadian towns you see in travel brochures. It's situated in the heart of Manitoba's most spectacularly scenic region known as the Parkland. It's the kind of place you'd expect to find Ukrainian milkmaids enjoying picnics in fields of sunflowers. Except, of course, in the winter when icy blizzards are legendary.

As promised, Perimeter's propeller plane—say that fast five times—deposited me at Dauphin's tiny, blue and white airport building precisely at 6:40 p.m. Once inside, I checked my email. Good old Anatole already had me booked on a 9:00 a.m. flight out of Winnipeg tomorrow morning, arriving in Toronto at 12:17. It was a tight connection, but there was another flight at 10:20 should I need it. Avis would have a car waiting there for me.

For tonight, he had me booked at Canway Inn & Suites, which offered private entrances, a pool, in-room coffee, and Jacuzzi hot tub suites. The hotel was also connected to a Smitty's Family Restaurant and, more importantly, the Internet.

Anatole's message said he was still working on getting information about Maryann Knoble but listed plenty of Dauphin residents, along with phone numbers and home addresses, who might have information about Hanna Billings's current whereabouts.

I took a few moments to study a map of the area, then jumped into a taxi. I gave the cabbie a $100 bill and asked him to stay with me for the night. We both resisted the obvious joke.

It was early evening. In the hope of catching someone there before they closed shop for the day, my first stop was Hanna's former place of employment. Bouffant Salon on Main Street looked like it had recently undergone a facelift. The colour scheme was dark chocolate, offset by a much lighter cream that reminded me of vanilla pudding. The air held on to a faint scent of paint, mixed with hair chemicals and flowery perfume.

"Who do you have an appointment with?" the receptionist, young enough for high school, asked me when I stepped inside. Her smile was uncomfortably seductive.

"I'm looking for Hanna," I told her.

"Hanna?" she said with a smack of her gum. "I'm pretty sure she doesn't work here anymore. Not for a long time. How about Denise? She's free right now. Or Shelley is just about done."

Behind the girl, I could see six cutting stations. Only

one was occupied by a stylist and client.

"Which one's been here the longest?"

"They've both been here forever. Long before me. They're both really good though. Shelley was Manitoba Stylist of the Year a couple years ago. But Denise does more men." She giggled at what she'd just said. "I mean, like, she does their hair."

"Okay, I'll give Denise a try then."

"Great. I'll take you to her chair." She did so, then, "I'll go get her. You can tell her what you want. She's in the back having coffee. You want some? Or some water?"

"No thanks."

"Okey-dokey."

A minute later, Denise was at my back. Our eyes met in the mirror in front of us. Before she even said hello, her fingers were running through my hair.

"You've got gorgeous hair," she said with a megawatt smile, rivaling the receptionist for sultriness. "I hope you don't want me to cut it all off. The shaved head look is really hot nowadays. You could totally pull it off too. But just between you and me," she whispered, leaning in so close I could feel her bosom pressed against my shoulder, "a girl likes something to hold on to." She pulled back. "What's your name, honey?"

"Saint. Adam Saint."

"Glad to meet you, Adam. So what'll it be?"

"Well, Denise, I'm not here for a cut."

Her confused face looked more like a pout. "Just a shampoo and blow then?"

"I'm looking for Hanna Billings. I thought since you

used to work with her, you might know where she is."

The pout stayed in place. "Yeah, Hanna used to work here. But that was a long time ago. She's been gone for quite a while. Left us in a real lurch too. Didn't give notice or anything. Just didn't show up for work one day."

"Were you a friend of hers? Or maybe Shelley was?" I could see Shelley at the chair across from Denise's, watching us in the mirror like a hawk on rabbit. She was mindlessly teasing the thinning hair of a nasty looking octogenarian.

"Sure. We'd all go out for drinks now and then. But we weren't real close, you know? She had a kid. So that kinda cramped her style, I guess. She really sacrificed a lot for that kid. Spent a lot of time with him. You have any kids, Adam?"

"No."

"You're single then?" Despite the fact that I wasn't there for service, she was still rummaging through my hair.

I was about to say no when I realized…I was. "Yeah."

"Is that why you're looking for Hanna? Are you an old boyfriend or something like that?"

"What do you want with Hanna?" Shelley brashly inserted herself into the conversation, her question sounding more like a warning.

"I'm an old friend. I heard she might be having some troubles. I thought I might be able to help."

"What sort of trouble?" Denise wondered. "Single moms are always having trouble, aren't they? Money. Men. Mortgage. You name it."

I kept my eyes locked on Shelley via the mirror. "I think this is a little more serious than that. I think she really might need my help."

Shelley sucked in her cheeks, then looked away, refocusing on the few strands of hair left on her client's head. "Can't help you. Like Tiffany told you, Hanna hasn't worked here in a long time."

Tiffany was the receptionist. Shelley didn't miss a beat around here. She'd obviously been listening in to that conversation as well.

"Is there someone else who works here who maybe spent more time with Hanna? A close friend maybe?"

Denise began to say something, but Shelley cut her off with precision as sharp as her scissors. "No, I don't think so. Denise, why don't you show Mr. Saint out? It's just about closing time. Sorry we couldn't help you out."

I doubted her sincerity.

"Listen," I said to Shelley as Denise herded me toward the front door. "I'm going to leave my card with Tiffany." I tossed a card with my cell number on it onto the receptionist's counter. "I'm at the Canway Inn tonight. Just in case you think of something, or someone who might help me. It's important, Shelley."

She acted as if she hadn't heard me, suddenly intensely interested in her customer.

Denise laid a hand on my bicep as she opened the door for me. "If you want a cut, or a shave, or anything at all," she winked, "you come right back here and ask for Denise, okay, honey?"

I winked back. "I wouldn't think of going anywhere else."

For a variety of reasons, Anatole was convinced that of all the Billingses in the Dauphin phone book, Ted and Gail Billings were the most likely candidates to be Hanna's parents.

Arriving at their home on Crocus Bay, the evening had grown dusky, the setting sun diffused in a feather blanket of clouds. I knocked on the door and waited. Just as I was about to try a second time, it opened. The woman looking out at me had a warm smile. Her greying, chestnut hair was styled into a pageboy that framed a square, pleasant face.

"Hello? Can I help you?"

"I hope so," I responded with an optimistic smile. "My name is Adam Saint. I'm with the International Intelligence Agency." A little white lie. "We were…working with your daughter, Hanna."

The woman's smile faded faster than a cheap t-shirt. After a false start or two, the woman said, "I don't understand what you want here."

"Could I come in and talk to you about Hanna?"

"I don't think so." She seemed nervous now. I could tell she was considering pulling back and slamming the door in my face. I had to say something to keep her talking.

"You're Hanna's mother?"

"Of course."

"I need to talk with you. I hope you can help us locate Hanna…."

"Locate her? Who are you?" Now she was alarmed. I'd played the game wrong.

"I'd like to see your ID please."

All I had was my driver's license. Somehow I didn't think that was going to suffice. "Mrs. Billings, I believe your daughter may be in danger. I really—"

The door slammed shut in my face. Just as I'd predicted. Shit.

I knocked again.

No answer.

Then again.

The porch light went out. My superior deductive skills led me to believe I was not about to get an invitation inside.

I turned to make my way back down the cement pathway that led to the curb and my waiting taxi. I was only halfway there when I sensed a massive force rushing up behind me. I whirled about and with reflexive action landed a chop in the crook between my attacker's neck and shoulder. I followed this up with a left uppercut to his gut, just as he was reacting to the sharp pain from my first hit. You kinda don't want to sneak up on a guy like me.

The man doubled over, stumbled, then fell to the ground with a grunt. At the same time, I heard an anguished cry coming from the front porch. Mrs. Billings. Then a rough "Hey! What's going on?" from the street. The cab driver.

Ignoring them, I lowered myself like a bat over the man who'd come after me. I filled his entire line of sight with my bulk. I placed my face in his. It was an old what-to-do-when-you-see-a-wild-animal-in-the-forest trick. I don't guarantee that making yourself appear big and menacing will work with a bear, but I know from experience, it often does the trick with more domesticated species.

The man lying on the ground, looking up at me with wide eyes, had to be in his seventies. His skin was tanned— probably from a lifetime of fieldwork in the sun, rather than lolling about on a beach—and loose around the jowls. What was left of his hair was an indecipherable colour between white and grey. He wore eyeglasses that were now askew and a plaid shirt beneath suspenders that held up dark brown pants. As we stared at one another, I had the sinking feeling I'd just taken down Hanna Billings's elderly father.

But he started it.

Despite his supine position, I saw the simmering rage in Ted Billings' face. His bottom lip was quivering, watery eyes washed over me with undisguised contempt. I was about to raise myself up and offer a hand to the man when suddenly his arms wrapped themselves around my neck like the tentacles of an octopus. Our faces were less than two inches apart. I could feel the damp heat of his breath on my cheek, his grip quivering but holding strong.

"How dare you?" His voice was hushed but powerful. "How dare you come to my home and ask for help finding my daughter? When it was *you* who took her away from us in the first place!"

"Mr. Billings, if we could jus—"

"Everything was fine. Then one day, she tells us she thinks something might be wrong. She calls you people. The next day she's gone. Forever. She and Jake. My only daughter. My only grandson. Gone. As if they're dead. No goodbye. No explanations. Just gone. Poof. Into thin air. And all you people can say is that it's for everyone's safety. You say it's best we don't know where they are. You tore our family apart! As far as we're concerned, you killed our daughter. You took her away without even letting us say one last pitiful goodbye.

"How would *your* father like that?" he kept at it. "Huh? If I squeezed tighter, I could kill you right now."

I highly doubted it but tried to pull away from the man anyway. With surprising strength, he held firm as if his own life depended on it.

"How would that make your father feel? No chance for one last hug. One last kiss goodbye. No last words. No chance to say how much he loves you. How about that, huh? What do you think of that?"

Ted Billings's eyes never moved off mine. And mine did not move off his. When he was done talking, I could see he was beginning to cry. His hold began to loosen. I could have easily broken free. But for some reason I felt I owed it to him not to. Instead I lay there, suctioned to him, taking the verbal beating, his words lacerating me with their sharp edges and brutal intent. Suddenly a horrible picture flashed into my head. Instead of Ted Billings on that lawn, it was my own father, his shoulders trembling with the force of unrelenting tears as he held on to me...to my dead body.

"Ted, no! Ted, please let go," Gail wailed, running toward us.

"What is this?" the confused cabbie wondered. He was out of the cab, inching toward the melee on the Billings's front lawn. "Should I call the police, lady?"

Billings released me. I fell backwards and rolled onto my back. We were now lying side by side on the ground, facing the darkening sky, breathing heavily.

"I think you should go, Mr. Saint," Gail Billings whispered.

Slumped over Smitty's bar, having washed down half a hamburger with two Labatt Blues, I mulled over my decision to come to Dauphin. I only had three days to find Hanna Billings. Had I just wasted one on a bad call?

I'd made seven stops that evening, questioning people whom Anatole suspected had a connection to Hanna. None had gone well. After the fourth or fifth stop, I began to suspect that a phone call, likely from Ted Billings, had preceded me. I'd been shut out. No one was telling me anything useful. They admitted to knowing Hanna. But when I asked if they had any guesses as to where she might be, the blank stares were carbon copies of one another. I couldn't decide if they were simply trying to protect their hometown girl or if they truly didn't know anything.

"Hi," said a female voice from down the bar, to my right.

I'd noticed the woman when I came in about an hour earlier. She'd nursed a single beer the entire time but downed several shots of something clear. Tequila likely. It was getting late. Most of the diners had departed, leaving only one or two tables occupied. Other than myself and the woman, there was one other guy at the other far end of the bar. He was a middle-aged, overweight, salesman type guy, who drank dark rum and Coke like it was water. I didn't want his hangover tomorrow morning.

I nodded at the woman and returned the greeting. She was attractive in a simple, understated way. She had big eyes—dark blue with flecks of green. Her hair was thick and lustrous, falling in heavy, auburn waves that framed a pretty, round face. She wore very little makeup—that I could tell. She'd started out in a light jacket over jeans. But as the evening progressed and shots added up, she'd peeled off the jacket, revealing a tight white t-shirt that did exactly what a tight white t-shirt should.

"You from here?" she asked.

"No."

"Same. I'm here on business. What about you?"

"Same." She wasn't a highly skilled interrogator, especially if she was looking for more than one-word answers from a guy like me who didn't want to talk. But something about the woman made me instantly like her. She had a compassionate face. I liked the sound of her voice. I had nothing else to do in Dauphin until my early-morning flight. I decided to make *her* talk. "What kind of business are you in?"

"Sales. I'm a traveling rep."

"What's your product?"

"Farm equipment."

I must have had a surprised look on my face, because she followed up with: "What? Were you thinking beauty products for Shoppers Drug Mart, or something like that?" Every fourth word bordered on slurred.

"Not at all. Actually I was thinking fertilizer or salt blocks."

She smiled and downed a shot, waving for another when she was done.

"Can I buy you a drink then, Misterrrrrrrr...?"

"Saint. And thanks, no. I think I'm at my limit for tonight."

The woman picked up her beer and closed the two-bar-stool distance between us, settling in next to me. She smelled great.

"I'm Theresa. You'll have to forgive me for being a little tipsy," she said, sounding flirty. "I'm celebrating a big sale."

"Congratulations." I signaled to the barkeeper as he delivered her next drink. "Put that on my tab."

The bartender looked at Theresa. She hesitated, then nodded.

"That's very nice of you. Thank you."

"You're very welcome."

She leaned in, so close I felt the skin of her lips against my ear. "Do you have a room here?"

My body immediately instructed me to say, "Hell yes, let's go."

But I didn't. The woman was inebriated. I had too many other things to focus on. Besides, who was I kidding? I was…emotionally screwed.

Theresa leaned back, awaiting my answer.

I smiled and kissed her on the cheek. "I haven't had such a wonderful offer in a very long time. But I think we've both had too much to drink. I wouldn't want either of us to wake up with regret tomorrow morning. But tell you what I'd love to walk you to your room."

Pulling back even further, Theresa's demeanour suddenly transformed. She straightened in her stool and squared her shoulders. Her eyes were clear, and her jaw was set tight. When she spoke, there wasn't a hint of drunkenness in her words. "That won't be necessary," she said. The woman was stone cold sober.

Chapter Twenty-Three

"You just paid for a shot of water, big spender," Theresa told me as she glanced at the bartender and said, "Mel, is it okay if we use one of your booths?"

The man bobbed his head.

Theresa faced me again. "Can we talk?"

I should have known something was up. Theresa was not a good enough actress to pull off being blotto. And when she moved closer to me, I couldn't smell hard alcohol on her breath or from the shot glass. But being a typical egotistical male with raging hormones and tight jeans, I ignored the signs.

I followed Theresa to a booth against the back wall of the dim restaurant.

"You're Adam Saint?"

I ignored the fact that she knew my first name (I'd only volunteered my last)—for the moment. "Care to let me in on what's going on here?"

"Shelley called me. From Bouffant. And so did Hanna's dad. They said you thought Hanna might be in trouble and that you wanted to help. Is that true?"

"You know Hanna?"

She nodded, her eyes abruptly threatening tears. "She's

my best friend. Hanna and I and another girl have been best friends since grade three."

"Is Sheila Shellbrook the other girl?"

Theresa's eyes widened. "You know Sheila?"

This was good. I finally had some leverage. "I'm afraid both Hanna *and* Sheila are in danger."

"What? Sheila too? How can that be? What do you mean?"

"Theresa, some not very nice men have taken Sheila captive. They won't let her go until I find Hanna."

"Oh God," she cried, torturing the napkin in her hands. "This is getting worse every second."

"Theresa, you have to tell me what you know."

She hesitated, weighing her options, wondering whether talking to me was going to help her friends or hurt them even more. Not an enviable position to be in. "Shelley and Mr. Billings told me you were in town looking for Hanna. They said if you came to see me, I shouldn't tell you anything. They don't know you, or whether you can be trusted."

"I understand that, Theresa. I just don't have the time to build that trust. Your friends are in big trouble. I need your help right now."

"It's gotten to the point where we can't trust anybody," she said, frustration evident in her voice. She held my eye. "When you didn't show up at my house, I just...I had to come see you. Shelley told me where you were staying. I thought if I talked to you, tested you somehow, I could decide for myself if I could trust you."

Now it was my turn to widen my eyes. "Are you saying

that if I had agreed to invite you back to my room for sex just now, you wouldn't have told me anything? That was your test?"

"And we most definitely would *not* have had sex either," she retorted.

"Theresa, do you know where Hanna is?"

A fat tear rolled down the young woman's face. She stared at me, seemingly unable to say a word. But her eyes were speaking volumes.

"Theresa, you have to tell me what you know. I know I'm a stranger to you. You already know my name is Adam Saint. I used to work for the organization that was looking after Hanna for all those years. I know about Jake. I know she has something—"

"Do you know Nigel?"

"Hanna fell in love with Nigel."

I could see Theresa's chest move faster. She was beginning to believe me. "Yes, she did."

"Nigel is being held with Sheila. In Las Vegas."

"What do they want with Hanna? Why is everyone after her?"

I shook my head. Apparently Hanna had been successful in keeping her secret, even from her best friends. She was a determined woman. But I was hoping she wasn't so determined that she'd abandoned her girlfriends altogether. Obviously Nigel thought Sheila knew something. It's why he went to Las Vegas in the first place. And now I was with the third in the trio of friends. Hopefully Hanna had confided in *both* of them.

"I can't answer that, Theresa," I lied easily. "All I know

is that Hanna knows something that the Canadian government wants to keep secret. But someone else found out about it. They want to get it from her. And they'll do anything."

She continued to stare at me, breathing heavy, considering, judging, assessing me.

"Theresa, we're running out of time. We have to find Hanna now."

"Wait, wait, wait!" she cried out, holding up a hand, stifling another tear. "I have to think. I have to be sure about this. I don't want to be the one to get Hanna into further trouble."

"Theresa, you might be the only one who can save her now."

"If these men want Hanna in exchange for Sheila and Nigel, exactly what are you going to do when you find her?"

Excellent question. I reached over and grabbed the woman's trembling hands and buried them in my own. "Theresa, I'm going to be honest with you. I don't know the answer to that yet. What I *do* know is that I will give my own life if it means saving Hanna, and Jake, and Sheila." Nigel, I wasn't so sure about yet. What Theresa didn't need to know was that the life I was so willing to give up wasn't worth what it once was.

Silence.

Then: "She called me."

"When?"

"A couple of days ago. She's been calling Sheila and me every couple of weeks or so. She just needed something to hold on to from home, you know. Someone to talk to. She was too scared to call her mom and dad. Or anyone else from the family. She was scared their phones might be tapped or something.

"After she left Nigel, she and Jake got in the car and headed first east and then west. She wanted to get lost. She thought she'd find some small town, where no one knew her or Jake. And it worked. At first. But then she started to talk about weird stuff."

"Weird how?"

"She thought someone might be following her. Or watching her. She started moving around more and more. From town to town. We started hearing from her less often. And when we did, she'd sound scared and tired and just… well, not the Hanna we knew. Sheila and I were getting so worried about her. We told her to come home. That we'd find a way to work it all out. But she said that was impossible."

"What happened when she called the last time, Theresa?"

"She sounded just horrible. She was sick. And she was so frightened." Theresa took a moment to swallow her tears. "She said someone tried to kill Jake. I just…I didn't know what to say or do about that. It all seems so…unreal. I mean stuff like this just doesn't happen in a life like mine. Do you think it could be true?"

I nodded.

She was silent for a moment, taking that in. Then, "Ever since then, they've been on the move non-stop. But the money had dried up. The last time she called, she said she was one…." She stopped, again choked by tears.

I went to the bar and brought back a glass of water. She gratefully swallowed some.

"She told me she was one meal away from not being able to feed Jake. Oh, God…." Tears threatened again. "It just tore me up to hear that. You don't know Hanna, but she is such a beautiful girl, inside and out. And more than anything, she loves that boy. To think she couldn't feed him, or keep him safe…it would tear her apart."

"Did she ask for money?"

"She needed help. She didn't know what to do. She said she couldn't reach Sheila…oh…maybe because those men already had her…?"

I nodded.

"This is so messed up."

I agreed.

"I asked her where she was. She told me. I have friends who live nearby. On an acreage. It's someplace I thought would be safe. I told her to go there and that I'd set it up with my friends before she arrived. She and Jake could have a place to stay, food, a bed. Whatever they needed. She's on her way there now."

"Where, Theresa? Where is Hanna?"

Back in my hotel room, I contacted Anatole on Skype and told him to cancel my travel plans to Toronto. I was coming home. Hanna Billings had headed west. She'd ended up in North Battleford, a small community an hour's drive from Saskatoon.

"Anatole," I said to my nephew, whose black hair seemed to have taken on a life of its own—or had he been asleep? "Does your mother Skype?"

"Of course. She says it's the only way she gets to talk to me, which she seems to like to do on a freakishly regular basis."

"Can you try getting her online?"

"She's at work, but hold on."

Within a minute, I saw my sister's face in a small screen at the bottom of my laptop screen. There was a great deal of noise and activity in the background. Funny thing about dives, they never seem to be short of business.

"What do you want?" she snapped, obviously distracted by other activities within her line of vision.

"Anatole, would it be okay if I spoke to your mother alone for a minute?"

"I'm an adult, you know."

"I know that. But this is…brother/sister stuff. Okay?"

"G'night." And with that, he was offline.

"Nice one, bro. You just hurt my son's feelings."

"I'll make it up to him. Alexandra, I need a favour."

"What is it?"

I hesitated, not quite sure if I was doing the right thing, on many levels.

"Alexandra, I'm coming home…."

"Great. I'll book a parade."

"When I get there…I'm going to need some guns."

She grinned. "Let me get a paper and pen."

I shook my head and wondered if this was going to turn out to be the worst decision of my life.

The moon was full and bright as a light bulb. The old kind, not a halogen. He swung open the terrace door and stepped outside. The coolness of the flagstone felt good on his bare feet. Chilled night air wrapped itself around his naked chest, but he didn't care. After the prolonged heat wave of the past few weeks, the bracing cold was invigorating. He leaned against a stone balustrade, drink in hand, staring at the marvel in the sky. Just as he'd done last night. And the night before that. And the night before that. He couldn't remember the last time he'd slept through the night. He didn't know if it was the medication prescribed by the new doctor he'd been forced to find after that damn fool Yelchin killed himself, or if something graver was to blame.

Life had become increasingly complex since his diagnosis. At first, the plan seemed foolproof. Well, as foolproof as you can get when putting matters of life and death in the hands of people other than yourself.

Almost at the exact same moment that Milo Yelchin broke the news to Ross Campbell that he was dying of cancer, the plan had begun formulating in his head. Campbell had known for years that IIA was hiding a cure. He didn't know why. Or what form it took. He had no reason to care. Until now.

In general, Campbell considered himself to be a moral man. There'd been only a time or two in his entire life when he'd seen fit to temporarily remould his morals in order to fit a very specific, one-of-a-kind situation. Every man in the world who held a position of considerable power, such as he did, had done the same. Whether or not they'd admit it was another story. It came with the territory. In this particular case, the decision was less difficult, for it had to do with personal preservation. His life, simply, was too good to give up. Ross Campbell had everything. Money. Career. Good looks. How could he possibly throw it all away without trying every possible means to hold on to it?

Somewhere in his past, he could hear someone blather on about "If you don't have your health, you don't have anything." He hadn't paid much attention to the words at the time. He'd always been superbly healthy and hearty, and had come from a long-lived family. His father lived to eighty-eight, his mother to ninety-three. There were no significant illnesses in his family history. Hell, he rarely even caught a cold. He ate right, exercised, drank in moderation, never smoked or did drugs. Whenever the stresses of his job—of which, admittedly, there were many—threatened to overcome him, he booked a long weekend someplace expensive and took advantage of his bloated bank account. Those weekends solved almost anything that dared to ail him.

Until Yelchin said the word.

Cancer.

Followed up by the only word worse to hear.

Terminal.

Beginning on that day, Campbell's sole goal in life became to find the cure. Which, providentially, proved to be more plausible than it sounded. It was preposterous to believe that it was simple happenstance that he worked for an organization that was hiding a cure for what was about to kill him. This was fate. Although, if he was honest, up until then, he was not a believer in fate. Or rather, he supported doing whatever you needed to in order to control your own fate, which was exactly what he'd decided to do.

Campbell spent the next weeks on his covert operation. He used at will, and often, his high clearance level at IIA to hack into Asset Protection Unit files. What he learned was troubling. It wasn't clear what the cure was, but he did discover that the lead agent assigned to the asset for many years, Nigel Congswell, had recently left IIA under muddled circumstances. Even worse, it appeared that IIA was no longer in control of the asset. Just his luck. For ten years, IIA had maintained the safety of a cure for cancer, only to lose control of it when he needed it.

Ross Campbell was an eminently intelligent man. Intelligent men are acutely aware of both their own strengths and weaknesses. Campbell recognized that the skills required to hunt down the cure, particularly given the time constraints, were not within his particular wheelhouse. He was a man who did his best work behind a desk. He needed someone else. Someone with the expertise to barrel into the world and blast his way through every obstacle until he met his goal. Someone who would be as steadfastly dedicated and committed to finding the cure as he. Someone he could control. Only one name came to mind.

A sudden noise jarred Campbell from his reverie. He spun about, spilling the drink he'd yet to taste.

"Sweetheart, you shouldn't be out here without a shirt on. God, Ross, you've gotten so thin. Come inside. The last thing you need is to catch a cold." It was Campbell's fiancée, standing in the doorway, wrapped tightly in a bathrobe.

I don't catch colds.

But that was his old life.

His heart melted a little each time he looked at the woman. If only they had met earlier. Perhaps, Campbell thought, he might be a different man today. Deep inside, he knew he *didn't* have everything. Not really. What he had was quantity. Not quality. This woman could change things. If only they could have more time together. If only....

"Couldn't sleep again?" she asked when he didn't respond.

"No."

She gave him the look. He was noticing it more and more. Sympathy. He hated it.

"It's four a.m. Come inside. I can make you something hot to drink."

"It's okay. I'll just stay out for a few minutes longer."

"You sure?"

He nodded. "You go back to bed. I'll be there soon."

Kate Spalding turned and headed indoors.

Chapter Twenty-Four

When Ross Campbell and Kate Spalding began dating, they kept it quiet. Although they rarely worked together, it still wouldn't be appropriate for IIA's second-in-command to be seen fraternizing with an employee. Plus, Kate was still married to another agent, Adam Saint.

It wasn't until much later that Campbell realized just how important his relationship with Kate would prove to be.

Choosing Saint to procure the cure for him was a slam-dunk decision. Whereas Campbell was a bureaucrat through and through, Saint, as IIA's most experienced and senior disaster recovery agent, had superior training in intelligence gathering, reconnaissance, physical combat, and international relations. Whatever expertise might be needed to find and deliver the cure, Saint had in spades.

There were two major obstacles.

The first was Saint's reputation. Yes, he could be tough, duplicitous when he needed to be, uncompromising when the situation called for it, but overall, he was known to be clean. Too clean to be swayed into treading morally unsteady ground. To do what Campbell needed doing would take someone who was not only willing to bend the rules, but disregard them altogether.

Which led to the second problem. Geoffrey Krazinski.

Saint took his orders from Krazinski. He trusted him. They were friends. Or at least as close friends as men like them had. If Krazinski said, "Saint, find the cure for cancer," Saint would do it. But Krazinski was nearly as bad as Saint. He was a frustratingly inflexible rule-follower. When it came to doing something even somewhat ethically or legally vague, even for a good cause—to save Campbell's life—he would never budge. At least not without a series of long, verbose, useless meetings. Meetings that Campbell did not have the time nor the patience for. This was his life on the line. And time was running out.

One thing became very clear early on.

Krazinski had to die.

To get to Saint, Campbell needed a clear path. Unfortunately, Krazinski was blocking it.

It was too bad really. Campbell genuinely liked Krazinski. But not enough to allow him the power to keep him from saving his own life. It was the age-old dilemma: you find yourself in deep water; you can swim, your partner cannot; what do you do? You swim to shore and save your own life. Or you try to save your partner. His flailing and panic will threaten to pull you under, deplete your strength, and increase the risk that neither of you will ever get to shore. What do you do? To Campbell, there was no debate; the answer was always clear. You save yourself, of course.

Killing Krazinski was not difficult. As head of CDRA, Krazinski, like Campbell himself, was more of a talking head than active agent. Even so, for him to find himself in an exceedingly dangerous situation would not seem unusual.

A fatal accident in such a situation would be lamentable but nothing to arouse suspicion. The—truly—accidental death of Canada's Governor General in the right place at the right time was the perfect impetus.

Saint, who normally would have pulled duty on such a high-ranking case, was out of reach. It took very little manipulating, and a few well-timed remarks to Krazinski—in Maryann Knoble's presence—to convince him to travel to Magadan himself.

Over the years, Campbell had become familiar with varieties of unsavoury characters throughout the world. Mercenaries, hit men, dictators, dirty politicians, Third World tyrants, autocrats, tormentors, martinets. Agree with their methods or not, such people were an undeniable part of the fabric of doing business on a worldwide scale.

Campbell had always expected that one day he might find himself in need of a favour from the dark side. So it was through these illicit connections that Campbell was first put in contact with Develchko, a dirty general with the Russian army. He was, Campbell's associates made clear, more than willing to broker a deal that would result in Krazinski's unfortunate demise when the opportunity presented itself.

What surprised Campbell was the price. International assassination was not cheap. Campbell did not have vast sums of money just sitting around. And certainly not stashed in such a way that it could not be traced to him should Krazinski's death, his dealings with Develchko, or both, ever be investigated. The negotiations were tense and in danger of failing.

It was Develchko himself who saved the day. When it became apparent Campbell could not pay the bill, Develchko inquired whether he had anything else of value he could give up instead. Campbell knew what Develchko was talking about. The General knew Campbell was a high-ranking official for an international agency with close ties to the Canadian government.

At first doubtful that Canada would have anything that he could possibly want, Develchko was keen to play the espionage game. He wanted secrets. Secrets that could propel him up the ladder within the ranks of his own government.

Although Campbell may have been willing to compromise in some areas, even contemplating murder in order to save his own skin, he had no intention of becoming a traitor. When his time came, Campbell intended to be remembered as a great statesman and patriot, not a turncoat. No, he would not give away secrets. There had to be another way.

Campbell knew that rushed plans are often full of holes. But this one was born of genius. Not only would he not have to pay Develchko anything, but the Russian would actually pay him. Campbell *did* have something of value to give up. The cure for cancer. Once he was done with it, once he had the cure, had used it for himself, what further need did he really have for it?

Develchko was willing to bite but not without proof.

Desperate again, Campbell went deeper into APU files. He used his unquestioned authority to find out more. He identified a susceptible target, Rebecca Castlegard, and manipulated the junior APU agent into revealing that, although the asset was indeed MIA, there was a small sample being cryogenically stored in the IIA vaults. That was the hard part. Getting access to the vaults and the sample was relatively easy.

Campbell had his proof. He overnighted the sample along with a description of a battery of tests pioneered by APU physicians that would confirm the sample's status. By late the next day, Develchko's team had verified the sample, Rebecca Castlegard was on her way to exile, and Campbell has his assassin in place.

Develchko promised to dispose of Krazinski. Then, upon delivery of the cure, he would also deliver 250 million rubles into a bank account of Campbell's choice.

Ten. Million. Dollars.

Free and clear. Not only had Campbell managed to save his own life, he'd set himself up to live happily ever after. It was understood, of course, that if Campbell failed to deliver the cure, repercussions would be grim. Then again, Campbell thought, if he were unsuccessful in acquiring the cure, his life wouldn't be worth a plug nickel anyway.

The plane went down. Within hours, Krazinski was on his way to Magadan. Develchko and his men, conveniently already in Russia, easily made it there ahead of him. Then poof! Krazinski was dead. Step one was complete.

Step two was convincing Adam Saint to go after the cure. Campbell knew of only one foolproof way to instill in the agent the same level of fanatical, zealous passion and dedication to the pursuit as he himself had. Saint also had to die.

Campbell planned his second murder. The lovely fringe benefit? His victim didn't *actually* have to die.

Adam Saint only needed to *believe* he was dying. From the same illness Campbell suffered. Despite the tiresomely gushing things people might say about Saint, Campbell knew he was still a man like any other. A man who, when faced with his own demise, would fight tooth and nail to save himself. Self-defence was part of his goddamned training after all. Saint would want to live. Campbell knew that, not unlike himself, Saint lived a charmed life. Fancy cars. Fancy house. Healthy paycheque. And with the way he looked, he could get any woman he wanted. When the other option is death, why shouldn't he use his talents to save himself?

Unfortunately it wasn't as easy as opening up a nice big can of cancer and feeding it to the man. He'd need to devise another way to convince Saint that he was dying. Campbell, ever resourceful, knew how. The secret behind any successful plot is to know who to use, when, and how. Campbell's plan entailed using three people. Krazinski and Saint were the first two. The third was Milo Yelchin.

Of all of them, Yelchin was the easiest. It didn't take much research for Campbell to discover the doctor's Achilles heel. Married, with two children to support, Milo Yelchin was in deep financial trouble. His predicament had been brought on by years of addiction to gambling and prostitutes. A costly combination, even if you did pull in a salary in the high six figures.

As with Krazinski, Campbell liked Milo Yelchin. Unlike with Krazinski, the plan necessitated Campbell having to reveal his treachery to Yelchin by way of blackmail instead of behind his back by way of murder. For a man like Campbell, the former was the lesser of the two evils.

With little choice, Yelchin went along with the plan. His role was to convince Saint that his days were numbered. With that accomplished, he'd offer to personally and privately oversee every step of Saint's treatment regimen until the very end. During the course of the "treatment," Yelchin would administer certain drugs that would convince the healthy agent that his body was beginning to succumb to his illness. Nothing serious, of course. Campbell didn't want his action hero to be incapacitated. But just a little dose here and there to keep the sham believable.

As it turned out, it didn't take long for Yelchin to identify a bevy of compounds—amitriptyline, diazepam, even morphine—that in the right combination and dose would do the trick nicely. Hooray for modern Western medicine.

Step two was complete.

Step three—convincing Saint to go after the cure for cancer—was immediately thrown into a tailspin. The strategy was that Yelchin would inform Saint that his life was about to end. While Saint rolled around in his own turmoil, Campbell would strike. He would reveal the existence of a cure for his malady, then persuade Saint to go after it. He had a big speech prepared about how, even though it might not exactly follow IIA protocol, Saint was too valuable to the organization to lose. By pursuing the cure—with "help" from IIA if he needed it—he would actually be doing everyone a favour, not least of all himself.

If Saint was stupid enough not to want to save his own life, Campbell had a Plan B in place. He would throw IIA under the bus. He would arrange a clandestine meeting with

Saint at a secure, offsite location. There he would reveal his personal suspicions that IIA was intentionally and callously refusing a cancer-stricken world a definitive cure. The reason: to appease behemoth drug companies whose deep pockets funded IIA through support of governments around the world, including Canada's, in the form of kickbacks, donations, and other under-the-table financial arrangements.

It should have worked.

Instead the unexpected happened. Stone-hearted Saint suddenly developed a soft side. He had allowed emotions, melancholy, homesickness, or some such shit to take over his once highly functioning brain. Before Campbell knew what was happening, Saint resigned from CDRA. Almost immediately, an infuriated Maryann Knoble stepped into the picture, flaunting her ability to abuse power by giving in to her temper tantrum. She decisively shut the rogue agent out of IIA and the life that went with it. Office. Car. Apartment. All gone.

With that ill-advised move, Knoble had effectively extricated Saint from Campbell's spectrum of control. Without access to IIA's considerable resources, not to mention Yelchin's continued presence as assurance of his terminal illness, Saint would have no reason, or ability, to carry out Campbell's desperate mission.

Campbell prided himself on being quick on his feet. The situation called for a speedy rethink of his plan. The first hasty course of action that came to mind was to kill Maryann Knoble. As second-in-command, Campbell would naturally take over the reins of IIA.

Who cared if it was a temporary or permanent promotion? He only needed access to her power for a short while. Once he was the IIA chief, he would reinstate Saint and yank the rest of the plan back into place. He'd gotten away with Krazinski's murder. But a second mysterious death of a high-ranking IIA agent so quickly on the heels of the first would more than likely raise suspicion. Suspicion he could not afford. Another tack was needed.

So, as with many great structures the world over, Campbell realized he would require a fourth support for his master plan. Kate Spalding.

Speeding up the winding, gravel driveway that led to Ken and Patti Kerchuk's ranch-style home, I wondered for the hundredth time that day why I'd allowed my sister to coerce me into bringing her along. I suppose it could have had something to do with the two rifles locked in the tool box in the bed of Dad's half-ton. She'd made it clear before she handed them over that one was for me, the other for her, and the two would never part.

Fortunately Alexandra was not in a talkative mood, and I was able to use the ninety minutes it took to reach the North Battleford area acreage to think.

Things weren't going well. Develchko expected me to show up at Sheila Shellbrook's Las Vegas condo tomorrow with the cure for cancer. Even if I did succeed in convincing Hanna Billings to come with me, what would I do then? There was no way I was turning her over to a ruthless killer whose plans for her likely included spiriting her out of the country to some godforsaken Russian butcher shop, where they would do who knows what to her.

My brain was roiling with possibilities, each one more far-fetched and fantastically impossible than the last. Anatole had remained on the farm, where I had him checking on a few things for me. But at this point, with the clock ticking, the best I could do was keep moving forward. I hoped answers would present themselves when I needed them to. This wasn't how I like to operate, but I wasn't exactly running the show here.

Parking in the yard, we stepped outside into dry, hot country air flavoured with sun-soaked leaves and freshly mown grass.

A long shaft of dark hair swinging at her neck from a topknot ponytail, Alexandra swung her legs up to get into the truck's bed. She was wearing a camouflage-patterned jumpsuit. And heels.

"No guns," I told her. "We're just going to check things out first. Say hello. Theresa called ahead. They're expecting us."

"I went to a lot of trouble to get those guns," she informed me—again. "We're taking them with us."

She was standing atop the truck bed, hands on hips, rooted there like a tree that wouldn't bend, not even for a prairie plough wind. I held out a hand to help her down. She ignored it. I hoped no one was watching us from the house. That would do a lot for their confidence—Hanna's rescuers involved in a sibling catfight.

"Alexandra, I appreciate your getting the rifles," I said through clenched jaw. "I really do. But they're for security only. I wanted them just in case."

"Just in case what?"

Anatole had filled his mother in on the pertinent details of what was happening, including the names of the key players. Like it or not, this had become a family affair.

"In case Develchko decides to go back on his promise to stay out of my business until day three. But the whole drive out here, I was keeping an eye out for tails. Nothing. For the last ten miles of country road, I didn't see anything moving except for a Black Angus bull. So unless you want to go hunting for supper, I don't think we'll be needing the firepower."

She rapped the lid of the tool box with the knuckles of her right hand. "Open it."

Wordlessly we glared at one another.

Two sharp reports tore apart the pastoral silence.

My sister tumbled off the truck bed and fell to the ground.

Chapter Twenty-Five

As I lay there, my face pressed into the gravel, staring into my sister's unblinking eyes, I tried to remember if I'd ever been this close to her before. It was an oddly intimate moment, this shared terror.

"You duck-fucking son of a one-eyed bitch," she growled.

And then it was over.

"I told you we needed the rifles. What are you? Some kind of anti-gun crusader now?"

Hardly. I reached in my pocket for the key fob.

"Why the hell are these assholes shooting at us? I thought you said they'd be friendly. I thought you said they knew we were coming. I thought you said you didn't need me to come with you because there was no danger involved," Alexandra ranted. "You know, brother dear, I'm beginning to have serious doubts about believing anything you say."

I turned to her and gave her one of my best grins. "I think we need the guns now."

"Now that," she said, pulling herself up against the side of the truck, "is the fucking understatement of the year."

Several outbuildings cluttered the yard—machine sheds, granaries, storage huts. But I was quite certain the gunfire originated at the house, from one of the front windows. Fortunately our trusty farm truck sat positioned between us and the house. For the moment, we were out of harm's way.

"We need a bit of diversion at the front end of the truck," I said. "While one of us climbs into the truck bed and gets the guns out of the tool chest. Hopefully they're not smart enough to shoot at both ends at the same time. What do you want, heads or tails?" I asked her.

Alexandra surveyed the area immediately behind us. She lowered herself flat against the ground and slithered forward until she reached a stick. "This will do," she said as she slithered back. "I'll take heads."

The next thing I knew, she was doing that freaky thing women do when it appears they can remove their bra without disturbing any other piece of clothing.

It was vivid pink.

I would have expected leopard print.

Attaching the bra to one end of the stick, Alexandra signaled that she was ready.

"One."

"Two."

"Three!"

Alexandra thrust the brassiere-festooned stick high into the air, bobbing it up and down with as much gusto as a marching band's flag bearer. At the same time, I slid along the side of the truck until I was at the tailgate. In one swift move, I launched myself up and over into the truck bed. I gingerly crab-walked over to the tool box, inserted the key, and pried open the lid, just wide enough for me to thrust in an arm.

A rattle of gunfire was the response to our actions.

"You shit-eating pigs!" Alexandra shrieked. Her bra had been hit.

Luck was not on our side. I could only reach one gun. I tossed it over the side of the truck to the ground and prepared to make a second attempt.

"Hurry up, for crissakes!" Alexandra encouraged me.

This time I had to put more of my torso at risk. I lifted myself up in order to get a deeper reach into the box. My arm extended. My fingers stretched. I could feel the metal of the second gun.

And then I was hit.

"Ugghhhh!" I grunted as I fell backward.

"Adam!" my sister yelped.

I'd gotten the second rifle. And a grazed shoulder. Gun firmly in hand, I slid my body back to the tailgate end of the truck bed. With no time to waste, I vaulted over and landed roughly on the hard ground below. I swore heatedly, then quickly maneuvered myself to the safe side of the vehicle.

"You've been shot! Oh shit, Adam, you're hurt. I'm fucking calling the fucking cops right now!"

I knew how scared she must have been to utter those last words. Alexandra and the police were not the best of buddies.

"It's okay. Just a scrape." I could see blood seeping into the frayed edges where my shirt had been ripped apart by the speeding bullet. But I was okay.

We sat side by side on the ground, backs against the half-ton. We wouldn't have much time before the people in the house tried something else.

"Something's not right here," I uttered.

"No shit, Sherlock."

"Ken and Patti Kerchuk from North Battleford can't possibly be such good shots."

"Did you miss the part where they missed both of us?" Alexandra wanted to know.

"Still."

"Maybe it's the chick. Maybe it's Hanna doing the shooting."

"I don't think so."

"You think it's Develchko?"

That didn't sound right either. I couldn't see any possible way that he and his men could have gotten to Hanna first. But I've been wrong before.

I pulled out my cellphone and dialed the number Develchko gave me.

"*Preveet!*" a voice barked.

"Develchko, it's Saint."

"You have the cure."

"I have one more day."

"Then why are you calling?" His voice was as still and calm as a frozen-over lake.

"I just wanted to make sure I had the right number for when I do call tomorrow. *Dasveedanja.*" I hung up and shot my sister a look. Of course, I couldn't be sure the cell I'd called wasn't mere metres away in the farmhouse rather than in Las Vegas. But I doubted it.

"Not him, huh?"

"Nope."

"So if it's not Ken and Patti, not Hanna, and not the

crazy Russian, then who?"

I was afraid the answer was becoming apparent to me. And if I was right, I didn't know if any of us would survive the day.

"Mr. Saint!"

The voice startled us. In unison, we turned so that we were now crouched against the side of the truck. Inch by inch, we raised our heads until our eyes were level with the top of the bed.

Shuffling toward the half-ton, hands in the air, was a man in his late fifties. His soft cotton shirt was untucked over a developing paunch and loose jeans. He wore cowboy boots and a terrified look on his face. I was suspicious. This could easily be a trick. I did not recognize the man. The description Theresa had given me of Ken Kerchuk wasn't detailed enough for me to rule this man in or out from this distance.

"Stop right there!" I yelled. He was about halfway between the house and the truck. "Who are you?"

"Ken Kerchuk. I'm a friend of Theresa's. I live here. She called to tell us you were coming."

"What does Theresa look like?" I asked.

"What? Why…?"

"Never mind why! Just tell me!"

He gave a fairly accurate description of the woman I met in the bar in Dauphin. My suspicion was lessening.

"What's going on in the house? Why are you shooting at us?"

"It's…." He stopped there. I couldn't be certain, but I thought he was getting emotional and trying to control himself. "It's not us!" he screamed, his voice ragged. "It's them!"

Alexandra and I exchanged worried looks. I was afraid of this. Nigel and the others who knew and loved Hanna had intimated that she felt she was in danger long before I came into the picture. Long before Develchko showed up in Canada. That could only mean one thing.

Someone else had discovered IIA's big secret. Someone else found out that Hanna was the key to something essentially invaluable. Possibly agents of another country. It could virtually be anyone. One of the sad realities of my line of work is that you collect a bounty of experience and personal knowledge that will forever jade your view of how the world works. Especially the world of big "B" business. I'd personally witnessed unimaginably despicable and cruel acts carried out by companies and organizations that to the world showed a face that seamlessly hid a wolf in sheep's clothing. There were men and women in the world who made, on a daily basis, decisions that affected countless human lives in adverse ways. Usually for one reason: money. The New Testament contains the phrase "The love of money is the root of all kinds of evil." I often believe this to be true.

Hanna Billings, unwittingly, had become the centre of a maelstrom of competing greeds. Were the men in the house from a drug company? Drug companies would have a vested interest in keeping Hanna's secret hidden. The best way to do that would be to silence her forever. Other organizations would rather keep her alive. They would use her to reap the endless rewards an appreciative world would gladly give up to them in order to be free of cancer.

I myself would happily give up a great deal.

But not at the expense of Hanna Billings's life.

"Who's them?" I volleyed back.

"I don't know who they are. I only know they have guns. They have my wife." He hesitated again. Choked up. "And Hanna. And Jake."

"How many of them are there?"

"I can't tell you that." I suspected as much. "They're listening to this."

"What do they want?"

"They want you to leave."

Fat chance.

"Just go!" Kerchuk cried, suddenly forceful. "Get out of here! If you don't, they're going to kill one of us."

"Ken, it's okay. We'll figure this out."

"How the fuck do you think we're going to figure this out?" Alexandra hissed at me from the side.

"Go! Just go!" he pleaded. "Oh please, you've got to go now!"

Kerchuk was losing it. He was beginning to hop from one foot to another, as if he was standing barefoot on hot coals. He kept twisting his head to look over his shoulder at the house.

"Go! Oh God! Goooooooo!"

"Okay," I yelled. "We're go—"

The sound of a single shot echoed through the air.

I'd seen the telltale dot of red on Ken Kerchuk's forehead just before he died and dropped. In that order.

"And now," a cold voice reeking of foul satisfaction came from behind us, "it's your turn."

Chapter Twenty-Six

"The danger to the rest of the world, Mr. Campbell, is not insignificant," a swarthy man with an eagle's beak nose announced loudly. "You cannot afford to take this offer lightly."

Ross Campbell sat at the head of a long table. It was made from sheesham, a hardwood found in India, used particularly for its grain quality. He calmly surveyed the half dozen men and women gathered around it. Each represented a city commonly known to be amongst the most dangerous in the world. Mogadishu, Somalia. Linfen, China. Caracas, Venezuela. Detroit, U.S.A., Johannesburg, South Africa. And, arguably the most dangerous of all, Ciudad Juárez in Mexico.

The "offer" proposed by the coalition was sound. Smart. Important. It made sense. These people were unswerving in their convictions. But there was no way IIA, the Canadian arm or any other faction, would accept their proposal. Campbell wasn't a fool. He knew this same group had been on a dog-and-pony show of every IIA organization the world over, peddling their "save us!" scheme.

"I've reviewed your budget very carefully, Mr. Garza," Campbell announced. "I'm afraid the amount you are proposing for IIA involvement is woefully inadequate."

Money was not the issue.

"You're requesting IIA to mobilize what amounts to a small army to march into each of your cities and declare war on your citizens. Is that about right?"

"No!" Linfen's Hui Cai responded vehemently. "It is a war, yes. But not against our citizens. Against our criminals!"

"As an international organization at arm's length from any specific government, IIA is uniquely positioned to do such a thing, is it not?" Andreina Rainusso, from Caracas, added via translator.

"*Perceived* arm's length," Campbell elucidated.

"That is what is important. Only you can help save our cities from certain ruin. Many of us are almost there already."

IIA would never touch this with a ten-foot pole. Campbell's job was to find a way to communicate this while still giving these people hope that IIA would do everything it could to help. Political double-talk. It was what he excelled at.

"More sweet tea, Jamilla?" Campbell offered to the representative of Somalia. He'd done his homework. If she was a typical Somali, she would drink four to six cups a day.

The woman nodded. She was uncommonly beautiful, with large, dark eyes that glowed like wet coal and skin that shimmered, even in the unnatural light of the IIA meeting room.

As Campbell indicated to his assistant, Alan, to pour more tea and refill water glasses and coffee cups for the others, he felt the first tingle. It began at his ankle, then ran up his calf and thigh. He'd had a bad headache since waking up at five that morning after less than three hours of sleep. But so what? He prided himself in knowing that no one in the room would be the wiser. Regardless of any physical discomfort, Ross Campbell was always on top of his game.

"If you are unhappy with our budget, let's discuss a new budget then," Cai suggested. The man aggressively thrust words out of his mouth, making it sound as if he were angry, perhaps even disgusted, with everyone around him.

"I don't know if that would be helpful at this time. I've already assigned a team to study your data and crunch numbers," Campbell lied easily. "This will take some time to complete."

"How much time?" Cai demanded to know.

"We haven't much time left," Rainusso and her translator added, ever the alarmists.

"Fuck!" Campbell cried out. The jab of pain to his temple was sudden and extreme.

The others gathered at the table stared at him in astonishment. Rainusso's interpreter debated whether to communicate the latest from Mr. Campbell.

Campbell pulled back from the table, reeling with nausea. *God, I'm going to throw up.*

His smile was sickly as he moved to stand up. The joint of his right knee went numb, causing him to stumble against the side of the table.

"Mr. Campbell!" this from a concerned Alan, midway through pouring water into glasses. "Are you all right?"

Campbell managed a swift recovery, standing up tall, chest out. "My apologies. Please excuse me. I've just remembered an important telephone call I must make. Perhaps it's time for a break, anyway. I'll be back in fifteen minutes." His jaw quivered with the effort it took to appear unfazed by his agony. "Alan, could you locate Kate Spalding? Have her meet me in my office immediately."

When Kate arrived at Campbell's office ten minutes later, she found he hadn't made it to his private bathroom. He lay in the shadow of his impressively massive desk. His body prone in the soggy mire of his own vomit.

Many things happened next, almost too fast to comprehend.

My sister and I turned our heads to face our attackers. A woman and a man. All in black. Black caps. Black shirts. Black pants. Black boots. Black guns. Pointed at our heads.

"Lower you weapons." Yet another voice. Forceful. Female. This time from somewhere unseen. "I have six snipers focused on you. Six on *each* of you. Two on your heads. Two on your chests. One on each kneecap."

I was particularly thrilled to realize the woman was not talking to us.

I saw the man hesitate.

The woman did not.

Her finger moved.

Twelve shots, nearly silent, sliced neatly through the air. Each met its mark, just as the voice had described.

The pair collapsed to the ground.

From the farmhouse came a sharp barrage of bellowed commands.

Then shouts of surprise, immediately turning to alarm,

then anger.

Gunfire.

Shrill cries of horror rang out as small bomb blasts reverberated throughout the structure.

Within seconds, dense, bluish grey clouds of smoke began billowing from every window of the house as tear gas and smoke bombs did their dirty business.

Doors and windows burst open as bodies began to evacuate the poisoned home.

It was difficult to tell the civilians from the marauders. All were being physically dragged out of the house by men in gas masks who were part of the SWAT team that had also just saved the lives of my sister and me.

A skirmish broke out between two of the evacuees. A woman with a silver-grey bob was beating on a SWAT member with the ferocity of a mother lion protecting her cubs. The man maneuvered her to the ground. He fell on top of her, trying to use his bulk to contain her. Simultaneously he attempted to place a restorative oxygen mask over her nose and mouth. She was having none of it, fighting him hard, flailing about wildly. She sliced at this face with her nails. The man finally gave up, rolling off her. As soon as he did, she rose up into a crouched run, dashed across the front yard, and threw herself against Ken Kerchuk's body. Her husband. Even though the noise of the counterattack was still considerable, I could hear the abject wails of Patti Kerchuck.

"Secure the asset!" It was the voice of the same woman who'd so precisely carried out her threat of deadly force.

Alexandra and I unsteadily rose to our feet. From

amongst the dust and smoke and great commotion, a figure began to materialize. The bulldog. Maryann Knoble. She approached us, never taking her hard eyes off the scene unfolding in the Kerchuks' front yard. The woman exuded indisputable power and authority.

With the smoke clearing, it was obvious that Knoble's forces had taken the day. Every black-outfitted enemy was in the hands of a SWAT member, or whatever God they believed in. The sounds of war began to diminish. Except for one.

Grief. Patti Kerchuk's unrelenting anguish continued to fill the air like an air raid siren.

"You let that man die," Alexandra accused, advancing on Knoble with a determined march.

Ignoring her, Knoble roared at her troops: "Is the asset secure?"

I turned to study the fracas. Hanna Billings. She was talking about Hanna Billings. Where was she? Had she survived?

Then, a revelation.

Deep down, it was something I'd begun to know quite some time ago.

A soldier yelled, "Yes, sir!" as he emerged from the house, carrying the asset in his arms. Carrying the cure for cancer. Carrying, not Hanna Billings, but her son, Jake.

Good Lord.

It was Jake Billings, not his mother, whom everyone was after. He was the cure for cancer. The asset hidden by IIA since his birth. The boy who could save millions. The boy who could save me.

Then, like an insidious disease itself, a dark thought consumed me. I began to wonder: What if it were me? What if it were me instead of Knoble's soldier, disappearing through the bushes, the cure for cancer under my arm? Under my control. Instead of ferrying him to safety, would I falter? Would I take him to a laboratory somewhere— maybe make a deal with Develchko and his team of crackerjack medical specialists—and steal from the boy whatever it is his body offers that cures cancer? Use the child so I could go on living?

"You! Loudmouth! You're in charge here, right?" Alexandra's voice, shrill.

My sister was not a woman ever prepared to be ignored. She was now in Maryann Knoble's face. Alexandra in her tight camouflage jumpsuit and heels. Maryann in a no-nonsense pantsuit and silk scarf. The scarf likely cost more than my sister's entire ensemble.

"You did this. You let that innocent man take a bullet to save your precious asset! While his wife watched! What kind of monster are you?"

Knoble was a big woman in most ways. Alexandra was no match, except in height. And, quite possibly, temperament. They were eye to eye. With a flick of her pinkie finger, I knew Knoble could have had one of her men take down Alexandra like a bowling pin. Instead she waited. She stood her ground and waited for my sister to take a breath. Then, rather than respond to Alexandra, Knoble turned the full power of her scrutiny onto me.

"We've been watching Antonio Pinella and his men for months. Pinella discovered the asset through a very temporary APU leak. When Billings went rogue, we continued to monitor them. Hanna called us, giving us her location. But by the time we got here, Pinella and his men had already arrived. And then…."

Inwardly I cringed. Suddenly I knew exactly what happened next.

Maryann's face reflected her contempt. "Then you and your…*sidekick* stepped right in the middle of our plan to take him down." Only then did she reposition her bulk to face Alexandra. "A plan that entailed extracting the asset, his mother, and everyone else in the house. Safely. And alive." She paused, pointing to the body being mourned on his own front lawn. "If anyone is responsible for that man's death, it's you…." Her glare moved to me. "…and you."

Mercifully Alexandra was speechless.

Knoble strode off to assess the situation at the farmhouse.

I moved to my sister's side. She was visibly seething.

"Alexandra," I soothed, "it isn't our fault. Maryann Knoble is a horrible woman. She's heartless, tactless, self-serving. We couldn't have known what was going on here. We were trying to save lives. Not end one."

But was that really what I was doing? Had I done all this for selfless motivations? Even after I discovered the nature of the cure, and IIA's reason for keeping it secret, for keeping it from being used by anyone, even me, I kept going. Was it just to save the lives of Nigel Congswell and Sheila Shellbrook? Or was there more?

I was a man drowning in the deepest, coldest, roughest of waters.

There was only one buoy available to me.

How badly did I want it?

Was the life I was intending to save today…my own?

As soon as Kate told me about the cure, I was off and running. What did I think I was doing? At that point, I assumed the asset was nothing more than some kind of formula, or pills in a bottle. Not a boy. I'd had no concept of why IIA would be hiding the cure. And, really, it didn't matter. Was I going to steal a few tablets for myself and hope no one noticed? Why not? The only one it would hurt, the only one I would be betraying, would be IIA. A massive, elite, government-subsidized giant without a morsel of soul or feelings.

Today I had to face a new reality. IIA had been protecting the life of a boy. I still wasn't completely sure of how or why it could be true that Jake Billings was the asset. But he was. And Maryann Knoble was retaking possession of the boy. She would hide him so well, bury him so deep, he would never be heard from or seen again.

If Jake Billings disappeared, so too would the cure for cancer.

My cure for my cancer.

My only hope.

Now what, Saint?

Deep down, I knew this journey would sooner or later lead me to this day. A day when I would be forced to show my hand. To answer the question: Was I a good man or a bad man?

Or maybe, instead, the question was: Was I a good man forced to do something bad to preserve himself, to live to prove himself good another day?

"Alexandra," my voice croaked, "how much ammunition do we have?"

She stared at me with unreadable eyes. "What do I care? I want to get the fuck out of here. Right now. Before I rip that bitch a new one."

"We can't leave, Alexandra," I told her.

"Why the hell not?"

"We didn't get what we came for."

Chapter Twenty-Seven

There are many secrets hidden in, around, and beneath Las Vegas and its surrounding desert. One of the best places to carry out a clandestine operation in a see-no-evil, hear-no-evil, speak-no-evil type of environment is in one of the ubiquitous off-strip motels that infest the city like colonies of cockroaches.

As long as you don't forget to grease the right palms.

I am a specialist at this. As a CDRA agent, greasing palms is a fact of life. It could mean the difference between ferrying your ward safely out of a country and having to tell his family they'd have to visit him in a Third World prison for the rest of his miserable days. Some people are offended by the practice. I see it as a cost of doing business, right along with office stationery and a coffee fund.

The Shady Palm Inn is the picture you'll see when you search Google Images for "scuzzy flea trap." Depending on my purposes, I kind of like scuzzy flea traps. They're usually cheaper than a carwash and within walking distance of surprisingly good diners. Not bad if you're in a bind and can put up with the smell of Lysol.

Today, Develchko's Day Three, the Shady Palm Inn fit my needs perfectly. I'd rented two rooms with an adjoining door. When we showed up after dark, our comatose "patient" in tow, Big Ed at reception merely smiled and pocketed his fifty. It wasn't exactly the easiest thing getting our "patient" across the U.S. border, but once again, CDRA training and tricks saved the day.

Although Develchko wasn't keen on my insistence that he come to us, rather than we go to him, when I explained the reason, he could hardly turn me down.

Without having the benefit of actually being in Las Vegas physically, by various methods that included cold-calling neighbours and recruiting local fellow geeks for reconnaissance work, Anatole had confirmed that Develchko was holding Sheila Shellbrook and Nigel Congswell at Sheila's condo. The General had far more manpower at his fingertips than I did, so he could well afford to leave behind some goons to watch over his captives while he paid us a visit.

I was about to investigate the peculiar odour emanating from beneath the room's Double Deluxe (according to the brochure) bed when a knock landed on the door. I glanced at my watch. 11:23 p.m. He was early.

I opened the door. Develchko still managed to appear as if he were in a land of frozen tundra and potato latkes, rather than one of heat mirages and topless dancers. He pushed his way into the room, assessing every inch of the place in a few seconds. Which wasn't difficult, given its size.

Cool as a frozen cucumber, the man said nothing. Instead his eyes found mine and silently demanded his prize.

"First things first," I said, indicating one of two plastic chairs next to a Formica table that looked to be a survivor of the Great Depression.

He ignored my invitation to sit. Into the space between us he raised a cellphone. A silent reminder. If I didn't produce the cure, he'd give the order to kill Congswell and Sheila Shellbrook. All he had to do was make a phone call.

"That's a good idea," I responded casually. "Call your men. You want proof I've held up my part of the bargain? Well, so do I. I want proof that Sheila and Nigel are still alive. I want to speak to them."

He didn't counter with the expected refusal. The look on my face must have convinced him it would be futile. Develchko was not a man to waste time. Or words. Instead, with cold, blue eyes never leaving my face, he hit a button on his phone with the thumb of his gloved left hand and lifted it to his ear. He ordered whoever answered to put Nigel on the phone, then handed it to me.

I waited almost a full minute before I heard a faint "Hello?"

"Nigel, it's Adam Saint. Are you and Sheila all right?"

"You son of a bitch, Saint! What have you done? Where are…where is the asset?"

Seems he was well enough to be annoyed. That was good enough proof for me.

"Let me talk to Sheila."

There was a bit of muffled swearing, then Sheila was on the line.

"Sheila, are you hurt?" I glared a warning at Develchko as I waited for the answer.

"No."

"I spoke with Theresa." That's all I would say. I hoped the message would give the woman some comfort. I'd been in contact with one of her best friends. Hopefully she'd believe that if I'd talked to an ally, I might be one too.

I heard sobs and mumbled words. I felt the smooth, cool leather of Develchko's glove brush against my cheek as he pulled the phone from my hands.

Not great, but it would have to do.

Develchko poked at the phone to disconnect the call. "Your turn," he said.

"I'm not done yet."

"Mr. Saint, you are trying my patience. In the case you are unaware, you should know that I am not a man whose patience you should toy with."

"Believe me, General, you are the last person I wish to toy with. But we have one more thing to discuss." I walked purposefully to a shelf where I'd laid out a bottle of vodka and two glasses. I poured one for myself and gave Develchko a questioning look.

His head moved a tick in the negative. I threw back the vodka and poured another.

"What is this *one more thing* you wish to discuss?"

"Our terms."

Eyes narrowed. "What is this, our terms?"

"You should recognize terms, Develchko. There are ten million of them."

The man's nose flanks began to flare. His lips were tight. His eyes bore into me like two ice drills.

He knew exactly what I was saying.

"I have the cure. You want the cure. You offered to buy the cure for ten million dollars. I am selling the cure for ten million dollars. Sounds like negotiations should go pretty smoothly, wouldn't you say?"

"I did not agree to buy the cure from you." His voice was stony as darkness fell across his face.

"Fine. Then I'll say goodnight. Go ahead and deal with your previous seller." I smirked. "But in the case *you* are unaware, I should tell you that I'm quite certain there is only one cure for cancer up for grabs here. And since I have it, I'd be a little suspicious of whatever goods your guy is trying to peddle." My voice turned heavy. "Your seller may have thought he controlled the cure. I'm here to tell you, he no longer does. Deal over."

"I will kill your friends." The words were said with unsettling steadiness. As if the taking of two lives were nothing more to him than throwing out garbage.

"Great. Go ahead. Then you'll have two murders to deal with on foreign soil. Plus, no cure to take home to a hero's welcome. Besides," I told him, "who said they were friends of mine? Go ahead. Kill them. I'll be busy settling on a price with another buyer. I've got a feeling that once news of what I have gets out, there'll be a lot of them out there." I tossed back another drink. "Sure you don't want one?"

He said nothing. I decided to take that as a yes. I poured out two more shots and handed one to my new best comrade.

"Besides, Illya Nikoleyevich…may I call you Illya?"

Develchko dashed the still-full shot glass to the floor, as if it were acid burning his fingers. He peered at me with venomous eyes.

I took that as a no.

"You were willing to pay ten million before. I'm only

asking for the same ten million. Which, by the way, is a heck of a deal. You've lost nothing. This is the way it will work. Tonight I will provide you with proof that I have the cure. It will take you however long to verify…what, a day, two? When you've substantiated that I have the bona fide goods, you will wire the ten million to an account of my choosing. When it hits the account, I will release the asset to you."

For a full minute, Develchko stood rooted there, staring at me, pulling in slow, deep breaths. I hoped he was considering my offer. And controlling his anger. I realized this was not how he imagined things would go.

"Where is the cure?" he finally muttered under his breath.

I tilted my head toward the door that led to the adjoining room.

"Do we have a deal?"

His eyes appeared to glitter as he beheld the closed door behind which was his glorious future. "*Da.* Let me see it."

I led Develchko to the door. I knocked lightly, then opened it.

The room was a mirror image of the one we'd been in. Except here the lighting was dim, the smell musty and medicinal. On the bed was an obscured figure, swaddled in layers of off-white bed sheets. Standing next to the bed, attending to an IV drip, was a nurse who barely registered our entrance.

"Who is this?" Develchko hissed, indicating the nurse.

"You wanted proof, didn't you? I expected you wouldn't trust me to be the one to provide it for you. Am I right? Besides, I have no medical training whatsoever. But if you'd prefer to do this yourself…?"

"No, no. Just do it quickly," he relented.

"Nurse," I called out to the woman. "This is Mr. De-velchko. Please commence with the procedure."

Alexandra, looking astoundingly compassionate and trustworthy in her demure nurse's outfit, turned toward us. She said nothing but gave Develchko an assessing look be-fore nodding her assent to comply with my request.

Develchko stepped closer as Alexandra pulled a bare arm out from under the covers. "I want to see the face," he said in a way that meant he would not take no for an an-swer.

Alexandra looked at me. I nodded. She moved aside.

Develchko moved in next to the bed. He leaned over the body.

As he beheld the face, his own registered modest sur-prise.

He stepped back. "He isn't awake."

"Did you really think he would be?" I asked. "Once he knew what was happening to him?"

"I see." The Russian moved back. "Continue," he or-dered Alexandra.

As Alexandra prepared the arm and needle for extrac-tion of a blood sample, the room was unnervingly quiet. Even the hoodlums and hookers who frequented the area and could usually be counted on to provide some colourful background noise at this time of night seemed complicit in the silence.

Develchko watched intently as the needle punctured the skin. Red liquid began filling the IV line.

"I assume you have DNA records of the tissue sample you originally obtained?" I said to Develchko.

"*Dah.*"

"Good. You can use it to match the blood we give you tonight."

"Blood? You only give me blood?"

"Did you want to find a surgeon to come in here and perform a little laparoscopic tissue removal? If you do, be my guest. I expect they might be a little suspicious, what with the lack of sterile environment and penny slots in the waiting room. But do your best. I have nothing but time."

He steeled his jaw, then decided, "The blood will do."

Alexandra handed him two vials. He searched her eyes as he accepted them. What was he looking for? Guilt? Weakness? Signs of someone who was about to run to the cops and blab about what was happening in this room?

He must have approved of what he saw. He pocketed the vials and headed back into the first room. I followed.

"This will take time," he said as he moved to the door. "I will send to Russia tonight. I will have confirmation to-morrow."

"You have my number."

He stopped at the door, turned, and looked at me hard. "Yes, Mr. Saint, I know exactly how to find you."

And then he was gone.

When Alexandra joined me in the first room, she'd abandoned part of her Florence Nightingale outfit, discarding the cap and sensible, white Skechers

I was on the ratty couch, attempting to contact Anatole via Skype but having a difficult time establishing a connection.

"What would I do with ten million big ones!" she crowed, palming the vodka bottle off the shelf and downing a healthy swig. "Or, no, wait, there's four of us, right? Me and you. Dad of course. And Anatole. Divided four ways, what is that? Two, three mil apiece?"

I snorted at her superior math skills. "Something like that."

"I could live on that."

Of course I wouldn't need my share. There's only so much money a person can spend in a reduced lifespan.

I couldn't help but wonder if this was a reasonable, defensible compromise. I couldn't morally bring myself to be the direct beneficiary of Jake's gift, to be party to his exploitation, to his very life's blood being syphoned off to his detriment. But couldn't I at least be forgiven one last semi-heroic, selfless gesture of providing financially for my family? If I didn't take the ten million, wouldn't someone else eventually? Realistically, wasn't the life of Jake Billings—not unlike my own—hopelessly ill-fated?

Alexandra plopped down next to me on the couch. "So how long do you think this is going to take?" She lit a cigarette, her eyes roaming the room for an ashtray.

"I don't know. Not long, I'd expect. He wants this over as quickly as we do. Tomorrow maybe. Next day after that at the latest."

"Do we really have to stay in this dump until then? It smells like a goat's underarm in here."

My eyes jumped to the connecting door. "I don't think we can check into the Bellagio with him like that."

"Shit. I guess not. What about the Hard Rock?"

Skype made its do-whoop noises indicating it was placing a call.

"What's up?" my nephew greeted us. The room behind him was dark, making his naturally ghostly appearance almost translucent in the unnatural glow of his computer screen. "My buddy in Vegas told me a man fitting Develchko's description left Sheila Shellbrook's condo earlier tonight. Did he show up? How'd it go?"

"Do you have this guy on twenty-four-hour surveillance or something?" I asked.

"You bet."

"He doesn't have to do that."

"Are you kidding? This is like the most exciting stuff to happen to him in his life so far."

Somehow I didn't doubt it.

"Hi, honey!" Alexandra sang out, a little high on vodka.

I could see Anatole's dark hawk eyes move to take in his mother. "Nice outfit, Mom," he commented dryly.

"Hey," she snorted, "I nursed you, didn't I?"

Suddenly the translucent skin turned a chafing pink.

"Anatole, do you have everything set with the bank account?" I asked, saving him from any further humiliation his mother might have had in store for him.

"It's ready, Uncle Adam. They know to expect the wire transfer within the next day or two. They'll confirm when it arrives."

"Good. And the travel arrangements?"

"Done. And I've rented a small house and a car. Don't worry, the way I did this, no one will ever be able to trace any of it. If they can, I want to meet them and shake their hand."

I pulled in a big breath. It was happening. I hoped I'd made the right decisions.

The sound of smashing glass brought us to our feet.

Two men in black, brandishing rifles, catapulted into the room through the window. Simultaneously two other attackers broke through the suite's door.

One of the two from the window grabbed Alexandra, pulling her into a chokehold. The other did the same to me.

The second set of two closed the door behind them. Not that they had anything to worry about from the neighbours in a place like this. Gunplay and breaking and entering was just another night in Vegas as far as they were concerned.

When the dust settled, I studied the faces of the invaders.

One of them was very familiar.

Chapter Twenty-Eight

Once upon a time, I'd stood in front of family and friends, a minister and altar, and pledged my love to this woman. Til death do us part. Today she was aiming a gun at me. She'd never looked lovelier.

"I can't allow this to happen, Adam."

"What the hell do you think you're doing, Kate!" Alexandra blurted, at the same time making things very difficult for the man who was attempting to keep her in his grip.

"Alexandra, I'm sorry you're a part of this…you too, Adam…really…but I need you to stop what you're doing."

"And what exactly do you think we're doing?"

"You have the cure. I know you do. I need you to give it to me."

"What makes you think we have anything?" Alexandra spit out.

Kate regarded Alexandra with sorrowful eyes, one mother to another. "He's a very sweet, young man…and trusting…."

"You fucking bitch! You used Anatole to get information? You're his aunt. He trusts you. I'm going to rip your throat out!" If it wasn't for the muscle man restraining her,

I had no doubt that was exactly what she would have done.

Although I know it affected her, Kate did her best to ignore Alexandra's venom, and faced me. "Adam, this doesn't have to be like·this. I just need the cure…whatever it is….I need it now. Just enough to—"

"Enough to what, Kate? Why the rush? I thought you wanted me to find the cure so I could be healed."

"Wha…?" This from Alexandra.

Crap. Cat out of the bag. Again.

"I did, Adam," Kate said. "I did want to find it for you…too."

"What did you mean by that?" Alexandra's voice was strained. "Heal yourself of what?"

I did the best I could—within the restraints of the giant who was holding on to me—to turn toward my sister. "Alexandra, I have cancer. It's terminal. It's over for me." I had to be blunt. There was no time for anything else. We had more important things to deal with.

In a matter of seconds, my sister's face changed in front of me. From angry and belligerent to disbelieving, dejected, then, as I suspected, back to angry again.

"And when were you planning to tell me about this? Huh? At your funeral? Oh yeah, sis, just in case you're interested, I'm dead! You puke-faced son of a bitch!"

"Alexandra, shut up. Just for the time being, okay? How about we deal with the people with guns first, all right?"

"There's nothing to deal with. You're here for the cure, right?" she asked Kate.

"Yes," Kate told her. I noticed she'd put away her gun.

"You want some. We want some. There's enough to go

around. Bro, I'm done with this plan."

Shit! My goddamned sister was about to blow everything sky high, because….

…*because she loves me and wants me to live.*

"It can't work that way, Alexandra. It just can't. Remember what we talked about."

Kate, sensing a shift in the axis of power, moved in for a face-to-face with her ex-sister-in-law. "Do you know where it is?"

A blast of steam escaped Alexandra's nose. She looked at me, looked at Kate, looked at the nearest wall. "Yes."

"No!" I warned off my sister.

"Good," Kate said, disregarding me. "Let's start there. Where is it?"

"Why *do* you want it?" Alexandra asked.

"Yes, Kate, tell us why you want it," I challenged.

We both knew the answer. She'd used me. She'd used the ridiculous coincidence of fate, where both her ex-husband and next husband were dying of cancer. She never meant to save me. Even when she was making love to me, watching the stars with me that night in the pasture, she knew what she was doing. Manipulating me into finding the cure so she could save Ross Campbell. I pointedly stared at the gleaming diamond on her finger.

"Of course I want to save Ross!" she yelled. "What's wrong with that? I love him. I loved you too…once. Why can't I save both of you? Why not, Adam, why not? Why can't we use this…thing, whatever it is, to save you *and* Ross? What's so wrong with that? There have to be some perks to dedicating our lives to these jobs." She stopped to catch her breath, then, "And how, I'd like to know, does this make me any worse than you? You don't want the cure to save a life. Not even your own. From what I can see is happening here, you want it to make money! That's as dishonourable as it gets."

"No, Kate. You're wrong."

Kate's eyes, the eyes I once knew so well, reached for me, beseeched me. "He's sick, Adam. He's really sick. He needs this right now. If he doesn't get it…I'll lose him."

I raised an invisible barrier between her and me. It was not lost on me that this was not an entirely unfamiliar move. "I don't know what she told you in order to get you involved in this," I addressed the three men who'd blasted into the room with Kate. "As you can hear, this isn't some mission you're on. She's doing this for personal gain. This mission has *not* been sanctioned by IIA."

I could see doubt creep into the men's eyes. I was right. She had misled them.

Kate bristled. I'd declared war. She was not the kind of gal to back down from a fight. "He's lying," she told her companions, fighting to regain high ground. "You know Adam Saint is a rogue ex-IIA agent." She was punching hard. "He is currently in possession of an APU asset of national and international significance. You know your orders. I need you to—"

"When did he do it, Kate?" I interrupted her spiel.

"Do what?" she shot back.

"When did he first tell you he loved you? Before or after he suggested the plan to get me to go after the cure?"

Her face froze. I had my answer. It was a hurtful blow.

But the fighting was getting dirty, and I was running out of ammunition.

"Adam," my sister beckoned. "I don't care about her. I don't care what she wants. But I can't let you frickin' die. Not if there's a way to save you right at our fingertips."

Kate took speedy advantage of the crack in our wall. "Take her to the car," she ordered the man who was holding Alexandra.

"What car? Where are you taking me!" Alexandra shrieked loudly.

"The parking lot. You're just going to the parking lot. I'll be right there. We can talk. It'll be okay, Alexandra," Kate told her. "I promise."

"Alexandra, don't!" I bellowed, feeling the veins in my neck threatening to burst. "Don't say a word to her! You don't know everything!"

It was too late. She was gone.

Except for the heavy breathing of the four of us left, the room fell into a hush. Noticing the vodka bottle Alexandra had left on the coffee table, Kate found a glass and poured herself two fingers. Eyeing me the entire time, she lifted the glass to her lips and downed the liquid.

"I know you won't believe this now," she said. "But I'm sorry about this. I'm not going to hurt anyone. Not you. Not Alexandra. All I care about is saving someone. I'm going to get Alexandra to give me the cure. Then I'm going back to Toronto. Ross is in a private clinic. They're waiting for me. They won't ask questions. After they administer the cure, I don't really care what happens to me."

"I guess you've changed then." Another dirty shot.

"What are you talking about?"

"You don't care what happens to you? As long as your man gets to live on, to screw over the world another day. When did you become so weak?"

Kate came closer, her shoulders thrown back. "Screw you."

Stepping back, she addressed the man attached to me. "Keep him here. Tie him up. Whatever you have to do. Just don't hurt him…unless he tries to leave this room. When I get what I want, I'll let you know. Then let him go."

"How generous."

"Goodbye, Adam." She and the other agent left the room.

The incessant knocking at the door began as a series of rolling knuckles against wood. Quickly they graduated into light pounding followed up by non-stop, drunken rambling: "Jimmy let us in we forgot our keys hey dude come on let us in we can't open the door it's locked or something we got the munchies now let us in dude where are you in the can why won't you open the door it's us come on dude it's Tommy and Kyle we're out here in the hallway…." It went on and on and on and on.

"You're going to have to do something about that," I said to my guard, who'd yet to share his name with me. I decided to call him Lackey. Because that's what he was, blindly following the lead of a superior officer without questioning the obviously suspicious underlying circum-stances. "Doesn't sound like they're going away. And pretty soon the neighbours are going to call management. Or the cops. I don't think you want that, right? I mean, I would. But I have to admit, it's beginning to get on my nerves." It really kind of was.

He hadn't had time to tie me up or find another way to restrain me. Other than the gun-in-my-face routine. Which, until now, had worked rather well.

He pointed at the couch. "Sit. Don't move."

I obeyed.

Lackey stepped up to the door and hollered through it. "Get away from the door. You've got the wrong room."

"Oh yeah sure Jimmy funny funny now let us in I gotta pee like crazy you want me to pee right here in the hallway the ice cream's melting all over the floor let us in…."

"I said step away from the door! Take a hike!" He was beginning to sound like a drill sergeant attempting to control a detachment of ducklings. "This is not your room."

"If you don't let us in we're going to get another key from the front desk and let ourselves in and you can get your own food dude this isn't cool this isn't cool at all…."

Lackey turned the lock on the door and reached for the chain. He pulled it out of its mooring. Just as he did so, I leveled the handgun I'd pulled from my ankle holster at his left ear. Stealth is one of my specialties.

"Drop your weapon to the floor and kick it aside."

He did as he was told. See? A lackey.

"Open the door."

"There's no need to involve civilians in this, Saint."

"Open the door."

He did it.

Behind it were three of the geekiest-looking young men this side of a comic book convention. Aaron. Darren. And Bob. My reinforcements.

"Great job, guys. Come on in."

Eyes wide, glasses steamed over, noses twitching with excitement, the trio of Anatole's digital buddies shuffled into the room. They looked at Lackey as if he might be the reincarnation of Darth Vader.

"Guys, can you find me something to tie up our friend here, please?"

The boys scurried about the room like foraging mice. A moment later, they returned with a towel, a pillowcase, and a spool of dental floss. None of which would work. "Sacrifice time," I told the team. "Darren, take off your belt. Aaron, let's have your t-shirt."

"Aw, man, it's an original *Game of Thrones* from Comic-Con. Signed by Emilia Clarke!"

There was further groaning, but they handed over the goods. After seating Lackey in a chair, I used the items to fasten his feet and hands.

"Bob, take off your socks." They were thick, white sport socks, the kind that went halfway up his skinny calves.

"Why?"

I gave Lackey a meaningful look. "Just in case our friend here decides to start bawling, I want something to gag him with."

The goon gave me a "fuck you" look but wisely said nothing.

Another knock at the door.

Barefoot Bob let in Kate, hands secured behind her

back. Behind her were Alexandra and two bearish biker dudes, complete with beer bellies, bandanas, and sunburned forearms and foreheads. Former riding buddies of Scruff's, Alexandra's deceased boyfriend.

Yes. Geeks and bikers. This was our backup team. And a damn fine one they turned out to be.

"Where are Thing One and Thing Two?" I asked.

"Gumbo and Duster are holding them in their car," Alexandra replied, looking as self-satisfied as a whippet who'd just won a fight against a fleet of pit bulls. With the ample help of four mighty mastiffs. "Thanks for escorting us in," she said to her two friends. "We can take it from here. We'll let you know when you can let the other two go."

They glared at Kate, then Lackey. After sharing knuckle bumps with Alexandra, they left, closing the door behind them.

"You can go too, fellas," I said to Aaron, Darren, and Bob.

"Uh…what about my socks?"

"And my shirt?"

"And my belt?"

I reached into my pocket and pulled out a roll of cash. Pulling off a fifty per geek, I led them to the door like donkeys jonesing for a carrot. They scampered off, no doubt to their respective dark caves to breathlessly report back to Anatole. Perhaps they'd tell their stories to others of their kind. But really, who would ever believe them? Three geeks in league with a posse of bikers, helping to take down a cabal of dirty government agents? Never happen.

"You have her gun?" I asked my sister.

"What do you think I am? An idiot?"

"We'll have to get that back to you at a later date," I told my ex-wife. Then to Alexandra: "Untie her."

I stopped my sister before she began to argue. "Just do it." She complied in unhappy silence.

"What now, Adam?" Kate asked, bitterness steeped in every syllable. "You're just going to let Ross die? He's your friend too, you know."

"Oh, Kate. You are so wrong about so many things."

"Tell me." She said it as a challenge.

A bone-weary fatigue washed over me. I sighed. Over the years, Kate and I had had our share of tough times. We'd had devastating fights. We'd said hurtful things to one another. We'd hurled insults and good china. But always, we'd bounce back. We remembered the love. We remembered the child we created together. We remembered our first heady days as young agents with IIA, hiding our relationship from everyone else, keeping a secret that could never survive. But I knew that from this—what happened in this room tonight—there would be no recovering. Some day in the future I might chuckle about this. Saint, I'd say to myself, if you ever needed a sign that your marriage was truly over, well, you got it in spades.

"I'm going to tell you two things, Kate. Two very important things. I want you to listen very carefully. Then do what you will."

"Go."

"There is no cure."

She began to dispute my words. I held up a hand to silence her.

"There *never* was a cure. It was a myth, Kate. You sent me to find Nigel Congswell. You wondered why he'd left APU so suddenly? He *was* hiding something. He was hiding the truth. The fact that for all those years he was protecting nothing more than a fairy tale. An urban legend. He was about to be found out. So he ran."

"That can't be. There were tests, there—"

My hand rose again.

"No, Kate. None of it was real. There is no cure. Not for Ross." I glanced at my sister. "Not for me."

Having my illness revealed to my sister had not been part of the plan. The plan was to have Anatole innocently reveal to his aunt where I was. And that I was intending on selling the asset (of which he claimed no further knowledge). I set the trap for selfish reasons. For reasons that any man with an ego—and face it, what man doesn't have one?—could understand.

I needed to know the truth behind my ex-wife's motives. Or…I thought I did.

Anatole would mobilize the geeks, Alexandra the bikers. When Kate and her men first burst into the room, Anatole would monitor the activity. Although he couldn't see most of the action via our Skype connection, he could certainly hear it. Particularly Alexandra cleverly getting Kate to say out loud where she was being taken.

As an experienced agent, I know that all plans, once underway, tend to reveal unexpected components. Such as Kate's spilling the news of my tumour. But I'd have to deal with that later.

Little by little, Kate's face began to crumple as she digested my news. First her bottom lip began to tremble. Then the skin around her eyes and jaw lost its usual tightness. Her hands began to quake.

"There's a second thing you should know," I continued.

"What is it?" The words were clipped. The voice did not sound like her own.

"Ross is no longer at the clinic."

"What are you talking about?" More animated now. "I saw him there myself. Less than two days ago."

I stared at her. She knew I spoke the truth.

"Where is he?"

"Kate, I'm sorry. Ross didn't make it. He's gone."

Standing alone in the middle of a filthy, seedy motel room, on the wrong side of the Las Vegas Strip, my ex-wife began to wail. She wrapped her arms around herself, as if protecting her body from attack. Alexandra stepped back, afraid of catching her sorrow. She stared at Kate, then at me, then at Lackey, then out the broken window.

I felt as if the oxygen had suddenly been sucked from the room. My chest moved up and down heavily, exerting muscles normally not required to breathe. Part of me wanted to move in, throw my arms around my wife, comfort her, tell her everything would be all right. But this wasn't my wife. This was a woman I'd betrayed in a way that could never be forgiven.

Everything wasn't going to be all right.

Then it was over. Kate straightened her back. She pushed a stray strand of hair off her face, an offending tear off her cheek. Kate Spalding was a proud woman. I had no doubt she had plenty more grief, but she'd show no more of it tonight. Not in this room. Not to me. Glancing at the bound man in the chair, then at me, she sighed. "Let him go."

Alexandra did the honours. When the man was free, Kate told him to wait for her outside.

"Why did you do all this?" Kate asked when he was gone. "If there is no cure. If you knew about Ross. Why lure me all the way here?"

"I think you know why."

The mantra in my head continued its steady, annoying rhythm. *How much did she know? How much did she know? How much did she know?*

"And do you have your answers now?" Angry? Resentful? Apologetic? Deceitful? I couldn't tell anymore.

I shook my head. I'd never have the answer. Maybe I never really wanted to. If the answer was the wrong one, I didn't know if I could take it.

The mantra would have to stop.

And so it would. In too short a time.

We stared at one another. I could feel the heat of Alexandra's presence behind me, singeing my ears.

"I'm going home." With that, Kate stalked out of the room.

"You're just going to let her go?" Alexandra was incensed.

Yes. I will.

Twenty-four hours later, I jolted awake to a ghoulish sound. I had my iPhone's ringtone set to play Bach's Toccata and Fugue in D Minor when Develchko called.

I pulled myself into a sitting position. My back ached from two nights on the Shady Palm's poor excuse for a couch. Alexandra was snoring on the bed. The bed next door was still occupied.

"Saint," I answered.

Develchko spoke four words: "We have a deal." Then hung up.

Suddenly the room grew cool. My head filled with a familiar ache.

God forgive me.

I'd just made a deal with the devil.

Chapter Twenty-Nine

It was an awkward arrangement for a business transaction but the best the Shady Palm Inn had to offer.

Develchko and I sat side by side on the lumpy couch that doubled as my lumpy bed. We were both staring at the screen of my laptop sitting on the coffee table in front of us. This time Develchko had accepted my offer of a shot of vodka. I'd thought we'd use it to toast our successful transaction once the money came through. Instead he'd downed it in one swift move and eyed me until I did the same.

We waited.

Alexandra was next door, again in her nurse persona. She was busily preparing the *patient* for transport.

Patient.

I couldn't bring myself to refer to him by name, not even in my head.

We waited.

The screen, displaying the current balance of the foreign bank account Anatole had set up, became quite familiar to us. Small talk was hard to manufacture and unnecessary. We had little more to say to one another. But in my mind, I was saying all the things this monster deserved to hear.

Then, with considerably much less fanfare than such an

event deserved, the computer binged, indicating the arrival of ten million dollars into the account.

Develchko stared at the number. He looked at it as if it were a favoured child whom he'd found necessary to sacrifice for the greater good. His own.

I punched a number into my cellphone. A voice answered, made a few identifying queries, then confirmed that indeed ten million dollars had arrived safe and sound into the account. I disconnected and nodded to Develchko.

Develchko retrieved his own phone from a coat pocket and made a call. When he was done, I made a second call. Nigel Congswell and Sheila Shellbrook had just been released. Develchko's men had left the condo. Every tumbler had fallen into place. Every promise met.

It was over.

My stomach growled with discontent. I felt nauseous. This wasn't the tumour speaking. No pill was going to help with this.

Worst of all was the sick feeling that I'd made the wrong decision. But it was too late. There were no geeks or freaks, bikers or IIA agents, outside the door ready to pounce and save the day. General-polkovnik Illya Nikoleyevich Develchko was about to walk out of here with his precious cure.

Develchko stood. He straightened the tie beneath his uniform jacket, then marched to the door that separated this room from the next. Without waiting for me, he turned the knob and walked inside. What was once mine, even for a short while, now belonged to him. He would waste no time taking it away from me. Fair enough. The man had paid my price.

"Is he ready to be moved?" Develchko barked at Alexandra.

"Yes," she said. "Your man outside the door…the one who claims medical knowledge… I've left instructions with him on how best to keep the patient asleep during transport. As I told him, I don't recommend going beyond light sedation. It could be dangerous over a prolonged period of time. And in the unlikely event of an emergency during your flight back to Russia—"

"Yes, yes," he said dismissively. "There will be no emergencies. We are flying privately, with pre-clearance for our patient. A nurse will be on board. There will be no problems, I assure you."

Develchko moved to the exit to call in his team.

"Wait," I said.

Develchko stopped. "What is it?"

"I'd like to…pay my respects before you take him." I didn't know how else to put it in a way Develchko was likely to respond to.

His eyes narrowed to slices of blue as he assessed me. He was likely expecting some kind of last-minute trickery. I stood still, trying to look as innocent as a guy like me can. His head shifted up, then down, just once.

I stepped to the side of the bed.

Holding my breath, I looked down at the slack, ashen face of Ross Campbell.

I lowered my face to his, bringing my lips next to his left ear. "If you can hear me, Ross," I whispered, "I want you to know…I know what you did. This is for Geoffrey. And Jean. And their daughters. You took a husband, and a father and a friend. And this is for what you tried to do to Kate. And now you are going to hell for it."

Was that a twitch at his cheek? I couldn't be sure.

I straightened and stepped back.

Develchko rapped sharply on the door. He shouted a string of orders in Russian, and a small flotilla of associates flooded inside. Alexandra and I moved away as they took over the room and its comatose inhabitant.

"He looks weaker than he did two days ago," Develchko growled, as he oversaw the transfer of the patient from bed to gurney. "His colour is bad. Is there something wrong with him? Is he ill?"

"Keeping him this way has stressed his body," Alexandra noted with an admirable tone of authoritative knowledge. "And he's weak from being fed by intravenous only. But your medical professional can attest, he is well enough to make the trip."

Over the next several minutes, my sister and I watched in grim silence as Develchko's men and women fussed like a flock of vultures over a helpless carcass. When they were done, the body transferred to a waiting vehicle, Develchko was the last one left in the room. He hesitated at the door.

"I understand you suffer from the same disease, Mr. Saint?" he said, his chin high.

"I do."

"Well then," he began, directing his intense gaze over my sister, then back to me, "I don't expect we will meet again."

"No, I expect not."

His gaze burned into me. He said a few words in Russian.

And then he was gone.

"What did he just say to you?" Alexandra asked when the door was closed behind him.

"Rest in peace."

"Fucking bastard."

"Is it going to rain?" the boy asked the man who held his hand as they traversed an uneven path down the steep trail.

"No. Maybe up in the mountains, but not down on the beach where we're going. What you see up there is called the *Khareef*," Nigel explained.

"*Khareef*. I never heard that word before."

Nigel grinned. "Well, actually, neither had I before we came here."

"What is it?"

"Remember when we told you that the country we're living in now?"

"Oman!" Jake announced proudly, as if answering an oral test question.

"Yeah, you got it, buddy. Remember we told you how Oman is surrounded by lots of deserts? In places like—"

"Yeah man!" His version of Yemen. "And Southern Arabian." Saudi Arabia.

"Have I told you how smart you are lately?"

"No. But Mom told me yesterday, so that's okay."

"So there are all of these deserts around us. You'd think it would be stinking hot. But it's not so bad, right?"

"Right."

"That's because at this time of year there are these really

big winds called…?"

Jake stopped, Nigel alongside him. He screwed up his face in thought, then answered: "*Khareef?*"

"Not yet, but close. They're called monsoons."

"Oh yeah. I knew that."

"Come on, let's keep on walking. Your mom is waiting for us."

"So what does a monsoon do?" Jake asked, scurrying after Nigel, reaching for his hand.

"It sweeps out over all that water in the ocean."

"The Arabian Ocean!"

"Yup, you got it. And when it does, the monsoon and the water get all mixed up together, and it makes that beautiful fog you see up there in the hills. That fog is called the *Khareef*. And that's what cools things down…a bit."

It was nearing twenty-eight degrees Celsius already, and it wasn't yet nine a.m. But like yesterday, and pretty much every day before today and every day after today, Nigel knew this was about as hot as it would get, while the surrounding region would bake in the high forties.

Rounding the final bend in the path, Nigel stopped short. He felt Jake's little hand slip from his. It was okay. Jake knew the way from here. Nigel had seen the remarkable sight before, but he couldn't imagine it ever not taking his breath away.

Mughsail Beach.

Eight kilometres of pure, white coral sand hugged by beautifully sculptured cliffs and rugged mountains on one side and a spectacularly turquoise ocean on the other. Crystal-clear waves crashed against the beach in a mesmerizing symphony of sound and seaspray. Towering palm trees, fronds swaying lazily in the breeze, lined the nearly deserted stretch of coastline. At the far end of the beach, silhouetted in black against the cloudless, azure sky, was a small caravan of camels. They were making their early-morning pilgrimage to a nearby village where they would find fresh water.

Pulling in a lungful of frankincense-scented sea air, Nigel felt his shoulders loosen. His chest grew lighter, his brain relaxed. It was a miracle what this place had done to him in so short a time. To his mind. His body. To Hanna and Jake. Up ahead he watched as the young boy, laughing, the wind whipping his long hair and light cotton clothing, sprinted toward the waiting arms of his mother.

Hanna Billings too had changed. Her once pale skin was tinged with colour. Her eyes were clear and bright. Her hair, beginning to grow out and lighten, was healthy and shiny. She was a happy, beautiful woman. His woman.

The house Anatole Saint had rented for them, in a remote village in the hills near Mughsail, was small but comfortable. The nearest city, about forty kilometres east, was Salalah. They could get pretty much anything they wanted there. All they really wanted was anonymity. Safety. A place to start a new life as a family. A place where they could feel free to love one another. A place where Jake would never be found. Oman, much of it untouched by tourism, was that kind of place.

Who knew what they'd end up doing here? Maybe he'd teach scuba diving to the occasional Middle Eastern tourist. Maybe Hanna would start up a little shop on the beach, selling handmade bracelets, or introducing slushies to the local populace. It didn't really matter. They needed to work only as a form of entertainment. Ten million dollars would last them forever in this hot, hazy, luxuriously exotic, secret corner of the world. The place they now called home.

When the cab pulled into the yard, both our mouths dropped. I could hear my mother's voice telling us to close them tight or risk catching flies.

"Looks like quite the shindig you got going on here," the cabbie commented.

That was an understatement. So many vehicles were crammed into the farmyard that there was barely room for the taxi to park. The house itself was lit up like a Las Vegas hotel. A fat summer sun kissed the horizon, tossing out shafts of orange, purple, and amber. In the dying light, I could see a group of kids playing tag. Even with the car windows rolled up, we could hear strains of old-time rock 'n 'roll—no doubt compliments of Anatole—blaring over a loud speaker.

I paid the fare, glanced at Alexandra, and said, "Here we go."

As Alexandra and I made our way through the house, judging by the general disarray of the place—empty wine bottles, beer bottles, pop bottles, casserole dishes, pie tins, and roasters—I'd say the festivities had been in full swing for quite a while. I'd checked the weather before we caught our flight home. Dad had lucked out. The forecast for his birthday party called for thirty-two and a light breeze.

"Look," Alexandra said. We'd stopped in the kitchen. She

was staring out the bay windows overlooking the backyard.

Fifty people of all ages were spread throughout the area. Some lounged on a collection of mismatched lawn chairs, others found comfy spots on the grass. Multiple strings of patio lanterns criss-crossed the air in haphazard patterns. At one far end of the yard, a folding table did duty as makeshift bar. At the other end, a small group of teens and young adults, including Anatole, were roasting marshmallows over a dug-out fire pit. Anatole appeared less than thrilled. But at least he was giving it a go.

"When did Dad learn to throw a party like this?" I asked my sister.

"You'd be surprised," she responded. "He's learned a lot of new things."

I knew better than to ask for clarification. Which was okay. I'd figure it out for myself.

Just then, the kitchen door burst open. Dad came through and registered surprise at finding us standing there. He'd had a toothy smile on his face like I'd never seen before. As it faded at the sight of us, I noted the redness of his nose and the sweet scent of something fermented on his breath.

"You made it," he said, taking a shuffling step forward, searching our faces as if needing intense visual confirmation of his statement. "You made it. I can't believe you made it."

"We could hear the noise from Toronto," I said in a mock admonishing tone.

Alexandra added, "And you know me, Dad. I never miss a good party."

"Anatole told me things were very busy for you two out there," he said. "He wasn't sure if you'd make it back in time."

Who knows what my father thought "very busy" and "out there" really meant. Whatever it was, he seemed to be dealing with it. Homemade hooch was a likely contributing factor.

"Wouldn't want to miss the old man's sixty-fifth," I said, trying my best to sound jovial. "We've alerted the fire station about the cake."

"I'm not dead yet! Not by a long shot!" Dad laughed, leaving behind the same toothy smile when it was over. "Adam, there's something you should know. That's if you're planning to stick around for a while? And you too, Alexandra."

We must have looked worried because he awkwardly patted each of us on the shoulder.

We said nothing, perhaps the first time my sister and I were speechless at the same time.

"It's not a bad thing," he promised. "Just something I guess you should know. You see…kids, I've invited a special friend to be here tonight."

"Oh," Alexandra uttered as she reached in a pocket for her package of cigarettes.

"That's good, Dad. Really. I'm glad," I added to my sister's verbosity, as usual confounded as to what to say to my father.

"Anyway, there's a lot to eat and drink. Come outside for a while. If you want."

As Dad headed back to the party, we watched through the window. He approached another man. Their arms slipped easily around each other as they shared a laugh about something or nothing at all. My sister remained maddeningly silent.

Suddenly all was clear. I shot Alexandra an inquiring glance.

Alexandra shrugged. "I figured."

"Really? Since when?"

"Adam," her voice had an edge of flint. "I live here. Dad is in my life. I see things. I sense things."

Message sent: I have not been in my father's life.

Accurate. But callous nonetheless.

"He's just starting to figure things out," she said, staring out the window at our father. "In his plodding way. It's probably why he hasn't always seemed too thrilled to have you here."

"Why is that again?"

"Oh come on. Look at his life. Look at yours. Look at who he is. Look at who you are. How's he supposed to know what you'd think about this? As much as you don't know him, he doesn't know you either. He's obviously got enough things to worry about without how you're going to react."

"Then why tell us now?"

"Adam, I think he wants you to stay."

Maybe my dad needed me.

Maybe I needed him.

"When are you going to tell him *your* secret?"

I sighed heavily. The weight of that secret was getting hefty. "I will, Alexandra. Just not tonight. I want him to enjoy this."

"Adam, what's going to happen when Ross Campbell gets to Russia and they start testing his blood and tissue? They're going to know I switched the blood I took from

Campbell with a vial of Jake's blood. I have no idea how long all this medical stuff takes, but I do know they're going to figure out sooner or later that nothing about him cures cancer. All they're going to find is that he's full of it himself and probably won't live long. Then what? Develchko is going to be pissed. He's going to come after you."

I shrugged. "It'll take a while for them to figure it out. If he dies before then, that's their problem, not mine. If not, it won't matter. By then...."

Alexandra's dark eyes were on me. Warning me. "Don't say it."

By then I'll be dead.

"The only real problem is if they let him wake up and he starts talking."

"What do you mean?" She sounded worried.

"Campbell and Develchko never met in person, only by phone. But even on his death bed, Ross Campbell is a powerful man. And a persuasive one. He could find a way to convince Develchko about who he really is. Regardless of what the initial tests and trials show, Develchko *has* to believe he has the real cure for cancer. If he doesn't, all of this falls apart very fast."

"What are we going to do, Adam?"

We.

"Don't worry, sis. I'll keep a close eye on things. In the meantime..." I grinned, eyeing the revelry on the other side of the window pane... "it seems I have a lot to catch up on right here at home."

There were few things Maryann Knoble enjoyed more than a late night in the office. No phones. No scurrying assistants. No murmur from the outside world. Sounds that, no matter how secure and cloistered her office was, still seemed to permeate her private space during regular work hours. At night, it was just her. Plus a damn good cigar. A glass of Scotch. And outside her window, the splendour of her adopted city, Toronto, spread out before her—for her—like a buffet of twinkling lights.

It had been a particularly productive week. For quite some time, Maryann had suspected two things. That Jake Billings was in danger from more than one credible threat. And that one of those threats came from within her own organization.

There were people who believed they knew most everything about IIA. Well, they didn't. Only she knew everything. For instance, only Maryann knew about her private force of agents. Some she used for their minds, others solely for their muscle. It was via this powerful combination of brain and brawn that she'd learned of Ross Campbell's duplicity. It really wasn't that difficult to ferret out once she'd learned of his terminal illness. Nor was she at a loss for how to deal with it. Or so she'd thought.

The final gambit had actually been proposed by Adam Saint during the Saskatchewan skirmish near the fittingly named North Battleford. He was correct in assuming Develchko could not be trusted. For all they knew, the man's own army could have had eyes and ears present in that farmyard. Saint suggested it be made to look—to *whoever* might be watching—as if he, and that cheap sister of

396 — Anthony Bidulka

his, double-crossed IIA.

They would overtake Knoble's man, who'd been tasked with the responsibility of getting the asset to safety, and escape with him themselves.

Although not the kind of woman who regularly—if ever—followed a plan not of her own making, Maryann was shrewd enough to see opportunity amidst chaos. She and Saint agreed on one thing. The asset had to be protected at all costs. And, Maryann relented unenthusiastically, the asset's mother too. Although that aspect of the plan, as far as she was concerned, was still negotiable, Maryann agreed to Saint's proposal. On one condition.

To Maryann's way of thinking, her idea of switching Ross Campbell for Jake was a stroke of genius. Saint, that exceedingly rare combination of both brain and brawn in one body, had already begun developing his own suspicions of Campbell. Even so, he balked at the idea. He felt it unnecessarily cruel. It was nothing short of sending a colleague to be tortured, with full knowledge and consent. So Maryann found it necessary to fill Saint in on some salient facts. She told him that Campbell's nefarious activities included the murder of his friend, Geoffrey Krazinski in Magadan. And, for good measure, she revealed that Campbell had been fucking his ex-wife, even before the two were separated. Whether or not the last was true, what did it matter? It did the job.

The plan proceeded.

And it worked. Oh, how it worked.

Laying aside her cigar in a S.T. Dupont ashtray, Maryann lowered the glasses on her nose, the better to study the file of papers on her desk. She opened the file and scanned the first page. It detailed the emergency laparoscopic surgery she'd ordered carried out at the IIA medical suite.

Vocal cord removal.

Maryann allowed herself a rough guffaw. For all intents and purposes, she'd seen to it that Ross Campbell had been de-barked. Even if the miserable sod ever did regain consciousness while he was in Russia, and managed to find someone who not only understood English but wanted to listen to him, he'd have nothing to say.

She'd seen to it that the asset was safe. IIA was safe. Maryann was safe.

When Saint asked about it, Maryann told him the scar was incurred during Campbell's initial medical trauma; his airway had been blocked, they'd needed to tube him.

Reaching over to the piece of equipment—one of her favourite—next to her desk, Maryann flipped the switch. She smiled as she fed the file into the shredder, listening to the sound she always found so comforting: "whirrrrrrr...."

Earlier in the day, using her higher-than-damned-well-everyone-but-the-Prime Minister clearance level, Maryann also destroyed all digital copies of the report, as well as supplementary files created by the IIA medical office.

For the next while, with her exceedingly comfortable and expensive leather chair swiveled so she could appreciate the view of the city, Maryann finished her cigar and Scotch.

Later, as she rose from her desk to leave, she noticed something odd at the top of her in-basket. Many years ago, she'd made peace with one blaring failure in her illustrious career. The fact that her in-basket would never be empty. No matter how hard she worked, no matter how diligent

398 — *Anthony Bidulka*

she was in reviewing the material that piled up there—especially preposterous given how so much information was received in elecronic copy only—there would always be more. The best she could do was to make time, every day, to deal with as much as she could, starting with the bottom of the pile and working her way up.

The item was odd only because it looked like something she hadn't seen in quite some time. A relic of the past. A dinosaur. It was a personal letter. Addressed to her. In longhand. It bore a stamp that someone had taken the time to buy, lick, and paste on the envelope. What a time-wasting fool, she thought of the sender, whoever it was.

She picked up the unopened letter and turned it over. No return address.

Using a diamond-studded, sterling silver letter opener, she sliced open the top.

A single sheet fell into her palm.

She read the handwritten letter.

Then again.

It was from Milo Yelchin.

It was, in many ways, his suicide letter. Or rather, an adjunct to the one they'd found with his hanged body.

With the letter, Yelchin was confessing to Maryann his role in Campbell's plan. A role that, until this moment, she'd been entirely unaware of. Milo Yelchin, under the duress of blackmail, had faked Adam Saint's illness. With the assistance of the faked diagnosis, pills specially engineered to encourage Saint to believe it, and the talents of a non-IIA special agent, code name: Eva, he'd assisted Campbell in convincing Saint to go after the cure.

Maryann swallowed her grudging respect for the dastardly but superlative plan.

Yelchin was sorry.

And for this—and his doubtless many other sins, Maryann noted to herself—he'd taken his own life. Milo Yelchin, Maryann decided, had been a fatally weak man.

He asked only one thing. When Maryann told Saint of his horrible deceit, she should ask him to try to find it in his heart to forgive him.

A minute later, Maryann Knoble strode confidently out of her office, listening to the sound she always found so comforting…"whirrrrrrr."

THE END

When the Saints Go Marching In

An Adam Saint Novel

Your best friend is killed. Your wife is leaving you. Your son hates you.

Then comes the bad news.

A Sukhoi Superjet carrying a Very Important Person, plunges from the sky over subarctic Russia. A Canadian Disaster Recovery Agent inspecting the crash site is murdered. CDRA sends in their best to investigate.

Man-of-the-world adventurer, Adam Saint, lives a fast-paced, often dangerous, always exciting life. When a passenger train crashes in Detroit, terrorists blow up a public building in Belfast, a cyclone ravages Bangladesh, or Angola descends into civil war, if Canadians are there, so is the CDRA. And so is Adam Saint.

Saint's Russian investigation is derailed when he receives devastating personal news. Suddenly, the ultimate man of action is thrown into emotional and physical turmoil that tests his moral fortitude to the limit. Thrust into a fight for his life, Saint embarks on a thrilling journey of danger and deceit from the bucolic prairies of Saskatchewan and high rise hotspots of corporate Toronto, through London's outer boroughs, to steamy Southeast Asia and Sin City itself, Las Vegas.

Failure is not an option. Until it is.

Anthony Bidulka is an award-winning writer enjoys traveling the world, giving back, and throwing parties. Please visit his website a www.anthony bidulka.com. *When the Saints Go Marching In* is the first book in the Adam Saint series. Bidulka is also the author o the long-running Russell Quant mystery series.